Acclaim for Christina Courtenay's enthralling dual-time romances

Christina Courtenay is an award-winning author of historical romance and time slip (dual-time) stories. She started writing so that she could be a stay-at-home mum to her two daughters, but didn't get published until daughter number one left home aged twenty-one, so that didn't quite go to plan! Since then, however, she's made up for it by having sixteen novels published and winning the RNA's Romantic Novel of the Year Award for Best Historical Romantic Novel twice with *Highland Storms* (2012) and *The Gilded Fan* (2014), and once for Best Fantasy Romantic Novel with *Echoes of the Runes* (2021).

Christina is half Swedish and grew up in that country. She has also lived in Japan and Switzerland, but is now based in Herefordshire, close to the Welsh border. She's a keen amateur genealogist and loves history and archaeology (the armchair variety).

To find out more, visit **christinacourtenay.com**, find her on Facebook **/Christinacourtenayauthor** or follow her on X **@PiaCCourtenay** or Instagram **@christinacourtenayauthor**

By Christina Courtenay

Standalones
Trade Winds
Highland Storms
Monsoon Mists
The Scarlet Kimono
The Gilded Fan
The Jade Lioness
The Silent Touch of Shadows
The Secret Kiss of Darkness
The Soft Whisper of Dreams
The Velvet Cloak of Moonlight
Hidden in the Mists
Shadows in the Ashes

The Runes novels
Echoes of the Runes
The Runes of Destiny
Whispers of the Runes
Tempted by the Runes
Promises of the Runes

SHADOWS IN
THE ASHES

CHRISTINA COURTENAY

REVIEW

First published in 2024
by HEADLINE REVIEW
An imprint of HEADLINE PUBLISHING GROUP

1

Cataloguing in Publication Data is available from the British Library

ISBN 978 1 4722 9322 0

Typeset in 11/14 pt Minion Pro by Jouve (UK), Milton Keynes

Printed and bound in Great Britain by Clays Ltd, Elcograf S.p.A.

HEADLINE PUBLISHING GROUP
An Hachette UK Company
Carmelite House
50 Victoria Embankment
London EC4Y 0DZ

www.headline.co.uk
www.hachette.co.uk

To Henriette Gyland,
lovely friend and fellow Scandinavian author,
thank you for awesome brainstorming sessions,
support and friendship!

Prologue

The ground was trembling, as if a giant was walking past, making everything around her quake. The walls shook, large cracks appearing, and items on shelves rained down, crashing to the floor. Plaster from the ceiling fell in chunks, spreading a cloud of dust throughout the room. She coughed and pulled her *palla* across the lower half of her face, trying not to choke on the particles.

The small child clinging to her whimpered, and she wanted to do the same, but for her daughter's sake she had to pretend to be brave. It was a good thing everything around them was moving, as this disguised her quivering limbs.

'Shh, sweetheart, it will be over soon. We just have to wait. Someone will come and help us.'

But she knew the likelihood of that was very small. Probably non-existent. They'd been left here all night, locked in, and while everyone else was running away as fast as they could, she and her daughter were stuck. She'd tried to force her way out. Had hoped the crumbling walls would open up a large enough gap for them to crawl through, but it was not to be. This would likely be their grave.

She had but one regret – she'd never see *him* again.

Chapter One

Frisia, AD 73

Raedwald

'Why do you want to go this way? We should be getting back before dusk.' Raedwald frowned at his younger half-brother, Osbehrt, who seemed inordinately pleased with himself.

'I think I saw that big stag here yesterday. You know, the one everyone's talking about with the huge antlers. Wouldn't it be wonderful if we manage to kill it and bring it back to Father? He'll be so proud of us. Come, it was this way.'

Osbehrt didn't slow his pace and Raedwald had no choice but to follow. He'd always been told to watch over his younger half-siblings. As the eldest, it was his duty, but sometimes, like now, it was a chore he could well do without.

It wasn't as though anyone gave him credit for it either, least of all their father, Raedwulf. After the early death of Raedwald's mother, he'd quickly remarried, and had fallen completely in thrall to his new woman. She'd done everything she could to promote the interests of her own offspring, while Raedwald was given all the hard or boring tasks. The only thing she hadn't been able to persuade his father to do was to have Osbehrt declared his heir instead of Raedwald. Some stubborn part of Raedwulf refused to give in on that point, but that didn't mean he liked his eldest son. Far from it – he was forever criticising, making Raedwald do more weapons training than anyone else, and expecting him to be at the beck and call of his stepmother in between.

It was unbearable, and Raedwald hated the pair of them, but he took it in silence. That was the only way he could thwart her – by not showing that she was affecting him in any way, nor giving up his rights as the heir. If she could, he was sure she'd insist on him being made a sacrificial offering to the gods. Fortunately, that wasn't up to her.

He sighed now as he trudged behind his brother. 'If you saw the stag yesterday, who's to say he'll still be there now? Deer roam far and wide. No doubt he'll be long gone.'

'No, no, it's not the first time, actually. I've spotted him several times, and there's a small lake nearby so he probably goes there to drink. It's not far now, I promise.'

Raedwald rolled his eyes, but Osbehrt wasn't looking so he didn't see that. Honestly, this was probably a wild goose chase, but best to let the boy learn that for himself.

The youth – a mere fifteen winters to Raedwald's eighteen – raced ahead as if eager to reach their goal. From time to time, he glanced over his shoulder to check whether his brother was following, but he didn't slow his pace. This was becoming very tedious, and it would soon begin to get dark. Not to mention that the tide would be starting to come in. The man-made island – or *terp* – they lived on, near the seashore, could only be reached at ebb across marshland that was treacherous at the best of times. They had left the coastal area behind and entered a forest inland, but they should definitely be turning back, not going forward.

Just as he had decided he'd had enough, Raedwald suddenly

felt something hard connect with the back of his skull. Shadowy figures materialised from the trees and surrounded him, one of them throwing some sort of net over his head while he was still stunned from the blow. What in the name of all the gods . . .?

'Run, Osbehrt, *run!*' he yelled, anger making his voice soar among the trees.

He tried to fight his way free of the net, galvanised into action by a fear for his brother, but although he was strong, he didn't stand a chance. They were too many against one, and he was grabbed from all sides and held in a tight grip while someone tied his hands behind his back. His head was pounding from the vicious blow. He squinted against the fading light as he looked up to see whether his brother had managed to escape. To his surprise, Osbehrt was standing in front of him, grinning, while tossing a clinking pouch from one hand to the other. Realisation hit him harder than that thump on the head.

'What have you done?' he growled, a fury greater than any he'd ever felt surging through him. Why, the little rat . . .

'Sold you. Mother thought it best.' The rat in question looked unrepentant. Triumphant, even. 'These men will take you away and sell you to the highest bidder, and they've guaranteed we'll never see you again. Father's hall and all his domains will be mine, as they should be. You've always thought you are so much better than me, but you're wrong. I'll make a great chieftain. And perhaps with you gone, Father will finally train me as he ought instead of giving all his attention to you.'

'You'll regret this, you little worm, and your bitch of a mother too. I will come back and kill you, *brother*, one way or another. You have my oath on it.' Raedwald spat on the ground and watched as Osbehrt jumped back, glaring at him.

Some of his swagger had left him, and there was uncertainty lurking in the youth's gaze, but he lifted his chin. 'No you won't.

These men will see to that. You'll die in a Roman arena some-where, torn to pieces by wild beasts. I only wish I could be there to watch. Farewell. I'll tell Father not to mourn you.'

'Don't be too sure.' Raedwald made his voice as menacing as he possibly could and had the satisfaction of seeing Osbehrt flinch. 'From now on, you'd better watch your every step, because one day I will be right behind you, ready to slit your throat. May the gods curse you!'

Another blow to the head cut off the sight of the snivelling little snake, but that was probably just as well or Raedwald would have choked on his rage. Oblivion was preferable for now.

Chapter Two

North London, 10 April 2022

Cat

'What did you buy at M&S today?'

Derek dropped his briefcase on the floor with a thump, and Cat flinched, then swallowed hard, trying to make herself speak normally. She plastered on a fake ingratiating smile, hating herself for it, even though she knew it was necessary.

'It . . . it was just a hoodie for Bella. They were on sale, really cheap, and she's grown out of everything else. She's been so cold these last few days. Who knew it would snow in April – crazy, right?'

He didn't so much as acknowledge her reply, but scowled at their three-year-old daughter, who took one look at his face and wisely ran to hide in her room. Even at such a young age, she'd learned that retreat was the better part of valour. And Cat hated that it had to be this way.

Derek continued in the arctic voice she knew meant big trouble. 'Didn't I warn you about not making any extra purchases? We're trying to save up for a holiday abroad, remember?'

7

Cat stayed silent and willed her limbs to stop trembling. She wanted to run and hide somewhere far, far away, and take Bella with her, but that wasn't an option. Having lost touch with her family and friends, she had nowhere to go, and no money of her own to live off. Besides, she was convinced he'd find them, and then things would be even worse. This evening he had swept into the house looking like an avenging Fury; Armani suit crumpled, tie askew. Now he was pulling on the top button of his shirt as if it was choking him. She could tell he'd had a bad day at work. His boss, who was a mean bastard at the best of times, must have been extra demanding today, and she was about to pay for it. Every particle of her body went cold at the mere sight of his expression.

She had tried to make light of the matter, but inside her the knot of dread was building to epic proportions. She'd known he would notice the purchase – he checked their bank accounts just about every day and made her give him all her receipts – but she'd had to do it for Bella's sake. The poor little mite had been trying to play huddled inside her duvet the day before. She'd not wanted to come out because the house was too cold. Another of Derek's 'economies'.

'No need to have the heating on during the day, is there?' he'd decreed back in November. Maybe it seemed unnecessary to him, as he was at work all day. But she and Bella spent most of their time here, and although the house was newly built, it didn't have much in the way of insulation. She suspected cowboy builders who had cut corners whenever they could. That must have been why the property was so cheap when they bought it.

Cat hadn't wanted to buy it at all. She disliked modern houses and would have preferred an old-fashioned property with original features and some character. But Derek had insisted. He saw no need for 'curly bits and draughty old fireplaces' when you could have plain walls and a gas fire. It was much more practical.

She'd almost told him it was soulless, but managed to bite her tongue in time. After all, it didn't matter where they lived – whatever the shape of it, their home would always be her prison. No point getting attached to it either, as he could decide on a whim that they were to move somewhere else. He'd already done that twice during their five-year marriage.

'And it was hardly cheap,' he was saying now. 'Eight pounds for an item that probably only cost a few pence to make? And in that vile shade of pink too. You know I hate pink!'

She did, but it wasn't the colour so much as the fact that he'd never forgiven her for giving birth to their beautiful daughter, when all he had wanted was a son.

'But it's Bella's favourite col—'

He cut her off. 'Either way, you should have asked me first.'

Although she'd been expecting it, the punch came from out of nowhere, catching her next to her left eye. It was a favourite spot of his and she sometimes worried she'd go blind on that side if it happened too often. A numb sensation spread from her temple down her cheek. She caught her breath with a hiss. Opening her mouth, she tried to flex her jaw to see whether it was still intact. It was, but a lightning bolt of pain shot down the whole length of it. She stifled a moan, knowing that would only earn his scorn.

'Well? Are you going to remember in future?' Derek loomed over her as if ready to repeat the punishment.

'Mm-hmm.' She wasn't sure she could open her mouth again just now, so the mumbled reply was all she could manage.

'What was that? I can't hear you.' He raised his fist and she cringed away from him, but he followed and hit her again. 'Speak up, Catherine!'

'Y-yes, I'll remember,' she said through teeth that had exploded with agony. 'I'm sorry.'

'Good. Now where's my dinner? Is it too much to ask that you

9

have it ready when I come home? It's not as if you do anything else all day, is it?'

Cat swallowed the angry retort that rose to her lips. She worked from home and had spent the day juggling an Italian translation job with trying to keep Bella occupied and happy. And dinner was ready. It was only that he'd prevented her from serving it by attacking her the minute he came through the front door.

'It won't be a moment. Please take a seat,' she said, turning to busy herself with extracting the casserole dish from the oven.

Please God, let it be tasty so he didn't have cause for complaint about that too, she prayed silently. And although she'd long ago given up on her mother's Catholic faith, she made a surreptitious sign of the cross when Derek wasn't looking. It couldn't hurt, could it?

Bella had the sense to stay out of the way; she'd already had her supper anyway. Derek felt children shouldn't join the adults until they were older and more civilised, as he'd put it. Cat ran upstairs to quickly check that her little girl was OK before taking her own seat. Derek hadn't waited for her, but was halfway through his portion already. They ate in silence, the meal apparently passing muster. When he'd finished, he stood up and announced that he was off to meet some workmates for a drink.

Once he was gone, instead of getting on with clearing up after the meal, and putting Bella to bed, Cat headed outside to the garden to breathe in some fresh air. She needed to calm down, stop her body from shaking, and for that to happen she had to be outside her prison. The house was suffocating her.

Drawing in the cold spring air, and pulling her cardigan tightly across her body, she closed her eyes and felt the metaphorical bands that were binding her chest loosen. The worst was over for now, and although she'd have to wear heavy make-up for a few days, she would have a reprieve until the next time Derek found fault with her. Thankfully, it only happened a couple of times a month. That was still too many, but . . .

'You really should leave him, you know.'

The quiet voice coming from across the hedge made Cat jump, and she forgot to cover her face as she swung round to see who was talking to her. Her neighbour, Suzanne, a woman in her late fifties or early sixties, was peering over the clipped yew. Her expression of quiet compassion turned into one of concern when she caught sight of Cat's rapidly swelling eye and cheek.

'The utter bastard!' she hissed. 'Honestly, what is it that makes some men think they can act however they like?'

'No, no, I . . . tripped. It was my own fault,' Cat whispered, putting up a hand to protect her face from view. 'Really, it was nothing.'

She'd had worse, but she'd never admit that, especially not to the only person in the neighbourhood who ever talked to her. They'd chatted occasionally across the fence, just small talk about the weather and such, but it made Cat feel slightly less isolated. And she had helped Suzanne out a few times by accepting deliveries on her behalf when she'd been out at work.

'Hmm.' The non-committal noise conveyed the woman's scepticism, and Cat cringed inwardly. How had it come to this? Why was she lying to protect a man who mistreated her? But she had no choice if she wanted to keep Bella from harm. If she wanted to keep her, full stop. So far, he had never hurt their daughter, but should she try to divorce him, he would be given shared custody of the little girl. Knowing him, he would use that to torment Cat endlessly. Perhaps even turn the child against her through bribery and lies as she grew up. She simply couldn't risk it.

'I'd better go inside. If I put some ice on it, the swelling will soon go down.' She turned away, wanting nothing more than to escape now. The embarrassment of being caught looking like this was more than she could bear.

'No, wait! Please, let me take a photo. It might help . . . one day, when you're ready to walk away. And I'd be happy to testify on your behalf any time you need me.' Suzanne shrugged and gesticulated towards their adjoining semi-detached properties, modern and purpose-built. 'These houses weren't made with thick walls, were they, so I'm afraid I hear a thing or two . . .'

Cat swallowed hard. This was getting worse and worse. 'Oh God,' she muttered, but then a small spark of defiance lit up inside her and she turned back towards Suzanne, lifting her chin a fraction. 'OK, then, take a photo if you want, but I doubt I'll use it. I can't. My daughter . . .'

Suzanne snapped a couple of quick pictures with her phone camera and nodded in sympathy. 'I understand. What's her name again? I've seen you with her in the garden, of course.'

'Isabel, but we call her Bella. She's, um, named after her grandmother, so we don't want to confuse the two.'

She shuddered at the thought, and sincerely hoped her daughter would be nothing like her mother-in-law when she grew up. The woman was as cold as a hoar frost; a control freak who had raised her son with an iron fist. It was no wonder Derek thought violence was acceptable, really, although it was still no excuse. From what Cat had gathered, he'd been subjected to corporal punishment from an early age. He had been just ten when his father had died, and from that moment on his mother had expected him to 'be a man'. No excessive emotions allowed. No weakness either. In fact, she'd done a fine job of turning him into an insensitive brute. It was a shame Cat hadn't realised that until it was too late.

'She's very pretty, your little girl. Is she asleep?' Suzanne asked.

Cat glanced up at the window of her daughter's bedroom. 'Not yet. She's probably watching a movie or cartoon She's a good girl.'

'I'm sure she is. I hardly ever hear her cry.' Suzanne put her phone in her pocket. 'Now, please, will you do me a favour? Whenever something like this happens, come out here and call for me and I'll take a photo. I'm usually in the kitchen or living room, so I'll hear you. I'll download the photos to my computer and date them, then if you ever want to, er . . . break free, I'll send them to you. Deal?'

She held out her hand across the low hedge and Cat felt compelled to shake it. There was something firm and reassuring in Suzanne's grip, giving her a tiny spark of encouragement. And an even smaller flicker of hope.

'Deal,' she whispered.

'And just in case you were wondering, you're not alone. I was in a similar situation some years back. It might feel hopeless right now, but it *is* possible to get away, trust me.'

Cat blinked away a sudden rush of tears and nodded. She'd probably never have the courage to leave Derek, but it didn't hurt to be prepared. Perhaps keep a few essential things ready to grab in case she ever had the opportunity to escape. Hide the few pieces of jewellery she owned in a safe place. There was no way she could take photos herself to keep for future use – he had access to both her phone and her email account and checked them regularly – but Suzanne was a different matter. He'd never even suspect her involvement, because he'd written her off as a 'dried-up old spinster' the one and only time they'd said hello across the fence. Cat was sure Suzanne was a lot more than that.

It had been so long since she'd talked to anyone properly. Since anyone cared. Her former friends had fallen by the wayside and she'd allowed it to happen. And she hadn't spoken to her mother in over a year. It was easier that way. If she kept them at a distance, no one needed to know the truth about her situation. She'd never had a best friend, and former college and workmates were easy to lose touch with, accidentally on purpose. Everyone was busy. But here was someone who seemed to see all too clearly what was happening in Cat's life. She wasn't sure whether that was a good or bad thing, but at least it was some form of human contact. A ray of light in the dark loneliness of her existence.

Perhaps she could do it. Break free. One day. But not just yet. 'OK,' she murmured. 'Th-thank you, Suzanne.'

She was too tired to say anything else, and just whispered a quick goodbye before heading back indoors.

Derek could come back from the pub at any time, and it would be best for both of them if she and Bella were in bed asleep when he did.

Chapter Three

Pompeii, 7 September AD *79*

Raedwald

'*Rufus, Rufus, Rufus!*'

The cry echoed round the amphitheatre arena and Raedwald closed his eyes for a moment, grounding himself. It was as though he was in the middle of some strange dream, and none of it was real. Rufus was the name he'd been given here – his mane of long red hair had made it a foregone conclusion – and now an audience of at least fifteen thousand people were egging him on to kill a man dressed in a ridiculous outfit.

With a crested helmet, bare torso, colourful loincloth, arm guards and greaves – armour that protected the shins – as well as a small, square shield and a curved sword called a *sica*, the so-called *thraex*, or Thracian, wasn't a worthy opponent in Raedwald's mind. Neither was the fighter next to him, the *retiarius*, who was even more naked, and carrying a fishing net and a trident. Luckily Raedwald wasn't expected to engage with him today, and if it hadn't been his task to hurt the *thraex*, he would have laughed at them both.

But this was not a jest; it was a matter of life and death.

Raedwald and the other gladiators of Pompeii were taking part in the Ludi Romani games, and blood needed to flow. Copiously. Apparently this would somehow appease the Romans' ancestors, although how or why, Raedwald had no idea and cared even less. He was tired and sore after a long afternoon of combat, and wanted nothing more than to go back to the gladiator barracks and sleep. Sweat poured down his back in rivulets. Like the *thraex*, he wore long metal greaves on top of quilted padding on his legs, and his helmet had large cheek guards and a long brim at the back protecting his neck. Heavy and made of bronze, it was making his head ache and his scalp itch with perspiration. Even though the hottest months of the year were behind them, it was still humid and much too warm for him. It had been over six years since he'd left Frisia, but he hadn't stopped longing for the cold, fresh air of his homeland. He had kept the memories alive in order to spur him on to withstand everything his so-called masters put him through. He also fuelled the flames of hatred towards Osbehrt and his mother constantly. Every indignity and any physical pain could be endured, as long as he used his determination and thirst for revenge as a shield to numb him from the inside out. He was going to punish them, but in order to do that, he had to survive this bout and the next few months.

And he would. He was Rufus the Barbarian, and he always won.

Aemilia

'I need to borrow some more of your jewellery. The taxes are due and the profits from the estate still haven't arrived.'

Aemilia Licinia turned to look at her husband, Lucius, who

had snuck up behind her without her noticing. They'd not long been back from the gladiatorial games, and she had just begun the work of putting together bunches of herbs to hang up to dry in the room she used for preparing tisanes and ointments. It was a task she enjoyed greatly, but the contentment she'd felt but a moment ago evaporated instantly. As did her daydreams of the handsome gladiators she had watched earlier . . .

'There isn't much left. You took most of it last time.' She tried to keep her voice even, although they both knew he'd promised faithfully to bring every last item back as soon as he was in funds and could retrieve them from the moneylenders. That hadn't happened, and wasn't likely to either. She'd never see those pieces again.

There was no point arguing with him, though. He was the *paterfamilias*, the master of the household, and everyone had to do as he commanded, Aemilia included. She put down her shears and, without waiting to see whether he followed, headed towards her *cubiculum*. The sleeping chamber was a small, dark room situated off the peristyle garden. It contained nothing more than a bed covered in a colourful quilt, a chair, a couple of shelves and two wooden chests. The walls were painted in plain ochre with red and black borders, and there was a small mat on the otherwise mosaic-covered floor.

She bent to lift the lid of her clothes chest. Nestled at the bottom was a small casket that had once held quite a lot of jewellery – all inherited from Lucius's mother, Flavia. He'd been her only surviving child, and she had insisted her new daughter-in-law should have her possessions.

Not that she'd been allowed to keep them for long.

What would Flavia have said if she'd known her son was going to pawn the lot? Nothing, probably, as she'd doted on him. It was no wonder he acted like a petulant child half the time, even though he was ten years Aemilia's senior.

She handed him the casket and watched as he surveyed the pitiful amount left – two pairs of earrings, an amulet and one arm ring of silver. Everything else had gone to pay his debts already. How he managed to spend so much was a mystery to her, but they were forever short of funds. She kept wondering how long they could remain here in Pompeii. They might be forced to go and live on the estate north of here that she had brought to the marriage as her dowry – the one that was supposed to be yielding enough produce for them to live off comfortably – and sell this house. She wouldn't mind, as she loved the countryside, but Lucius would hate it. His whole world was here in this small provincial town where he'd grown up.

'Are you certain this is all there is?' He grabbed her upper arm with fingers that dug painfully into her flesh. 'You're not hiding any of it elsewhere?'

'No! Why would I? There is nothing to hide,' she protested, gritting her teeth against the pain. She bruised easily, and the marks of his fingers were bound to show later. That meant she wouldn't be able to go to the public baths for days, not until they faded. It was a small price to pay, though, because in truth she *was* hiding things from him. And she'd suffer a lot more rather than admit it.

The last time her father, Titus Aemilius Licinius, had visited them, just before his death, he'd passed on her own mother's jewels. 'Keep them safe, Aemilia,' he'd told her. 'You won't inherit anything else from me, as you've had your dowry. I'm afraid I've used up all my wealth and there is nothing left but debts, but I kept these for you.'

'Thank you, Father.' She'd been extremely grateful. No matter what happened, she'd have a dowry for her own daughter when the time came. As long as she could keep it hidden from Lucius, and she would.

A sharp stab of guilt assailed her, but she suppressed it. She had to think of her child first and foremost. Lucius had already had more than enough from her family. The fact that he'd squandered it somehow was not her fault, and she hardened her heart. He glared at her now, his face mere inches from hers as he invaded her personal space with barely controlled aggression. His grip on her tightened even further and she drew in a hissing breath.

'You'd better not be lying to me. Things are becoming desperate. I had to sell a slave this morning just to pay some of those taxes.'

Aemilia almost curled her lip. She guessed he hadn't sold either of the two nubile new females he'd brought home recently after he'd won at the gaming tables. He was more likely to have got rid of one of her attendants, and his next words confirmed as much.

'That old Claudia wasn't much use anyway, and I received a pittance for her, but it's better than nothing.' He let go of her at last, raked up the few pieces of jewellery remaining in the casket, and threw the box back into her clothes chest with scant regard for its fragile hinges. 'You'd better hope the estate overseer arrives soon with funds, or I'll be forced to divorce you and marry a woman with a large dowry. In fact, it might come to that anyway . . .'

Aemilia said nothing, just watched him storm out of the door while she rubbed absently at her arm. He was becoming more violent by the day, and in truth she was grateful for the two new slave women, as they kept his attention away from her at night. He hadn't come to her bed in ages. *Thank the gods for that!*

In a way, she could understand and sympathise with his anger and frustration. His family had been prominent in Pompeii for years, but following a huge earthquake sixteen years earlier, they'd lost all the rental properties they had owned in the town. The buildings had collapsed, and without the wherewithal to rebuild them, they'd had to be sold for next to nothing. That meant the income Lucius had been used to each month was no more, and all he had left was her country estate. An estate on the slopes of Mount Vesuvius that, like everyone else's, was apparently doing badly this year.

The summer months had brought a mysterious drought to the countryside. Natural springs and wells had run dry even though there had been normal amounts of rain. No one could explain this strange phenomenon, and there were rumours of smoke rising from the ground, as well as vines wilting and fruit shrivelling. There was also talk of dead fish floating in the nearby river Sarno, whose water levels were currently very low. Aemilia wished Lucius would go to the estate himself to find out what was going on, instead of relying on the overseer to come to them with his reports and the profits. But her husband was too busy with his social life to do any such thing.

He had lofty ambitions to join the local council, and spent most of his time currying favour with men of higher rank. Without riches, however, that was merely a dream. Being more of a realist, Aemilia knew he had no hope of ever achieving it, but Lucius had yet to acknowledge that fact. He wasn't ready to settle for anything less than what he felt was his due. His single-minded pursuit of it had turned into an obsession.

It was all very worrying. She couldn't shake the feeling that they were balancing on a knife edge and something would have to give. And now he was threatening to divorce her. In principle, she'd be glad to be rid of him, as she'd been unhappy in her marriage for a long time now, but she had no family of her own left to turn to. With an estate that seemed unlikely to be able to support her, how was she supposed to live? And worst of all, she'd have to part with their three-year-old daughter, Caia, as Lucius would be within his rights to keep her.

That was something she'd never agree to. Not in a thousand years.

No, if it came to a parting of the ways, she'd have to find a way to bargain with him. Perhaps he'd take part ownership of the estate in exchange for letting her have Caia. She simply couldn't live without her child.

Chapter Four

North London, 7 September 2022

Cat

'For God's sake, child, watch what you're doing!'

A high-pitched scream from Bella made Cat almost drop the pot of pasta she was draining, and she slammed it down onto the kitchen counter before dashing into the living room. 'What's the matter?'

Derek was holding Bella's upper arm in a vice-like grip, giving her a vicious shake, while pulling her away from a rapidly forming puddle of blackcurrant squash. The red liquid was dripping from the coffee table down onto the beige carpet, making a stain that probably wouldn't ever come out. Cat didn't care about that, though. The sight of her husband's big hand on Bella's thin arm made her maternal instincts go into overdrive. Every other emotion came second.

'Derek, please! You're hurting her!' She rushed over and pulled the child out of his grip and into her arms, where Bella found her voice and started howling fit to wake the dead. 'Shh, shh, sweetie, it's OK, we'll clean it up. It's not the end of the world.'

She was talking to herself as much as the child, but Derek's face twisted in fury.

'Are you completely stupid, woman? The carpet is ruined! You'll never get that stain out and it's going to cost a fortune to replace. How could she be so clumsy? And what are you about, giving a three-year-old a mug without a lid? It was an accident waiting to happen.'

Bella was almost four now and had long since grown out of drinking from cups with lids. She was usually very careful, but Cat didn't point this out. The little girl was still crying, shaking with the force of her sorrow and fright. It was all Cat could do to hang on to her as she fought to be put down for some reason. Perhaps she wanted to run away from her father. And who could blame her?

Derek hadn't finished ranting. 'Besides, haven't I told you not to give her that stuff? It rots the teeth, my mother says. Water is good enough for children, or milk at the most.'

Ah yes, the saintly Isabel. Cat had been waiting for her mother-in-law to be brought into the conversation. Despite having only raised one child – and very badly at that – she was apparently the fount of all knowledge when it came to childcare. You'd think after what Derek had gone through himself, he'd be more understanding. Would wish to raise his child in a completely different manner. Sadly, that did not appear to be the case.

'It's the weekend. She deserved a treat,' she protested feebly, but in the next moment, Bella was yanked out of her arms and her head exploded with stars and pain.

'What the . . .? Derek, no! Stop it! I was only . . . *Ow! Argh!*'

Cat held up her arms to try and protect herself from further blows, but they rained down on her in the most vicious attack she'd yet sustained at his hands. Somehow she managed to remain standing, and Bella wrapped her arms around her mother's thighs from behind, so she knew the child was safe at least. But at the same time it hindered her from escaping.

'Don't . . . *ever* . . . tell me . . . what to do . . . with my own . . . *child*!' Derek's fury seemed to know no bounds, and Cat fought to disentangle Bella's arms from her legs.

'Run up to your room, B-Bella, there's a . . . good girl. Go! *Ouch!*'

The urgency in her voice must have got through, because the little girl turned and sprinted for the stairs. Cat doubled over and fell to the floor as a particularly hard blow caught her in the solar plexus, knocking the air out of her lungs. She gasped like a newly landed fish, and fought for breath, panicking when she couldn't manage to inhale. In the end, she just whimpered and curled into a foetal position. Sobbing and crying out with pain each time a blow hit home, she put her hands over her head to try and avoid the worst of Derek's assault.

At last he ran out of steam.

'Let that be a lesson to you, useless bitch,' he snarled, panting, before giving her one last kick that made her right thigh go numb. 'I'm going out for a drink, and you'd better have this mess cleared up by the time I get back, or else . . .'

She wasn't capable of replying, so just lay there until she heard the front door slam shut.

'Ohmigod, *ohmigod*! Are you OK? No, of course you're not. What a stupid question!'

To Cat's astonishment, Suzanne had come rushing in from the kitchen and now kneeled by her side, trying to help her into a sitting position. 'Suzanne? What are you . . .?'

'Never mind that. I heard screaming, and the back door was open. Is anything broken? Should I call for an ambulance?'

'No, no, I don't think so.' She wasn't actually sure, but right now there were other more important things to consider. 'Bella . . .'

'Oh, yes, of course, I'll go see to her. Don't move, I'll be right back.'

24

Cat drew in a couple of steadying breaths and found that it hurt. Probably some broken ribs, but at least she was alive. And she intended to stay that way. This was the last straw. *That bastard hurt Bella!* She couldn't get over that. The sight of him shaking the child had made something inside her wake up. It was as if she could suddenly see her life with much greater clarity, and she knew one thing – this couldn't go on. They had to get away, and fast, before it was too late.

By the time her neighbour came down the stairs with a tear-stained Bella, Cat was on her feet, although swaying slightly.

'You should be sitting down, dear. Don't try to get up yet, it's too soon.' Suzanne cast her a worried glance, but her voice stayed calm, presumably for Bella's benefit. The little girl seemed to be accepting the comfort the older woman was offering, although she was still sobbing intermittently.

'I'm fine.' Cat gritted her teeth. 'I mean, there's no time. We have to . . . leave. Now, before he . . .'

Suzanne nodded, as if she understood instinctively. 'Of course, yes, you're right. Go and pack quickly, if you can, and I'll stay here with Bella. If I hear him coming back, I'll let you know.'

Cat didn't argue, but limped upstairs. Grabbing two holdalls, she began filling them with everything she thought they might need. Unconsciously she'd been planning this for weeks, she realised. Every time she'd opened a cupboard or drawer, she'd looked at what it contained and decided which items were vital and which were not. Now she was able to operate on automatic, following the decisions her subconscious had made. Essential clothes, toys, a few items of jewellery, toiletries, night-time nappies, extra shoes, and the few possessions that were truly hers – photos and a couple of ornaments. It didn't take long. On top she packed her laptop, USB pens with all her clients' work, and her wallet.

In the bathroom, she caught sight of herself in the mirror and recoiled. She looked awful. Her face was swelling up, a bruise developing on one side, while blood ran from her nose and a cut above her eye. Dear God, but she never wanted Bella to see her like this again. *This is the last time, damn it!* She quickly wiped her nose with toilet paper and stuffed some cotton wool up her nostrils to stem the flow. Finally she put her mobile in her pocket and pulled on a warm fleece, bringing the new pink hoodie downstairs for Bella.

'Here, can you put this on her, please?' She handed the garment to Suzanne, who efficiently threaded the little girl into it while Cat put on Bella's sneakers. 'That's it. I think I have everything,' she said, standing up on shaking legs. 'I've just got to call a taxi.'

'No need for that, we'll take my car,' Suzanne said.

'But—'

'No buts. I'm taking you wherever you need to go, but first we're going to A&E. This . . .' she gestured at Cat's battered face and body, 'needs to be properly documented. Let's go out the back way, then we can get into my car while it's still in the garage so none of the other neighbours will see us. What they don't know, they can't tell your husband.'

'Good plan.'

She followed the older woman through the kitchen, and at the last minute remembered to grab the packets of birth control pills that she'd hidden in a tin at the back of the spice cupboard. She didn't want Derek to find them, as then he would know that she'd deliberately denied him the chance to have another child. No point giving him even more ammunition for his rage. His obsession with having a son was something she'd never understood. It was perhaps a desperate need to reinforce his masculinity, as if he'd never felt that he was enough. No doubt that was another legacy of his mother's strange child-rearing tactics. But she'd been certain of one thing – she was not willing to bring any more children into the world with him as their father.

She glanced at the dinner congealing in pots and pans. The hob was switched off and she didn't care about anything else right now. Derek could clear up the mess himself. That would serve him right. In fact . . .

'Sod him!' With a fury she'd never thought herself capable of, she swept the pots off the cooker and onto the floor, jumping out of the way at the last second. Red pasta sauce splattered every-where, mixed with long, oily strands of spaghetti. 'Deal with that, you bastard,' she muttered, then slammed the back door after herself. She hoped it would take him hours.

The doctor on duty at the local A&E was a woman, and when it was Cat's turn she took one look at her and hustled her inside an examination room.

'Please, get undressed and put on this gown for me. Would you mind telling me what happened?'

Cat clenched her fists, embarrassment making her cheeks heat up. 'I was . . . attacked.' There was no other way to describe what had happened, and she was done lying. To herself and to others. It was time to tell the truth. She couldn't let Derek get away with it any longer.

'Are you able to say by whom?' The doctor's tone was gentle and non-judgemental, which helped.

'My husband.' Cat slowly extricated herself from her clothes and managed to get into the hospital gown. It took a while, as her body seemed to have seized up now the adrenaline rush of anger had gone. Her head and ribs were throbbing, but the doctor waited patiently until she was done.

'Right, now let me have a look at you.'

The woman prodded and poked, shone a light into Cat's eyes and checked her blood pressure. When she touched her ribs, Cat inhaled sharply, and the doctor tutted. 'I'll send you down to have that X-rayed in a minute, but first . . . are you going to press charges? You do realise I will have to write a report about this, don't you?'

Cat nodded. She'd briefly discussed this with Suzanne on the way to the hospital, and her neighbour had pointed out that it might be her only chance to get sole custody of Bella, if and when she obtained a divorce. It would be humiliating, but for Bella's sake, she'd do whatever it took.

'What if the police don't believe me?' she had asked. 'Derek can be very persuasive. He's in sales, you know. Talking people round is his forte. He can be incredibly charming as well, when he wants to be.'

As she'd found out to her cost.

'Oh, they'll believe you,' Suzanne had said through gritted teeth. 'I filmed some of it with my mobile. I'm sorry, I should probably have stopped him, but I felt it was important to have proper evidence. And it was only for a few seconds, then he left anyway just as I was about to intervene.'

'You did?' Cat was grateful for Suzanne's clear thinking. 'Thank you. That could be invaluable.'

'Right then,' the doctor said now. 'I'll need to take some photographs, if that's OK?'

'Yep, go ahead.'

That was humiliating too, and Cat felt naked and exposed as the doctor snapped shots of her face and body from every angle. She gritted her teeth. It was a necessary evil. A means to an end. Bella had to be protected from her father for the rest of her life. Nothing else mattered.

'Has this happened before?' The doctor glanced up from typing some notes.

28

'Yes, but nothing quite this . . . extreme.'

It was true. Derek had lashed out with increasing frequency, but it was usually just one or two blows and then his temper cooled. This time he'd seemed totally out of control, and she had wondered if he would stop before he killed her.

'Do you have any proof of that? I mean, have you had to see a doctor about your injuries before? There's nothing in your file.'

'Oh no, but my neighbour Suzanne, the lady who brought me, has some photos and a . . . video. She's been keeping some sort of diary for me, taking pictures and noting the dates.'

The doctor looked at her keenly. 'So you've been expecting something like this to happen for a while, then?'

'Well, no, not exactly, but a while back Suzanne said I might need the evidence one day and she persuaded me it was a good idea.'

'She was right. Now, I'd like you to sign this form and I'll pass it on to the police, together with the photos I've just taken. I'll ask your friend to forward hers as well. The police will want to interview you in due course, but I'm not sure when that will be. What address should I put?'

'Um, Suzanne has offered to let me use hers, in case I have to move around. She'll get in touch with me. I'll need to go somewhere Derek can't find me.'

'I can recommend some shelters for you. The staff there will be able to help you.'

'No, it's fine, thanks. I'll just go and stay with my mum for now.' Although whether her mother would even want to speak to her was debatable after a whole year of no contact between them. She would just have to wait and see. If not, she'd find a hotel somewhere while she regrouped and tried to come up with a way forward.

She rattled off Suzanne's address for the report, then she was given some papers to take down to the X-ray department.

'They'll send me the images and I'll forward those to the police as well. I'm fairly certain you have a couple of broken ribs, but there's nothing to be done about that except rest. They will heal of their own accord. Here's a prescription for some painkillers, just in case, but don't take too many. Good luck. And whatever you do – stand your ground. Promise me? We can't let him get away with this.'

'Thank you, I will.' Cat felt tears welling up in her eyes at the kindness and sympathy she glimpsed in the doctor's eyes, but she willed herself not to cry. She was done with being pathetic.

After the X-rays were completed, they were free to go.

'Now, where to?' Suzanne asked as they exited the doors and headed towards the car park. 'Perhaps a shelter? We can google and see if there are any in the area.' She was carrying Bella, who had fallen asleep on her lap in the waiting room.

She glanced at her watch. 'No, the doctor mentioned that too,' but I'd rather not. It's very late, but I've got one place I can go – my mum's. Well, maybe. I'll have to call her and wake her up.'

She pulled her phone out of her pocket, but before she'd had time to start dialling, Suzanne snatched it out of her hand and threw it to the ground, stamping on it hard with the heel of her boot.

'Hey! What are you doing? That's—'

'For goodness' sake, Cat! You can't walk around with that. You might as well tell your husband exactly where you are. I'll bet you anything he's had that app installed that shows him where your phone is at any time. Being the controlling type, I'd be very surprised if he hasn't.'

'Oh. Of course.' She felt stupid. Why hadn't she thought of that before? It would explain the times he seemed to have known which days she'd been out, even when she hadn't told him. 'Sorry, I'm an idiot.'

Suzanne's expression softened. 'No, dear, just . . . Never mind.

Here, borrow mine, then let's go. He could arrive here at any moment. We're lucky he hasn't already.' She shuddered visibly and walked towards the car while Cat dialled her mother's number. She answered on the second ring.

'Hello?'

'Mum, it's m-me.' Cat's throat constricted and she had to swallow hard to stop herself from breaking down at the sound of her mother's voice. It had been so long since she'd heard it.

'Caterina? Are you OK? Has something happened?'

She gripped the phone tightly. Somehow Derek had managed to come between them, and had eliminated Giovanna from Cat's life with cunning and ruthlessness. Just like he'd done with all her friends and anyone else she'd ever known. She could see it now – it hadn't really been her own choice at all. God only knew what he'd said to her mother, but the last time they'd spoken she had sounded very cold and offended.

'Yes. I mean, no, not exactly. Please, Mamma, can Bella and I come and stay with you for a short while? Right now? I'll explain when I see you, if that's all right.'

'Of course, come, come. I'll be waiting. *Ciao.*'

Her mother didn't sound angry, and Cat hoped she'd be able to patch things up between them. She'd do whatever it took.

As they didn't have a child car seat, Cat strapped herself into the back of Suzanne's car with Bella on her lap.

'There's a vehicle approaching,' Suzanne warned as they swung out onto the road. 'Duck down, just in case. Sorry to be paranoid, but . . .'

Cat didn't argue, just did it. 'What kind was it?'

'A white BMW. I think it might have been your husband's. Doesn't he have one of those? Hope he didn't see me,' Suzanne muttered.

The familiar fear pooled in Cat's stomach, but she fought it off.

Derek couldn't possibly know that she was with Suzanne, so even if he had seen her, he shouldn't put two and two together. Thank goodness her neighbour had known about the phone tracking device, though. Cat would never have thought of that.

'You can sit up now. You'll have to give me directions, or should I stop and turn on the satnav?'

'No, it's fine, I'll tell you how to get there. It's a bit far, though, sorry . . .'

'Not a problem. Left, right or straight on here?'

Chapter Five

Pompeii, 8 September AD 79

Raedwald

'Leave me alone, boy! It's not even light yet.'

Raedwald was being shaken awake, and he very much resented anyone disturbing him before dawn. The young slave should know better.

A deep chuckle made him open his eyes and glance towards the other mattress in the small bedchamber. It was one of many similar such rooms in the *caserma*, the barracks where he lived and trained.

'What?' he groused, although he realised almost immediately that no one was near him. Had he been dreaming?

'It's an earthquake. It is the gods who are waking us, not Marcellus.' The voice of his friend and fellow gladiator, Duro – known here as Drusus – came out of the darkness, and his amusement could clearly be heard.

'Huh.' Raedwald sat up and dry-washed his face, trying to wake himself. 'We've had an uncommon number of them recently, wouldn't you say? And they seem to be growing in strength.'

As if to confirm this, another quake shook the building, stronger than the previous one, and the sound of falling masonry came from outside. It was disconcerting to feel the floor trembling without visible cause. Flakes of paint and plaster rained down on him, and he shook his head to dislodge the debris from his hair. 'Curse it!' he muttered.

It was bad enough being woken at dawn every day and made to exercise and practise weapon skills. Now the gods had seen fit to disturb them even earlier for no good reason.

'They could at least have waited until morning,' he grumbled, eliciting another chuckle from Duro.

'Maybe you should go to the temple and tell them?' he suggested.

Raedwald picked up his lumpy pillow and threw it at the other man. It came back almost as quickly, and he caught it and held it to his chest. 'You know very well I'll not be praying to any Roman gods. My own are good enough, and I don't think they're responsible for these tremors.'

Frisia might be far from the region of Campania, where he now resided – to the north of Belgica and north-west of Germania – but it was not as barbaric as some Romans seemed to think. The gods he had grown up with were every bit as powerful as theirs, of that he was convinced. And why would foreign deities help him when he didn't wish to stay here in their domains?

When a third quake shook the floor, they both grew quiet and readied themselves to dash out the door, should it be necessary. Neither of them wanted to die through being crushed by a ceiling, which sounded like a very real possibility right then.

'Whoa, that's . . . quite powerful.' It was as though the gods had decided to shake the whole building. The walls were fairly undulating. Raedwald put a hand on the nearest one and pushed, even though he knew it was a futile gesture.

'The Romans must have been misbehaving even more than usual,' Duro commented. 'The gods are punishing them.'

'Good, but I'd be grateful if they could leave us foreigners alone. We've done nothing wrong.'

Duro lowered his voice to a mere whisper. 'Perhaps they know about our plans and don't approve?'

'Why wouldn't they? It is justice and we are in the right.' Raedwald was absolutely certain about that. 'And our own gods will help us.'

Ever since he'd been taken from his homeland, his only goal had been to return and wreak revenge on Osbehrt and his snake of a mother. There was no doubt in his mind that it was the accursed woman who had organised the abduction. His half-brother didn't have the brains to come up with such a plan on his own. But they would both suffer for it as and when Raedwald got his hands on them. And he would, he was determined about that. It was merely a question of time.

Duro and Marcellus, the fourteen-year-old boy from Gaul who'd been assigned to look after them in the barracks, were the only two who were aware of his plans. The three of them had been amassing coins and jewels for the past few years, a growing hoard of treasure currently well hidden in a secret place. The two men had won every single gladiatorial bout they'd taken part in, and the usual reward was a purse full of coins.

Unusually, the *lanista* – their owner and master Marcus Antonius Varro – didn't confine most of his gladiators to the barracks, as was normally the case, but allowed them to go out and about on their own. Of course, they'd taken an oath of loyalty to him, and breaking it would have dire consequences – a flogging at the very least, possibly even branding or worse. Antonius Varro appeared to consider this enough insurance. He didn't worry about a possible revolt, although the tale of Spartacus was still told throughout the land. This meant that even though training took up a lot of their time, Raedwald and Duro still had many hours of freedom, which they took full advantage of to earn more silver. Some of their gains had been put to good use in the local taverns, where games of chance were a regular feature. Both Raedwald and Duro were good at these. There were often bets on such games, and by betting on each other – secretly, with the help of Marcellus – they had increased their wealth considerably.

Antonius Varro had also recently begun to hire them out as bodyguards and escorts to rich citizens of Pompeii, giving them a percentage of the pay as an incentive. These wages were entrusted to Marcellus so that the boy could place bets on their behalf before every gladiatorial game as well. They usually knew the other fighters, and could make accurate guesses as to who would win each bout. A tidy sum could be made that way, and they were pleased with their success.

'Not long now until we have enough, right?' Duro's voice interrupted his thoughts.

'Yes, thank the gods! I can't wait to leave this place.'

'Me neither.'

Duro came from Britannia and was just as keen to go home, although not for the same reasons. Together they would succeed. They must.

'Was it really necessary to send us out at midday? This couldn't wait until the sun starts to go down? I'm sweltering!'

It was many hours after the earthquake had woken them, and they were walking through the streets of Pompeii under a burning sun. It scorched their skin and beamed down with intensity upon the top of their heads.

Raedwald glanced at the normally even-tempered Duro,

whose face was glistening in the heat, and shook his head. 'We're slaves, remember? We just do as we're told.'

This was greeted with a snort. 'Well, who is it we're going to see? Another lazy rich man, I suppose. If they did some actual training in the exercise area of the baths, instead of just gossiping and preening like women, they could defend themselves and wouldn't need us.'

'Yes, but then we wouldn't be paid. Every coin gets us that much closer to our goal,' Raedwald reminded him.

'True.'

After a gruelling morning's workout under an increasingly hot September sun, they had been called into Antonius Varro's chambers as soon as they had washed the sweat off their bodies and changed their tunics. He'd informed them he had a task for them, and they'd have to set off at once to meet with the prospective employer.

'Look on the bright side – at least we don't have to help clear up after the earthquakes.'

They'd left Marcellus grumbling about the amount of debris he had to sweep up and cart away, and the reminder of this made them both smile. The boy was likeable and a hard worker, but he was a skinny little thing who could do with the hard work. The sooner he grew in strength, the better it would be for him.

They fell silent and continued along the scorching pavement, raised more than a foot above the street. The warmth of the stone slabs could be felt right through their leather sandals, but they were used to it by now. Despite the heat and humidity, there were people everywhere scurrying about their business – ladies on their way home from shopping, merchants crying their wares from open shop fronts, delivery men leading donkeys laden with goods or gingerly steering their mules and carts along the ruts in the paved road surface, and customers spilling out of the many taverns and eateries. Those establishments had begun to open around the fourth or fifth hour of the day, the wooden slats that covered their doorways at night having been slid back to reveal the marble counters and seating for customers. There was a lot of jostling, some frayed tempers and snarls – including from stray dogs lurking around – but also laughing, joking and ribald comments. When it came to Raedwald and Duro, however, the crowds parted and they weren't bumped into a single time.

Most people recognised the so-called gladiator double act known as 'Rufus and Drusus the Barbarians', and Raedwald had grown used to it. It was a fairly small town, after all. Taller and more muscular than anyone around them, they would have stood out even if Raedwald's hair hadn't been so red, or they hadn't been wearing strange trousers made out of a chequered material. Although the latter contributed to the feeling of overheating, he was pleased he'd managed to talk their master into letting them dress this way when out and about. He'd argued that it made them even more noticeable and piqued the interest of their potential audience. Everyone here knew that barbarians didn't dress like Romans, so why not play up to that? He'd omitted to mention that he absolutely hated walking around with his legs bare, on display for all and sundry. It was undignified. Bad enough that he had to wear a loincloth in the arena, although at least there he had leg guards. And in these trousers, rather than the Roman *braccae*, he was himself; a man of the Frisii tribe and proud of it.

He stepped around a trench that was being dug in the pavement. 'Gods, are they ever going to finish all these excavations?' he grumbled.

The lead water pipes buried underneath the paving slabs were in the process of being replaced all along this stretch of the street. A huge earthquake some sixteen years earlier had caused widespread damage. As far as Raedwald understood, it was hoped this could be avoided in future by burying the pipes deeper. It appeared to be an endless task, and only one part of the construction work constantly going on around the town. There were still a lot of buildings being repaired or replaced as well, and it would probably be many years yet before all the damage was fixed.

He caught sight of a newly painted *edicta munerum* – a message inscribed on the outer wall of a nearby tavern advertising upcoming entertainments in the local amphitheatre – and pointed it out to Duro. 'Oh look, Antonius Varro has been busy. No sooner have we finished one lot of games than he's promoting the next. Greedy pig. What will he do without us, eh?'

Duro smirked. 'He'll be livid to find us gone. Serves him right.'

The writing described the next gladiatorial games being held in Pompeii, and his and Duro's names were mentioned prominently. Raedwald knew he should have been happy to be one of the star attractions, but he wasn't. It was no better than being a lion, there for the amusement of the audience. At the end of the day, the gladiators' lives weren't worth any more than those of the animals, and he, for one, couldn't wait to get away from here.

And he would escape, there was no doubt in his mind. He just had to stay alive long enough.

Pompeii was not a particularly large town, but it was easy to get lost among its streets and back alleys. Raedwald had heard tell of cities with street names and numbered buildings to help guide visitors – like Alexandria, for example. Here one had to make do with following directions and noting specific landmarks. He'd memorised the way as told to him by his master, and a few blocks further on, he and Duro turned off the main thoroughfare into a slightly less crowded street. About halfway along were the doors he'd been instructed to look for. Painted black, with a phallic symbol carved into the masonry above the lintel, there was no mistaking them, even though they stood open at present. Through them he could see a short corridor with painted plaster walls, leading to a large, bright room. More artwork attracted the eye there, the colours vivid and brash, almost overwhelmingly so. It was the norm here, intended to impress the viewer. Raedwald barely glanced at it.

Duro burst out laughing when he caught sight of the decoration above the door. 'By Belenus, another Roman who feels the need to advertise his size to the women around here. Although methinks he exaggerates somewhat.'

A chuckle escaped Raedwald, although he gave his friend a small shove. 'You know it's just a symbol for luck. Or so they say . . .'

'Of course it is.' Duro grinned, but Raedwald shook his head at him. The man never missed an opportunity to poke fun at their masters, and it would get him into trouble one of these days if he was overheard. They couldn't afford for that to happen.

As they approached the doors, an officious-looking slave materialised in the opening, barring the way. 'How can I help you?' he enquired, studying them as if they were beneath him.

Raedwald squashed the impulse to push past the rude man, and instead said, 'We're here to see your master, Lucius Caius Merula. He's expecting us. We were sent by Antonius Varro.'

The slave sniffed, as though he doubted this statement, but he reluctantly led them along the passage and into the *atrium* they'd glimpsed from the street. 'Wait here.'

They stood by the wall and looked around the room. It was huge, with a square, shallow pool of water in front of them – the so-called *impluvium* – made out of white marble. An opening in the roof above it let in the bright sunlight and allowed rain to refill the pool from time to time. As they'd seen already, all the walls were painted. Some bore frescoes with motifs of mythical tales, or gods and goddesses, while others had pretend columns and other architectural details on them. Mostly the colours were a garish red, black and yellow, with a few bits of white, but Raedwald could see that the paint was flaking in a lot of places, and some of the plaster beneath had fallen out. There were cracks, too, possibly from that morning's earthquake, or perhaps left over from the long-ago quake that had devastated the town. In fact, the entire room was shabby, as if its owner couldn't afford to have the decorations redone. The space was almost devoid of furniture, but there were marble busts, statues and other artwork dotted around. Several doors opened into smaller chambers, all dark and seemingly not in use at present.

Their perusal was cut short by a voice, echoing across the small pool of water. 'Ah, the famous barbarians, there you are.'

A Roman man, perhaps around the age of thirty, came towards them with a jovial smile on his face. It didn't reach his eyes, however, and highlighted the fact that he had a couple of bad teeth. Romans had a penchant for sweet treats, which apparently caused a lot of them problems in this regard. Raedwald was glad he seldom partook of such foods. He'd hate to lose his teeth too early.

Lucius Caius Merula, known to most people in the town as just Caius Merula, was almost a head shorter than the two gladiators, but good-looking in a typically Roman way, with short dark hair, tanned complexion, a sharp nose, full mouth and determined chin. He was precisely as Raedwald had expected, except perhaps for his age – they were normally asked to escort much older citizens. It mattered not, as long as they were paid. Although he appeared to be in fairly good shape, without the paunch some of their other charges had sported, he had nowhere near the bulk of muscle they themselves carried. Presumably he only exercised in order to look good, and had no fighting experience. That was often the case, Raedwald had found.

41

The slave who'd let them in followed in his master's wake, looking sulky, and threw the gladiators a disgruntled look before going back to his post by the front door.

Raedwald and Duro inclined their heads slightly, but didn't speak. A slave only spoke when commanded to do so, and as yet the Roman hadn't asked for a reply.

'Now then, I expect your master told you why I have need of you? I desire an escort in the evenings when I go to and from the houses of friends to dine. And also if I wish to go elsewhere afterwards.' The man tutted. 'Such lawlessness on our streets these days. A man isn't safe after dark. A shame, but there we are, and one must take precautions. I shall expect you here just before the hour of *cena* each evening, and you will wait to take me home whenever I am done. Understood?'

'Yes, *domine*.'

Raedwald waited for permission to leave, but to his surprise Lucius continued as if he hadn't finished. 'There is another task for you as well. I wish you to escort my wife and daughter whenever they venture outside this house. I have been . . . er, threatened, shall we say, by some of the more undesirable elements of our town. That threat included my family, and I won't have any harm come to them. But my wife doesn't need to know this, as it would only worry her, so I expect you to keep silent on that point.' He fixed them with a stern gaze and they both nodded their acquiescence.

It was interesting, though. What could this man possibly have done to merit threats from Pompeii's underworld? But it was not for them to enquire, obviously, so they kept silent yet again.

As if he knew there were problems with this plan, Lucius added, 'I know you likely have training during the day, and perhaps other tasks, but my wife will simply have to fit in with your schedule. She doesn't need to be gallivanting about all the time in any case. Come with me, and you can agree suitable times with her yourselves.'

Duro and Raedwald exchanged surprised looks behind the man's back, but followed him through a sort of anteroom and out into a peristyle garden at the back of the house. A colonnade enclosed it, with a roof overhanging the walkway underneath, and there were stone benches and statues set at intervals. The centre of the square contained flowers and shrubs, planted inside clipped hedges. Rosemary, thyme, salvia and other herbs scented the air with their sweet perfume. It was an oasis of tranquillity and beauty, although yet again rather shabby if one looked closely.

In the middle of the opposite side to where they had entered, an opening led into another garden with more of the same, and even a few fruit trees. At the far end there was a back wall that seemed to have been painted with scenes of exotic animals – it was hard to tell at this distance. A fountain tinkled nearby in the middle of a pond, and a small child was running along the paths, shrieking with laughter as a slave woman gave chase half-heartedly.

On one of the benches under the colonnade sat a young woman, who stood up as they approached. Raedwald's breath stuttered at first sight of her, and he had to swallow a gasp. She was as beautiful as a goddess, and he'd never seen her like. Shiny hair, black as a raven's feather, was coiled on top of her head and secured with *vittae*, coloured linen bands. She wore a simple sleeveless tunic gown with another one – he believed it was called a *stola* – on top. This had shoulder straps that matched the bands in her hair and was belted. The garments fell in graceful folds around her luscious figure, exactly like the statues of Venus in the town. Her skin was as pale and smooth as marble as well, giving the illusion that she wasn't real. When he returned his gaze to her face, he could only describe it as perfection. Large amber eyes, surrounded by sooty lashes, only slightly emphasised by face paint, and topped by beautifully shaped, delicate brows. She had a straight nose, high cheekbones and a mouth so ripe he was gripped by an insane urge to kiss her then and there as a bolt of pure lust arrowed through him.

He shook himself inwardly. By the goddess Nerthus, what was the matter with him? She was a hoity-toity Roman matron and he should *not* be attracted to her one jot.

'Aemilia, why aren't you teaching the child some manners?' Lucius had come to a halt in front of his wife and scowled at her. 'She's turned three. It's past time she became more human and less of a savage.'

'I have been giving her lessons all morning. She's merely having a short break.' The woman looked uncomfortable, and the defensive tone in her voice was clear. Raedwald's gaze fell on a set of bruises that covered her upper arm and thought he understood why. The purple marks were the exact shape of fingers that had gripped too hard.

'Well, see that it is exceedingly short,' Lucius commanded. 'There's no time for this . . . this abandonment.' He gesticulated towards his daughter, who was still gurgling with laughter.

Raedwald wondered what on earth the man was on about. Surely a child that small could be left to play? Life became serious all too soon, but at three she was still entitled to enjoy herself. What was savage about that?

As if recalling their presence, Lucius turned to indicate Raedwald and Duro. 'I have decided I don't want you and Caia to go out and about without a proper escort. There have been too many daylight robberies recently, so I have hired these two. You're not to set foot outside this house without them in attendance, is that understood?'

Aemilia's eyebrows rose slightly, but she inclined her head. 'If that is your wish.'

'It is, but they also need to train each day, so you must come to some agreement with them about suitable times for your little excursions. Perhaps you could refrain from going out unless it's strictly necessary.'

'I suppose.' It was clear she wasn't happy about that, but Lucius ignored the hesitation in her voice.

'Good, I'll leave you to it. You can have someone show them out the back way when you're done.' He nodded curtly to the two men. 'Until tonight. Don't be late.'

Chapter Six

Putney, 7 September 2022

Cat

Cat had been living in north London, conveniently close to a train station in case Derek didn't feel like taking his car to work. Although since he was inordinately proud of his BMW company car, he mostly used that. She had a driver's licence, but hadn't driven in years. He wouldn't let her anywhere near his pride and joy, and she didn't want to touch it in any case. Since everything she needed was within walking distance, a car of her own had never been necessary. Or rather, he'd never considered it a priority.

She knew now that there was a difference.

Her mum lived on the outskirts of Putney, a borough south of the river Thames in west London. Getting there took a good half-hour even late at night. At last, though, they crossed Putney Bridge and drove down the quiet high street towards Giovanna's house. As Suzanne parked on the street outside, Giovanna already had the front door open, and Cat carried a sleeping Bella into the living room before turning to her mum.

'Mamma, I'm so sorry, I—'

But Giovanna just opened her arms and pulled her in for a big hug. 'I hope you have left that scumbag for good, *cara*, otherwise I might have to commit a murder,' she murmured. She pulled back to look at Cat's face. '*Ay, ay, ay*, what has he done to you?' Her fingers lightly skimmed over the bruises, but she was careful not to push too hard.

Silent tears flowed down Cat's cheeks – delayed reaction, she supposed – and her body shook with sobs. Eventually she calmed down and remembered her manners. 'Sorry, I forgot . . . This is Suzanne, my lovely neighbour. She's been helping me. Suzanne, my mother, Giovanna. I . . . I really don't know how to thank you enough.'

'No thanks necessary, honestly. It was my pleasure, trust me. But I'd better be getting back now. Your husband is bound to come round asking questions at some point, and it might look strange if I'm not there.'

'You think he'll go looking for me among the neighbours?' Cat blinked. He'd never wanted to have anything to do with them, preferring his own circle of friends from work.

Suzanne shrugged. 'If he can't find you anywhere else. He'll probably come here first, though.' She looked at Giovanna. 'What will you do?'

'Lie through my teeth.' Her mother sounded so fierce and determined, it made Suzanne smile.

'Excellent. Well, best of luck and I'll be in touch when I hear from the police. You will let me know if you move elsewhere, won't you?'

'Yes, I promise. Thank you again, Suzanne, you're a wonderful person.' Cat gave the woman a hug, although gingerly so as not to hurt her ribs. 'I hope that in future, perhaps we can spend some more time together?'

'I'd like that. Take care now!' With a small wave, Suzanne was gone.

Giovanna made them both a cup of tea, but she didn't ask any awkward questions and Cat was grateful. She knew she had a lot of explaining to do, but it was as if all the air had gone out of her, and she simply couldn't summon up the energy.

'We'll talk in the morning. Get some sleep now,' her mother said, turning off the lights and ushering her towards the stairs as soon as she'd finished her hot drink. As Cat went to fetch Bella, who was asleep on the couch in the living room, the doorbell's shrill ringing reverberated around the house. The two women looked at each other, and panic gripped her, paralysing her completely.

Derek had found her already.

'Go into the garden. I'll lock the back door. And give me those.' Giovanna picked up the two holdalls.

Opening the back door, she shoved the bags outside, then almost pushed Cat bodily into the dark back garden. She heard the key turn in the lock, and soon after, her mother's footsteps on the stairs. She guessed Giovanna had sneaked up and was now coming down noisily, turning on the light in the hallway.

'I'm coming, I'm coming,' she shouted. 'What's-a all dis noise? Oh, is you. What you want?' Her accent had turned more Italian, probably because she knew it irritated Derek, who'd never liked the foreign connection. He'd even said once it was a shame Cat looked so much like her mother, having inherited her amber eyes and black hair. Thankfully, he hadn't voiced this opinion in front of Giovanna.

Cat held her breath as Derek started shouting, demanding to see his wife and threatening to go to the police if anyone tried to stop him.

'What-a you talking about?' Giovanna sounded sleepy and dumbfounded. Cat had never realised what a great actress her mum was and silently cheered her on. 'You wake-a me in de middle of de night for no-thing? I no see Cat for a year, thanks-a to you.'

'I don't believe you. I'm going to search the house.' There was a crash as if he'd barged past Giovanna, slamming the door into the wall, then angry footsteps stomping around.

'Hey! This is my house. You can't just-a barge in. But OK, search and then go. Fine with me, *cagacazzo*.'

Bella, who was wrapped in a blanket and held tight in Cat's arms, stirred and murmured something. 'Shh, baby, shh. Go to sleep again. It's fine,' Cat breathed, and thankfully the little girl snuggled closer and kept quiet. They couldn't be found now. They just couldn't, not when she'd finally come this far. She didn't think she'd ever muster that amount of courage again.

Derek's furious shouting could still be heard echoing through the house as he clomped up and down the stairs and opened doors and cupboards. Hopefully he wouldn't look for them outside, and there was no sign that they'd been here at all. An extra mug in the sink could just mean Giovanna hadn't felt like doing the washing-up, right? Right. The voices of several neighbours now joined the chorus, demanding to know what was going on and threatening to call the police in their turn if the noise didn't stop. Eventually Derek seemed to realise that he'd been wrong, and he shouted a final warning.

'If you see my bitch of a wife, you'd better tell me, or I'll make you very sorry!'

'That's-a my daughter you talking about!' Cat didn't catch the rest of Giovanna's muttered reply, but guessed it was something extremely uncomplimentary in Italian.

A car door slammed and the BMW roared off down the street

with squealing tyres, then peace returned at last. Neighbours placated, her mother came to unlock the back door. 'You OK, *cara*? He's gone now.'

'Yes. Thank you, we're fine. Just a bit c-cold.'

'Come in, I'll make another cup of tea. And then I think maybe you better take a taxi to the nearest hotel. That man will be back, I'm sure. I don't trust him.'

'You're right.' No matter how exhausted she was, they weren't safe yet and she had to keep going. 'I'm sorry, I shouldn't have come here. He could have hurt you too.'

'Don't be silly, of course you should. I'm your *mamma*. I will help you, and tomorrow we go and see a lawyer, yes?'

'Definitely.'

After a tense night, when Cat woke at the slightest sound, panic squeezing her insides, she met her mother in a café in Putney High Street. They'd thought it best not to be seen anywhere near Giovanna's house, just in case Derek started asking the neighbours if they'd noticed anything.

'So, I have the details of a good lawyer,' Giovanna began, once they'd ordered coffee and cake. Bella was quietly doing some colouring in between taking bites out of a giant cupcake. 'A very good friend of mine recommended her.'

'Thank you, that sounds great.' Cat was grateful, because she'd had no idea where to even start looking for someone reliable and trustworthy. 'I hope she's not too expensive? Or perhaps she'll agree to wait for payment until the divorce comes through. I should be entitled to half the value of the house, right?'

She hadn't any savings of her own, but before going to bed last night, she'd gone into hers and Derek's joint account and transferred half the amount to an online bank account she'd been using for her translation invoices. Thankfully he hadn't thought to block her yet. Perhaps he'd believed he would catch her out when she tried to use her card to pay for something, as then he'd know which area she was in. She wasn't that stupid though.

He'd had access to her work account in order to check the amounts against her invoices each month before transferring the money to the joint account. It was in her sole name, however, as she'd set it up before their marriage, and she'd already changed the passcode on it. Derek could argue with the bank till he was blue in the face, but she doubted it would do him any good. Either way, she was going to set up a new account with another bank that afternoon and move the money again, then he'd never find it.

Giovanna answered her now. 'Yes, of course you should. But don't worry about payment. I will take care of that for now, and you can pay me back.'

'Can you afford that?' Cat had always thought of her mother as fairly poor, as she was careful with money and never spent huge amounts.

'Of course. I've been saving for years and I have a pension now. Also, I'm in the process of selling my house. I'm thinking of moving back to Italy. I was going to tell you once I had everything sorted out. I hoped to persuade you to leave Derek and come and live with me. I really wanted to discuss it with you, but . . .'

'But you couldn't get hold of me?' Guilt settled in Cat's gut like an indigestible ball of dough. 'I'm so sorry, Mamma. I . . . It was difficult and it seemed easier just to keep my distance. Derek would have—'

Her mother cut her off by putting her hand over Cat's on the table. 'It's OK, *cara*, I understand. And it is in the past. We will not think of it again, yes? Now we move forward, make plans.'

Cat swallowed past the lump in her throat and nodded. 'Yes, forward.' She sighed. 'But how? Lawyer first, then what? Should I find a shelter for abuse victims?'

'I don't think so. Listen, I've been thinking – do you have your passport with you?'

'No. Derek has our passports locked in a safe I didn't have access to, and Bella doesn't have one yet anyway. We were going to get one when we booked a holiday for this summer, but then he decided we couldn't afford to go this year after all.'

'That's fine. I have an idea.' Giovanna rooted round in her capacious handbag and brought something out. 'Look, I have your Italian passport. You left it behind and it still has one year to run before it expires.'

'Oh, I'd forgotten I left that with you.'

Cat had been born in Italy, as Giovanna had gone home to her mother to give birth because she'd been scared. When she had returned to England, Cat's father had registered her birth there as well and made sure she had dual nationality. Whenever they'd visited relatives in Italy, she'd used her Italian passport as it made things easier. Since marrying Derek, however, those visits had ceased.

'Well, lucky you did. With this, you can get an Italian passport for Bella, and we can both travel to Naples to stay with my brothers. They will protect us until the police deal with Derek.'

'You think? Is that allowed?'

'Maybe not, but we don't tell them. Just go. If you are needed here, your friend Suzanne will let us know and you can fly back quickly.'

Cat glanced at the passport her mother handed over. 'This has my maiden name on it, though. I never got round to changing it.'

It also had her original Christian name, Caterina. Derek had decreed that Cat was a ridiculous nickname for a grown woman, and her real name, chosen by her Italian mother, was too foreign. He'd made her change it by deed poll to the English version, Catherine. It hadn't seemed worth fighting over at the time, but now . . . *Oh God, she'd been such a fool!* Why had she ever fallen for this man? But she knew the answer.

She had been an awkward teenager, shy and self-conscious about what she considered her excessively curvaceous figure and puppy fat. As the only child of two strict Italian parents, she'd always strived to study hard and be a good daughter. That meant she didn't party like most of her schoolmates, and had few friends apart from the class nerds. She didn't really fit in, and kept to herself for the most part. By the end of senior school, she'd never had a boyfriend, although she'd been on a couple of awkward dates. And then along came Derek.

He'd been so charming at first. Handsome and exciting. The perfect gentleman, treating her like she was a princess, solicitous of her comfort and never pushing her too far. Five years older than her, he had seemed worldly-wise and confident, all the things she was not. If he sometimes verged a little towards domineering, she didn't mind. It only added to his allure – the alpha type of male she'd often read about in romances. Subtle warnings from her parents had been brushed aside. She felt they were simply being overprotective of their little girl. She had fallen under Derek's spell, and when he asked her to marry him, she had thought all her dreams had come true. And they had, for a while . . . until Bella was born.

He'd been so disappointed she wasn't a boy, although he tried to joke it off, saying they'd have a son next time. But from then on, he'd started finding fault with everything, from the way Cat looked to how little she was earning and how much she was spending. He had begun to alienate her from her family and friends. Since all her energy went towards looking after a baby by herself, while also trying to keep up with her job working from home, she had barely noticed. By the time she did, her father had died, and she was crippled with grief. In any case, she'd started to feel that it *was* all her fault. She was incompetent, stupid, a bad mother and wife, not to mention unattractive, even though the puppy fat was long gone. Derek had, quite simply, brainwashed her, and one by one the bars of her prison closed in on her because he had access to her phone, her emails and her bank accounts. His control was absolute.

And then he'd hit her . . .

The first time it happened, she'd been so shocked she had just stared at him. Then she had gone to pack a bag, put Bella in her pram, and headed for the nearest Tube station. Derek had caught up with her halfway there, apologising profusely and begging her to return home. He had appeared so sincere, so contrite, she'd fallen for it. It was a while before it happened again, but by then she was more or less estranged from her mother and had nowhere to run to. And he had almost convinced her that she deserved it. Things only got worse from then on, a vicious downward spiral, and suddenly there she was – alone and stuck in an abusive relationship with no way out. What was she to do?

Well, no more. She had escaped at last, and she wasn't going back.

'Doesn't matter,' Giovanna was saying now, bringing her back to the discussion about passports. 'You've been using your maiden name for your translation work anyway, haven't you? I saw on your website.' She was clearly fired up about this whole idea, and it did have merit.

It was true Cat had kept her original name for work. It had caused an almighty row with Derek before he'd accepted that her clients knew her by that name and she'd built up a solid reputation as a good translator. The fact that it was Italian merely seemed to inspire confidence in her abilities.

Giovanna continued, 'So you can just say you've been using both, and now you're getting divorced you prefer to only have this one. We give them the lawyer's name and they can check if they want.'

'But where am I going to get an Italian passport for Bella?'

'At the embassy, of course. I will take you. Maybe you can just add her to this one for now instead of getting her one of her own?' Her mother's smile was triumphant, as if she was pleased she'd worked it all out.

'Ah, but I don't have her birth certificate. Derek has that as well.' Cat's hopes crashed. Hiding out in another country had sounded so appealing, but nothing was ever that easy.

'Pfft!' Giovanna gestured with her hands. 'You send for a new one. I checked online. You can apply, say the old one was lost. You are her mother, it's allowed. And it doesn't cost much. Have it sent to my house.'

That was genius, Cat had to admit. And the fact that her mother had found all these things out online stunned her slightly. It would seem she didn't know her very well any more, but that would change from now on, she vowed. Giovanna was in their lives again and that was where she would stay.

'OK, first things first – the lawyer. I'd better phone and make an appointment.'

'Already done. If we leave in ten minutes, we'll be right on time.'

Cat shook her head and gazed at her mother in wonder. 'You are full of surprises today. But in the best possible way. Thank you, Mamma.'

'Actually, I have one more.' Giovanna opened her large handbag and withdrew something wrapped in wrinkled old tissue paper. 'I want you to have this. It's been in our family for generations and is supposed to give luck. If anyone needs it right now, it's you, *cara*. Wear it always.'

Cat opened up the layers and gasped at the gold bracelet that was revealed. It glimmered brightly compared to the dull sheen of the tissue paper. It was in the shape of three narrow leaves in a neat row – laurel, perhaps? When she slid it onto her arm, they wrapped around her like a clingy vine. It almost felt as though they tightened their grip on her so as not to let go, but that was probably just her skin reacting to the feel of the smooth metal against it.

'Is it real?' She stared at her mother, who nodded.

'*Sì*. It is pure gold. One of our ancestors found it. He said it was probably Roman.'

'Er, shouldn't it be in a museum then?' Cat frowned, but couldn't stop looking at the beautiful armband. It was calling to her on a visceral level, and something inside her protested that she never wanted to let it go.

'No, it was a long time ago. Who will know? There are lots of copies these days. His wife liked it and wanted to keep it, so she did. Now it is yours. Enjoy.'

'Thank you, Mamma. I don't know what to say. It's magnificent! I will treasure it, I promise.' And she was never taking it off, ever.

'Good, that is all I ask. I can feel in my bones it will help you.'

Giovanna sounded so sure about that, Cat didn't have the heart to argue that an inanimate object couldn't do anything. She was just pleased to own it.

Chapter Seven

Pompeii, 8 September AD 79

Raedwald

When Lucius had disappeared back into the house, Aemilia gestured towards the bench where she'd been sitting. 'Please, take a seat.'

Raedwald and Duro exchanged another glance. She wanted them to sit in her presence? With her?

'But we're slaves,' Raedwald ground out, too shocked to remember not to speak unless invited to.

It went against the grain to refer to himself as a slave, and he hoped he wouldn't have to for much longer, but it was the truth. Had she missed that? Not to mention the fact that gladiators were looked down upon by the rest of Roman society. Theirs was among the lowest of occupations because they hired themselves out for money, just like whores, and were therefore considered *infames* – disreputable or unsavoury.

'You are also famous. Celebrated gladiators, no less. I believe that entitles you to some courtesy. I saw you in action yesterday.

We should be honoured to have you in our house.' She smiled, something that hit him almost like a blow to his midsection.

He truly hadn't imagined she could become even more beautiful, but that smile lit up her eyes and gave her a radiance that was difficult to turn away from. Somehow he managed it, and looked out over the garden as he sank down onto the bench a good two feet away from her. Duro remained standing, leaning against the nearest pillar, but he was regarding the woman with a curious expression.

'Thank you, *domina*,' Raedwald said reluctantly. He felt her courtesy demanded politeness in return.

'Would you care for some refreshment?'

She didn't wait for their assent, but clapped her hands. Two surly-looking slave girls came out of a nearby room and sashayed over towards them. Raedwald frowned. What was the matter with the slaves in this house? They all seemed grumpy and uncooperative in the extreme. Although he fully understood the frustration of being at someone's beck and call, he'd seldom seen this level of insolence.

'Fruit juice for three, and some figs, please,' Aemilia ordered, and the two girls nodded and walked off, seemingly not in any hurry. 'Two of Lucius's recent acquisitions,' she muttered, perhaps having noticed Raedwald's questioning gaze. Her cheeks flushed, as if she realised she'd given away too much, and she abruptly changed the subject. 'So, what time of day do you train?'

'From dawn for at least two hours, and then again late afternoon.'

'Could you be here by about the third hour then? As my husband said, I shan't need you every day, but occasionally I have to be out and about.'

'That would be fine. Tomorrow?'

'Yes, please. I must buy new sandals for little Caia. She's growing so fast.' Aemilia's eyes sought out her daughter and her features softened with love. Raedwald tried not to let this influence his opinion of her. She was still a rich Roman woman, good mother or not, and he hated them all with a vengeance. His first owner had seen to that. She had been a cruel wealthy widow who had tried to break him in every way, physically and mentally. She hadn't succeeded, but the experience had scarred him for life, and he wasn't likely to ever forgive or forget such treatment.

They remained silent while the slave girls eventually brought the requested juice and figs, which were placed on a small table in front of Aemilia. She personally handed the two men a glass each and Raedwald cradled his carefully. He'd never held anything made of such exquisite material before and was afraid of dropping it.

'So what are your real names?'

'I beg your pardon?' He blinked at her, startled by the unusual question. No one here had ever asked him that before, and the only one who called him by his real name was Duro.

Another beautiful smile, accompanied by twinkling eyes, had him drawing in a sharp breath, but he tried to concentrate on her words. 'I assume you are called Rufus here because of your hair colour, but presumably where you came from it is not an unusual feature. And I know most slaves are simply assigned names when they arrive on our shores.'

It was true – he'd almost been offended when he had learned that Rufus meant red. His first mistress could have been more imaginative in deciding what to call him. It was reminiscent of the way one named a dog. He shook himself inwardly – that was neither here nor there now. The lady had asked a question.

'I am called Raedwald, and this is Duro.' He indicated his companion, who seemed to be leaving it up to him to speak for both of them. To cover the fact that he felt uncomfortable giving her his real name – it was too personal somehow – he drank some of the sweet juice he'd been given, enjoying the taste of it immensely. It was one of the things he actually appreciated about this place, made from delicious fruits unlike any he'd had in his homeland.

'And where do you come from?' At his raised eyebrows, she added, 'I am familiar with most of the conquered territories. My father travelled widely.'

'Well, as far as I know, my tribes are not yet conquered,' he retorted drily, and he was proud of that. 'Here we are known as Frisii. Duro is from Britannia, of a tribe called the Icenii.'

She nodded. 'Then if you don't mind, I shall call you by your real names. It will be less intimidating.'

He couldn't help himself, he just had to ask. 'Why would you find our Roman names intimidating, *domina*?' She was in charge and they were at her beck and call.

'Because they are associated with you as gladiators. As I said, I have seen you in the arena, and what you do is terrifying, brutal.' She glanced at the cuts and bruises that decorated every visible area of his skin, as if to demonstrate her point.

There was some logic to this, but he didn't want to try and unravel it right now. Besides, he didn't care how she viewed them or what she called them. They were merely here to perform a task, and the sooner they did it, the faster they would be paid. He finished his juice and fidgeted slightly. As if sensing his impatience to be gone, she stood up. 'I shall see you both tomorrow then. It is probably best if you enter by the back door.' She gestured towards a door set into the far corner of the garden wall.

Best for whom? But Raedwald didn't voice that thought either.

Before they could move, the little girl came hurtling along the walkway and cannoned into Duro's legs.

'Whoa! Careful there,' he murmured, smiling down at her.

She held out a hand that contained a scraggly bunch of flowers. 'I picked flowers! Do you want one? Here.' Choosing a sadly drooping one, she held it out towards him. Raedwald almost laughed out loud at his friend's flummoxed expression. He doubted the man had ever been offered such a gift before, and by so tiny a female.

'Caia, my sweet, I really don't think . . .' her mother began to say, but Duro swiftly hunkered down in front of the girl.

'Thank you, *dominula*,' he said to the little miss with a smile. 'I shall treasure it always.'

To Raedwald's further surprise, the youngster then turned to him and held out another bloom. 'You too?'

He bowed to her and accepted the gift. 'My thanks.'

Aemilia swept in and scooped the child into her arms. 'That was very kind of you, Caia, but we must let our guests go now.' She nodded at them. 'Thank you for humouring her. Until tomorrow.'

It was their cue to leave, and they did, each carrying a some-what wilted flower. When they were standing outside the back door, in a narrow, foul-smelling alley, they looked at each other with raised brows.

'What on earth just happened?' Duro chuckled. 'That must be the youngest admirer we've ever had.'

Raedwald smiled. 'Yes, definitely. At least guarding that one won't be boring.'

If only she didn't come with such an alluring mother, their assignment would have been just perfect.

Pompeii, 9 September AD 79

Aemilia

Walking down the busy street, Aemilia stopped every fifty paces or so to turn around and check that everyone was following her – the slave women she'd brought, her daughter, who was in their care, and the two gladiators bringing up the rear. There were so many people out and about, it would be easy to become separated. Or so she told herself.

Yet each time she couldn't help but glance at the red-headed man, Raedwald. In the sharp morning sunlight, his hair was shining like newly polished copper mixed with burgundy Frankish wine. He wore it long, flowing over his shoulders, and far from making him seem effeminate, as most Romans would say, it was absolutely magnificent. Add to that his impressive physique, battle scars and general air of ferocity, and she wasn't surprised that he was garnering a lot of attention as he passed by. She didn't know why he drew her gaze more than the other barbarian, whose dark golden curls were just as long and his body as perfect, but she hadn't been able to stop thinking about Raedwald since their first meeting the day before.

She'd known who he was the moment she set eyes on him. Having attended quite a few gladiatorial games in the town this year, she'd seen both barbarians in action in the arena. Then, as now, she'd been mesmerised by the one they called Rufus, although she couldn't explain it even to herself. There was just something about him that made him stand out. He'd fought with incredible valour, vanquishing all his opponents. She was embarrassed to recall that he'd featured in quite a few of her dreams immediately afterwards.

She knew she wasn't the only woman in Pompeii who daydreamed about the amazing gladiators. At the baths, she'd heard the whispered gossip about young Roman matrons who attempted to gain entry to the gladiator barracks for what they called 'a rough tumble'. The mere words made her cheeks heat up, even though she didn't quite understand what they meant. Obviously it had something to do with what happened between men and women for the purposes of procreation. It wasn't an act she enjoyed, however, and although Lucius usually seemed satisfied, it was always over very quickly, thank the gods. It wasn't that she found her husband distasteful – he was handsome enough, and could be charming when he wished to – but she'd never relished his attentions in the marriage bed. She gathered that some women liked it immensely, but she had no idea why. Still, she'd had a vague sensation of excitement when watching Raedwald in action. A deep thrill that made her insides flutter – and even more so up close – so perhaps it was different with a different man?

'Watch your step!'

An angry voice and a hard shoulder bumping into hers brought her back to the present. She should be paying attention and not mooning over a man who wasn't her husband. With a mumbled apology and a sigh, she tried to steer her thoughts into more acceptable channels.

'Did he hurt you, *domina*?' Raedwald had caught up with her and was looking down on her with a frown. He had a slightly foreign accent, and a deep but melodious voice, which for some reason sent a shiver down her spine.

'No, it was nothing. Ignore him.'

'As you wish, lady.'

He fell back again and she forced herself to continue walking without peeking over her shoulder. She couldn't help but think about the last time she'd seen him in the arena, victorious, his torso naked and covered in blood and bruises. The crowd had chanted his name and she'd joined in, mesmerised by the sight of him – all muscles and raw male power. She'd never imagined she would come within two feet of the man, or that he'd be assigned to follow her around. It was disconcerting in more ways than one.

They made their way down the *decumanus maximus*, one of the two main streets running east to west through the town. As usual, it was uncomfortably crowded and busy. Most of the townspeople spent a large part of their day outdoors, especially those of the poorer class. They lived in cramped accommodation and no doubt appreciated every moment they didn't have to be cooped up indoors. At a crossroads, she passed a shrine at the corner of a building – a simple altar with a few sacrifices scattered on its surface – and in the centre, where the two roads met, a public fountain. Water brought from faraway mountains via an incredibly long aqueduct flowed into a square trough and gushed through the open mouth of a god's head carved out of stone. Women and slaves congregated around it to fill their vessels, and while they waited, gossip and laughter ensued. Aemilia envied them; she had no true friends to really share her thoughts or laughter with.

The tempting smell of newly baked bread hung in the air, as well as the delicious aromas of cooking from the various eating establishments. These competed with the stench from a nearby tannery, and the even more noxious odours of animal and human excrement that coated the streets. It hadn't rained for a while, and they could definitely do with a torrential downpour to clear the roads of filth. Aemilia made sure to use the stepping stones placed at intervals whenever she needed to cross the street so as not to soil the hem of her garments.

Deep in thought, her musings were cut short by a high-pitched scream. At the same time a string of curses rent the air. She swivelled instantly, and felt her heart stop beating altogether as she watched Raedwald plunge into the road and scoop Caia out of the way of the flailing hooves of a mule. He was just in time – one single moment longer and the child's head would have been crushed. As if it was equally terrified, the mule brayed loudly and tried to buck. The driver, red in the face and clearly furious, swore again and pulled hard on the reins to bring the animal under control.

'Keep your child away from the street, you imbecile!' he shouted, making a rude gesture towards Raedwald. As Raedwald was holding Caia, and clearly busy, Duro reciprocated in his stead with an even ruder hand sign.

'And you shouldn't drive so recklessly on a busy thoroughfare,' he called back.

Aemilia couldn't move. She just stared as the barbarian swung her daughter up into his arms, one hand protectively cradling her small head. Caia had clearly had a fright, and her bottom lip was wobbling, but Raedwald was having none of it. He smiled at her and threw her up into the air, catching her with a laugh. The threatening tears stopped abruptly, and Caia looked at him with big eyes and the beginning of a smile. When he threw her up a second time, laughter gurgled out of her and she seemed to immediately forget what had just happened.

'Again!' she demanded, and that one word finally galvanised Aemilia into action.

She rushed over towards her child. 'Caia, are you—'

'She's fine.' The barbarian's deep voice interrupted her, and when she blinked at him, his green eyes appeared to be trying to convey something. 'We're playing a game,' he clarified.

'Yes, watch, Mater. Again!'

Obeying this order, Raedwald sent her flying into the air once again, eliciting more laughter. Something inside Aemilia unfroze, and she drew in a huge breath. Her heart began to slow its rapid tattoo, but it was by no means back to normal yet. She understood what he was doing, distracting Caia so that she'd forget the terrifying experience of a moment ago, and she was extremely grateful. For herself, it wasn't as easy to let the fear go.

'Thank you,' she breathed, the words heartfelt.

'It was nothing.' The barbarian had now put Caia down on the ground between himself and his companion. 'Would you like to ride on my shoulders the rest of the way, *dominula*?' he asked her. 'Or maybe Drusus's?' He nodded in his companion's direction.

'Yes, yes! Yours.' Caia jumped up and down eagerly, while Duro sent his friend a quizzical glance. But he too was smiling at Aemilia's daughter, and she was finding it difficult to take this in – two grown men being kind to a small child that wasn't theirs.

Perhaps they had children they'd had to leave behind? Or even wives and families at the gladiator barracks? Such things were not unheard of. The thought made her inhale sharply again, and she blurted out the question before she had time to think. 'You have little ones of your own?'

They both frowned and shook their heads. Duro spoke quickly. 'Younger siblings, *domina*. Lots of them.'

She nodded. They'd clearly been used to helping with them. She became aware that passers-by were throwing them curious looks. 'We had better continue.' Should she insist on Caia returning to the slave women, who were supposed to be looking after her?

As if he'd read her thoughts, Raedwald said, 'She's safe with us. We won't let any harm come to her.'

'Very well.' Aemilia fixed the women with a stern gaze. 'As for you, we will be having words upon our return.'

They were both looking very pale, their eyes shimmering with unshed tears. 'It was an accident, *domina*,' one of them whispered. 'The little one, she just suddenly pulled her hand out of mine and darted off the pavement. I—'

'Later. Come.' This was not the place for a discussion like that.

Raedwald lifted Caia and swung her effortlessly onto his shoulders. 'Hold on to my head, yes?' he ordered, although Aemilia could see he had a firm grip on her daughter's legs so she couldn't fall off either way. The smile on the little girl's face as she looked out over the crowds from this vantage point was nothing short of blinding.

They reached the Forum without further mishap, the large rectangular colonnaded open space just as crowded as the main street at this time of day. It was the heart of the town, both marketplace and political centre, and surrounded by formal edifices of various kinds. Many of them were still being restored following the massive earthquake over a decade ago, but they were no less imposing for that. Travertine slabs paved the square, the white limestone bright in the sunlight. There were three main public buildings to the south, where the local magistrates – the *duoviri* and *aediles* – met, including the lofty Basilica. On the west side stood the Temple of Apollo, adjoined by a colonnade where street vendors had set up their stalls as it was market day. To the north, the impressive Capitolium, a temple dedicated to the gods Jupiter, Juno and Minerva, was flanked by arches of brick and marble. And on the final side, more public buildings could be found, as well as the so-called Macellum, where various foodstuffs were sold. In the distance to the north, the shape of Mount Vesuvius could be glimpsed, its slopes covered in vineyards and olive groves.

The noise and bustle was deafening, sellers hawking their wares by shouting at the top of their lungs. Aemilia was jostled several times, but she was used to it. There were merchants selling everything from expensive cloth to cheap trinkets, but today she was mainly interested in the shoemaker's wares. She waited her turn, then sat down with her daughter while the man found a few pairs that might fit the child. She tried on three different ones, and Aemilia settled for a pair of *carbatina* sandals, with soft leather soles and an upper part made of lattice work, tied around the ankles with laces. They were practical in the heat and wouldn't fall off. Besides, Caia would grow out of them quickly, so there was no point buying anything more elaborate.

'I don't like them.' The little girl's mouth set in a mulish line and she crossed her arms over her thin chest. 'Want those.' She pointed to a pair with lots of unnecessary embellishments that wouldn't be suitable at all and were much more expensive.

'Not today. Perhaps next time.' Aemilia tried for a reasonable tone, but she was still shaken from the earlier incident and her patience was at an all-time low.

'Don't like them!' Caia repeated, her voice rising and the lower lip making an appearance.

Aemilia sighed and bit her teeth together hard. She'd prefer not to chastise her daughter in public, but she couldn't let her have her way over this either. To her surprise, Raedwald, who'd been standing like an impassive statue behind them, bent down and whispered something in Caia's ear. Aemilia only caught the words 'shoulders again', but whatever else he said, it worked.

'We can buy them,' Caia conceded, and jumped off the chair as if the transaction was already concluded. 'Want to go now.'

'Er, right. Good.' Aemilia gathered her wits and, after a quick glance at Raedwald, began to haggle with the shoe seller.

They had a few other purchases to make at the Macellum, but Caia behaved impeccably the entire time and didn't complain once about having to wait. Normally Aemilia would leave her at home with the slaves, but she'd had to bring her today since she was the one who needed shoes. And thanks to Raedwald, it had been a surprisingly smooth process. It would seem she was in his debt yet again.

And she wasn't sure how she felt about that.

Chapter Eight

Sorrento, 26 September 2022

Cat

Less than three weeks after her escape from Derek, Cat found herself walking along a paved street in Sorrento, the famous town near Naples in Italy. She was alone, with just a small suitcase and a capacious handbag containing her laptop and USB pens. Butterflies danced in her stomach, and her hands shook slightly. She was about to embark on a new phase of her life. Alone.

It had been a nerve-racking few weeks, but at last everything had been sorted out. The Italian embassy had very kindly issued Bella a passport quickly when Cat lied and said she needed to go to Italy for a funeral and couldn't leave her daughter behind. The fact that Bella didn't yet have a British one helped, as there was no cross-checking required. The flight from Heathrow had gone without a hitch, and her fears that they would be stopped had proved unfounded. Hopefully that meant Derek hadn't suspected her of leaving the country, and had refrained from reporting her missing. He'd turned up at her mother's house on several occasions, before she left to fly to Italy with Cat and Bella, each time searching the place thoroughly. It was clear he was still looking for them in the UK, but he hadn't found a single trace of them. Just to be on the safe side, Cat had moved from one cheap hotel to another every few days, paying in cash.

Today she'd left Bella ensconced with Giovanna at her uncle Pietro's roomy apartment on the outskirts of the Old Town in Naples. It was over an hour away from Sorrento by train, but still close enough that she would be able to visit a couple of times a week. Although saying goodbye that morning had been painful for Cat, her daughter had barely noticed her leaving. She'd been busy playing with a whole horde of second cousins around her own age, and it was clear she'd never been happier. At home, Cat had never dared to take her daughter to play dates, as she couldn't reciprocate without Derek finding out. By the looks of it, Bella had definitely been missing out.

'She'll be fine,' Giovanna had whispered. 'And you can come and see her often, as long as you're careful.'

They had decided that Derek might eventually figure out that they'd gone to Italy, since he knew about the connection there. He'd only ever met her Italian relatives once, at their wedding, but he hadn't been here and didn't really know them. Hopefully that meant he was unlikely to find them. Rossi was a common surname and Bella was easily hidden among Pietro's many grand-children. She and Giovanna would move from one relative's house to another each week. It seemed safer not to stay in one place for too long. One more tiny girl in a group wouldn't merit a second glance, and she was dark-haired like the others. After a week with Giovanna, she'd even picked up some Italian.

Cat, however, needed to stay out of the way. To that end, she had taken a temporary living-in job as a waitress and chamber-maid in a small boutique hotel in a former seventeenth-century *palazzo* overlooking the coast in Sorrento. It meant she'd be earning some money to pay for herself and Bella as well. They couldn't sponge off Uncle Pietro, and for now, she didn't dare take on any translation work from her usual sources. She'd told the agency that she was on sick leave for the foreseeable future.

It was amazing what could be achieved when you put your mind to it. Cat had seen a solicitor and started divorce proceedings. She'd been interviewed by the police and pressed charges against Derek for causing grievous bodily harm. The kind doctor had been as good as her word and wasted no time sending her report. And Suzanne had emailed them the video of that last attack. Cat couldn't believe she'd snuck in and filmed from behind the kitchen door without Derek noticing, but thank goodness she had. The police said this would help enormously and they were sure to get a conviction. The lawyer agreed and told Cat not to worry about a thing. She'd ask for a restraining order too, although secretly Cat doubted that would stop Derek if he ever found her.

'He won't care about that,' she'd commented to her mother.

'No, probably not, which is why you need to disappear.'

Giovanna was right. The main thing was to go somewhere he couldn't trace her, and nowhere in England seemed far enough. Unfortunately, taking Bella out of the country without Derek's agreement was illegal, but Cat deemed it worth the risk. She simply couldn't stay in the UK. With a bit of luck, he would never find out, since she hadn't applied for a British passport for Bella. The Italian embassy had granted one only because Cat herself had dual nationality.

Her Italian passport was now safe at her uncle's apartment. She'd had no trouble entering Italy, and her new employers were satisfied that she had the right to work there. Giovanna's other brother, Luca, had pulled some strings and got her this job, as he knew the owners of the hotel.

'I have given them some background details, but they can be trusted to keep their mouths shut,' he'd promised.

She told herself stoutly she'd be fine. She had to be.

As for Derek, Suzanne had told her that the police had come to question him, and she'd overheard him in the garden a few days later on the phone.

'He was furious,' she reported gleefully. 'I gathered he'd been given the sack and he was vehemently denying any wrongdoing, trying to hang on to his job and his car. I'm guessing his boss must have been sent a report by the police, and who'd want an abuser on their sales team? I think he wrecked what was left of your living room after the call ended.'

This news made Cat smile for the first time in days, perhaps months.

She hoped the loss of his job and that shiny company car would hurt. A lot.

As for herself, she would have to be very careful. Even here in Sorrento, she might not be safe. She couldn't help but glance over her shoulder every few yards, expecting Derek to pop up at any moment. What if he'd followed her? Or worse, knew where Bella was? He would be dangerous in the extreme, now that his whole life was unravelling.

She shivered and took one final look around before stepping into the hotel. No one was looking at her, but she still couldn't shake the ominous feeling of doom. Would she really be safe here? And for how long? Only time would tell.

Sorrento, 28 September 2022

'Caterina, can you take the corner table, please? There's an *inglesi*, and you're so much better at that than I am!'

Cat put down the heavy tray full of dirty crockery and glanced across the small dining room. Over by the open French doors, next to an ornate Juliet balcony, sat an auburn-haired man. He was deep in thought, drumming his fingers on the table as if he was impatient. 'Oh, has he been waiting long?'

Her fellow waitress, Pia, shrugged. 'Not that long, but he looks a bit . . . dangerous.' She smiled and wiggled her eyebrows. 'He's quite big, isn't he. Anyway, he's all yours.'

'Thanks for that,' Cat muttered, but she didn't mind really. He didn't scare her, despite the rather intense look on his face. In fact, she almost felt as if there was something familiar about him, but she didn't know why. She was sure she'd never met him before.

She smoothed her hands on her apron, then fished her notepad and pen out of the pocket. As she came closer, the man looked up and blinked, as if he'd been far away. Thick dark lashes framed his green eyes, highlighting their intense colour. There was a frown creasing his brow, but he made an effort to erase it when she addressed him.

'I'm sorry, sir, my colleague didn't quite catch your order. Her English isn't all that brilliant. Would you mind repeating it, please?'

His eyes crinkled briefly with amusement, and when he replied, she understood why Pia had had such problems. The man was Scottish. Very Scottish. 'Och, no' at all. I take it you've no problem understanding me?'

'Er, no, I think I can manage, sir,' she murmured, waiting with her pen poised.

'I'd like an espresso with plenty o' sugar on the side, and no milk, please. I cannae abide hot milky drinks, although I dinnae mind the white stuff cold. Some toast with jam and butter, and fresh fruit, if you have any. I don't suppose there's porritch?'

She'd been writing furiously, but looked up at that. 'If you mean oats cooked with salt and water, I'll see what we can do. Sugar and milk on the side with that as well? Or honey, perhaps?'

The hotel prided itself on its excellent service, and even if the chef had never cooked Scottish porridge before, Cat could do it herself if need be. She'd often eaten it, because it was cheap and she liked the taste.

He smiled and nodded, then said in a perfectly normal English accent, with just a slight trace of the Scots, 'Thank you, that would be very kind, Miss . . .?' He peered at her name badge, 'Caterina.'

It was her turn to blink. 'You were having us on? Are you an actor or something?'

'No, sorry, it was just a wee joke.' He held up his hands in a placating gesture. 'I really am half Scottish, but I barely spoke with an accent at all when your colleague came to take my order. I just thought I'd see if you were made of sterner stuff, and clearly you are. Seriously, I apologise. It was badly done of me.'

Cat stared at him for a moment. She couldn't decide whether to be charmed or annoyed, but it wasn't for her to take offence if the guests wanted to joke with the staff. And at least he'd had the decency to apologise. 'No worries,' she said. 'I'll go and place your order now.'

She returned shortly afterwards with his espresso and a big bowl of white sugar lumps. 'Here you go, sir. Your food will be out shortly.'

'You speak very good English for an Italian.' He cringed as he realised how that had sounded. 'I mean, no offence. God, I seem to be putting my feet in it right royally this morning.'

Cat's mouth twitched. Perhaps he wasn't a morning person and his brain wasn't quite in gear yet.

'None taken. I grew up in the UK, that's why. My dad had some English relatives on his mother's side, so my parents decided to emigrate from here just before I was born.' Not that it was any of his business, nor the whole truth, but there was no harm in telling him either.

'Ah, I see. You're very lucky, being bilingual. I so wish I could speak Italian right now.'

She raised her eyebrows at him, hesitating. She shouldn't really fraternise with the guests, but he'd made her curious now. And her ribs hadn't quite healed and were aching, so any excuse to stand still for a while was extremely welcome.

'Any particular reason?' Perhaps he was marrying an Italian woman and her relatives were talking about him behind his back. Or there was someone he wanted to woo, but she didn't speak English, or . . .

He interrupted her wayward thoughts. 'I'm here to do some research, and I've been given a load of reports to read, but the people here haven't had all the documents translated as they promised. Apart from a few graphs and charts, I can't make head nor tail of most of them.' He sighed and raked his hands through his hair, drawing her attention to it. It was cut very short on the back and sides, but the top part was a mass of glossy waves, the colour a deep, dark red that glowed in the autumn sunlight. She had a sudden urge to run her own fingers through it, but that was crazy.

'I see,' she said, busying herself with removing some dirty crockery from the next table.

'You wouldn't happen to know of any reliable translators here, would you?' he asked. 'I know I could probably find one by googling, but it's really important that the translation is correct, or it could ruin everything.' He sighed again. 'I suppose I'm just going to have to send the documents back to someone in the UK and get it done over there. More delays.'

Cat stopped what she was doing and regarded him with her head tilted to one side. 'Would it be so bad to spend a few extra days here? The hotel isn't fully booked at the moment, so I'm sure we'd have room for you. And there is a lot to see here – Naples, Pompeii, Herculaneum, Vesuvius, Capri . . .' She gestured to the window, where the volcano loomed to the right, in the centre of the Bay of Naples. That was what most people came here for.

'Oh, I didn't mean I'd be short of things to do – there's other stuff I can get on with. It's just that those reports sort of form the basis for what I'm doing. It's hard to explain. Anyway, needs must.'

She came to a quick decision. 'If you think you might be able to trust me, I could do the translations for you in my spare time. Might be slightly faster?'

'You could?' He fixed his moss-green gaze on her, making her stomach flutter ever so slightly. His eyes were beautiful, there was no other word for it. Like peridots in sunshine. But she didn't have time to stand here and admire them. She had work to do.

'Think about it,' she said. 'The offer is there. If you're worried about accuracy, I can give you my CV and some references. I have worked as a translator before, in England. For many years, actually. Now I'd better get your food before it goes cold.'

When she returned with his breakfast, he smiled and thanked her. 'And yes please, I'd like to take you up on your offer, if I may. How soon can you start? And what are your rates?'

She quoted the sum she normally charged her English clients, adding the percentage that the agencies she used to get work from would have claimed. There was no way she dared go via them. She had to handle this by herself. Derek would have found her through the agencies in an instant, but he'd never know about a private arrangement. And doing some extra work in the evening here wasn't a hardship. It would save her from feeling depressed and lonely.

'I have time off between two and five, and then again in the evening. If you could leave the documents with the receptionist, I'll pick them up later.'

'I'd rather hand them to you personally, if you don't mind. I'll meet you in reception at two. And Caterina – thank you so much, you're a life-saver!'

'Hardly.' She nodded at him. 'See you later. Enjoy your "porritch".'

As she walked away, she heard him chuckle at her hammed-up Scottish accent and it gave her a warm feeling inside.

He was waiting for her as agreed and his eyes lit up at the sight of her, as if he'd been worried she wouldn't turn up.

'I'm Connor Drake, by the way. Please just call me Connor. No need to be formal, is there?'

'Caterina Rossi. My friends in the UK usually shorten it to Cat.' Not that she had any friends these days, but it would be so nice not to have to answer to Catherine. She was going to legally change her name back at the first opportunity.

'Cat. I like it.' He gave her a quick smile that lit up his features, then got down to business. 'Right, here are the documents. I've got a computer copy saved on this USB stick, in case you prefer to work from that. Just don't lose the paper one or I'll be in trouble. Oh, and needless to say, this is all confidential.' He handed her a plastic document wallet with the memory stick tucked inside, together with a sheaf of papers.

'Understood, and I won't lose any of it. I'll go and get started straight away. I . . . um, won't be able to print it out for you, but perhaps the manager can help with that if I save the translated version on the USB as well?'

'No need. As long as I know what the damned papers say, that's all I need. Thank you again. Do you know where to find me when you're done? Room 224.'

She nodded. 'I don't know how long it will take, but I'll let you know how I'm getting on. Bye for now.'

Translation work had felt like a slog ever since Bella was born, as it was almost impossible to concentrate properly when you had to look after a small child at the same time. Today, however, Cat was actually excited to start. She took her laptop out of the safe in her room as soon as she got there, as well as her trusty old dictionary. There were dictionaries online, but the old-fashioned book version was more reliable.

The documents turned out to be some sort of reports about volcanic activity, and she glanced out of the window at Mount Vesuvius every so often. No one living in the Bay of Naples area could be unaware of its brooding presence, and although she didn't want to admit it, the possibility of an eruption scared her. Something like six million people lived hereabouts, and if anything happened, they couldn't possibly all escape. It would be a catastrophe of epic proportions.

Thankfully, there were scientists who monitored the slightest cough made by the mountain. It would seem Connor was one of them. Or at least, someone interested in the data collected. A lot of it was beyond her understanding, but she became immersed in some of the more basic conclusions she was translating. It was fascinating stuff.

After two and a half hours of non-stop work, she had finished at last, and stood up to stretch her cramped muscles. Hotel chairs were not meant to be sat on for this length of time, and she realised she should have moved to the bed at some point. Still, it was done now.

She saved the new document to Connor's USB stick, and gathered up the papers into the plastic wallet. Then she let herself out of her room in the staff wing and made her way towards the guest part of the hotel. Here, the height of luxury was the order of the day. Real antiques were everywhere, including a chaise longue that Cat would have killed for, and Chinese vases almost as tall as herself. It gave the impression of a *palazzo* that hadn't changed much over the centuries, as if the aristocratic family still lived here and were sharing their home with the guests. Most of them loved it, and why wouldn't they? It was charming and quaint in the extreme.

Room 224 was one of the larger ones, facing the front of the building, and the decor was opulent, with more genuine antiques dotted about. The ceiling was high, with original features like stone corbels, and there was a lovely view of the bay from the tiny balcony.

'Wow, finished already?' Connor stood back to let her in, closing the door behind her. He was wearing faded jeans and a T-shirt that showed the contours of his muscular shoulders and arms, and he was barefoot. She averted her gaze so he wouldn't catch her staring. He might be some scientist geek, but this man clearly knew his way around a gym as well.

In the enclosed space, he seemed even larger than he had downstairs. His size and power ought to have scared her witless, considering what a smaller man like Derek had done to her, but for some reason it didn't. Instead, she felt safe in his presence. There was nothing intimidating about him at all. She had a moment of indecision, wondering if she could trust her instincts. Should she really be alone with a stranger in his hotel room like this? But then she made up her mind. He was a client and she was a professional. If he tried anything, she'd scream for help – there were always chambermaids or other staff around the place, and the hotel wasn't large.

'Yes, all done. Here you go. I've taken the liberty of adding my invoice to the USB pen. I hope that's OK? As I said, I'm not able to print anything at present. No rush with payment, though, obviously.' She handed him the document wallet.

'Thank you so much! I owe you big-time. This will enable me to crack on. Honestly, you're a life-saver.'

'No problem. Glad I could help, and if there's anything else, just let me know.'

She was about to turn and head off when he called out, 'Wait! Please.'

'Yes?'

'I, er . . . was just wondering – could I buy you a drink? As a thank you? Downstairs, or wherever you prefer. I'm here by myself, and to be honest, I'm a bit bored with my own company. I don't know about you, but I find sitting in a bar or restaurant alone somewhat pathetic. Only if you don't have anything else on, of course. Or, er, someone else to see.' He glanced at the third finger of her left hand, where a pale sliver of skin showed the mark from the wedding and engagement rings she'd removed so recently.

She hesitated. This was verging on dangerous territory. Technically she was still married, and she was supposed to be lying low, but in truth, she wasn't looking forward to an evening on her own in that small, cramped room. If she could have visited Bella and her mother, it wouldn't have been so bad, but they only dared risk a meeting once or twice a week, and she hadn't been here long enough to go yet.

She gave in. Who was she kidding? She wanted to spend more time with this man, for reasons she couldn't quite understand herself. His job was intriguing, for one thing, and for another . . . No, she wouldn't go there. But in any case, she needed to be bolder, stop being a mouse. Just look where that had got her in the past.

'Well, I have to help serve dinner first, and technically I'm not supposed to fraternise with the guests, but . . . if we go somewhere else, I suppose that would be OK. I get off at half past eight.'

He grinned. 'Fraternise, eh? We'll be sure not to do that. How about if I meet you over in the next square at nine?'

'Nine it is. See you then!'

She left before she had a chance to regret her decision.

Chapter Nine

Pompeii, 9 September AD 79

Raedwald

'That was interesting,' Duro commented as they headed back to their barracks. 'I didn't know you liked children.'

'I don't.' Raedwald shrugged, but in truth he was lying. It was only his younger half-siblings he had disliked, and even that wasn't fair. They couldn't help who their mother was, and the smallest of them had been rather appealing, following him around like a puppy. He'd always imagined he would be a father himself one day, and was resolved to treat his offspring better than he himself had been treated. *Curse Father!*

'You could have fooled me.' Duro laughed and elbowed him playfully in the ribs, his eyes twinkling. 'Though I'll admit she's a fetching little thing.' He shot Raedwald a sly glance. 'Just like her mother.'

'Don't.' The warning came out like a snarl, but it sounded half-hearted even to his own ears.

There was no denying the lady Aemilia was stunning. Any man with eyes in his head would have to admit as much. How someone like Lucius had been fortunate enough to end up with a wife such as that, he had no idea. The gods must have been smiling on him, that was for certain. Raedwald had seen other men eyeing her during the walk to the Forum, and had felt like snarling at them too. That was ridiculous; she wasn't his to protect – except in the sense of being her bodyguard – and anyway, she herself seemed oblivious to the almost blatant ogling she received.

Duro laughed again, pulling Raedwald out of his thoughts. 'Very well, I won't state the obvious. Just know this – I won't fight you for her.'

'What?' Raedwald sidestepped an unwary passer-by while frowning at his friend.

'I've told you, my preference is for blondes, like the silver women from northern Germania. Beautiful or not, the lady Aemilia is not to my taste. Not that I wouldn't bed her if she offered . . .'

Raedwald growled, and Duro put both hands up as if to ward him off. 'Calm down! It's not as if she would, and I'm sure you know what I mean.'

He did calm down, and shook his head at himself. Of course he understood. Duro rarely said no to the Roman matrons who paid to be sneaked into the barracks. He said he preferred them to finding a whore in town, as presumably they hadn't been used by all and sundry, and they were free. They even gave him gifts on occasion, adding to the gladiators' accumulated riches. Raedwald, however, avoided them all. He'd take a wife when he returned to his homeland, but until then he'd make do without female attentions.

Swallowing hard, he allowed himself to dwell briefly on a scenario where Aemilia asked to bed him. Would he be able to refuse? In all honesty, probably not, but he'd do his utmost to resist. Still, it was a moot point. Why would she? He was a slave and a barbarian, and she was a respectable married woman. Nothing about her – that he'd seen so far at least – suggested that she was immoral in any way. On the contrary, she appeared virtuous and good in the extreme. She'd kept her head meticulously covered with her *palla* the entire time they were outside, and hadn't so much as glanced at any man.

Except him, of course.

Looking into those amber eyes, huge after the fright she'd sustained, he'd had the insane urge to take her into his arms to comfort her. His own heart had been beating triple-time after the near-accident. He could only imagine how she must have felt seeing her tiny child so nearly killed. The way she'd stared at him had been intense, as if he was some hero from the legends, and her thanks came from the bottom of her heart. They both knew she was in his debt, but he'd never hold her to it. To him, what he'd done was part of his duties as guard and escort.

And yet . . . No, he would put the incident out of his mind. She had probably done so already.

Pompeii, 14 September AD 79

Raedwald

'By all the gods, he thinks a lot of himself, doesn't he?'

Duro's whispered comment made Raedwald's mouth turn up involuntarily, and a quiet chuckle escaped him as he watched their employer. The two of them were standing by the door of an *atrium*, but this one was on a much grander scale, and not nearly as run-down as the one in Lucius's own home. The man they were guarding, and his wife, had been invited to supper – *cena*, as they called it – by a rich man Lucius had been fawning over that very morning. The two gladiators had escorted him then too, and neither was impressed.

'He doesn't seem half as deferential now. Just kissing the man's arse in a different way.' The amusement in Duro's voice was loud and clear, and Raedwald could see why.

'Oh yes. The gods forbid he should actually dirty his hands with some work in order to earn his keep.' They had gathered that Lucius and his kind thought trade and manual labour vulgar. Income earned that way was beneath them.

Lucius was by far the loudest member of the supper party. He and the other guests were soon escorted to a large *triclinium*, an al fresco dining room facing the building's peristyle garden. It was still balmy enough in the evenings to eat outdoors in this way. Slaves removed their shoes – as if they couldn't manage that small task for themselves – and they took their places. The master of the house lay on his side on a bench covered in mattresses, with cushions for extra comfort. It was one of three surrounding a small pond on which yet more slaves placed plates of food that floated on the surface.

Lucius was soon holding forth again, in between mouthfuls of wine and various delicacies grabbed as they drifted past. Aemilia sat with some other women on chairs around the men. Her expression was impassive, with what looked like a fake smile pasted on her face. Raedwald wondered if she was embarrassed by her husband's behaviour. He and Duro had attended other men at such functions, and he'd gathered that the purpose of the meal was relaxation. The Romans appeared to love spending time together this way, and usually all the guests worked hard to make the atmosphere lively and convivial. Being in a good mood was a must, and conversation was supposed to be sparkling and animated. It was as though they were talking to each other for the sake of it, not because they particularly wanted to exchange views or news. Raedwald found this extraordinary and strange.

Back in his homeland, everyone would gather in the largest house of an evening to listen to tales and music, gossip, play games or simply enjoy each other's company. The Roman way, however, appeared forced, and he couldn't see any true joy in it. Occasionally these get-togethers included flirtatious behaviour, but no outright coupling, although apparently that sometimes came afterwards in a darkened room with whichever slave was available. Everything followed unwritten rules, and he couldn't understand the pleasure in it. But then he didn't particularly want to fathom the Romans and their ways in any case.

'We'll never see the sense in the way they act,' he commented quietly.

'No, but we don't really care, do we?' came Duro's reply. 'As long as he pays us for our services, he can do what he likes, as far as I'm concerned.'

'True.'

Earlier that day, they'd accompanied Lucius when he went to pay a call on the owner of this mansion. They gathered it was a custom called a *salutatio*, where lesser men asked those above them for various favours. It was a common practice and something they'd previously only heard about. Apparently upper-class Roman men spent most of their time trying to climb higher in society, and the best way to do this was through patronage. Everyone wanted power and riches and worked continuously towards this goal. Each morning they would go to someone above them in the hierarchy, waiting patiently on stone benches outside their house to take their turn at begging for assistance. This could take the form of coins, help with finding employment for their children, having a good word put in for them or similar. In return, the patron demanded that their client voted for them in local elections or escorted them places to show their prestige. Sometimes, like this evening, they would invite their supporters to lavish dinners.

Lucius hadn't been the only man there by a long stretch. The *atrium* had been crowded with others aspiring to the same thing, vying for a morsel of attention. Although Lucius had arrived with a retinue of his own, it hadn't taken the gladiators long to realise he was having to work very hard to gain the more important man's attention.

'I heard tell he wants to be elected to serve as an *aedile*,' Duro had sneered under his breath. 'The gods help the people of Pompeii if the likes of him are set to rule over them.'

'I don't think it's that important a task. And he doesn't have the coin for it, which is why he's here trying so hard to be noticed.'

The Romans had a leader they called emperor, but he lived elsewhere, and it seemed small towns like this one were more or less left to their own devices when it came to governing their affairs. Most things were run by two so-called *duoviri*, the most senior men. The *aediles* and decurions, who were some sort of councillors, helped. These were at the top of the local society, and most men of Lucius's class aspired to be part of that. Unfortunately for him, their duties included giving lavish gifts to the city, as well as paying for games, processions and theatricals. If a man didn't have the wherewithal for that, he simply couldn't be one of the ruling elite.

Most of this was of no interest to Raedwald, but he was vaguely impressed that the rulers were elected by the townspeople as a group. Messages painted on the walls of houses all over the city encouraged votes for this or that particular candidate, but of course only free men were allowed to cast a vote, so it didn't concern him.

As he glanced at the diners once more, Aemilia looked up and straight into his eyes. He almost took a step back as her gaze hit him square in the chest. There was something in it, an almost tangible connection that he didn't want to ponder.

'Uh-oh, she likes you.' Duro laughed and shoved him playfully with one shoulder.

'Shut up.' But Raedwald didn't put any anger into his words. He was too busy staring back at her and he couldn't seem to avert his eyes.

She was looking particularly beautiful this evening in a gown of rich saffron yellow, with matching bands in her glossy hair. She wasn't dripping with jewellery, like the other ladies present, but she was more stunning without embellishments. In the flickering light from dozens of oil lamps, her eyes burned bright, deep amber pools of mystery and allure. Her cheeks were slightly rosy, and her lips parted in a genuine smile when she saw him returning her gaze. Then she looked down, as if embarrassed to be caught staring.

'Are you sure you're not on the lookout for a bed partner?' Duro teased.

Raedwald just glared at him, but the heat heading towards his groin told him his friend wasn't far off the mark. Aemilia was too tempting by far, and it was agony standing here having to watch her. She was way out of his reach in every way, and yet there was a connection, he'd swear to it. Not that he wanted one. He was leaving. Soon. And he didn't need any complications.

'Let's go outside for a moment. It's too hot in here.' He shoved Duro towards the doorway, and his friend only smirked slightly before moving.

Just as well, or he would have earned himself a punch.

Aemilia

Aemilia swallowed a sigh. She hated these formal dinners and couldn't understand why everyone else loved them so much. She knew they were necessary for Lucius to advance up the social ladder, but it would have been so much better if she hadn't had to come along. It was embarrassing to watch him; he was trying so hard it was painful. If their host had even the slightest common sense, he'd see through her husband in a trice.

She fiddled with the thin copper bangle on her wrist, wishing she could have worn one of the thick golden ones her father had left her instead. One in particular, one of her mother's favourites – three laurel leaves wrapping snugly around the forearm – made her think of happier times whenever she touched it. There was no way she would let on to Lucius that she owned anything that valuable, though. He'd have it off her faster than she could blink, and little Caia would never inherit it. No, best to stick to the pathetic pieces of jewellery she was wearing tonight, even if it made her feel inferior to the other ladies, who were flashing theirs for all to see.

'I saw you arrive with the gladiators,' Claudia, the matron seated next to her whispered, her eyes brimming with curiosity. 'I'm sure it's not exactly a hardship having them following you around.' She gave a low, throaty laugh that grated on Aemilia.

'They are simply guarding us from thieves,' she said calmly, although the mere mention of the two big men made her glance over at them. They were like gorgeous statues, their marble skin and features partly in shadow. She had an almost irresistible urge to go over to them and check whether they were warm to the touch, or as cold as the carved gods in the temples. As before, Raedwald drew her gaze, and she imagined she could see the green of his eyes glinting even at this distance. But that was ridiculous; she had to stop looking at him.

'I'm sure they'd do more than guard you if you asked,' Claudia murmured with another laugh. 'At least one of them. I've heard that Rufus refuses all offers of . . . shall we say, comfort.'

Aemilia turned to frown at her. 'Really?' She shouldn't be asking, but her curiosity was piqued now.

'Oh yes. Lots of women have tried, believe me, but they never get further than Drusus.' Claudia's smile turned into a knowing smirk. 'Perhaps he prefers young boys?' She shrugged delicately. 'A great shame.'

Not wanting to let on that she had no idea what that entailed, Aemilia just nodded. Raedwald's preferences were none of her business in any case, but she couldn't help a tiny thrill of satisfaction at knowing he wasn't sleeping with anyone. Why that should matter, she refused to contemplate. And if he truly did prefer males, it was a moot point anyway.

She swallowed a sigh and turned to the lady on her other side, doing her best to make witty conversation. But her heart wasn't in it, and she had a horrible suspicion it was heading in the wrong direction altogether.

Chapter Ten

Sorrento, 28 September 2022

Cat

'That's a beautiful bracelet you're wearing.'

'Er, thank you. My mother gave it to me. It's been in her family for donkey's years apparently.'

Cat was sitting perched on a bar stool, feeling supremely self-conscious. It had been so long since she'd dated, she had forgotten how to relax in a man's company. If she'd ever known how to begin with. She'd always been socially awkward, hiding in the background. That was why Derek had managed to fool her so completely. He'd ignored her natural reticence and just pulled her along, not taking no for an answer. At first, that had felt exciting, but she knew better now. He'd been confident he could dominate her utterly because she was a mouse.

'More like two thousand, I should think,' Connor said, taking a sip of his cold Nastro Azzurro beer. He was drinking it out of the bottle, and for some reason that seemed sexy. It drew her gaze to his mouth, which was surrounded by a couple of days' worth of dark red stubble. That was a good look on him.

'I'm sorry, what?' She forced herself to concentrate on what he'd just said, and not the image in her mind where she raked her short fingernails along his jaw. What was wrong with her? She barely knew the man, and ought to stay as far from the opposite sex as possible. She was still technically married.

His mouth lifted in a lopsided grin and he nodded towards the bracelet. 'Looks Roman. I'd bet you anything one of your ancestors dug it up around here somewhere. Pompeii, maybe?'

'Oh, well . . .' Since that was more or less what her mother had implied, Cat didn't have an answer for him.

She hadn't realised it could be as old as all that, though, and it made her feel uncomfortable. That would definitely make it a museum piece. She put her hand around the smooth metal and gripped it hard, the thought of parting with it almost physically painful. When she looked up, Connor's face seemed to shimmer for a moment in the dim lighting of the bar, and she saw a different one superimposed on it. The same general features, but surrounded by a mane of hair that was a much more vivid red. The green eyes of both men bored into hers, and she felt pinned to her seat, limbs unable to move so much as an inch.

'*You are so beautiful, domina . . .*'

She heard the words as if from afar and blinked. 'Excuse me?' Had he just said she was beautiful? It was a bit soon for chatting her up, wasn't it? They'd only been here for a quarter of an hour.

'I said it's beautiful craftsmanship. Your bracelet?' Connor clarified, lifting his eyebrows, as if wondering whether she was all there.

Cat was beginning to ask herself the same thing. 'Oh yes, thank you.' Self-consciously, she tugged at the gold and freed it from her skin. It was like dislodging a creature with suction cups, but that was probably only because it was hot in here and it had been sticking to her. She took a deep breath and decided to change the subject.

'Tell me what you're doing here exactly,' she demanded, then cringed at the bossy tone and added a 'please'.

Fortunately, Connor didn't seem to notice. 'I'm working on a PhD in volcanology. I've been spending time in places where there is volcanic activity of various kinds, and this is my last stop. Collecting data, like in that boring report you had to translate.' At her startled glance, he held up a hand and smiled. 'Don't worry, I don't think Vesuvius is about to blow any time soon. I'm just interested in studying the local earthquakes and so on. There's a research centre in Naples where they are constantly monitoring things, and I've been allowed to join their team for a short while. It will help with my thesis.'

'I see.' It did sound interesting, if a little scary. 'And have you been to other places where the volcanoes are more active?'

'Oh yes. Iceland, Hawaii and Sicily, to name a few. They're all fascinating, and I don't mind travelling. But I don't want to bore you. Apart from seeing actual flowing lava, it's not all that exciting. Tell me about yourself instead.' He put his fingers under her left hand and lifted it up into the light. 'Recently divorced?'

Cat felt her cheeks turning scarlet. 'Um, not quite. Working on it.' She swallowed hard. If she was going to have any chance of finding a new relationship with anyone – although not necessarily this particular man, attractive though he was – she should probably start by being honest. 'And I have a three-year-old daughter. Well, she's almost four now, actually.'

'Sweet.' He looked slightly confused. 'She's not living at the hotel with you, is she?'

'No, no. My mother is looking after her while I work. They're staying in Naples, with my uncle.' To make sure he didn't think she was the worst mother on the planet, she added, 'This is only a temporary job, and I go and see her on my days off, a couple of times a week. But I have to live in at the hotel, otherwise I'd be getting up at four a.m. in order to be on time for work. She and Mamma get on really well, thankfully.'

She'd FaceTimed with them several times, and to her relief Bella didn't seem at all bothered. The little girl had just chattered on about what she'd been doing with her new friends, and what they were going to do the next day. Her speech had been peppered with Italian words, which amused Cat no end, even if it felt wrong that her daughter was happy without her.

Connor held up a hand. 'Hey, I'm not judging. Just trying to get to know you.' He gave her that slow smile again, and something inside her fluttered.

'Oh. Why?' she blurted out, then felt extremely foolish. He was hitting on her, and she was too naïve to even recognise it. Perhaps he thought she'd be game for a one-night stand. Had she unwittingly given that impression? Damn. She shouldn't have entered his room that afternoon.

'Because you are a very attractive woman, Cat, and I like your company.' He tilted his head to one side. 'I can see you're a bit spooked, though, which was not my intention. In case you're worried, I have no expectations other than talking to you and enjoying an evening out. Does that sound OK?'

'Um, sure.' She fiddled with a long strand of hair that fell over her shoulder. 'You must think I'm really silly, but I . . . This is all new to me. In fact, I haven't really talked to anyone other than my husband for ages. Well, until recently. Not properly.'

He was frowning now. 'Why? Did he keep you imprisoned or something?' His tone was joking, but there was a steely undertone.

When she replied, 'More or less, yes,' his scowl deepened, so she hastened to add, 'But I've escaped now. I mean, I've left him, and soon it will all be in the past. I hope.'

He reached out to take her hand, and she couldn't help her instinctive flinch. That made him narrow his eyes. 'Wow, he really did a number on you, huh?' He held on to her hand firmly and stroked it gently with his thumb. 'Please don't ever be afraid of me, Cat. I know I'm a big guy, but I swear on my mother's grave, I've never hurt a woman in my life, and I don't plan on starting now. Do you believe me?'

His green eyes were fixed on hers intently and she couldn't look away. There was something so solidly reassuring and familiar in their depths, she relaxed almost immediately. It was as if she knew and trusted this man, was sure he'd never harm so much as a hair on her head.

Which was probably crazy, since she'd only met him that morning.

'Yes,' she whispered, letting out a breath she hadn't realised had been trapped inside her.

'Good.' He gave her hand a quick squeeze, then let go. 'How about another drink, and then I'll walk you back to the hotel. I'm assuming you need to get some beauty sleep if you have to be up cleaning rooms before dawn.'

'Thank you, that would be great.'

Being with him felt so easy and uncomplicated, Cat wasn't sure if she could trust that it was real. But she couldn't shake the feeling that she knew this man and was safe with him. It was a sensation she'd not had in a very long time. This was how normal people interacted, she told herself. Derek and his power games had to be left in the past, where they belonged.

Even if that was going to take some time.

Connor

Connor glanced at the woman walking by his side, only huffing slightly as they climbed the steep incline of the narrow alley leading up from the seashore to the main part of town. He'd felt an instant connection to her that morning, and couldn't believe his luck when she'd turned out to be a translator. Before handing over the assignment, he'd checked her out online and found her website, where there were lots of glowing reviews from satisfied customers. He could see why – she'd done a quick and thorough job, and had saved him a lot of time.

The woman herself, however, was an enigma.

He'd noticed the pale mark on her ring finger almost immediately, and knew it was stupid to get involved with someone who was on the rebound. Been there, done that, and didn't want another T-shirt. Still, he'd found himself asking her out without even thinking about it, just because he wanted to spend time with her. Why, apart from the obvious? Sure, she was beautiful as all hell, and had a sexy, voluptuous figure, like a young Sophia Loren. Not that he watched a lot of old movies, but his gran had sometimes made him sit through a few. But there was something else about Cat that attracted him; her earnest but guarded expression, perhaps. And the way she'd reacted with humour to his silly prank that morning.

God, what had possessed him to tease the waitresses like that? Boredom, most likely, but it was no excuse. He wasn't twelve.

She had gone through something pretty tough, that much was clear from the way she'd reacted to his touch. And she wasn't even divorced yet, just 'working on it', whatever that meant. It spelled trouble with a capital T. He'd be stupid to get involved.

'So how long have you been working at the hotel?' he asked, making sure he walked beside her without touching her. He wanted her to be at ease in his company, and suspected she was finding it difficult. He was fairly sure her ex hadn't just been a bastard – he'd been a violent one. Her flinch earlier was reminiscent of how a dog would behave when it had been repeatedly mistreated. He knew, because he often volunteered at a local dog shelter. And Cat's eyes held that same fearful mistrust, coupled with a deep yearning.

He found himself wanting to be the man she could depend on, which was crazy since he didn't even know her.

'I started on Monday,' she told him with a small smile. 'Until a week ago, I was living in the UK.'

'Wow! That was . . . sudden.' He hadn't expected that. She must be stronger than she looked to have organised such a quick change.

'I had help. My mother has umpteen relatives around here. Family is everything, and when I was in need, they didn't hesitate. I'm unbelievably grateful to them all.'

'Sounds wonderful.' He couldn't help a bitter note from creeping into his voice. He hadn't seen his own family for over a year, apart from one very stilted lunch with his father at the Oxford and Cambridge Club in Pall Mall.

Sir John Drake was a baronet and a KC. He'd also remarried only a few months after Connor's mother died. Connor couldn't forgive him for that, despite the fact that he'd known his parents had been heading for a divorce anyway. He had been fourteen at the time, grieving, but trying his best not to show it at the posh boarding school he attended. Any sign of weakness was pounced on there, and he had no wish to become a punching bag. The new wife, a younger woman by the name of Amanda, had no idea how to handle her stepson. She had an eight-year-old daughter from a previous marriage, and soon added to the nursery with two more sons. To Connor, it all felt like a huge betrayal.

His comment made Cat stop and look at him. She tilted her head to one side. 'You don't have a family?'

'Oh, I do. Or rather, I did.' He filled her in on the bare facts, and added, 'I turned into the kind of rebellious teenager who got expelled from three different boarding schools. As you can imagine, that didn't endear me to my father. I think I was an embarrassment to someone in his position. He routinely puts delinquents behind bars, but he didn't want to admit that his own son should probably be there too.'

'That must have been tough.' Cat reached out and put a hand on his arm, squeezing it.

Connor had been wondering why he was telling her all this, since he didn't normally talk about it with anyone. That small gesture, however, gave him the answer. He wanted her to know him, really know him. Why, he wasn't sure yet.

He pushed his hand through the thick hair on top of his head. 'Yeah, well, thankfully I had a grandmother who understood me better and took my side. She stepped in, offered me a home, and sent me to the local comprehensive for my final year. She refused to take any crap, and we came to an understanding. In fact, it was her idea for me to study volcanology when she caught me watching loads of programmes on the Discovery Channel.' He smiled at the memory. 'Typical Gran. I was just passing the time, vaguely interested, but her enthusiasm was infectious.'

Cat nodded. 'She sounds like a lovely old lady.'

'She was,' he said. 'I lost her five years ago, but even then she helped me. She left me everything she owned so I wouldn't ever be dependent on my dad again. She was amazing.'

'I'm sorry for your loss.' She was quiet for a moment, then said almost wistfully, 'I always wanted siblings. Being an only child means there are a lot of expectations too. I tried my best to be a good daughter, but it's not easy.' Sending him a quick glance, she added, 'Do you ever see your brothers and sister? Or has your stepmother driven a wedge between you?'

'We don't often meet up, but whenever we do, we get along OK. I mean, it's not their fault what happened. My half-brothers are much younger than me, although now they're becoming adults it's easier to relate to them. As for my stepsister, she's at uni, and recently she's been texting me quite a lot. I don't think she gets on too well with her mother.' He smiled. 'She's joined the club.'

Cat returned his smile, and even in the darkness of the alley, it lit up her features. He had to force himself to turn away and keep walking, rather than standing there and gawking at her like a love-struck moron. And why was he even thinking about the L-word anyway? He didn't do relationships. They were messy, and he travelled a lot. Most girlfriends didn't appreciate that. He shook himself inwardly. Nothing was going to happen between him and Cat, even if he felt extremely attracted to her. He had a few weeks in Naples and then he'd be gone. End of story.

Chapter Eleven

Pompeii, 28 September AD *79*

Raedwald

'No Duro today?'

Aemilia looked behind Raedwald as if his companion might be hiding there, but he'd come alone.

'No, sorry, *domina*. He ate something last night that didn't agree with him. I hope you don't mind?'

There was nothing wrong with Duro other than a sore head and a need for sleep, but he wasn't going to let her know that. Hopefully she wouldn't tell her husband and they'd still both be paid, even though Raedwald was quite capable of escorting one woman and her retinue by himself.

'No, no, that's fine.' She seemed slightly flustered, but he merely waited to do her bidding. 'I wish to go to the baths today and I think I'll bring Caia. It's good for her to get out and about a bit.'

He nodded. She hadn't asked for his opinion, so he didn't give it. He couldn't care less who she took with her or where she went.

It took her a while to get organised, and while he waited, the little girl came running towards him through the back garden. One of the slave women was huffing along behind her, looking fed up with chasing someone so energetic. Caia had a ball in her tiny hands and turned to try to cajole the slave into playing with her, but the woman was taciturn and just sat down on a bench, ignoring her charge's pleas. For some reason, this angered Raedwald. As he was bored anyway, he walked over and playfully snatched the ball out of Caia's grasp.

'Catch me if you can,' he said, pretending to run away from her. She squealed with delight and gave chase along the paths. He allowed her to win the ball back eventually, then encouraged her to throw it to him, teaching her how to catch it in return. From what Lucius had said, the girl was only around three years old, but she had quick reflexes and learned fast.

'Throw!' she demanded, and he felt himself smile in amusement. Another domineering little Roman lady in the making, but at least she was young enough for him to cope with it at the moment.

If only they were all this sweet.

Aemilia looked startled to find him playing with her daughter, but soon recovered her composure. 'You shouldn't bother Rufus, Caia,' she murmured to the little girl.

He noticed that she used his Roman name when talking to her daughter. That was wise, as children absorbed everything adults said and she'd be likely to blurt things out to her father. Not that there was anything wrong with Aemilia calling him by his real name, but it might seem suspicious to Lucius. He glanced at the lady. She was astute, that much was clear.

'She didn't bother me,' he told her. 'I offered.' He didn't add that he'd enjoyed the interlude. That was something he didn't want to admit even to himself.

'Next time I'm going to show you my tortoise.' Caia beamed at him and placed her tiny hand on his trouser leg to steady herself as she gazed up at him. 'He's very slow and he likes to eat leaves.'

'You have a tortoise?' He probably shouldn't encourage her to keep talking to him, but she was so small and earnest, he couldn't ignore her. 'I've never seen one of those.' Although he'd heard of them and seen depictions in paintings.

'Yes! My pater gived him to me.'

'You are very lucky.'

The group set off for the Forum Baths – Aemilia, Raedwald and the little girl, plus two slave women. As before, he brought up the rear so that he could keep an eye on everyone, but to his surprise, Aemilia beckoned him forward.

'You may walk next to me, Raedwald. You're not a guard dog, and I don't want you looming behind my shoulder.'

His mouth twitched, but his expression remained impassive as he briefly stepped forward to walk beside her. 'If you don't mind, I prefer to bring up the rear. That way I am better able to see any dangers, as last time.' He gestured towards her daughter, and she flushed pink.

'Oh yes, of course. I merely thought to converse with you, but you're right.'

He wondered why she wanted to talk to him. As a slave and a hired bodyguard, he could have nothing to discuss with her, but she did seem rather unconventional and curious. Still, it was best if they kept their distance. Nothing good could come of them getting to know each other better, and she didn't press the issue.

Thankfully, there were no incidents this time, and one of the slaves kept a tight hold on Caia's hand. Although Raedwald was alert to every danger, he still had the opportunity to watch Aemilia from behind. She walked with a smooth and graceful gait, as though she was gliding along the street, and the gentle sway of her hips under her layers of clothing was enthralling. He tried not to notice, but it was proving very difficult. His gaze strayed that way far too often, making him curse under his breath.

They soon arrived at their destination. Surrounded by shops and bars, the Forum Baths were situated behind the Capitolium, the temple dedicated to the great god Jupiter and two other Roman deities. It was the largest and most lavish of the public baths in the town, and Raedwald had been there many times before. Taking frequent dips in pleasantly warm water was one of the few things he really enjoyed about the Roman way of life. Slaves were allowed to mingle with free men and nobles alike, and societal norms were ignored for the most part. Being naked made everyone more equal somehow.

The men's section was very ornate, with exquisite stucco designs on the barrel-vaulted ceilings. There were mosaic floors, and in the changing room, the niches for storing clothes were divided by male terracotta figures. The detail of these statuettes always amazed him, and he couldn't help but be in awe of Roman sculptors.

The separate women's section was around the corner from the main entrance, where there was a door in an alley marked *Mulier*.

'You may go to the men's section and do what you please for a while. We will be here at least until the seventh hour.' Aemilia handed him a few coins: a silver *denarius* and a couple of copper *asses*. 'Here, this is for the entrance fee. Meet us outside this door later.'

Raedwald nodded, then watched his charge walk into the bath house, followed by her daughter and the two slaves. One of them was carrying fresh clothing and whatever else the lady might need here – oils, ointments and a strigil, presumably. It was a relief to see the back of her, if only temporarily, because she'd stirred an interest in him that he didn't wish to acknowledge. He shouldn't find anything about her enticing. She was married, and he wasn't staying in Pompeii. Not for much longer, anyway.

And he hated aristocratic Roman ladies.

Since his capture, he'd been through a lot, but he hadn't died, and he most definitely hadn't forgotten the oath he'd sworn. Osbehrt and his duplicitous mother would rue the day they were born, he was determined about that. When he'd first arrived on these shores, he hadn't been thrown into an arena with wild animals, although at the time, he sometimes wished he had. Instead, he'd been bought by an older woman, a widow rich beyond belief and used to getting her way in every last thing. What she had wished for was Raedwald's body. And that of every other young slave boy she could get her hands on.

'I will use you for my pleasure until I tire of you,' she'd decreed, after having him stripped naked and bound to her bed. It quickly became clear that she'd had a lot of practice in how to arouse male bodies, but fortunately – or unfortunately, perhaps – Raedwald was so disgusted by her that nothing she did to him could make him want her in that way. His body had simply refused to cooperate.

She was lithe and agile for someone her age – he guessed her to be fifteen or twenty years his senior – and her body was in good shape. When younger, she must have been stunningly beautiful, but now she wore an excessive amount of face paint. It was as if she didn't believe that her slightly older features could be as attractive in their natural state and tried to overcompensate. The result was a disaster, a grotesque mask that was as fake as it was repulsive, but Raedwald wasn't going to be the one to tell her that. She also stank of strongly scented perfume, as if she'd bathed in vials of it. The virtual miasma made him gag. He'd forced himself to concentrate on the disgust he felt at this, as well as her overweening vanity and the cruel glint in her eyes that hinted at her ruthless and violent nature, rather than what she was doing with her clever hands. That way she never succeeded in keeping him hard for long enough to violate him.

Unsurprisingly, she was incandescent with rage.

What followed was best forgotten, but it involved extreme pain and a leather lash that nigh-on stripped his back bare to the bone. Once he'd recovered enough to be able to move without wincing, she'd had him taken to a slave dealer in the Saepta Julia area of Rome, near the Pantheon. With iron fetters around his ankles that chafed, and his wrists bound tightly, he'd been displayed naked and with a label hanging around his neck. At the time, he wasn't able to read it, but he'd gathered it was information such as his age, where he was from, and any defects or bad characteristics prospective buyers needed to be warned about. Flaws the slave trader played down in favour of bragging about his strengths.

'A perfect specimen of manhood,' the man had claimed to those who came to look him over. 'Almost a head taller than most men, and just look at that physique.'

He'd known being a slave would be difficult, but in his homeland they were not treated this harshly. Rather than being kept in chains or locked up, they were loaned land on which to build their own huts, grow crops and keep livestock. They then gave their masters a portion of that. There was none of this deliberate cruelty, and he couldn't fathom the need for it.

Standing on a raised platform, poked and prodded like an animal for sale, Raedwald had retreated inside his mind, ignoring everything that was going on around him. He had ruthlessly suppressed the burning rage and humiliation coursing through him, and concentrated on survival and the future. A future where he escaped and returned to wreak vengeance. This determination kept him sane when a *lanista* bought him for over a thousand *sestertii* and made him take an oath binding him to the gladiator owner.

An oath he had no intention of keeping, since he owed these people nothing.

The *lanista* fortunately allowed him to heal before putting him through his paces. He'd been a gladiator ever since, and he was lucky to still be alive. As he made his way to the main entrance of the baths now, he sent up a quick prayer of thanks to the gods – his own deities, not the Roman ones. Soon, very soon, his patience would hopefully be rewarded.

'I'm coming for you, Osbehrt,' he murmured. 'And you'll rue the day you conspired against me.'

He passed through a vestibule and into a colonnaded court-yard, which was the porticoed *palaestra*, or exercise area. Turning right, he continued along a corridor into the *apodyterium* – the changing room – where he left his clothes in a small hamper in one of the niches on the wall. This was situated above a bench that ran around the perimeter of the changing area. There was no need to be embarrassed about nudity in this place, as most of the patrons shed their clothes, although one or two kept their loincloths on. Raedwald knew his body was a work of art, with muscles honed through hours of training each day, and it no longer bothered him when people stared. Here, he could stare right back.

'You there, will you keep an eye on my clothes, please?' he called to one of the attendants. The man came over and eagerly accepted a couple of *asses* while nodding his agreement. Theft was always a possibility here unless you paid someone to watch your possessions.

He figured he might as well do a bit of light exercise, since he had some free time. It was unfortunate that these baths didn't have a swimming pool, like some of the others did, but he could head down to the sea later if he wanted to. He'd always loved water, having grown up next to the sea, and never wasted an opportunity to immerse himself. After briefly washing all over using a marble basin in the *calidarium*, he bypassed the warm plunge pool, wrinkling his nose at the sight of the oil and scunge floating on its surface, and went straight outside to the *palaestra*, where men were engaged in various types of exercise. Some played ball, lifted weights or worked up a sweat in other ways, while others sunbathed to acquire the healthy tan that was considered necessary for a man to look his best. Almost all were chatting, laughing and exchanging news and views, the social aspect of this place crystal clear. But Raedwald wasn't here to talk to anyone.

He picked up some weights and concentrated on pushing his muscles to their limit. Later, he'd jog around the perimeter of the courtyard for a while, working up a sweat before going inside to wash again. There was plenty of time, and he might even have a massage, although gladiators could enjoy those at the barracks whenever they wanted. It was part of the *lanista*'s way of keeping their bodies in good working order, as well as having a physician on hand for any ailments.

Aemilia would be a while, he guessed, as she was no doubt being pampered in every way after passing through the various types of bath, hot and cold. Roman women seemed to need a multitude of treatments in order to feel beautiful – they were massaged, plucked, trimmed and perfumed. It seemed vain and silly to him, and someone like Aemilia didn't need it, in his opinion. He was sure she'd be lovely no matter what she did to herself.

But it was nothing to him. She could please herself.

Aemilia

Aemilia emerged from the *laconium*, where she'd been relaxing wrapped in soft towels after her bath and beauty treatments. Having her body plucked free of every last hair except those on her head was painful, but the hot water of the *caldarium* and steam rooms afterwards helped to soothe her smarting skin. And she felt wonderfully smooth and clean, almost as though she glowed.

She was now wearing a clean tunic and was making her way back to the changing rooms when she heard giggling. A group of women jostled each other by the back wall, and one seemed to have her face right next to it.

'What is going on?' asked Aemilia, recognising Claudia, the woman she'd spoken to at the dinner the other night.

Claudia sent her a mischievous grin. 'We owe you thanks for bringing the barbarian for us to look at.' She nodded to a small peephole Aemilia could now see in between the stones of the wall. 'He's just finished his exercise regime, and dear gods, but he is sheer perfection! See for yourself.'

The woman pushed the others out of the way and ushered Aemilia over. She was reluctant to spy on someone in this fashion, but at the same time she couldn't quell the curiosity surging through her. Besides, the others would laugh at her if she turned tail. Putting her eye to the hole, she stared through it and her breath caught in her throat. Raedwald was striding completely naked across the *palaestra*, his body displayed for all the world to see, and she knew she'd never be able to erase the image from her brain. He was, quite simply, magnificent. Muscles played under his skin as he moved, along his arms and shoulders and across an impressively ridged abdomen. It was as though a Greek statue had come to life, except this one was lightly covered with copper-coloured hair in between the pectorals and arrowing down towards the V of his groin. She swallowed, hard, and tore her gaze away from this sight.

She felt her cheeks turn crimson, but forced herself to calm down before she relinquished her place to someone else. By focusing on her breathing, she got herself under control, at least partially, and attempted a smile.

'I see what you mean,' she told Claudia. 'Is this something you all do a lot? Spy on the men?' She'd never noticed the peephole before.

'No, we've only just discovered the crack in the wall. Must have been from that earthquake the other day.' Claudia laughed. 'I have a feeling it will be in use quite a lot from now on, though. Do bring the barbarian again soon for our delectation.'

Aemilia nodded, but had absolutely no intention of doing so. It felt as though she'd violated him in some way, even though she couldn't possibly have known what would happen.

It was a relief to finally leave the baths a while later. Raedwald was waiting for them, lounging against a wall, but she avoided meeting his eye. It would be best if she escaped his presence as soon as possible, or she was bound to blush profusely. At the same time, she realised she didn't want their outing to end yet.

'How about we buy something to eat on the way home?' she suggested. Since she was the one in charge, the two slave women merely looked at her, while Raedwald shrugged. Caia started jumping up and down.

'Yes, yes, I'm hungry.'

'Very well, let's see what we can find.'

They ended up at a small tavern, where Raedwald found them a table inside. It smelled of lamb stew, which made her stomach growl. She stayed by the counter at the front of the establishment, checking to see what was available. A sixth sense told her he had come to stand right behind her, shielding her from other customers and passers-by on the pavement. He was so close, she could feel the heat emanating from his body. A tremor shot through her, and she bit the inside of her cheek, trying to suppress the images of him that rose in her mind. This was madness. She mustn't let him affect her in any way.

'What shall we have?' she asked, half turning to look up at

him. The movement made her shoulder brush against his chest, which was solid and warm.

He raised his eyebrows. 'That is for you to decide, *domina*.'

She knew it was, but for some reason she wanted his opinion. 'Well, is there anything you don't particularly like?' she persisted.

A smile tugged at one corner of his mouth, and his eyes glinted with amusement. 'Dormice, songbirds, snails and sea urchins. I'd rather eat dirt than touch any of those.'

'Oh.' She blinked at him, surprised at the vehemence in his voice. 'I was thinking more along the lines of lamb stew. Will that do?'

'Certainly. But if the meal is coming out of my pay, I would ask to decline. I will be fed upon my return to the barracks.'

That made her frown. 'Of course not. I'm paying.' Why would he think she'd be that miserly?

After she'd ordered, he escorted her to the table, where she busied herself with Caia, who was fidgeting. The whole time, she was supremely aware of him next to her, and as the space was cramped, their thighs occasionally touched under the table. It was unsettling, yet thrilling at the same time, and she didn't know what to make of it. No man had ever affected her in any way, so why was this one the exception? Was it only because she'd seen him in all his glory? No, surely she wasn't that shallow.

Once the food arrived, silence descended on the table as they all ate. It felt uncomfortable, however, and Aemilia found herself turning to Raedwald while the two slave women tried to cajole Caia into eating everything in her bowl.

'Is this the sort of food you would eat in your homeland?' she asked.

He chewed and swallowed before replying, as if he wasn't sure he should. She wondered why he was so reluctant to talk to her, something she'd noticed right from the start. Perhaps it was because he was a slave. Not everyone took well to servitude, and he was clearly a proud man, strong and capable. To be a slave – even a popular gladiator one – must be demeaning. Did he hate all his oppressors? Did he hate her? A shiver went through her as she found she didn't want that.

'We ate lamb, certainly, but not prepared in this way with herbs and spices. And no garum. Mostly we had a lot of fish – I lived near the sea – and beef from our cattle. Hardly any bread.'

His voice was gruff, as if he was telling her this against his will or better judgement, but at least he didn't refuse outright. She appreciated that.

'Not everyone enjoys garum, I gather,' she commented. 'I've heard tell that foreigners dislike it intensely.' The sauce that was added to most dishes here was a rather foul-smelling concoction, fishy and strong, she had to admit, but she was so used to the taste, it didn't bother her.

Raedwald's eyes crinkled in amusement. 'As I said, I was used to fish, and I've had worse.'

'Like dormice?' She couldn't resist teasing him. The little creatures weren't to her taste either – she'd only tried them once – but his revulsion had been clear.

She felt him shudder, his warm thigh burning hers through their clothing. 'Exactly.'

There wasn't much more to add, so she resigned herself to silence, but he surprised her by asking a question of his own. 'Did you grow up in this town, *domina*?' He'd finished his food and sat back, leaning against the wall, and regarding her with that keen emerald gaze.

'Er, no. I lived in Rome with my father until my marriage. We often came down here to spend time in the summer, though, and became acquainted with my husband's family.'

She didn't add that her father had been dazzled by what he thought was Lucius's exalted status. His family name was ancient and respected, but they hadn't realised that the rest was all lies and he had very little actual wealth. He'd needed the income from her dowry in order to stay out of debt. But by the time Aemilia found out, it was much too late, and her father had died before they could do anything about the situation. She had no one else who could help her. No other relatives whatsoever, in fact.

'Ah, yes, I gather rich Romans come to this area to enjoy themselves.' There was something about his expression that showed his disdain for such luxurious living.

Aemilia saw nothing wrong with it, but perhaps people in other countries did not have that kind of privileged life. She shrugged. 'Yes, some. They like to escape from the big city for a while each year. Who can blame them? Rome is very noisy and there is no peace.'

'Noisier than here? It couldn't possibly be,' he joked, and she almost laughed.

'Oh yes, much worse.'

'Actually, I know. I've been there,' he confessed, a brief frown marring his features.

She glanced at him, but some instinct stopped her from asking about his time there. Instead, she said, 'I gather there aren't as many people where you come from.'

He gave a short laugh. 'No, there were perhaps fifty of us on our *terp*, that's all.'

'*Terp*?'

'A sort of man-made island by the coast. The land is very low, so unless you can raise it somehow, the sea would devour you.'

'Oh, right. I'd like to see that sometime.'

'I doubt it. You'd find the accommodation way below your usual standards,' he told her drily, almost mockingly.

Was he insinuating that she was spoiled? Perhaps she was, but she'd never blame anyone else for the way they were forced to live.

111

'That is for me to decide, don't you think?' she retorted tartly. Yet the thought of going with him to his home country was not one she should entertain. It was time to bring this conversation to a close, so she stood up. 'Let's go home. Caia should be going to bed soon.'

Raedwald didn't comment on the abrupt departure, just followed behind like a faithful guard dog. For some reason, that irritated her, but then what had she expected? That they could be friends? That was out of the question.

Chapter Twelve

Sorrento, 29 September 2022

Cat

The man's eyes were a clear green in the sun, like pale emeralds catching the light, and twinkling with intelligence and humour. They were shielded by long dark lashes – not black, but a deep auburn, the same as his eyebrows. His hair was an even more vivid colour; a dusky, rich reddish-brown, with copper and burgundy highlights that shone every time he tilted his head. She was mesmerised by the sight of him, even though she knew she ought not to stare.

She couldn't stop herself, though, and watched his mouth as he talked. The words washed over her, unheard, as she stared at those lips. They were firm, but beautifully shaped, the lower one slightly plumper than the top. Surrounded by reddish stubble that glinted like shards of coloured glass as he moved, they looked eminently kissable. She wondered what they would feel like melded with her own. Would the stubble tickle or prick her, or would it heighten her awareness of him as a man?

But wait – she knew what they felt like. The sensation was etched into her brain, and it was one she'd never get enough of. She needed to kiss him now, this instant, and hold on to him before he disappeared . . .

Cat turned over in bed and registered the fact that her mobile was blaring out a wake-up signal. 'Shit, what was that?' she muttered, sitting up to grind the heels of her hands into her eye sockets.

The dream had been so vivid. She could still smell the exotic scent of the man, his warmth radiating towards her. He'd been standing so close. She'd wanted to reach out and touch his muscular forearm and pull him in for a kiss. And those eyes . . . They reminded her of someone. Connor.

Her cheeks grew hot. Was she dreaming about him already? She couldn't be that attracted to someone she'd only just met, could she? Besides, the man in the dream had had long hair. It had reached past his shoulders, and had been buffeted by a breeze, the copper-burnished tresses swirling around his cheeks and jaw.

She took a gulp of water from the bottle she kept beside her bed. 'This is crazy,' she told herself. 'Connor is a guest at the hotel and a temporary client, nothing more.'

Whatever silly visions her brain was coming up with when she was asleep, during the day she was in charge. And she didn't want to become ensnared by any man right now. She needed to sort her life out first. Best to keep out of Connor's way.

That proved easier said than done. He was there in the restaurant when she clocked on for her morning shift, sitting at his favourite table by the window. Of course fate would have it that he was in her section. She had no choice but to go and take his order.

'Good morning.' He smiled in a way that was eerily reminiscent of the man in her dream. 'I trust you slept well? No ill effects from your limoncello spritz?'

'No, I'm fine. Thank you.'

In all honesty, the lemony liqueur mixed with Prosecco and soda had given her a slight headache, as she seldom drank alcohol. Derek had always been very sparing with wine at home, and hadn't taken her to the pub for years. Not since before Bella was born, in fact. But she didn't want to think about that. She had a job to do, and pasted on a smile.

'What can I get you for breakfast?'

Connor's eyes narrowed a tad, as if he could tell she was trying to keep him at arm's length, but he went along with it. 'Same as yesterday, please. And if making porridge is a pain, I can have something else instead.'

'It's no problem.' She snapped her pad shut, and stuffed it into the pocket of her apron, then walked off to fetch his espresso.

She returned a while later with his breakfast, and Connor watched in silence as she set it out in front of him. When she'd finished, he spoke quietly. 'Did I do something wrong? I hope I haven't offended you. If so, I apologise.'

His expression was one of genuine concern, and Cat felt bad. He'd been nothing but kind to her so far.

'What? No! Not at all. I just . . .' She glanced around to make sure no one could overhear them, but thankfully the neighbouring tables were all empty at the moment. 'I enjoyed last night, but I don't think I should be going on dates with anyone until I've, um, sorted out my life. Not that it was a date . . . I mean, probably . . . It's complicated. The truth is, I'm a mess. You should stay well clear.'

He smiled gently. 'It's OK. No worries. I understand. And like I said yesterday, I won't pressure you in any way, I promise. I do wonder, though . . .' He paused, his eyebrows lowering slightly. 'Could you use a friend? I don't really know anyone here, and my colleagues have all been too busy to socialise with me. I'd love to have someone to have lunch with, or an ice cream. This place is famous for those, isn't it?'

Cat regarded him and saw the honesty in his gaze. He wasn't trying to bamboozle her, or trick her into anything she wasn't ready for. And there really was loneliness lurking in his eyes. She bit her lip, then nodded. 'You're right. Friendship and a few meals together I can do. But nothing more.'

'Excellent! Thank you.' His smile widened, making his eyes shine. Cat was instantly reminded of that green gaze she'd admired in her dream, but shook the thought away. 'Do you finish at two today as well? We can grab a late lunch and some ice cream. Deal?'

She couldn't help the answering smile tugging at her lips. 'OK, I'll meet you in the piazza at two fifteen.'

Connor

Connor didn't know why he'd been so persistent, but he was glad that he had. They'd had lunch at a small family-run restaurant, having been waved inside by an enthusiastic greeter. To his surprise, Cat had engaged in some light-hearted banter with the man, smiling and laughing at something he said. Their rapid Italian was all gibberish to Connor, but it was clear that she was in her element, the Italian side of her coming out in force. The man had promised them 'the best food in all of Sorrento'. Although that might be taking things a step too far, it couldn't be denied that their seafood platters had been delicious. They were accompanied by the most amazing freshly pressed orange juice he'd ever had. He was now pleasantly full, and needed only a dessert to make the experience complete.

'I love this place,' he said, looking around at the buildings they passed. 'It's so quaint and serene.'

They were walking along narrow lanes paved with lava stone that had been worn smooth over time by thousands of feet. The dark grey colour contrasted beautifully with the pastel hues on the painted stucco facades of the surrounding houses. Some of these could be described as 'faded grandeur', with fancy doorways carved in stone. Others were newer and fresher, but still in that unmistakably Italian style. Everywhere was clean, though, unlike some parts of Old Naples, where the dilapidation was more severe. In some places, the buildings overhung the alleyways, wreathing them in shadow, but that was welcome whenever the sun became too hot.

The lanes were lined with shops, most of them geared towards the tourists who thronged the streets. Leather goods – expensive handbags, shoes and belts – and clothing in a particular indigo colour predominated, but there were other stores as well. Majolica-ware was on offer, exquisite marquetry in the shape of music boxes and plain ones, as well as jewellery made out of coral and turquoise. Occasionally the alleys opened into tiny piazzas, ringed with cafés and trattorias.

'So how about that ice cream then?' Connor said, stopping outside a shop that proclaimed itself to be a *gelateria*. It was one of many, but it looked inviting.

'You mean a *gelato*,' Cat teased, her eyes sparkling. 'There is a huge difference between what you call ice cream in the UK and this.'

She indicated a counter crammed full of the most amazing-looking home-made ice cream of every conceivable flavour. Banana, mango, pistachio, lemon, strawberry, chocolate . . . the choice seemed endless.

Connor loved seeing her so happy and carefree. It was a long way from the wary woman who had come to take his order at breakfast that morning. He'd worked hard to relax her during lunch, telling her about his travels, and some near-misses with boiling hot lava flows. It seemed to have worked.

'OK, OK.' He laughed. 'Whatever you call it, I want some. The only problem is which one to choose. What will you have?'

'Chocolate.' She didn't hesitate for a nanosecond, and that made him laugh again.

'I see. Your favourite, I take it?'

'Of course. What woman doesn't like chocolate?' She grinned at him, and warmth spread inside him. Cat was truly beautiful with her eyes shining like that, and her mood playful. It was as though she was letting out her inner self for the first time in ages, and it was wonderful to behold.

'Very well, I'll take your word for it that it's good. I'll have that and plain old vanilla. Can't go wrong with the basics.'

They sat down with their desserts at a rickety wrought-iron table on the pavement. There were people all around them, passing in a steady stream, but it didn't bother Connor, and Cat appeared oblivious. She was laser-focused on her *gelato*, moaning as the first spoonful slid down her throat. Connor almost choked on his when he caught the expression on her face. *Holy cow* . . . He wished he could have been the one to cause her to look and sound like that, but it wasn't an appropriate thought and he blinked it away.

He turned to watch the tourists surging past and cleared his throat. 'You were right, this is divine.' The creamy concoction melted on his tongue in the most amazing way, and he couldn't remember when he'd last had anything this good.

'Told you.'

'Fine, I'll allow you to be smug, just this once.'

She finished her *gelato* in silence, then licked her lips, causing him to turn away again. 'How long are you here for?' she asked.

'About a month, I think. It depends how quickly I can collect the data I need, and also on the people I work with. There are questions I need to ask them, but they aren't always available. They're busy with their own work, you know. It doesn't matter, though. My deadline for the thesis is flexible.'

'I see.' She tilted her head at him, as if she was trying to solve a puzzle. 'How come you're not renting an apartment or something then? It's going to cost you an arm and a leg to stay at the Palazzo for that long.'

'It's not too bad. They gave me a good deal, as it's not the busy season. And I prefer not to have to shop and cook for myself. It takes time out of my day that I could be spending on the research and writing.'

He didn't add that money wasn't an issue for him. She was working as a chambermaid and waitress, so presumably her circumstances were substantially less fortunate than his own. No point bringing that up.

'I guess that makes sense.' She changed the subject and stood up to throw away their empty paper ice cream cups. 'I'd better be getting back. I'm starting work again in half an hour. Thank you so much for lunch and this. It was lovely!'

Not as lovely as you, he wanted to say, but he merely smiled. 'You're very welcome. Any time. Perhaps we can do it again later in the week?'

She smiled. 'Yes, that would be nice.'

Connor was pleased that she looked as though she actually meant it. That was progress, and he couldn't wait to spend more time with her. That thought brought him up short. What on earth was happening to him? Usually, if a woman was interested in more than a casual short-term fling, he'd be off in a flash. Yet here he was, trying to get to know someone he should be running a mile from. A woman who was still married. It wasn't logical and made no sense, but he couldn't stop himself. She was already getting under his skin. An enigma he had to solve. And being with her felt all kinds of right, despite everything. He simply had to see her again, that was all there was to it.

Naples, 30 September 2022

Cat

'How are things at the hotel? Are they working you hard?'

Cat was sitting on a park bench next to her mother while Bella played on a nearby slide. It was wonderful to see her daughter so happy, and she had no trouble climbing up and whooshing down by herself. Going to outdoor playgrounds was the one thing they'd been able to do back in the UK without Derek getting cross. He'd forbidden them from attending playgroups, or making friends in their local area, but going to a park was allowed. It meant Bella was confident on the various pieces of equipment, which was a relief. There was no need to watch her like a hawk.

'The job is fine. I'm used to getting up early with Bella, so that's not a problem. Cleaning rooms can be a bit yucky, but most of the guests aren't slobs. And waitressing is easy, apart from the fact that I'm on my feet all day. That takes some getting used to.'

'Good, good. I'm glad you're settling in. No difficult guests to deal with?'

Cat almost smiled. Connor had been a bit of an arse that first day, but he'd apologised and explained he was just bored. And now? Now they were becoming friends, or so she thought. She'd been supremely comfortable in his company the day before. He was so easy to be around, so laid-back. Their lunch had been relaxing and fun. *Fun!* When was the last time she'd been carefree and enjoyed anything as frivolous as a simple meal with someone? A conversation where she didn't have to tread on egg-shells and watch her every word? She couldn't even remember.

'No, they're all nice. A bit demanding, some of them, but the Palazzo Rossi is a five-star hotel. They're allowed to expect only the best.'

'Of course.' Giovanna took her hand and squeezed it. 'Everything is working out. Soon we will hear from the lawyer in England and you'll be free. It would be a lot faster if Derek agreed to it, but I don't suppose that's likely.'

'No, definitely not. This divorce is going to be far from amicable. He'll fight me every step of the way.' Cat trembled at the thought of his wrath. No doubt he was furious that she'd dared to challenge him, and that he was being charged with causing her bodily harm. She had no idea if that would affect the divorce process, but she hoped it would speed it up. 'The lawyer said it's likely to take at least six months before it's all finalised. Maybe as long as a year because we have to sort out the finances. I don't know if I should stay here that long.'

What if he'd already figured out where she was? She gave her surroundings a quick glance, feeling as though she was being watched, but there was no one there.

'Perhaps not. We'll have to see about finding you a safe place in the UK.' Giovanna glanced at Bella. 'It's a good thing she's still so young. You don't have to drag her from one school to another.'

'Yes, thank goodness for that!' Cat sighed. 'I'm sorry you're having to look after her all the time, Mamma. It can be very tiring. Bella is a quiet child, but she still has a lot of energy.'

'Oh, don't worry about that. I'm happy to help and she's a very good girl. I feel like I'm making up for lost time.' Giovanna must have seen the chagrin on Cat's face, because she held up a hand. 'No, stop blaming yourself for that. I understand that it was hard to break free. Like I said, it's in the past. Now we look to the future.

And Bella is having a lovely time playing with her second cousins every day. She's only asked after you once or twice. She's fine, so stop worrying.'

Cat hugged her mother. 'Thank you, you're the best! I don't know what I'd do without you.'

Giovanna laughed. 'Well, lucky you don't have to, then.'

Chapter Thirteen

Pompeii, 1 October AD 79

Raedwald

'Guess we're not going to any fancy supper gatherings this evening,'
Duro whispered as they accompanied Lucius along the streets after
dark, each carrying a lantern on a pole to light the way. They were
headed towards the area of town with the most taverns, and by the
look of it, the man was eager to get there. He was striding a lot faster
than when he'd attended the *cena* the other week.

'Not unless he changes direction. And he's not dressed in that
long sheet either.'

Raedwald knew it was called a *toga*, but the garment seemed
silly and unnecessary to him. What was wrong with a tunic and a
cloak if it was cold? All that drapery would just get in the way. He
watched as Lucius glanced into a *caupona* – a place that sold only
drinks – halfway down the busy street, only to change his mind
and carry on. This part of town came alive after dark, with taverns and brothels staying open until all the customers had decided
to leave. That could be any time between now and dawn, most
commonly the latter.

Night-time here was dangerous, and the man had been wise to bring an escort. Crime was rife and rumours of violent gangs abounded, as well as the more common pickpockets and muggers. There were no soldiers or guards making sure the streets were safe for ordinary citizens. They'd left Lucius's home via the back entrance after he'd made sure the front doors were securely locked. Not just with a stout bar, but with several metal bolts and a thick plank leaning against the back of the door, one end stuck into a specially cut stone to hold it in place. As a final precaution, a guard dog slept just inside. These seemed like extreme measures, but they were necessary to protect what you owned.

'Looks like he's heading to Asellina's place again,' Duro commented. Her *popina* was well known, the sort of low-class establishment where you could enjoy both a meal and a girl, as well as plenty of wine and gambling. Lucius's visits had become a nightly occurrence in recent weeks, so their destination wasn't a surprise.

There were several similar inns along this street, with enticing aromas wafting from the wide doorways, mixed with the reek of cooking fat and too many people crammed into a small, hot room. Some customers queued for their orders, while others sat at the tables inside. As space was limited, quite a few people spilled out onto the pavement, blocking the way. Lucius swerved around them with a muttered curse.

As predicted, they entered Asellina's tavern, and Lucius elbowed his way past the long masonry counter with four large terracotta *dolia* built into it. The innkeeper herself presided behind it and she nodded her welcome. To the right of the entrance was a painting of a man with an animal head, holding a huge phallus. Nearby were other scenes depicting fighting, wenching and gambling. The noise level inside was deafening, all the tables filled with customers drinking, chatting or playing games. A mixture of local politics and gossip could be heard, as well as snatches of drunken singing and laughter.

Raedwald couldn't help but remember the time he'd spent at an inn with Aemilia. Their visit had been a lot more demure, but sitting so close to her had still been difficult, to say the least. He'd felt trapped by her presence somehow, as if she was drawing him in with her graciousness and beauty against his will. He didn't want to desire her, and yet he couldn't help it. So far he'd not detected an ounce of malice in her, only kindness. How was he supposed to hate that?

They extinguished their torches and left them by the door as Lucius headed straight for the back room, where the rattling of dice boxes could be heard. He glanced at the two gladiators. 'You two, settle down to wait. I'll be here for a while as usual. But stay alert. I'm not paying you to enjoy yourselves.'

It was clear that was what he intended himself, since the table he chose had three men seated there with a game of dice already in progress. They greeted him effusively, as if they'd been expecting him, and slapped his back as he sank onto a stool. Lucius wasn't just out to drink with friends, he was here to gamble. A lot, judging by the gold coins Raedwald spotted. This was nothing new, and he and Duro were becoming used to the routine.

They found seats on a bench along one wall, underneath another series of wall paintings depicting life inside an establishment such as this one. They were lifelike and colourful. He'd never seen their like before coming here, and admired the skill it took to create such art. These people were excellent builders and craftsmen, he had to give them that. It was going to feel strange living in a draughty wooden house with crude wall hangings after this. Still, that was home.

A serving wench came and handed them each a cup of wine, nodding towards Lucius. 'He told me to bring you these,' she informed them.

'Thank you.' Raedwald ignored the flirtatious glance she sent him, and the way she leaned forward to give him a glimpse of what was under her tunic. Duro smiled at her, but didn't act on the invitation either. The girl might be willing to take them upstairs for a few *asses*, but neither of them was interested.

She took the hint and marched off, chin a fraction higher and her mouth tight.

'She'll get over her pique in a moment,' Duro said. 'Although she won't find anyone as fine-looking as us in here, so it's bound to be a disappointment.'

Raedwald snorted and elbowed his friend, who was undoubtedly handsome. 'By Baduhenna, but you're vain! I have a good mind to rearrange your face the next time we fight in the arena. Then the wenches will stop ogling you.'

'It wasn't just me she was batting her eyelashes at,' Duro retorted, giving him a good-natured shove in return. 'And the ladies don't seem averse to a few battle scars. Quite the opposite.'

'Well, that can be arranged.'

But they both knew it wasn't up to them, as they weren't usually allowed to fight each other. They were both exceedingly skilled, and pitting them against one another could result in a lethal injury. Their owner wanted them hurt, but not killed. They always hoped to be spared the worst injuries. Blood must flow, but that didn't mean it had to come from a man's face or other vulnerable parts. The two of them had practised fighting so that when they wounded someone it looked a lot worse than it really was, while still giving the spectators what they wanted. Some of the other gladiators were in on this ruse too, and trained accordingly.

They sat in silence, studying their surroundings. This particular tavern wasn't one they frequented when they were out by themselves. Most gladiators favoured one down by the Nuceria gate, but they were all fairly similar. Noisy board or dice games

126

were being played at nearly all the tables, and by the looks of it, quite large sums were being won and lost. Lucius's cheeks were becoming redder by the moment as excitement had him in its grip. When he won a round, his raucous laughter rang out, but when he lost, his expression turned vicious and sulky.

'I'd never play with him,' Raedwald muttered. 'Sore loser.'

'Mm, not to mention reckless. Can he afford to lose such sums every night?' Duro eyed the heap of gold and silver coins now placed next to one of Lucius's opponents, while his were dwindling.

'Who knows? He lives in a fine house. Must have coin coming in from somewhere.'

But something about this whole scene bothered Raedwald. Lucius wasn't just enjoying himself. It was as though he was in the grip of a fever, and the game had him by the throat. Raedwald had seen such behaviour before, usually from men who were desperate to play with any opponent. It was an illness, and he thanked the gods he and Duro didn't suffer from it.

'It's going to be another long night.' Duro sighed and crossed his arms over his chest before leaning back against the wall, closing his eyes. 'Let's take turns watching him, then I can catch up on my sleep.'

'Not yet. How about you go and chat to the serving wench instead. See if you can glean anything from her. Lucius comes here a lot. She ought to know whether he can afford it.'

'What? Why? It makes no difference to us.' His friend frowned at him.

'No, but it might matter to Aemilia.' As soon as he'd said it, Raedwald knew he would never hear the end of it.

Sure enough, Duro laughed out loud. 'I knew it! The pretty matron has caught your eye. Even the mighty Raedwald isn't as immune to all women as he'd like to be. Oh, this is priceless!'

'Shut up! Let's just say she deserves better than a man who's probably gaming away her very home at this moment.' He nodded in Lucius's direction. 'Look at him. He's not going to stop till they've bled him dry. It was the same thing yesterday, and the night before. And he probably hasn't got the wits to know they're cheating.' He'd seen a few subtle moves that Lucius, by now several cups of wine down, hadn't noticed.

'Sure. Keep telling yourself that.' The Briton was still chuckling, but got to his feet to escape the light punch Raedwald aimed at him. 'Fine, I'm going, I'm going. But don't think I'm letting you off the hook. I've waited a long time for this.'

'Fool.'

But Raedwald wasn't sure who was the lackwit here – it could conceivably be him.

Aemilia

The pounding on the back gate woke Aemilia, and she stumbled out of her room and along the peristyle colonnade, not bothering to slip on her sandals. She slept in her tunic, and it fell to the floor, covering her feet so that only the toes peeked out. Irritation flashed through her. Where were the slaves? They should be opening up, not her. This was what came of selling the best ones and keeping those who pleased Lucius. The remainder were lazy and insolent, doing only the bare minimum when prodded.

'Who is it?' she asked, leaning towards the thick wood to hear the muffled answer.

'Rufus and Drusus with Lucius Caius Merula. Let us in, please.'

She lifted the heavy bar off and slid the bolts to the side with some difficulty. This entrance was almost as heavily locked as the front one, but she didn't know why Lucius was coming in this way. Normally he'd wake the guard at the other end of the house when he'd been out of an evening.

Opening the gate just a sliver, she peeked out and saw the two barbarians holding lanterns in one hand while propping up a slumped Lucius between them. She hurried to widen the gap so that they could pass through. 'By all the gods, has he been hurt?'

Duro chuckled, while Raedwald's mouth was set in a grim line. He didn't look pleased to see her, although why, she couldn't fathom.

'No, but he'll be in pain come the morning, that's for certain,' he ground out.

'Oh.' She could smell the wine fumes coming towards her in waves now, and understood. Lucius had imbibed too much, to the point where he couldn't even stand up straight. She sighed. It had happened before, and seemed to be becoming a more frequent occurrence, but it was not for her to tell him what to do. 'This way, please. I'll show you to his chamber, then I'll wake one of the slaves.'

'They should be awake already,' Raedwald muttered, but she ignored that, even though it was the truth.

They followed her to Lucius's quarters, a room off the *atrium*, where the two gladiators dumped him on his bed. He groaned, but didn't open his eyes, and barely moved when Aemilia shouted for one of his slaves. The man came sloping into the room, reluctantly, and glanced at his master without bothering to hide a yawn.

'You'll stay with him tonight,' Aemilia ordered. 'Fetch a bucket and a jug of water. He might need it.' In fact, there was no doubt about it, and she was thankful she didn't share a room or a bed with him. Married couples of their class usually had separate quarters.

What on earth possessed him to drink to this extent? Was it the worries about debts? The thought made her feel guilty, since she had a way of alleviating that, but at the same time, she knew it would never be enough. If she gave him the jewellery her father had handed her, Lucius would just squander it and they'd be no better off.

For some reason she was embarrassed to have the two barbarians bringing her husband home like this. She hustled them back to the garden gate, where they'd left the poles of their lanterns stuck into the soil of one of the flower beds. Duro picked his up and slipped outside with a quick 'Goodnight', but Raedwald turned to her and hesitated.

'Will you be all right, *domina*?'

'Me? Of course.' She crossed her arms over her chest defensively, and glanced up at him, acutely aware of how little clothing she was wearing. He didn't leer at her or ogle her body, however. She was grateful for that.

'He won't . . . take out his bad humour on you in the morning?' His eyes were holding hers, and it was as though he was looking straight into her soul.

Aemilia shivered. 'No.' She wanted to ask why he should care. Why he was asking. But she couldn't get the words out.

'Good. I'll see you tomorrow then.'

'Tomorrow?' She couldn't think while he was staring at her like that. His gaze shifted and he was caressing her with his gaze now. She could feel it skimming her skin. Heat travelled through her and pooled in her stomach, and there was a hitch in her breathing.

He smiled. 'The baths again? Or so you told us.'

'Oh, that. Yes. Of course.'

Her cheeks caught fire, and she didn't know whether to run away or just stand there staring at him. The flickering light of the lantern gilded the planes of his face and made his glorious hair shine like amber in the sun. There was so much of him, it was overwhelming, but not in a threatening way. And when he reached out and took one of her hands in both of his, she didn't pull it back. She breathed out, a sensation of safety enveloping her.

They stood like that for another moment, her small hand engulfed in his, and just looked at each other. He didn't say anything, but he didn't need to. She understood that he was concerned about her, wanted to protect her, perhaps even cherish her. And she knew she'd remember this for the rest of her life, even if it was wrong.

Finally he gave her hand a squeeze.

'I must away. Until tomorrow, *domina*.'

He had probably added the courtesy to remind them both of who they were, but right then, Aemilia didn't care. Not one bit.

Chapter Fourteen

Pompeii, 1 October 2022

Cat

'Thank you so much for coming with me. It is much more fun sightseeing with someone else, rather than on your own.'

Connor smiled at Cat as they walked out of the train station at Pompeii. It was shabby and run-down, and much smaller than she had imagined, with only two platforms. But as they headed down the street towards the entrance to the ancient city, she forgot about it, the man by her side taking up all her attention.

She nodded at him and smiled back, but she wasn't convinced she ought to be here. Not that she didn't want to spend time with him, but she should have been with Bella again today, as she had another day off. However, that morning her mother had called and put her off.

'Luca thought he saw someone lurking outside, watching the house. It could be a coincidence, but it would be stupid to take the chance, no? Better to wait till later in the week, *cara*.'

It made sense, but it was a huge disappointment, as she'd been looking forward to spending another day with her daughter. As a consequence, she'd felt a bit lost, and decided to go for a walk down to the harbour in Sorrento. On her way out of the hotel, she'd run into Connor, who had persuaded her to come to Pompeii instead. Perhaps it would take her mind off things, although she couldn't help worrying about the potential stalker. Was it Derek? Had he figured out where they'd gone? She hoped not.

'A photo, *signora*!' A huge man dressed as a Roman centurion called out to her. He'd been posing for selfies, for a fee, with a couple of giggling teenage girls, and was obviously touting for more business.

'No, thanks.' Cat hurried after Connor, who was already striding off down the street leading into the ruined town. Something about the pretend Roman soldier made her uneasy, although she couldn't for the life of her figure out what.

'Wow, this is just amazing, isn't it?' Connor's face was alight with wonder as he studied their surroundings.

According to the map they'd been given at the ticket office, they were passing through a gate near the so-called Quadriporticus. As they entered a spacious rectangular grassy area surrounded by Doric columns, they stopped to take it in.

'This is where the gladiators lived, apparently,' Connor said, scanning the information booklet he'd bought. 'It's believed they originally had their barracks in the north-eastern part of town, but after a huge earthquake in AD 62, they had to move here temporarily.' He nodded towards the lawn in the centre. 'That must be where they did their training. And look, all these little rooms around the courtyard are where they slept.'

There was a walkway under a roof all the way round the area, with doors opening into small, cell-like rooms. Cat peered into the nearest one while adjusting her gold bracelet, which was sticking to her skin since it was a warm day. 'Must have been rather cramped,' she commented. 'Not to mention dark.'

She could imagine it quite vividly – a couple of mattresses on the floor, the light from a Roman oil lamp casting flickering shadows across the walls, while the small window was shuttered.

'Mm,' Connor agreed. 'They probably didn't expect luxury. To all intents and purposes, they were slaves after all.'

'Slaves? I thought gladiators were famous.'

'Yes, but they were owned by some sort of manager and had no choice but to fight. I've read about it. Most of them didn't live long. And who in their right mind would want to battle for their lives like that? No, I think they were forced into it.'

Cat shuddered. He painted a bleak picture, and for some reason it bothered her more than it should.

'Let's go look at the theatres instead,' she suggested, leading the way to the theatres adjoining the Quadriporticus. The larger one had once held four or five thousand spectators, and they tried the stone seating, taking turns to snap photos of each other like most of the other tourists. From there, they continued along a narrow alley that led to a wider street, paved with huge stones of volcanic rock.

'Wow, these are amazing!' Connor exclaimed. 'I can't believe how well preserved they are.'

The sun was beating down, although it wasn't as fierce as during the summer months. Cat was glad she'd put on a baseball cap, as her dark hair always felt extra hot when it hung heavy down her back.

'It's really something,' she agreed.

She'd only been here once before, when she was a child, and didn't remember much about it. Now she looked around in awe at everything that remained from that fateful eruption back in AD 79. For a moment she closed her eyes and could almost hear the screams of panic and chaos as the townspeople tried to flee to safety through the gate they'd entered earlier. *A stampede of terrified humanity, almost engulfing her as she battled to go in the opposite direction . . .* She shook her head and blinked at her surroundings. Her imagination sure was working overtime today.

They checked out the usual tourist sights – the House of Menander, the brothel, the main street and the Forum – and finally sat down on a high kerb, taking swigs from the bottles of water Connor had bought. He dug out a packet of biscotti and offered her one.

'I figured we'd need sustenance. There's a lot more walking involved here than people think, or so I read.'

'Thank you.' She appreciated his forethought, and also the fact that he wasn't telling her what to do every five seconds, the way Derek would have done. Instead, he'd allowed her to lead the way after consulting the tourist map. He seemed content to go wherever she wished.

When they'd rested for a while, they stood up and Connor asked, 'Where next?'

Cat looked around, then pointed down a side street. 'That way?'

She didn't know if there was anything to see there, but something was urging her to head in that direction. Her steps were sure as she set off, with Connor following closely on her heels. She had no idea what she was looking for, but halfway down the street, she stopped suddenly and stared at what had once been a fairly grand house. The wooden doors were gone now, as was the upper floor, but it was possible to look towards what would have been the *atrium*, or main reception room. The walls there still had some paint on the lower parts, but in her mind's eye she could see exactly what they would have looked like originally. She recognised them.

Startled, she retreated a few steps and blinked at the doorway.

Connor chuckled. 'Did you bring me here just to show me a prime example of a phallus? Way to make a guy feel inadequate.'

'What?' She swivelled to frown at him, and he nodded towards the lintel above the door. 'Oh.' She felt her cheeks become suffused with heat. 'I . . . No! I had no idea it was there.'

'Mm-hmm. Sure you didn't.' Connor sent her a teasing smile.

She shook her head at him and turned back to study the house again. It felt familiar, almost like . . . *home*. A voice whispered inside her head and made her shiver. What was wrong with her? But she had the eerie sensation of having been here before. She even remembered the colour of the doors that were no longer there – black. She looked for the guard who she knew ought to be waiting there to intercept any visitors, and the dog chained to the wall at night. Then her gaze was drawn to the *impluvium*, what had once been a sunken pool. Without thinking, she stepped through the doorway and wandered towards it, looking up for the large hole in the roof that should have been there. It was gone now, but she still saw it, and that scared the living daylights out of her.

She wrapped her arms around her torso and bent double, trying not to hyperventilate.

'Cat? Are you OK? What's the matter?' Connor put an arm round her shoulders and drew her upright, his expression concerned as he peered at her.

'I . . . I don't know.' She took a deep breath and tried to stop her heart from going ballistic. There was something weird happening here and she didn't understand it. 'I'm not ill, just . . . confused.'

'How so? Come, let's sit down for a minute.' He led her through an anteroom and towards a low stone wall in a peristyle garden. 'Are you dizzy?'

'No, but . . . Oh God, I don't know how to explain.' He was going to think she was nuts. *She* thought she was nuts. 'It's the weirdest thing. I feel as though I've been here before. And I don't mean recently, but when this house was intact. Like, before the eruption in . . . in Roman times. I know what it looked like, what each room was for and how it was furnished. I can see it in my mind. It's . . . creepy.'

'Oh-kaaay?' He was studying her with a nonplussed expression, and she suddenly wanted to cry.

His face was also familiar, beloved even, but she had no idea why. She didn't know him, not really, and yet a part of her was saying she loved him. Or an older version of him. Was there such a thing? Souls that had been reborn? She'd never believed in anything like that until now.

Her gaze fell on the gold bracelet gripping her forearm. It was burning hot in the sun now, somehow radiating energy into her body. She had a flash of another arm wearing it . . . *while holding on to a strong hand, being pulled along the back of a building . . . then the scene changed, the arm ring was gone, but the same hand guided her through the house and out into the street. The world around her was grey and it looked as though it was snowing, but when the flakes fell on her they made smudges on her skin. She heard screams again and there was terror rising inside her. Her heartbeat was frantic, uneven, but she clung to that large hand as if it was the only thing keeping her alive. He'd save her, she knew he would. He would always come for her . . .*

'Cat? You're worrying me now. Do you want to go back to the hotel?' Connor's voice came from a long way away at first, but slowly it came into focus, as did his face.

She almost grabbed him to plant a kiss on his lips, but remembered at the last moment that he wasn't the man whose hand she'd been holding. That was someone else. Someone long gone.

Burying her face in her hands, she shook her head. 'No, I don't want to leave yet. I need to process this.' Peeking out from behind one hand, she asked him, 'Do you believe in reincarnation?'

'Uh . . .' He was clearly flummoxed. 'I've never given it much thought, to be honest.'

'Yeah, me neither.' Cat sighed. 'Listen, you're probably wondering why on earth you chose to spend the day with a crazy person, but I swear I'm not. I really didn't know this was going to happen, but I'm definitely seeing things.' She swept a hand out to indicate the rest of the house. 'I could tell you what all this was like before the eruption, the colours, ornaments, everything. I just have to close my eyes. And it's freaking me out no end.'

Again he slung an arm round her shoulders, but this time he pulled her in for a hug. 'I believe you, and I don't think you're unhinged. It could be the sun, but I doubt it. From your reaction, I think what you're seeing is genuine somehow, but I'll be damned if I can explain it.' With a lopsided smile he added, 'Not sure I want to, to be honest.'

She gave a shaky laugh and allowed herself to snuggle against him for a moment. 'Me neither.'

Breathing in the scent of him – subtle cologne, shampoo and clean clothing, plus his own unique smell – her panic subsided. Whoever he'd been, her protector, he was still here in the shape of Connor, and nothing bad was going to happen. She was safe. And what was more, he hadn't laughed at her or shouted. He was holding her instead of hitting her.

They stayed like that for a bit longer, then she wriggled out of his embrace. 'Do you mind if I just walk around for a bit? I need to see it all.'

'Of course. Go ahead. I'll wander down the street. Just give me a shout when you're ready to move on.'

She appreciated the support he was radiating. The mere thought of how Derek would have reacted to something like this had her shrinking inside herself, but Connor had taken it in his stride. It was incredibly comforting. Although she probably should have run screaming from this place, she knew she'd always regret it if she didn't allow the strange memories to surface.

Closure was needed; whether it was for herself or someone else didn't matter.

Connor

Connor didn't go far. Although Cat seemed OK now, she'd scared the living daylights out of him earlier when she had just crumpled like that. He'd thought she was going to faint or something, and had visions of having to carry her all the way back to the main gates. Not that he couldn't do it, but it would have taken a long time and might have done more harm than good.

What he definitely hadn't expected was her having some sort of hallucination. Nor the question about reincarnation.

He sat down on the kerb opposite the main entrance of the house, the stone warm through the fabric of his jeans. The phallus carved above the door was giving him ideas he shouldn't be having, even though he knew it was just a symbol for good fortune. When he'd first caught sight of it, though, his brain had exploded with images of Cat next to him, beneath him, around him, naked. Where had that come from? Sure, he was a normal, healthy male, and fantasies of what he'd like to do to Cat had vaguely flitted through his mind ever since he'd met her, but nothing that explicit.

Then she'd mentioned seeing things as well, and it seemed like too much of a coincidence. Was reincarnation possible? Or possession? There was definitely something strange at work here, and he wasn't sure whether to be angry or scared.

Or to enjoy it. Where had that thought come from? He shivered, despite the warmth of the afternoon sun.

Maybe they should leave. He hadn't felt like this with her at any other time, so perhaps it was this place. There could be some ancient magic at work, or maybe spirits tethered to this exact spot.

'Jesus,' he murmured, and speared his fingers through his hair. Was he really even thinking something like that? He didn't believe in ghosts or anything that wasn't scientifically proven. At least, he never had in the past. He was a scientist, for goodness' sake.

'Connor? I think I'm ready to go on now.' Cat came out of the door, and he had a sudden image of her dressed in long, flowing drapery like a Roman lady, her tantalising curves clearly outlined. It disappeared as quickly as it had come.

He stood up and tried to get a grip. 'Sure. Need any more water, or a biscuit?' Concentrating on practical matters might help.

'No, I'm fine, thanks. Let's just move on.' She was smiling, but it was a tremulous effort, as if she was afraid of him judging her. Or even striking out at her for being foolish.

It made him spitting mad that someone had done that to this beautiful woman. If he ever got his hands on the bastard . . . No, it wasn't his problem and he shouldn't get involved. He couldn't help but reach for her hand, though, and she didn't protest when he plaited his fingers with hers. 'Come on then. What do you want to see next?'

'The amphitheatre?'

'Sure. This way, I think.'

There was definitely a connection between them, and for now, he'd be happy to follow her anywhere.

Cat

The amphitheatre did not prove to be a better choice. The enormous oval edifice towered over them, and as soon as they drew near, a sensation of dread pooled in Cat's stomach. There were stairs on the outside, rising to what had been the upper tiers of the seating, but they didn't venture up there. Instead they followed other tourists down a sloping tunnel paved, according to the guidebook, with basalt blocks. It was dark and ominous, sending a chill down her spine. How many people had walked this way knowing they would never leave the place alive?

The thought made her positively nauseous.

They emerged into the arena itself, which was vast and covered in gravel. Standing there made Cat feel very small, and she could imagine how intimidating it must have been for those condemned to fight or die here. She closed her eyes, and her mind flooded with gory images of men fighting, weapons flashing in the sunlight and blood flowing freely. The metallic tang of it hung in the air, along with the stench of sweat and fear. She wrinkled her nose and recoiled. The shouts of encouragement from the crowd baying for a kill assaulted her, almost deafening in volume.

'Good grief!' She covered her ears with her hands and staggered over to the nearest wall. There she sank down to sit with her back against it, knees drawn up so that she could lean her forehead on them. She wrapped her arms around her legs and shivered as the sounds inside her head faded away.

'Cat? Are you having another weird episode?' Connor kneeled next to her, gripping her shoulder. His touch anchored her, and the strange smells disappeared as well.

'Y-yes. I saw fighting. Killing. It was horrible! Why are humans so cruel?' She shuddered, despite the warm sun trapped in the enclosed area.

When she looked up, she expected Connor to be staring at her as if she'd lost her mind, but she saw only understanding and sadness in his gaze. 'I know,' he murmured. 'I felt it too. This place has seen a lot of evil. It's embedded in the very stones.'

She nodded. 'I think I'd like to leave now, if you don't mind. Feel free to stay if you want. I don't want to ruin your day.' Bracing her hands against the wall, she levered herself upright.

Connor took her hand again and twined his fingers with hers. 'No, I'm happy to go with you. I can always come back another day.'

With her mind all over the place, she barely said goodbye or thank you upon their return to the hotel. The strange happenings had thrown her completely, and she needed time to process them. Thankfully, Connor seemed to understand. He merely kissed her on the cheek and let her go.

Chapter Fifteen

Pompeii, 2 October AD 79

Raedwald

Raedwald followed Aemilia as she made her way home from the baths at a leisurely pace. He guessed that she was feeling languid from the pampering and hot water. Much as he hated to admit it, having someone massage your body, using a strigil to clean every inch of your skin, then immersing yourself in a hot bath was an enormous pleasure. One of the few things he would miss when he left this place.

The child wasn't with them today, and Aemilia had only brought one slave woman, who was even slower than her mistress. She looked downright sulky, in fact. He recognised her as one of the two who had been introduced to him as Lucius's latest acquisitions that first day. Presumably she resented having to look after her mistress, as well as sharing the master's bed whenever required. He had some sympathy for her, but at the same time it wasn't Aemilia's fault, so he felt cross on her behalf.

'Did her husband say anything about going out tonight?' Duro asked quietly. He'd been walking next to Raedwald, lost in his own thoughts up until now.

'Not yet, but I would be surprised if he stays at home.' Raedwald shrugged. 'More coin for us, so I'm not complaining.'

Although he'd like to knock some sense into the man, they were profiting from the nightly excursions to the gaming taverns. As Lucius was useless at whatever game he attempted, and lost more often than not, they'd secretly been betting against him and had won a tidy sum already. Raedwald only wished he could be sure all these losses weren't affecting Aemilia. Her husband was getting increasingly desperate, and that didn't bode well. Since he had already been threatened – presumably by moneylenders or whoever he was borrowing funds from – he must be trying to win enough to pay them back. Instead, he was digging himself into a deeper hole every day. This could only end badly, for both him and his family.

They had emerged from the baths a little later than usual, and dusk was falling. As they walked past a dark alleyway, a group of four men suddenly emerged, rushing to grab Aemilia and the slave girl. The latter let out a piercing scream, while her mistress only blinked in fright and confusion. The men all had dark material tied around the bottom half of their faces, giving them a sinister look. Hired thugs who didn't want to be recognised, was Raedwald's immediate conclusion.

He and Duro had been hanging back, not wanting to crowd the women, but now they sprang forward as one. Instinctively, Raedwald headed for Aemilia, and punched one of the men holding her, hitting him so hard the man's head snapped back audibly and he sagged to the ground. The attacker had been holding a knife to her throat, but it fell from his lifeless hand without touching her. Raedwald kicked it out of the way as he set about releasing her from the other man.

As soon as his friend went down, the second man pointed his

own dagger at Aemilia's torso. 'Don't come any closer, or she dies,' he hissed, pulling her against him and backing up against the nearest wall while inching his way towards the alley.

'That's not what you were paid to do, I'll wager.' Raedwald tried to keep calm, even though the sight of that sharp weapon pressing against her was making him want to tear the man to pieces with his bare hands. 'Let her go, or I swear to all the gods I'll hunt you down and kill you very slowly and painfully. Trust me, it's not worth it for what little you were probably paid. I'm sure you know who I am,' he added, for once using his fame to advantage.

The man's eyes flickered uncertainly as he took in what was happening behind Raedwald. A quick glance over his shoulder showed the gladiator that Duro had the other two men beaten and was attempting to shut the slave girl up by a combination of cajoling and shaking. That only left the man holding Aemilia.

'Let. Her. *Go*.' His voice was so cold it should have frozen the man's innards, but it had no immediate effect. The attacker was cornered, and probably scared without the backup of his companions, which made him unpredictable and even more dangerous.

Aemilia's eyes were fixed on Raedwald, and he tried to imbue her with calm through sheer willpower, looking deep into her eyes. It seemed to be working, as she relaxed visibly, her wide gaze becoming less frantic. He calculated that he could yank the man away from her with a quick lunge, and although she might be pricked by the knife, he'd be so fast the injury would be minimal. He had to take the risk, otherwise everything could turn out much worse.

Just as he was about to make his move, however, she suddenly flung herself to the side, away from the dagger. Her movement took the attacker by surprise, and it was exactly what Raedwald needed. Surging forward, he had the man's wrist in his grip in the blink of an eye, knocking it against the wall behind him with such force the bones splintered. The dagger fell with a metallic clatter, out of harm's way.

The man howled with pain, but Raedwald didn't wait for him to counter-attack, even if he'd been capable of it. He punched him repeatedly, in the jaw, on the side of the head and in the gut, until he collapsed like a sack of turnips, sliding down the wall onto the pavement. When he was sure the assailant wouldn't wake any time soon, Raedwald picked up both knives and turned to Aemilia, who was standing next to Duro with her arms wrapped around herself.

'Are you well, *domina*?' He peered at her to see whether she was hurt. The sleeve of her tunic had been torn, and her *palla* had slipped off her head. She had some ugly bruising on her upper arm, but he didn't see any blood. He cursed out loud. 'I should have killed him,' he hissed.

She glanced down to see what he was looking at, then pulled the sleeve back in place. 'It is nothing,' she said, her voice a little shaky, but composed. 'I'm fine.'

Something about the way she was avoiding his gaze made Raedwald frown, but he decided he would mull that over later. For now, he needed to get the women home.

'Let us go,' he ordered. The attackers, who were still slumped all around them, could stay there till sunrise for all he cared. He hoped they'd learned their lesson.

Aemilia

'You should go and lie down.' Raedwald followed Aemilia through the back gate and along the colonnaded walkway surrounding the garden. 'You've had a fright.'

'Thank you, but I'll just sit out here for a while. I'll recover in a moment.'

The slave woman had been led away to the kitchen by Duro, and loud sobbing could be heard coming from that direction. Aemilia turned and walked through the flower beds to a bench at the end of the garden, hidden from sight behind an arch of climbing flowers and a dense bush. She was shaken to the core, but most of all, she wanted answers. She sat down and patted the seat beside her. Raedwald looked as though he would refuse, but her frown must have convinced him she wasn't in the mood to argue about it. With a sigh, he followed suit.

'What was that all about?' she demanded.

'What do you mean? They were robbers.' His gaze was fixed on a nearby fruit tree, avoiding hers, which made her instantly suspicious.

'No, they weren't. They could have taken my coin purse or arm rings at any time, but they didn't so much as mention them. They just wanted to hurt me.' She laid a hand on his forearm and willed him to look at her. 'Please, Raedwald, tell me the truth. I would rather know than be kept in the dark.'

She saw rather than heard him sigh again, his broad chest rising and falling, and the muscles under her fingers jumped. They were hard to the touch, with the softness of skin and fine hairs added, and for some reason the sensation calmed her. Those muscles had saved her, and she was grateful. Very grateful.

Finally he swivelled round to face her, his expression bleak. 'They were sent to scare you. Or your husband, rather. I believe they'd been hired by one of the moneylenders to frighten Caius Merula into paying what he owes them. Duro and I were employed to protect you from just such an attack. Your husband knew it might happen – he'd been warned.'

'Oh no . . .' It all made sense now. Why Lucius should

147

suddenly care about her welfare to that extent. He'd never been bothered about possible robberies before. Such things happened, and if you just let go of your coin purse, all would be well. This, however, was much more serious. 'How much does he owe them?'

Raedwald shrugged. 'I have no idea, but judging by the way he plays dice and other games every evening, I would guess a considerable amount.' He dry-washed his face. 'I'm sorry, I didn't want to have to tell you. I promised him I wouldn't, but you're right, it is not fair to keep it from you. You can be on your guard better if you know.'

'Thank you. I agree, and I promise I won't let on to Lucius that I'm aware of the situation. I will merely tell him we were attacked by robbers.' She shook her head. 'I knew I shouldn't have gone out today. The calendar said it was an unlucky day, but I wanted to get out of the house . . .'

'For the love of all the gods!' Raedwald shook his head. 'Unlucky day? That had nothing to do with it. I don't understand why you Romans place so much faith in that rubbish. We all have good or bad fortune, but we're not going to have it on the same day as everyone else just because the calendar says so. That is ridiculous.'

Aemilia stared at him, surprised by his vehemence. His words made sense, but she'd grown up with the notion that certain days were bad – marked on the calendar as *nefastus* – and it was best to avoid doing anything on such a date. For important occasions, it was the custom to check and make sure. She hadn't considered that not everyone would have bad luck at the same time.

'Well, I . . . No, maybe you are right.' She fiddled with the torn sleeve of her tunic, which had fallen down again. Raedwald's gaze fixed on it. The bruising in particular.

'That man wasn't holding your arm,' he stated, watching her as a flood of heat suffused her cheeks.

'Wasn't he?' She tried her best to sound ignorant, but he wasn't fooled.

'Those bruises are your husband's doing. And it's not the first time, is it.' It was not a question and she didn't bother to deny it.

Lucius had tried yet again to make her give him something of value – anything – the look in his eyes half crazed. She'd been afraid he would beat her black and blue, but fortunately he had stomped off in a temper and taken his ire out on an ugly statue in the *atrium*. She had felt sorry for him. He was a proud man, and to have to scrabble around for small amounts of coin was undignified and demoralising for someone in his position. The scion of a once great family. And yet she'd held fast to her conviction that she was right not to tell him about her mother's jewellery. Giving it to him would be pointless.

'I want to wring his scrawny neck,' Raedwald muttered. 'Can't you leave him? I know marriages can be dissolved here.'

Aemilia felt tears seeping out of her eyes as desolation swept through her. 'No,' she whispered. 'He would keep Caia, and I couldn't bear that. Although I might not have a choice. He was muttering again this morning about divorcing me. He . . . he wants to marry a woman with a large dowry. Now I understand why he's so desperate to do so.'

She buried her face in her hands and tried to compose herself. Here she was, breaking down in front of a gladiator, of all people. A man who faced death every time he set foot in the arena. He must think her pathetic, her problems small in comparison. And they were, she knew that.

'Oh Aemilia, don't cry. Please.' His voice was gruff, but in the next instant his arms wrapped around her, and he pulled her close so that her cheek rested against his shoulder.

He smelled of clean linen and pine-scented soap, and she felt the heat of his skin through his clothing. His embrace was a safe haven, a cocoon keeping her away from everything that was bad in her life. She wanted to stay hidden there for ever. He pulled away slightly and looked down at her, searching her eyes for something, then his gaze dropped to her mouth and awareness tingled in her veins.

He lifted a hand to cup her cheek, and his thumb stroked her bottom lip. 'You're so kind and beautiful,' he murmured. 'He doesn't deserve you.'

When she didn't draw away, he leaned down slowly to capture her lips with his. It was a mere touch, like a whisper of silk, but it sent shock waves right through her. She grabbed his tunic with both fists to tug him closer. She wanted more, so much more, and she couldn't bear it if he stopped now.

He seemed to understand, and tilted her face with his fingers as though to gain better access. Slanting his mouth across hers, he deepened the kiss, cajoling her into opening for him so his tongue could stroke hers. She made a noise deep in her throat, enjoying the sensation and the taste of him so much it made her tremble. Boldly, she kissed him back, digging her fingers into his glorious hair to keep him anchored to her. It was thrilling and delicious, and she'd never wanted anything as much as she wanted this kiss.

Eventually they came to their senses, and he leaned his forehead on hers, breathing in short bursts. 'Aemilia, we can't . . . Someone will see. I should go.'

'I know.' But she didn't let go of him yet. She needed to skim her hands along his strong shoulders and arms down to his hands, where she plaited her fingers with his. 'Thank you for saving my life earlier.'

He retreated, eyebrows drawing together as he regarded her. 'Is that what this was? A thank-you kiss?' He sounded offended, and that made her smile and punch him lightly on the chest.

'No, Raedwald, it most certainly wasn't. I've never thanked anyone like that before, and if you'll recall, you started it.'

His mouth drew up into a lopsided grin. 'So I did. Forgive me, but I don't make a habit of mauling married women. Or any women, for that matter. I'm out of practice.'

'Oaf.' But she was joking, and stretched up to give him one last kiss. 'I don't know what this was, but I don't regret it. Now go, please, before I make an utter fool of myself.'

He gave her a fierce kiss back, then stood up. 'As you wish, *domina*. I hope you sleep well tonight.'

As he walked away, she wanted to shout after him that he knew very well she wouldn't. She'd be thinking about that kiss all night, until it drove her crazy.

Chapter Sixteen

Sorrento Beach, 2 October 2022

Cat

Cat felt so guilty about ruining their day in Pompeii, she could barely meet Connor's eye when she took his breakfast order the following morning. He smiled as if nothing was amiss, but that made her feel even worse, so when she brought his porridge, she bent to whisper to him.

'I'm so sorry about yesterday. I . . . obviously wasn't feeling like myself.'

'No problem. I enjoyed our outing.' He kept his voice down as well. 'It's just a shame you probably won't want to go anywhere with me ever again.' Although he made light of it, she could tell this genuinely bothered him.

Did she want to go out with him again? The answer was yes, she couldn't deny that, but quite apart from the embarrassment of having weird visions, he was only here for a short while. The wise thing to do would be to avoid him altogether, but her mind protested vehemently at that idea. And was spending a little time together really so bad? They had agreed to be friends, and although a part of her had already started yearning for more, she could stick to that. Couldn't she? She had to.

'Um, I should think it's the other way around,' she replied. 'Why would you want to be around a complete nutcase?'

'Cat.' His voice was a caress, low and slightly husky. 'I don't think that about you. I believe you might be under a lot of stress right now. Obviously I don't know all the details, but it doesn't make me want to stay away from you. Quite the opposite. The fact of the matter is that I like spending time with you, no matter what. And I want to be there for you if you need someone to have your back.'

There was only deep sincerity in his green eyes, and she couldn't resist their magnetic pull. She wanted to see him again, talk to him, drown in that gaze. But she was afraid it would lead to heartache, and she needed a buffer.

'Actually, I've unexpectedly got the afternoon off and I'm taking my daughter to the beach. Mamma will bring her there before meeting up with a friend. Would you like to come?'

When she'd talked to her mother the previous night, Giovanna had told her that the man Luca had seen hanging around was just some local drunk, so there was nothing to stop Cat from seeing Bella today. But would Connor want to come? Most likely he'd be busy. He was supposed to be working while he was here, after all.

His face lit up. 'I'd love to. Where should I meet you, and when?'

'Wait for us at the top of the cliff and we can walk down together,' she said, before hurrying off to serve another table.

It had probably been a mistake to invite him, but it would give her a chance to see how he reacted to Bella. Any man who took Cat on in the future would have to be vetted by her daughter first, no question about it. Never again would she have her little girl feeling afraid of a man. *Never.*

And the two of them came as a package. Take it or leave it.

It would be interesting to see how Bella interacted with Connor too. Before coming to Italy, she'd been shy around strangers, and the mere thought of introducing her to a possible future partner would have seemed almost impossible. But now she'd been around Cat's Italian relatives for a few weeks and had gained confidence. Hopefully, meeting Connor wouldn't be too scary for her. Deep down, Cat was desperate for them to get on. She refused to reflect on why that was.

Connor

It was a beautiful sunny day, and quite warm despite it being October already. Cat was waiting by the walkway that led down towards the seashore. There was a sheer drop to the beach, maybe fifty metres or more, and the view from the top was spectacular. Blue waters as far as the eye could see, verging on turquoise closer to the shore, where jetties lined the edge next to a narrow band of dark volcanic sand. To the left, the coast continued along the peninsula; while in the other direction the bay curved round towards Naples at the far end, with Vesuvius more or less in the middle. There was no mistaking the shape of the mountain, and today it was free of the mists that sometimes shrouded it.

Connor kissed Cat on the cheek in greeting, then turned to smile at a small girl who had her hand in a death grip. She looked to be an enchanting copy of her mother. Long dark hair caught up in a ponytail under a floppy sunhat, big eyes in an elfin face, and olive skin already sporting a slight tan. The only difference was in the eyes – where Cat had deep amber ones, her daughter's were blue.

He took a deep breath, squatting down in front of the child. 'Hello, I'm Connor. What's your name?'

'Bella.' The word came out as a whisper, and she was watching him with solemn eyes, as though she wasn't sure whether he could be trusted. He resolved then and there that he'd make her unafraid of him if it was the last thing he did.

'That's beautiful,' he said gently. 'Are you ready to build a sand-castle? I fancy something huge with turrets, like in a fairy tale. Perhaps your mum will help us?' He glanced at Cat and saw her shoulders drop as she relaxed her almost defensive stance. Had she really been worried he'd be horrible to her child? That made him spitting mad, because he guessed why.

'Yes, please.' Bella's eyes lit up and she jumped up and down with excitement. 'I've never built a castle before.'

'Never? Then what are we waiting for? After you, ladies.' He swept out a hand to indicate that they should lead the way, then followed them down the walkway.

It was paved with lava stones, worn smooth like the ones they'd seen in Pompeii, and sloped gently at first, then more steeply. At one point, the route doubled back into a cave of sorts in the rock face. Their steps echoed along the roughly hewn walls, and Bella shrank against her mother, blinking against the sudden loss of sunlight. When they finally reached the bottom, they took a right along a paved boardwalk, until they reached a small beach next to a rickety pier. The cliffs towered above them, making the space feel safe and secure somehow.

'This will do,' Cat declared, and Connor nodded. He couldn't care less where they were, as long as he was near her. Closing his eyes for a moment, he tried to get a grip. This was all happening too fast; he had to rein his feelings in. They were only supposed to be friends. Cat was clearly on the rebound from some pretty harrowing experiences, and the last thing she needed was him pushing her into something she wasn't ready for.

It was hard, though, because she was so damned enticing. He tried his best not to stare at her amazing figure squeezed into a black bikini with a colourful sarong wrapped around her waist. He'd dreamed about those curves, but he hadn't seen them on display before. The effect was like a blow to his chest, leaving him breathless. Even though the bathing suit wasn't overtly sexy or skimpy, she filled it out so completely, he would have had to be blind not to find it tempting. He forced himself to look away or his board shorts would soon give away just how much she was affecting him.

They found a spot not too far from the water's edge and spread out their towels. The tourist season was almost over, so the place wasn't crowded. Cat had brought a bucket and a couple of spades, and seemed happy to let him take charge of the building work. She watched him while he set about teaching Bella how to shape the moist sand, and Connor felt as if he was being judged. He supposed it was only fair. A mother had to put her child first, and if he'd been some kind of monster who hated kids, she would have been right to leave as quickly as possible.

As Bella went to fetch a bucket of water to pour into their newly dug moat, he turned to Cat. 'Do I pass?' he asked, trying to make his question sound light-hearted and joking.

'What?' She blinked at him.

'You're trying to decide if I can be trusted with your daughter.' He held up a hand. 'I don't blame you. I'm just curious whether I've passed muster.'

Her cheeks turned a deep red. 'Oh dear, am I that transparent? It's just . . . She's been through so much. I don't want her to get hurt.' The hitch in her voice told him this was serious.

He put a hand over hers and squeezed her fingers. 'That's

totally understandable. Want to talk about it? I swear I won't tell a soul. Did your ex-husband hurt her too?' He wanted to add 'the utter bastard', but thought it best not to say that out loud.

Cat hesitated, and waited until Bella was making another trip to the sea. 'Only the once, and that was when I realised I couldn't stay. It was one thing for him to hit me, I'm a grown woman, but someone as small and vulnerable as Bella . . .'

Connor swore under his breath. 'I'm so sorry. That is . . . I don't have words.' It most definitely wasn't OK for the man to hurt Cat either.

She gave him a tight smile. 'Thank you. He didn't hit her or anything, but he shook her, and I could see that it wouldn't end there. She's always been a quiet child, but as she gets older, she's bound to become more difficult, and things would have escalated. Derek . . . doesn't tolerate opposition in any way. He was raised by a very domineering mother, who put him on a pedestal while at the same time being extremely harsh with him. Both physically and mentally. I don't think he understands that her treatment of him wasn't normal. That little children need love and care, not just discipline.' She shivered despite the heat of the afternoon sun, as if remembering the violence. It made Connor want to take revenge, even though he realised how hypocritical that would be.

'Well, I'm glad you're both here now, and I hope the courts decide in your favour. I take it you're seeking sole custody?'

'Oh yes, definitely. And I'm lucky I have proof of Derek's actions.' She told him about her neighbour's quick thinking.

'Wow, I'm impressed. I don't think I would have had the presence of mind to do that. She sounds like quite a lady, this Suzanne.'

This time Cat's smile was broader. 'She definitely is. I think she's coming to visit us here quite soon. She's been amazing, and I owe her.'

Their chat was interrupted by Bella. 'Mummy, can I have an

ice cream, please, please, *please*?' She had come running over to throw herself at her mother, who toppled over onto the towel with a laugh, giving her daughter a hug and a kiss. They were a lovely sight, and something inside Connor tightened.

'That sounds like a good idea.' Cat grabbed another towel to dry Bella's hands and brush some of the sand off her. 'Let me get some money, and then we'll go in search of a proper Italian *gelato*.'

'What's that?'

'Ice cream, but better,' Cat assured her daughter. 'Isn't that right, Connor?'

As he'd had more than a few by now, he nodded with a grin. 'Absolutely. Do I get one? I have worked very hard here, don't you think?'

Bella smiled, seemingly relaxed in his company now. 'Yes. He can have one, can't he, Mummy? He's been a good boy.'

That made Cat laugh. 'Of course. What flavour?'

'Hmm, I'm not sure.' Connor pretended to think it over, rubbing his chin. 'What do you think, Bella? Which one is best?'

There was no hesitation. 'Chocolate!' Like mother, like daughter, it would seem.

'OK, sounds great. I'll have one of those then, please. I'm just going for a quick swim to wash off all this sand. See you in a bit.'

He watched as Cat and Bella walked off hand in hand. A warm feeling spread inside him and he found himself smiling. Life was looking up.

Cat

'Again, Connor, again!'

Cat floated on the waves while watching her daughter being

thrown into the air, then whooshed along the water to create a small tsunami. Bella was shrieking with laughter and having the time of her life. It made her sad to think how much she had been missing out on. They'd been to the beach during a short holiday in Devon once, but Derek had left it up to Cat to entertain their child while he chatted with whoever was sitting next to them. In fact, she couldn't recall him ever playing with Bella at all.

Now here was this gorgeous man, who'd only just met her, being so kind. Cat's throat constricted. She wanted to cry, but at the same time she knew this was a turning point. She and Bella deserved someone like Connor in their lives. Respect and consideration should have been theirs, and she vowed it would be in future. Whether that came from him or someone else didn't matter. She was done being downtrodden.

'Do you think we should throw your mum up too?' she heard Connor say, quickly followed by Bella's enthusiastic 'Yes!'

Before she had time to so much as turn her head, he had come up next to her and hoisted her up with one arm under her thighs and the other across her back, then tossed her back into the water with a laugh. She came up for air, spluttering and pushing strands of wet hair out of her eyes. Fixing him with a mock-glare, she growled, 'Oh, this is war! Bella, splash him!'

They began a water fight, which helped to keep them all warm. Although October could be changeable, weather-wise, with the occasional rain and thunderstorms, today was a fairly hot day. The sea was somewhere around twenty-two degrees Celsius, which wasn't freezing, but was still a bit on the chilly side. After the splashing session, however, they were all breathing heavily and flushed with the exertion. Bella laughed so much, Cat had to pick her up so she wouldn't swallow half the sea.

'OK, OK, I think that's enough. Time to sit down now.'

'Here, come and ride on my shoulders,' Connor offered,

plucking Bella out of her arms as if she weighed nothing at all. The muscles in his shoulders bunched as he settled the little girl comfortably, gripping her ankles so she couldn't fall off.

Cat remembered how those strong arms had felt when they'd briefly lifted her – smooth, warm and hard. He'd caught the sun, and his skin had turned golden with a smattering of freckles. For some reason they made her want to reach out and caress them, following their path down to well-defined forearms. She'd never realised before how downright sexy a man's forearms could be, but she longed to touch those too.

'Let's get you dry, sweetie.'

She turned to practical matters, rubbing Bella and changing her into a dry swimsuit and a T-shirt. There was the endless chore of applying more sunscreen as well, a job she hated. Although Bella had inherited her Italian colouring and tanned nicely, Cat would never risk her burning in the sun.

Connor flung himself down on his towel and watched them with a smile. 'I should probably have some of that stuff on me too. I'm a lot paler than either of you. The curse of redheads the world over.' He reached inside his rucksack and brought out a bottle of sunscreen.

'It's not a curse. You just have to be a bit more careful, that's all. And I wouldn't say your hair is red exactly, just an amazing auburn colour,' Cat protested. It was beautiful, actually, glinting with highlights in the sun. In fact, all of him was incredibly attractive, and she couldn't help but wonder what he was doing with her. Surely he could do better than a single mother with more baggage than a diva?

'You haven't seen my whiskers when they grow into a proper beard, or my . . . er.' His cheeks turned ruddy as he realised what he'd been about to say in the presence of Bella. 'Sorry, ignore me.'

But Cat laughed. 'Sounds intriguing.' She had no idea where

this was coming from, but she was actually daring to flirt with the man. And she was curious, no doubt about it. The mere thought of what he'd been talking about made her flustered. She didn't recognise herself.

'Oh yeah?' Surprise and something else flared in his eyes. He stared at her mouth for a fraction of a second too long before giving her a slow smile. 'Maybe I'll show you sometime.'

Cat didn't know how to reply to that without sounding as though she was angling for an invitation to his bedroom. Which she definitely wasn't. She couldn't be. It was too soon and . . . well, there were surely many reasons why it wouldn't be a good idea. But it was tempting. Very tempting. She busied herself with putting on Bella's sunhat.

'There, now you can go and play again. Looks like you'd better repair your castle. That corner is falling down.'

As the little girl sprinted off to fix it, Connor asked, 'Would you mind doing my back, please? As your hands are greasy anyway. I'd be happy to reciprocate.'

'Um, sure.' She took the proffered bottle and squirted some lotion into her hands before smoothing it down his back. He made a small contented noise as she rubbed it into his skin with a circular motion. She was mesmerised by the silken feel of him against her palms. She swallowed hard. This was getting dangerous.

'That feels wonderful, thank you,' he murmured. 'I'm not flexible enough to reach the middle.'

Cat was sure he was very supple in other ways, but didn't comment. 'There, you're done,' she announced instead. 'My turn.'

She turned her back on him so she wouldn't have to look him in the eyes. If she'd done so, she was sure he would have seen the longing in hers. They barely knew each other, though, and she had to be careful. There was more than her own wants and needs at stake here.

As he began to massage her back and shoulders with a gentle touch, she couldn't help but enjoy the sensation. And when he leaned forward to whisper, 'All done,' into her ear, a delicious shiver ran through her as she thanked him. He must have noticed, because he added a quick kiss on her neck, in that one spot guaranteed to send even more tremors through her.

'My absolute pleasure,' he said, and by the husky note in his voice, she knew he meant it.

Chapter Seventeen

Raedwald

'Here we are again.' Raedwald sighed, rolled his shoulders and stretched his muscles, trying to ignore the irritating weight of the bronze helmet he was wearing. He and Duro were standing just outside the main ceremonial entrance of the amphitheatre, waiting to take their turn to entertain the crowd with possibly lethal games.

'Mm-hmm. Hopefully for the last time,' Duro whispered. 'If we both win our bouts today, we'll have more than enough riches to leave this place behind for good.' He chuckled. 'And that fool Caius Merula has inadvertently added to our stash considerably these past few weeks. If only he knew how much we've earned by secretly betting against him . . .'

Raedwald hid a smile. They had indeed profited from the man's incompetence, but it still nagged at him that this wasn't helping Aemilia at all. The more her husband gambled, the more he lost. He seemed to be in a downward spiral and in the grip of an obsession. Any sane person would have desisted by now and tried to recoup their losses some other way, but the man remained convinced he would soon win big.

'It's merely a question of time,' they'd heard him tell a friend.

Raedwald knew better. Caius Merula was doomed, but it wasn't his problem. He needed to concentrate on the here and now, where his own life was at stake. Literally.

As for Aemilia, he didn't want to think about her and the fact that he was leaving soon.

The amphitheatre in Pompeii was an imposing edifice, one of the oldest such venues in the country. There were others in the nearby towns of Nola, Capua, Herculaneum and Cumae, where Raedwald had fought a couple of times, but this one always drew big crowds. None were as large as the new arena currently being constructed in Rome, however. Raedwald had once caught a glimpse of it, and although it hadn't been even close to finished at the time, he could tell it was going to be huge.

Pompeii's gladiatorial arena was situated on the edge of the town, in the south-east corner, and could apparently seat upwards of twenty thousand spectators. Raedwald didn't care how many there were, as he was always focused on his own role and the need for survival. The roar of the crowd egged him on, but ultimately he was indifferent as to whether they liked him or not. As long as they were satisfied with the entertainment, that was all that mattered. If they hailed him as some sort of a hero, so much the better. It meant his owner and trainer was more likely to keep him alive for the next fight, and that was paramount.

He couldn't die now. Not when he was so close to attaining his goals.

The amphitheatre had been cleverly constructed, the structure partly dug into the ground and supported by the town walls and an embankment. The so-called *cavea* was made up of rows of seating divided into three sections horizontally. These in turn were split vertically by staircases so that it looked as though each block of seats was a wedge.

The lowest part, the *ima cavea*, was comprised of flat terraces where special wooden seats for the most prominent citizens were erected. The *media* and *summa cavea* were larger, and consisted of stone and wooden seats for everyone else, with the top part reserved for women and slaves. Those seats could only be reached via the external double staircases that rose against the outside of the building in an inverted V. These led to an upper passage with stairs down on the inside. On hot days, a *velarium* – a type of awning supported by poles – could be rigged over the uppermost seats to give welcome shade, but that wasn't necessary this late in the year.

The arena itself was a spacious oval bordered by a high wall and parapet to keep the audience safe. Frescoes in bright colours covered the wall's inner surface all the way round with scenes of gladiatorial combat, mythology and wild beasts. The ground was strewn with sand to give the combatants a good grip with their bare feet, and to soak up the copious amounts of blood that would flow. Unlike some, this arena didn't have any underground rooms or passages, and the only way in or out was via a gate at either end. Dark tunnels paved with smooth basalt led down from these into the open space beyond.

A special dais halfway along the northern side of the oval was reserved for the *editor*, the man who had paid for the entertainment. He was responsible for the programme, and had agreed the order and magnitude of the event with the *lanista*, Antonius Varro, beforehand. Raedwald knew he was also the one giving out prizes, and he hoped the man was feeling generous today.

As the games went on all day, there were stalls set up outside the venue to cater to the audience's needs. Some were under the arches of the stairs, others on the flattish area in front. Food and drink of all kinds was on offer, and the sellers never ceased hawking their wares.

'I do wish they'd be quiet,' Raedwald muttered grumpily.

He really needed silence while he readied himself mentally, but knew that was an impossibility. He wasn't tempted by the cooking smells wafting his way either. Together with all the other gladiators taking part in the games, he'd attended a large banquet the night before and eaten his fill. This so-called *cena libera* was a dinner traditionally hosted by the *editor*. As far as Raedwald could make out, it was more to show off the combatants to the public beforehand than to reward them, as it was usually held somewhere people could come and gawk at them. Sure, it was a free meal with sumptuous dishes of every kind, but with this came an unspoken obligation to chat to anyone who approached them. Duro was much better at that sort of thing. Raedwald preferred to keep to himself.

'Yes, and by Teutates, I wish the *lanista* would hurry up. I hate standing around waiting in this cursed get-up,' Duro grumbled.

'You know no one is ever in a rush here.' The pace of life in this town was much slower than Raedwald had been used to at home. That was fine during the hotter months, but by now it was cooler and felt wrong to him.

The entertainments were in progress. They had begun much earlier in the day with musicians performing and then the *venatio*, the wild animal hunt. The cages for this remained near the entrance, but they were empty now, their occupants dispatched to the next world. The various animals used in this provincial little town were mostly unremarkable. Resources rarely stretched to anything as exotic as lions or elephants. Instead, the audience had to make do with dogs fighting wild boars, or gladiators battling bulls and the occasional bear. Raedwald had watched this part of the proceedings in the past, but saw it as pointless slaughter. Why kill a beast if it wasn't to be eaten or its pelt used? He preferred the animals that had been trained to do something, like dance or perform in some way.

Next on the agenda were acrobats and men who tried to be amusing. Again, Raedwald didn't see the point, but he enjoyed the musical interludes in between. Around midday, when most of the crowd were ready to eat something, and the *editor* and his guests went off to enjoy a lavish meal, it was time for the *noxii*. This was the truly vicious part of the programme, when condemned criminals were put to death in the most creative ways possible. Raedwald understood that punishments had to be meted out, but the Romans appeared to delight in drawing out the suffering for the sake of it. Not that he wouldn't like to do something similar to his accursed half-brother and stepmother . . . Crucifixion, burning alive or being torn to pieces by a lion were all too lenient for Osbehrt and his devious mother, but he'd settle for killing them any way he could. As long as they both died knowing their evil schemes hadn't succeeded.

Some of those executions were ongoing right this moment. The noise from the crowd rose and fell in accordance with what was happening in the arena, punctuated by unearthly shrieks from those suffering. Raedwald blocked it out; the criminals were not his concern.

At long last, slaves began hauling fresh sand into the arena to cover the worst of the gore in preparation for the gladiatorial part of the games.

'Line up, please!' someone shouted.

Raedwald and Duro took their places as part of the twenty pairs of gladiators who would be fighting today. They'd already participated in an official procession earlier, featuring the *editor*, musicians, some of the town's magistrates, and all those who were to take part in the proceedings. Now they strode into the middle of the arena, heads held high and armour throwing off sparks from the rays of the sun. The space appeared vast from down here, the tiered seating rising towards the sky. At the front sat those who could afford ringside seats; men such as Caius Merula and those he fawned over each morning. Raedwald barely spared them a glance.

He took his place with the rest of the gladiators while the referees and other attendants filed in behind them. Some carried weapons and armour, and he grabbed a spear that one of them held out to him, as well as the shield that would protect him from potentially lethal blows.

'They're in good voice today,' Duro commented, sweeping the audience with a cool gaze. They were shouting, cheering or jeering, according to their preferences, and some were banging on drums or clapping hands and stamping their feet.

'Indeed.'

Raedwald followed suit, but refused to acknowledge to himself that he was looking for one particular face in the crowd. He hoped she wasn't there, as things could get ugly, but at the same time he craved her presence. He hadn't been able to stop thinking about the kiss they'd shared, but he knew he had to put it out of his mind for now. He couldn't afford to become distracted, and tried to suppress the urge to look for her. Thankfully, it was impossible to make out individual faces in the upper tiers.

Someone produced a large bowl containing the names of the gladiators written on wooden tablets. These were drawn in pairs to see who was to fight whom, although Raedwald was convinced it was all decided beforehand, as the pairings were complicated. The crowd seemed not to realise this, however, as each name read out was greeted by cheers.

A horn blared one long note to signal the start of the fights, and the gladiators gripped their weapons. They each had a specific part to play, like actors in a theatre, with particular accoutrements assigned to them. Raedwald was a so-called *hoplomachus*, his shield round and made of thick bronze that gleamed in the sunlight. He'd learned to use it as a weapon in its own right and could do considerable damage with it. The spear he carried was almost as tall as himself, and as backup he had a short sword. Like all the other fighters, his torso was bare, and he was parading around in a loincloth. It seemed demeaning somehow, and he wished he could have worn his barbarian trousers instead, but at least his legs were partly covered by the quilted padding and metal greaves.

Duro was a *murmillo*, wearing a large helmet like Raedwald's, although his had a crest of horsehair. He wielded a *gladius*, the short Roman sword common here, and used a large rectangular shield for protection, like the legionaries and Gauls did. He had arm guards, shin guards and a wide belt over his loincloth. His equipment was much heavier than Raedwald's, especially the shield, which made things more difficult for him. It meant his fighting style was different, but he was no less dangerous for all that.

Unusually, the two of them had been drawn to fight each other, the starting pair for the day. All the fighters were matched with someone armed differently to themselves. These odd combinations made for more exciting bouts, which were supposedly more enjoyable for the spectators, but Raedwald and Duro knew how to put on a show in their own way. While training, they had worked out who would wound whom, and how, and an acceptable amount of blood flowed without either of them becoming incapacitated. Their moves were practised and smooth.

The audience roared their approval each time one of them was hurt. Raedwald inwardly shook his head at them. He couldn't understand this bloodlust for the sake of it, rather than in pursuit of something that mattered, like holding on to one's ancestral lands. To him, the audience were like silly children who hadn't been taught any better. And the worst thing was, they didn't seem to see the gladiators as humans, just a different species of animal to be slaughtered for their amusement. That made him furious.

'Rufus, spear him!'

'Drusus, faster!'

They each had their own group of vocal supporters. After a while, their fight was declared a draw, and Duro moved on to do battle with someone else. They had expected this, as it wouldn't be in the *lanista*'s best interests for either of them to die. Raedwald had to wait his turn as Antonius Varro drew out the entertainment by only allowing one pair of fighters at a time. Standing off to one side, he was offered some refreshment by the ever-attentive Marcellus. As he took a drink of water, he scanned the seating area once more. He still couldn't see Aemilia. *Curse it!* He shouldn't be looking for her at all. Shouldn't care whether she was present or not. And yet he did.

Duro jogged up to lounge next to him, panting slightly after his exertions. 'That new recruit Octavius just got himself killed,' he muttered. 'He should have paid more attention during practice. I didn't mean to run him through, but he turned the wrong way and forgot to block my thrust to his torso.'

'Bloody fool!'

'Yes, but the crowd are loving it, and maybe I'll get a larger prize as a consequence.' They exchanged a glance; neither of them was very happy about this turn of events, but both knew they had to be pragmatic.

Good potential gladiators were expensive, and most owners wouldn't want to waste their resources, so they tried to keep deaths to a minimum. Inevitably, though, novices had to be brought in to replace men who had been killed. With these sometimes being unwilling slaves or condemned criminals, however, it wasn't always possible to train them properly, and accidents happened. There were more where they came from, and a substitute would quickly be found.

Raedwald's next opponent was a *thraex*; a man wielding a short curved sword and clutching a square shield. Quick and nimble, he was difficult to pin down, but Raedwald was confident he could take him. He just needed to be patient and watch for an opening. Soon the man was fighting for his life, the noise levels around them almost deafening and the atmosphere sizzling.

'*Rufus, Rufus, Rufus!*'

The chanting spurred Raedwald on to wound his opponent further, but the *lanista* had given them orders not to kill anyone else unless it was absolutely necessary. The *thraex* raised his left arm in surrender and threw his shield on the ground. Raedwald stopped pursuing the man, who kneeled in the sand and waited for the *editor*'s verdict. The organiser had the final say in whether those defeated lived or died, although sometimes he listened to the crowd. Would this particular gladiator be given *missus*, and allowed to leave the arena alive? He had fought bravely, but that wasn't always a guarantee of survival.

Part of the audience were shouting, '*Iugula, iugula!*' Kill him. Cut his throat. The word sent a shiver down Raedwald's back. It had never happened to him, but that was not to say it was impossible.

The majority of those present, however, seemed more benevolently inclined, and calls of '*Mitte!*', mercy, drowned out the more bloodthirsty members of the crowd.

The organiser nodded and gave the sign for clemency. While the *thraex* was helped out of sight to have his wounds tended, Raedwald went to collect the palm branch that signified his win, and the purse of coins that accompanied it. The latter was quickly passed on to Marcellus, who would keep it safe.

Later, when it was his turn again, Raedwald battled a sneaky little *retiarius*. He wasn't normally asked to fight this type of gladiator, but the *lanista* must have been short of suitable opponents today. The *retiarius* should have been an easy adversary. He had no shield, helmet or armour; just a metal shoulder plate and some quilted padding. But the long trident he carried was sharply honed, and he knew how to wield the circular fishing net tied to his left wrist. He was fast, too, his reflexes sharp, and appeared to have a large part of the audience on his side. The female part. Raedwald knew it was because the man was handsome. Often the best-looking gladiators were picked for this role, since their faces weren't covered by a helmet. He'd been offered the part himself, but had turned it down. Fighting men as if they were fish did not appeal to him.

The *retiarius* kept on trying to trap Raedwald's sword in his net, while jabbing at him with the trident. It was a tiresome game, and one he didn't relish much, but it had to be endured. At one point, his sword was caught up for longer than he would have liked, and his opponent managed to stab him in the thigh with one tine of the trident.

'Curse you!' Raedwald hissed, as pain radiated down his leg and a large bloodstain spread across his thigh.

He retaliated as soon as he'd freed his own weapon, and slashed at the other man's arm. The audience went wild at seeing them both bleeding freely, but Raedwald swore again. This was a much deeper wound than he would have liked, and his leg throbbed with a dull ache. Thankfully, the fighting came to an end soon after that when he landed another blow to the man's arm. The *retiarius* conceded defeat, and Raedwald collected another palm branch and a fat purse of coins.

At long last, the afternoon drew to a close. Raedwald was relieved to have survived yet another day in the arena. Hopefully his last. Musicians began to play as he limped out, trying not to let on how much pain he was in. Duro sent him concerned glances, but didn't comment until they were outside the entrance.

'Are you about to faint? Here, let me support you.'

'No, just get me out of here. I'll manage.'

Raedwald bit his teeth together. His thigh was burning like a blazing furnace now, but the last thing he wanted was to allow anyone to see him as weak. One final glance at the audience had shown him Aemilia at last, his eyes meeting her frightened gaze. She'd been accompanied by a slave woman, but he hoped she'd have the sense not to let on to anyone that she cared one way or another whether a gladiator had been hurt. If that was reported to her husband, she could be in trouble.

'Let's go back to the barracks. I need to have this wound cleaned, and fast.'

Chapter Eighteen

❧

Cat

'Wow, this is so different to Pompeii, isn't it!'

Cat hadn't seen much of Connor since their outing to the beach three days ago, but this morning he'd asked if she wanted to come along on a trip to Herculaneum. It was Wednesday, and she had unexpectedly been given half a day off. She had hoped to meet up with her mother and Bella, but they'd been invited to visit a friend of Giovanna's who lived on a farm. No little girl could resist the prospect of petting goats and other animals, and Cat knew it was good for Bella to experience things like that more.

Going on an outing with Connor sounded a lot more fun than moping around on her own, missing her daughter, so she readily agreed. They'd taken the Campania Express train to Ercolano Scavi station, which took approximately forty-five minutes, despite the name. It was only called express because it was faster than the ordinary commuter train, the Circumvesuviana, which was rather grotty, stopped at every station, and took for ever. That one was cheaper, and Cat would normally put up with the extra travelling time in order to save money. Connor insisted on paying for both their tickets, though, and she didn't protest. It was nice to be spoiled occasionally.

So here they were, walking down a steep hill towards the excavated parts of Herculaneum, a neighbouring city to Pompeii, which had also been destroyed in the eruption of AD 79. As they passed through a gateway at the bottom of the street, the ruins were immediately visible on the right-hand side. They followed a walkway along the edge of the excavation, and stared down twenty metres, if not more, at some of the remains of the city.

'What an awesome sight! I can't believe how deep down the ruins are.' Cat gazed out over the ancient streets that had been revealed so far below them.

'Yes, the whole town was covered in a thick layer of volcanic ash,' Connor said. 'There's a lot that hasn't been dug out yet, but I think it might lie underneath the modern town so can't be reached.'

They'd purchased entry tickets online and made their way to the site entrance. The excavated parts were accessed via a steep walkway that led down to what used to be sea level. Here they passed a set of rooms carved into the cliff that had apparently been boathouses. A few decades earlier, archaeologists had made a gruesome discovery there of two hundred and eighty-six skeletons. People who had tried to take shelter from the volcanic eruption but had perished all huddled together.

'That's so very sad,' Cat whispered, glancing at the bones that could be seen through the open doorways. 'They must have been absolutely terrified.'

'Yes, but at least they died quickly.' Connor steered her towards the town itself. 'Let's go and look at something more cheerful.'

Herculaneum proved to be a much smaller site than Pompeii, with narrower streets that were less worn, and tightly packed buildings. Everything was incredibly well preserved. There were even ceilings, upper floors, staircases and some folding doors to be seen. That hadn't been the case in Pompeii. Roofs overhanging the pavements lent the whole area an intimate feel, and it was much easier to imagine yourself back in Roman times here. As it was much more intact, it gave the visitor a better sense of what life had really been like in a town such as this back in the first century.

'I love all these mosaic floors,' Cat commented, as they entered one of the town's public baths. 'Just look at this!'

They were standing in what had been a changing room for women. It had little niches to leave their clothes, a vaulted roof, and a magnificent mosaic of a man whose lower half seemed to turn into octopus tentacles below the knees. He was surrounded by fishes and other sea creatures, and the design was exquisitely done.

She closed her eyes and breathed in deeply of the humid air that seemed to swirl around her. It made her gold bracelet cling to her arm, and she adjusted it slightly to loosen its grip. In her mind, she could picture the scene – women in various stages of undress sitting on the stone bench below the niches to remove their shoes, gossiping, whispering, laughing. Many of them were damp from the *caldarium* next door, tendrils of hair curling on their foreheads. The mosaic floor was a little slippery, and someone gave a tiny shriek as they almost went flying. It smelled of soap, scented oils and sweat, and she longed to throw off her clothes and head into the bathing areas . . .

'Mater, are you coming?'

Cat looked down to find a small girl with amber eyes tugging at her clothing. Love and tenderness for the child welled up inside her, and she was just about to answer her when a big hand landed on her arm.

'Cat? Are you all right?'

'Hmm?' She blinked at Connor, who was tugging on her wrist, his hand clamped over her golden bracelet. When she looked down again, the little girl had disappeared and the bath house was quiet, the scene gone. 'Oh, sorry. Just . . . er, daydreaming there for a bit.'

She had wondered if she would have any strange episodes here, like she'd had in Pompeii. The sensation of déjà vu wasn't as strong, but there were still ancient memories tugging at her brain. As if she'd been in a bath house such as this, although not this particular one perhaps. It made her shiver.

Who was that little girl?

'It's cool in here. Let's go back out into the sunshine.' She didn't wait for him, but marched out into the street and strolled along the pavement.

He soon caught up with her and took her hand. 'Did you have a strange vision again?'

Cat felt her cheeks heat up and ducked her head. 'Maybe. I don't know. It's probably just my imagination working overtime. I mean, it's easy to picture what it must have been like in a place like that, right?'

She was grasping at straws, but she didn't want to acknowledge that something weird was happening to her. That she might be remembering things from a time gone by. It made no sense and shouldn't be possible.

Whose memories were they? She didn't want to know.

'Yes, I suppose that's true,' he acknowledged, but he didn't sound convinced, and neither was she.

What the hell was happening to her?

Connor

Connor didn't know what to think. He'd hoped that Cat's strange behaviour at Pompeii had been a one-off, he supposed. It would have been easy to blame it on too much sun, excessive amounts of exercise, or some temporary dizziness perhaps.

That theory didn't hold today. It was sunny, but not particularly hot. This place wasn't very big either, so visitors weren't tired out by walking too far. And Cat had seemed perfectly normal until they set foot inside the bath house. There, her expression had turned dreamy and her gaze unfocused. It was as if her soul had left her body, and only the husk remained.

Creepy.

But she seemed fine now, and if she didn't want to talk about what had happened, he couldn't force her. He held on tight to her hand, just in case something else triggered another weird episode. She could be hurt if she wasn't paying attention to her surroundings, and he didn't want her harmed in any way. His protective instincts came to the fore whenever he was with her. He couldn't help it, she just brought out the caveman in him.

At the end of the street, they turned left, and stopped to admire the paintings on a wall outside what had been an inn of some sort. Cat was about to walk off, and pulled her hand out of his, but he gripped her wrist to stop them from becoming separated.

'Wait, please, I want a closer look at this,' he said, and felt her gold bracelet digging into the palm of his hand. When he looked up at the wall again, he could see that the frescoes depicted wine flagons of various types, with the prices charged for each written underneath. Even now, after two millennia, it was easy to read the words, and he felt a frisson travel down his spine. It was as though he'd been transported back in time.

A distant memory flickered at the edges of his mind, of standing outside a similar place, waiting to go inside. Cat and the tourists around him faded away, and instead he thought he heard chatter and raucous laughter, as well as a strange rattling sound. He peered in through the doorway and saw men sitting around crude wooden tables, small piles of coins next to them. One man, who had a crooked nose and a bald pate, shook a box and emptied it with a flourish. Two dice rolled onto the table, and a huge smile spread across his face. He lifted a fist in the air, in the age-old sign of success, and cheered loudly. His companions grumbled under their breath, but pushed piles of coins toward the winner. He called a woman over and asked for another flagon of wine.

'Make it the best kind, from Falernia. Not that piss you normally serve,' he ordered.

She nodded and sashayed away, ignoring the playful slap to her buttocks she received to hasten her progress.

Connor felt someone tugging on his arm, and blinked down at Cat. 'What?'

'I said shall we move on? There's more to see over here.' She frowned slightly, but didn't question his distracted mood.

He swallowed hard and turned to look through the doorway one more time. There was nothing there, only the ruins of a serving counter and part of a doorway to a back room.

'Jesus!' he muttered, letting go of her wrist to take her hand instead. What had he just seen? And how had it been so clear? He could have described every last detail if he'd been asked to, and it was freaking him out. Was he having visions too now? What on earth was going on?

He followed Cat down the street, staring at the back of her head as if he could find the answers there, but none of this made sense. It should have been impossible, but he couldn't unsee the scene he'd just witnessed. It had been as real as the woman in front of him.

And that was scary as hell.

'So what did you think? Pretty impressive, huh?'

They were seated by the window of a small pizza restaurant

close to the station, having decided to grab an early dinner before they took the train back to Sorrento. There had been waiters outside trying to entice them in, probably believing them to be just another tourist couple. Connor knew that was what he was, but somehow he didn't feel like one right now. He had a deep-rooted sense of belonging, which was disconcerting. Cat, of course, fitted right in, and had ordered drinks for both of them in rapid Italian.

'It was, but I felt more at home in Pompeii.' She was fiddling with the menu, trying to decide on her choice of pizza. Her cheeks turned slightly pink. 'I mean, it had more of an emotional effect on me, if you know what I mean. I really felt the scale of the tragedy there, whereas Herculaneum seemed as if it hadn't been devastated to the same extent. I know that's not the truth, but . . .' She shrugged as if she couldn't explain it.

'Yes, I think you're right.' Connor didn't want to put into words the fact that Herculaneum seemed familiar, yet not nearly as much as Pompeii. 'We'll have to go back again soon to really compare the two.'

He saw Cat shiver as she shook her head. 'Not too soon, if you don't mind. There was something there that . . . scared me. Silly, I know.'

Taking her hand across the table, he gave it a squeeze. 'No worries, I understand.' And he did, probably more than she'd imagine, but he didn't want to talk about it.

Time for a change of subject. 'Have you heard from your mother?' he asked. 'Was their excursion a success?'

'Oh yes.' Cat laughed and picked up her phone, holding it up to show him some photos of her little girl with a euphoric grin on her face. 'Bella had the time of her life, petting every animal in sight. Mamma could barely get her to leave. She'll probably start demanding that we go and live on a farm when we're back in England. Or at the very least, get a dog or some other pet.'

'And would that be so bad? I love dogs.' He allowed his thumb to stroke the soft skin of her hand, needing to touch her even in a small way. She didn't pull away, which felt like a tiny victory of sorts.

She sighed. 'No, I love them too, but it's going to be hard enough to be a single mum without pets entering the equation. I do work from home, but a dog will need walking, and I'm not sure where we'll end up living. Probably in a flat, and pets might not be allowed.'

'Why don't you just take it one step at a time, see how it goes. It might work out fine, but if not, you can always have an indoor cat or a guinea pig or something.'

He refrained from saying that he wanted to be part of that equation. To look after both her and Bella, if he was honest. He had no idea how it had come to this so quickly, as he barely knew them, but he would love a future that included both of them. And several dogs. But would Cat want him in her life?

There was definitely chemistry between them, but she'd been hurt. Badly. He had to go slowly so as not to scare her away. He could do that. For her, he was coming to realise, he'd do anything.

Chapter Nineteen

Pompeii, 8 October AD *79*

Aemilia

Aemilia saw the smaller gladiator sink his viciously sharp trident into Raedwald's leg and stopped breathing for a moment. Her lungs didn't expel the next breath of air until he disentangled himself from the fishing net and fought back, expertly bringing the *retiarius* to his knees with a few swift blows. There was blood flowing from his thigh, though, all the way down to his foot, and seeping through his padding into the sand of the arena. The sight of it made her nauseous.

Not that she was afraid of the sight of blood under normal circumstances. She was quite simply terrified for him, but she couldn't show it. Lucius had already commented on the fact that she was very quiet that morning, asking if she was sickening for something. She'd blamed a headache, and lied when he had asked if she was going to the games. There was no way she'd let on that she was desperate to attend, and to watch the man she'd kissed just a few days ago. That she feared for his life. It was better if Lucius didn't connect her and Raedwald in any way. He didn't know she was here, as she'd snuck in halfway through the day, and she didn't want him to find out either. She had to pull herself together and hurry home before he returned.

When the crowd cheered for Raedwald's victory, she forced herself to join in, then again when another gladiator dispatched his opponent. Her eyes returned to the red-headed barbarian again and again, but although he was still bleeding freely, he appeared able to carry on. But for how much longer? Loss of blood made a man weak, and he'd be easier to kill.

She couldn't bear the thought of that.

It was ridiculous really. They'd shared one kiss and he had been kind to her, that was all. It did not constitute some great love story, and nothing could come of it in any case. She was a respectable married woman. It wasn't in her nature to go sneaking into the gladiator barracks in search of a bed mate, the way some of her friends did. But although she'd never been tempted before, she couldn't deny that she was now. The mere thought of that kiss had her trembling.

The stampede of feet thundering up the stairs towards the exits roused her from her jumbled thoughts, and she hurried to join them. Her gaze had been fixed on Raedwald and Duro as they left the arena carrying their palm branches of victory. Was it her imagination, or did he walk with great care, as if every step pained him unbearably? She shook herself inwardly. He was alive and still standing; that should be enough for her.

'Come.' She threw a glance at the slave girl she'd brought with her for the sake of propriety. The two of them shuffled out behind everyone else, joining the throng of spectators leaving the amphitheatre. Thankfully, she didn't see Lucius among them. Knowing him, he'd probably headed for a tavern with friends to either celebrate winning bets on the bouts they'd watched or drown his sorrows if he'd lost. She was afraid it would be the latter.

It was broad daylight and the streets were crowded, so there was no need for a brawny escort today. No self-respecting thug would accost her with hundreds of witnesses around, and Aemilia felt safe walking home with just the slave. They made it back without mishap, and she was greeted by an exuberant Caia.

'Mother, Mother, come and see how far I can throw the ball! And I catched it every time too!'

Seeing her little girl calmed her, and for a while she tried to forget her concerns.

Several hours later, however, she hadn't been able to stop thinking about Raedwald. He'd been seriously hurt, of that she was sure, and she needed to know if he was all right. She couldn't send a message to the gladiator barracks, for obvious reasons, but perhaps she could go there quickly to enquire about his health? He might be in need of healing herbs or a poultice. Was there even anyone looking after him?

'Oh, stop it,' she admonished herself. Duro would make sure he received care. They seemed inseparable, and clearly looked out for each other.

And yet . . .

By midnight, she'd worked herself into such a state, there was no way she would be able to sleep a wink. She had to do something. She had dismissed the slaves, claiming she had a headache again and wanted to be left alone. Usually at least one of them slept on a pallet in her chamber, but unlike most of her countrymen, she preferred to be by herself at night. Now she got up and, moving stealthily, pulled on her *stola* and a pair of soft sandals, then went to grab a *palla* to cover her head with, and her coin purse.

Then she stopped to think. Going out alone at night was incredibly dangerous, especially for a lone female, and a high-ranking one at that. There were thieves and rapists who wouldn't hesitate to slit her throat and dump her body somewhere. Perhaps even slave catchers on the lookout for easy prey. Dressing as herself would be foolhardy in the extreme. The least she could do was to find a slave's garments to hide her own.

She discarded what few pieces of jewellery she was wearing, despite them not being worth much, then peeked through the doorway and tiptoed out. The house was quiet, although she heard snoring from a couple of the smaller chambers leading off the peristyle garden. Thankfully no one stirred as she made her way to a room used to store freshly washed laundry. Fumbling around in the darkness, her fingers encountered the coarse material of a slave's long-sleeved tunic and cloak. She put these on, making sure she was well wrapped up, her hair safely hidden. Finally she headed for the door set into the back wall.

She managed to undo the bolts and lift the bar out of the way without making a sound. Slipping through, she pulled the door shut, praying to all the gods that no one would find it unlocked and draw the bolts while she was gone. There was no way she'd be able to explain how she came to be outside in the middle of the night. It was very dark in the back alley, but once she reached a larger street, the moon was enough to light her way. Keeping to the shadowy edges, she hurried from doorway to doorway, trying to remain unnoticed. A few groups of people passed by, but they seemed to have imbibed freely and were busy chatting and laughing to each other.

A couple of times, men called out suggestive remarks, but she ignored them, and fortunately they didn't follow her. Her heart was beating so loudly, she could barely hear anything else. And her breath was uneven, her lungs so tight she wasn't sure she'd have enough air to reach her destination. Her eyes kept flitting around, checking her surroundings for possible dangers. Was there someone lurking in that alleyway? Would that man over there grab her? Why was he looking at her like that? Her mind raced, her imagination working overtime, and she had to swallow down a sob as a dog shot out in front of her, almost giving her a heart attack.

She had never been so scared in all her life.

It seemed an eternity before she finally arrived at the door to the gladiator barracks, and when she saw the huge man guarding it, her courage almost deserted her completely. But she'd come this far; she couldn't turn around now.

'I've come to see Drusus,' she announced haughtily, as if she came here every night and had an arrangement to do so. She had no idea if her friends made their intentions so blatantly clear, or whether there was some stealth involved. Cursing herself for a fool, she knew she ought to have listened more carefully. Perhaps there was some secret way of gaining access? But when she held out a large silver coin – one of the few she had left – the guard grunted and opened the door.

'Fourth door on the left,' he muttered.

Almost fainting with relief, she hurried through the gap and heard the door slam behind her. She had to stop for a moment to catch her breath, and put a hand to her chest to slow the frantic beating of her heart. It felt as though she'd run all the way here, the blood pumping around her body at great speed. After a while, her eyes adjusted to her surroundings, and she saw that she was standing at the edge of a huge courtyard. It was surrounded by a colonnade, and there were doors all around, presumably leading to the gladiators' sleeping chambers. Lights burned in a few of them, seeping out underneath the ill-fitting doors.

She turned left and made her way to the fourth one, knocking softly. After only a heartbeat, it opened a crack. 'Yes?'

'Duro?' she whispered.

'*Domi—*'

'Shh!' The last thing she wanted was for anyone to hear her addressed as one of society's elite women since she was disguised as a slave. 'Can I come in, please?'

Without another word, he opened the door and ushered her inside. The room was small and cramped, with two straw pallets on the floor, and a niche in the wall where an oil lamp stood. Its light bathed the space in a soft glow, and bounced off the large form stretched out on one of the mattresses.

Aemilia's eyes flew to Duro's. 'Is he . . .?'

'He'll live.' The Briton was watching her curiously, as though he couldn't quite believe she was there. She couldn't either, but she'd come this far, and she refused to leave without seeing for herself.

'Can I look at his wound? I have some experience of healing.'

Duro grinned mischievously. 'Ask him yourself. I'll be outside.' And before she had time to reply, he was gone.

She stared after him, then turned to find Raedwald pushing himself into a sitting position. '*Domina!* What are you doing here? You shouldn't have come.' He was frowning mightily, but something in his eyes told her she wasn't altogether unwelcome.

Kneeling by his pallet, she stretched out shaking fingers to feel his forehead. 'I saw you get hurt and I was worried about you. Do you have a fever? Has your wound been cleaned and bandaged properly?'

He grabbed her hand and gazed into her eyes as he kissed her fingers one by one. 'I'm fine.' His voice was gruff, but there was a husky undertone that made her heart flutter.

'Can I see? Please? I won't be able to rest otherwise.'

'Stubborn woman,' he muttered, but his mouth had turned up at one corner, and he watched her as he flipped off the blanket to reveal his near-naked body.

Aemilia drew in a hasty breath at the sight of him clad only in a loincloth. His muscular frame was displayed in all its glory, albeit marred by various cuts and bruises, as well as a large bandage around one thigh. Her senses were overwhelmed, and she had the urge to run her hands over every last patch of smooth skin, as well as the smattering of copper hair on his chest, which led downwards in an intriguing darker red trail. Instead, she focused on the bandage.

'Can I undo it to have a look?'

'The loincloth? Well, I don't usually allow that sort of thing, but for you, I might make an exception.' He sent her a teasing look and she almost punched him, only remembering at the last moment that he was injured.

Her cheeks heated up to a scorching level. 'Raedwald!' she admonished sternly, and he chuckled.

'Very well, feel free.' He gestured to the bandage, then lay back down and put his hands behind his head while keeping his eyes on her.

She tried not to notice how this movement made the muscles in his arms bunch and flex – not to mention those in his abdomen – and concentrated on her task. To her relief, the deep gash had been expertly stitched and didn't look too angry. There was blood on the bandages, but it appeared to have stopped flowing. If only he didn't develop a fever now, all would be well.

'Thank Aesculapius for that,' she breathed.

'Who?' One raised eyebrow told her he wasn't a follower of her gods.

'The Roman god of healing. I pray he will keep you well.'

Without warning, he brought his hands up and snaked them round her waist, pulling her so that she was flush against him, her face mere inches from his. 'And does it matter to you?' he asked, his moss-green gaze searching hers.

With his distracting mouth at such close quarters, she could only nod. It did matter. A great deal. And that scared her.

He didn't give her time to ponder it further, as in the next moment his mouth crashed onto hers. Hot and fierce, this kiss was as far from the gentle one he'd given her in the garden as it could possibly be, but she revelled in it. Twining her arms round his neck, she leaned forward even further and kissed him back with all the pent-up relief of finding that he wasn't as badly hurt as she'd feared. His tongue demanded entrance, and she granted it gladly, euphorically, almost sobbing with the exquisite feel of it.

This was what she'd needed. This was what she craved.

It lasted ages, but still wasn't nearly long enough.

'Aemilia,' he whispered, tearing his mouth from hers and holding her still against his chest, where she could hear his heart thumping wildly. 'You shouldn't be here.'

She drew back slightly, and pushed her fingers through his glorious hair. It was like skeins of the finest embroidery silk, shimmering in the light. She gazed at him, memorising every last detail of his face. The high cheekbones, straight brows, long auburn eyelashes, and an impish nose that tilted up at the end, so unlike her husband's. Then there was that sensuous mouth, surrounded now by reddish-gold stubble as if he'd recently trimmed his beard very short. He was a glorious statue brought to life and gilded with fire.

'I couldn't stand not knowing what was happening to you. I had to come.'

'Well, much as I appreciate your concern, I am mindful of what you have risked for me. You must return to your house before anyone notices that you're gone. I take it you came alone?' At her nod, he shook his head and kissed her, gently this time. 'Foolish woman.' But it sounded more like an endearment, so she didn't protest.

'Duro will take you back,' he declared. 'Please don't ever come here again.'

Disappointment rushed through her. How could he kiss her like that one moment, then reject her the next?

His lips caressed hers again. 'I'll find another way for us to meet,' he clarified. 'If that is what you wish?'

'Yes.' She'd never been so sure of anything in her life.

'Then trust me, and go home now. I'll see you as soon as I have recovered, I promise. And Aemilia?'

'Hmm?' She'd been lost in the happy daze of knowing she wasn't the only one feeling this attraction that sparked between them.

'Thank you.' He smiled and tugged her close.

She had no idea what exactly he was thanking her for, but right then she didn't care. Instead, she leaned forward for one more bone-melting kiss, and she might have stayed there for the rest of the night if he hadn't gently pushed her back onto her knees.

'Go now, before I do something we might both regret. Goodnight, my *domina*.'

Warring with the desire to throw herself back into his embrace, she stumbled to her feet and headed for the door. 'Goodnight, Raedwald.'

Duro was waiting in the darkness outside and guided her to the outer door without saying a word, as if he'd guessed what his duty would be. They were let out by the surly guard and set off down the street.

As they neared her home, he said, 'I take it you used the back door?'

'Yes, of course. I only hope it hasn't been barred in my absence.'

He flashed her a smile. 'Doesn't matter. I can scale the wall. Haven't you noticed the part that is broken?'

She had. There was a section of the back wall that had been

half crumbled since the last big earthquake, and Lucius hadn't got around to having it fixed. It had been that way for so long, she'd almost forgotten. But if Duro had noticed, what if robbers had too?

Fortunately, climbing over the wall didn't prove to be necessary, and Aemilia shuddered to think how lax her slaves were when it came to security. This time, it was to her advantage, but in the future she ought to make sure things changed. She whispered a quick goodbye to Duro, who was still regarding her quizzically, but he didn't question her and merely waved before melting into the night.

As she sank onto her bed, having made it to her chamber without waking anyone, she forgot about everything except the bliss of being held in Raedwald's arms, and the feel of his mouth on hers. She fell asleep with her fingers on her swollen lips, reliving every moment.

Chapter Twenty

Mount Vesuvius, 8 October 2022

Cat

'I have no idea how you talked me into this. I'm actually terrified! How can you even contemplate going near a volcano when it's erupting?'

Cat was on yet another outing with Connor, and despite her words, she was loving every minute. He'd persuaded her she couldn't live in this region and not climb to the top of Mount Vesuvius. Since she wasn't planning to visit Bella and her mother until the following day, she'd agreed. They'd taken the train to Ercolano station again and, after waiting around for a while in the small square outside, had boarded a bus that took them up the mountain. She had no idea how the driver managed to man-oeuvre such a large vehicle up the narrow roads, navigating around hairpin bends with zero visibility while honking his horn loudly. They'd been let out at the bottom of a trail, as the bus couldn't go any further.

'Please be back here in two hours,' the driver had instructed everyone before they spilled out into the small parking area, grateful to have arrived in one piece.

They were now walking along a volcanic ash trail, the greyish dirt road strewn with sand and stones. It snaked up to the rim of the crater at the top of Mount Vesuvius and was steeper than Cat had imagined. On one side it was bordered by a fence, and on the other by scrubby bushes and hillside. The view across the Bay of Naples grew progressively more amazing the higher they went. A large plain covered in a sprawling urban landscape spread out before them, with the glittering sea in the distance. The cloud-filled sky provided a spectacular backdrop, seeming to be closer than should be possible. It was quite simply breathtaking.

Connor had said he needed a quick trip up here to take some measurements, although she wondered if it was just an excuse to spend time with her. The thought heated her cheeks and made excitement buzz through her. It shouldn't. It felt like it was too soon, and she hadn't even extricated herself from her marriage yet, but she couldn't help it. Being with him made everything seem right. As if it was meant to be.

'The hike up won't take very long, twenty minutes tops,' he'd assured her, but as she struggled to keep up with him now, her lungs about to burst, she muttered under her breath about fit men not having any idea. On his own, he would probably have made it in less than ten minutes, but he was staying with her and going slowly for her sake.

'The mountain is sleeping.' He smiled and took her hand, again twining his fingers with hers like he'd done at Pompeii. It felt so good, she didn't protest, even though she wasn't sure why he was doing it. Were they dating? Or just friends who held hands when they went places? She couldn't say and wasn't sure she wanted to put a label on it. For now, she would merely enjoy the sensation of his warm fingers interlaced with hers and live in the moment. And she couldn't deny it helped to be pulled along up this infernal track.

'Hah, that's what the Romans thought in 79 AD too. And look how that ended.'

Connor's smile turned into a full-blown grin. 'You really trust me that little? I'm supposed to be an expert, you know.' He patted the bag he carried, which contained lots of measuring instruments and other equipment. 'If it's about to erupt, I'll let you know, I promise.'

'Yeah, a lot of good that will do when we're standing on top of it,' she shot back, but she couldn't help grinning too. She knew she was worrying for nothing. If there had been any danger whatsoever, no one would have been allowed up onto the mountain, and they weren't the only people here. Busloads of tourists walked ahead of them and behind, chattering away in various languages. No one, apart from Cat, seemed at all anxious.

'Has anyone ever told you you're adorable when you frown?' Connor's question made her swivel towards him.

'What? No! I mean, I'm not . . .' Confusion filled her. He was flirting again, and she didn't know how to react.

He let go of her hand and put his arm across her shoulders instead, drawing her to his side. 'Relax, I'm just teasing. And for the record, you're beautiful all the time.' He gave her a side hug, then released her and took her hand again.

'Er . . . thank you?' It came out as a question, which made him chuckle and shake his head.

'You're going to have to get used to compliments, Cat. We're in Italy, for goodness' sake. Don't you get whistled at all the time, or am I stereotyping Italian men?'

She *had* received her fair share of admiring whistles, but she hadn't given it much thought. It was just something the men here did automatically, or so she'd assumed. As did some men back in the UK – in fact, it was probably a universal thing. Peeking up at Connor, she tried to determine if he was serious about finding her beautiful. He stopped, as if he sensed her inner turmoil and saw the question in her eyes.

'I meant it. I do find you incredibly attractive, but I also know you're vulnerable and I don't want to rush you. For now, do me a favour and start thinking of yourself as worthy of admiration, OK? Because you are.'

His words warmed her right to the core, and on impulse, she stood on tiptoes to give him a kiss on the cheek. 'Thank you. You're pretty amazing yourself.' She tugged on his hand. 'Now let's get this torture over with.'

He laughed and started to drag her with him again without further comment.

There were a couple of huts along the way with little shops selling souvenirs, drinks and snacks. Each one had a few benches outside, but Connor didn't let her stop. Lava formations began to appear on the inner side of the trail, covered in moss and lichen. This was followed by glimpses of the volcano's crater. It was vast and deep, and Cat paused to look down in awe. The sides looked like they were layered, and there was sand in places, apparently sliding down towards the bottom. Surrounding the entire area was a wooden fence, with people leaning on it taking photos. She took some of Connor, and he reciprocated, laughing when her long hair blew out around her in the cold wind.

'It was a good thing you told me to wear a jacket,' she commented. 'It's freezing up here!'

'Well, I wouldn't go that far, but I'm glad I didn't wear shorts,' he replied.

She was pleased when the track evened out, and followed Connor around it as far as they were allowed. They passed yet another café-cum-tourist shop, and a row of picnic tables, the kind you saw in every beer garden back in the UK, with benches tacked on either side. Once they'd reached the other side of the mountain, Pompeii could be glimpsed in the distance, as well as Sorrento and some islands far out at sea.

In a couple of places, mist or smoke was wafting out of the earth inside the crater. It was as though it was steaming gently, letting out puffs because the mountain was too hot to bear it. The wisps drifted into the air, moving lazily, and in her mind, Cat thought of them as the mists of time.

'Fumaroles,' Connor said, indicating the closest one. 'Can you smell the sulphur?'

'Only vaguely.' To be honest, she'd expected the odour to be stronger.

While Connor went to carry out his scientific readings, she strolled around taking more photos and gazing down into the heart of the mountain. The crater really was incredibly deep, and kind of scary when you considered what was lurking underneath. When she'd had enough of being a tourist, she bought herself a cappuccino and sat down at one of the tables, watching all the excited people around her. As she lifted her cup, the cuff of her jacket fell back and the sunlight caught her gold bracelet with a flash that almost blinded her. She covered it again and took a sip of coffee, then closed her eyes, but jumped when the earth started shaking and there was an almighty boom behind her.

Startled, she turned around and stared with horror as a huge cloud of smoke and ash erupted from the crater, spewing its contents straight up into the air. She ducked instinctively, putting up an arm to shield her face from any debris, but she knew it wouldn't do the least bit of good. If the volcano was erupting now, they were all doomed. Panic flared inside her. She wanted to get up and run down the mountain as fast as she could, but her limbs were paralysed with fear.

But . . . hold on. Where was everyone? Connor?

Cat suddenly realised she was all alone, and she wasn't sitting at the picnic table any longer. Instead, she was perched on a boulder with a bird's-eye view into the angry crater. The fence was gone, as was the café and all the tourists, and the trail was no longer there either.

'What the . . .?' She lifted a hand to touch her arm and found that her skin was cool. Shouldn't it be unbearably hot? And why hadn't she died already? Or was she dead, and her soul had remained behind as a spectator?

The earth trembled once more and she leaned forward, covering her face with her hands. This could not be happening. What was going on? None of it made sense.

A warm hand on her shoulder made her jerk upright.

'Cat? Are you OK? I'm sorry it took me so long.' Connor slid onto the bench beside her, and when she looked up, the scene was back to how it had been when she'd sat down.

She blinked at him, opening and closing her mouth a couple of times without being able to make a sound.

'Having another weird vision?' He reached out to push a strand of her hair behind her ear.

Instead of answering him, she threw her arms around his neck and buried her face in his shoulder, letting out a sob. He pulled her close and stroked her back, the way Cat did to Bella when she needed soothing. 'Shh, I've got you,' he whispered. 'You'll be fine.'

After a while, her heartbeat slowed down and she stopped shaking. 'I . . . God! I thought the mountain erupted. I *saw* it, Connor. Heard it and felt it too.' She leaned back and stared up at him. 'An enormous column of smoke and ash, heading into the sky. It was terrifying. I was sure we were all d-dead.' Her voice caught on the last word and she bit her lip to stop it wobbling. 'I'm sorry. I don't know what's the matter with me. I've never had this much imagination before.'

He cupped her cheek with one hand and looked her straight in the eyes, his green ones keeping hers spellbound. 'I don't think it's you,' he told her gently. 'Something is obviously happening, but I doubt it's your imagination. My gran always said there were things we humans don't understand. I scoffed at her, quoting scientific theories and what have you, but she just smiled at me as if I was deluded. I'm guessing she was right.'

'I don't like it.' Cat drew in a deep, shaky breath. His words were reassuring, but at the same time not what she wanted to hear. 'And why me?' None of the other tourists were acting strangely.

'Who knows? But you're not alone. I'm here for you.'

His thumb grazed her cheek, moving slowly as if he didn't want to spook her, but it felt good, so she leaned into it. That made his gaze more intense, and after a small hesitation, he bent down to give her a tender kiss. It was only lips meeting lips, not seeking anything more than a brief touch, and to Cat it wasn't enough. She scooted closer on the bench and tipped her head up in invitation, trying to show him without words what she wanted. He got the message.

Moving his hand to the back of her head, he kissed her again, but this time as if he meant it. Not a reassuring peck, but a proper, sensual caress of his hot mouth on hers. He took his time before delving inside, teasing her lips apart with his tongue and sending little darts of lust right down to her toes. She loved the taste and feel of him, their tongues learning the steps of this new dance. The kiss was so all-consuming, the mountain could have erupted for real and she wouldn't have noticed. Or even cared. This was what she wanted, nothing else.

They had to come up for air in the end, and he gathered her close, holding her head against his chest. 'I should make sure I'm always around when you have your visions if that's what happens afterwards,' he murmured jokingly.

She clung to him for a moment longer, then let go and put some space between them. 'I'd rather do without the scary part first.'

'Agreed.' He smiled at her, then stood up as if he knew she needed space to process what they'd just done. 'I could use a coffee. Want a fresh one? I bet yours is cold by now.'

'Yes, please.'

She watched him walk into the café and tried to breathe normally. That kiss had definitely been worth the fright she'd had. And then some.

Connor

Connor wasn't sure he should have taken advantage of Cat when she was in a state of terror, but he hadn't been able to resist her inviting mouth, and she seemed OK with that. More than OK, judging by the dreamy state of her eyes afterwards. He pushed his fingers through his hair and tried to tamp down the lust raging through his body. He was absolutely certain he'd looked exactly the same as her, and he hoped the people around him couldn't tell.

He had only seen Cat in passing at the hotel the last few days, and had been growing desperate to spend some more time with her. It probably wasn't wise, as he kept telling himself he didn't want a woman who was on the rebound from a real mess of a marriage, but he couldn't help it. He needed to be with her, it was as simple as that.

When she'd agreed to come on this trip with him, he'd felt like a teenager on a hot date, even though they were going to be in a crowd of people and not doing anything remotely romantic. And now . . . well, he couldn't care less about everyone else. The only person he saw was Cat.

By the time he returned with their hot drinks, he had himself under control, more or less, and was able to talk rationally about the fumaroles and the readings he'd taken. Cat's cheeks were a bit rosy, and she kept peeking at him under her eyelashes as if she wasn't sure whether he was going to pounce on her again. He decided not to. Better to take things slowly. He wasn't a brute, like her ex, and it was clear that she needed gentleness. That didn't mean he'd back off completely, though.

'How would you like to have dinner with me this evening?' he asked on the walk down to the bus. 'My colleagues were telling me about this restaurant that serves authentic Roman food. I guess one ought to try it at least once.'

'Um, sure, that sounds nice. My mum didn't want me to come over today. She's convinced my ex is stalking the house where she's staying. But she's got my uncles on the case, so if he is, they'll soon know for sure.'

Connor frowned. 'That doesn't sound good. Can't she call the police?'

'Not really.' She sighed and bit her lip. 'Can you keep a secret?' When he nodded, she continued, 'We're not supposed to have taken Bella out of the UK without Derek's approval. As we're not divorced yet, I don't have the right to decide that on my own. In fact, if anyone found out, it could jeopardise my appeal for sole custody. It's a crime.'

'Ah, I see. Are you sure it was worth the risk then?' It sounded dicey to him.

Cat's mouth tightened into a stubborn line. 'Oh yes. Trust me when I say that she's much safer here. If he got his hands on her, I'd never see her again.'

'Whoa, that's . . . intense.' The guy was obviously deranged. No wonder Cat had wanted to escape him.

They didn't discuss it any further, and a couple of hours later they arrived at the restaurant, whose interior looked just like the houses they'd seen in Pompeii. It was located not far from the ancient ruins, in a tiny side street under a flyover. Not the most appealing of locations, but still . . . The outside was painted white, with deep terracotta along the bottom half. There was writing in Latin and some frescoes painted on the upper part, and the wide doorway was covered by a small roof overhang. Inside, the walls glowed a deeper red, mixed with panels of black and mustard yellow. These too were painted with frescoes and fake architectural details like pillars and moulding. It was enchanting and rather dark, not to mention run-down. Faded grandeur was probably too kind a description – crumbling would have been more apt.

'Welcome, *signore, signora*. Would you like to dress like a Roman, like this?' The waiter showed off his own outfit.

Connor and Cat looked at each other and smiled. 'Sure, why not?' he told the man, and soon they were both kitted out in supposedly authentic clothing. Cat looked adorable in some sort of flowing tunic with a shawl draped over her shoulders, and Connor himself had been given a shorter tunic and a toga that kept slipping off.

'Looks like we've got the place to ourselves,' he whispered as they were seated at a table for two in one corner of the restaurant. The furniture was rustic in the extreme, but sturdy. 'I hope that's because we're early, and not an indication of the state of their cooking.'

Cat giggled. 'I guess we'll soon find out.'

Burning candles in old-fashioned candlesticks added a romantic ambience, which was perfect. On the recommendation of the waiter, they ordered a five-course Roman meal, which began to arrive on shiny terracotta-coloured pottery. The wine was drunk out of mugs of the same material, and tasted good. The waiter brought them bread first, a whole round loaf divided into eight sections ready for tearing, exactly the way the Romans had baked them. They'd seen fossilised versions of this at Pompeii.

'*Focaccia* with rosemary and honey,' he explained, then left to fetch their starter.

'That looks and smells amazing,' Cat said to Connor. He watched as she grabbed a piece of the still warm bread and closed her eyes with an expression of bliss as she took her first bite. 'Oh my God, it's delicious!' She blinked open her eyelids and frowned at him. 'Aren't you having any? Here, you've got to try it.' She broke some off from her own piece and held it out to him, then seemed to realise what she was doing. 'Oh, sorry, you'd probably prefer a chunk of your own.'

'No, it's fine. I'm happy to share.' He couldn't stop looking at her sensuous lips. They reminded him of that spectacular kiss and made him want to pull her across the table and do it again.

Her cheeks turned dark red when he opened his mouth and she popped the bread inside. As if she couldn't help herself, she took another bite and moaned softly. 'So good,' she murmured.

While he chewed and swallowed, Connor drank in the sight of her. In the candlelight, she was even more stunning than normal, the planes of her face accentuated to perfection. He winced. 'Please don't make noises like that or you're going to give me ideas,' he muttered.

'What? Oh!' She blushed again, and he reached across the table to take her hand.

'Hey, don't be embarrassed. I'm having a natural reaction here, OK? Any heterosexual man with a pulse would be the same. That doesn't mean I'm going to leap over there and jump you, much as I might like to.'

She looked down and pulled her hand away from his. 'It's just . . . I don't know how to react. I'm not used to this. It's all Greek to me.' She laughed. 'Or Latin I suppose would be more appropriate here.'

He grinned at her, glad she could joke a little. 'Why don't you just say what you feel, the way I am? It's better to be honest, and I'd rather you told me straight out to stop flirting if it makes you uncomfortable. If not, I'm going to keep trying, especially after what happened today.' He shrugged. 'Sorry, but I for one enjoyed it. A lot.'

'I did too, and I don't want you to stop. But I'm scared you're going to find me . . . unsophisticated and naïve. It's not like I've been with loads of men.'

Her eyes were huge pools of worry, and he wanted to erase that look so badly. 'Listen, nothing you say could put me off you. I don't mind unsophisticated, although I don't think you are. I would call it genuine, and believe me, it's refreshing. I like it. I like *you.*'

Her amber gaze softened and she nodded. 'Very well, I'll take your word for it. I guess if you didn't want to be here, you wouldn't have asked me out.'

'Exactly. Now let's enjoy the meal.'

The first course was some type of chicken brawn, along with boiled egg, sesame seeds, seared greens and black olives. This was followed by the best lentil soup he'd ever tasted, accompanied by more bread with a garum crust, and a piece of deep-fried cauliflower. After that, the waiter brought the main course – lamb stew with broad beans, cabbage and walnuts.

'Wow, this lamb is simply divine,' Connor enthused. 'It literally melts in your mouth.'

'Yes, incredible,' Cat agreed. 'Who knew the Romans were so good at cooking?'

Dessert was ricotta with honey and figs, and Connor leaned back in his chair, sighing in satisfaction, sipping the last of his wine. 'That was excellent. I have to admit I was a bit dubious when we first arrived.' He indicated the less than perfect area outside. 'But this makes up for it.'

'Definitely.'

They sat in silence for a while, each of them lost in thought. When next he looked up, Cat was staring at him and had tilted her head to one side.

'What?' he asked with a smile. 'Do I have ricotta on my nose or something?'

'No, I was just thinking . . . Have you ever worn your hair long? It's amazingly thick and I love the colour.'

His eyebrows shot up in surprise. 'Er, thank you. And yes, I used to until a couple of years ago. Want to see?' He chuckled and pulled up some photos of himself on his phone, taken a while back.

He expected her to laugh, but instead she drew in a sharp breath. 'Oh my word! You look so much like him.'

'Who?' A tendril of unease shot through him.

'This man I keep seeing in my visions and . . . I think, in my dreams. It's uncanny.' She looked across the table. 'He's Roman. Or at least I think so, because he's dressed vaguely like you are now. And I have no idea what he wants with me, but I think he . . . loves me.'

'That's what your visions were about? A man?' Connor wasn't sure how he felt about that. It wasn't as though the man was real, but he still couldn't suppress a stab of jealousy.

'Yes, but not always. I sense that I'm . . . someone else. His love. I'm seeing things through her eyes. And when we were in

Herculaneum, there was a little girl as well. She . . . she was at the baths with me. I had the same feeling towards her as I do with Bella. As if she was mine.' Cat's gaze was troubled. 'I don't know who these people are. Or were. And what do they want with me? Why are they in my brain? It's all so weird. And scary!'

'It does seem strange,' he agreed. 'There must be a reason for it.' He debated whether to tell her about his own vision, but decided against it. She was already spooked enough. 'Did you ever have dreams like that before moving to Italy?'

'No, never.' She hesitated, then added, 'I think they're definitely connected with this area. As I said, the people must be Roman, judging by the way they're dressed.' She glanced at the bracelet she wore, as if it was to blame, then shook her head. She shuddered visibly and covered her face with her hands, leaning forward. 'I wish I knew what was happening to me.'

'I wish I knew too, but one thing is for sure – we're in this together.'

When they left the restaurant, Connor kept a tight hold on her hand, and on the train he put an arm around her shoulders, nestling her close. He craved the contact between them like he needed air to breathe, and sensed that she felt the same. She snuggled into him and gave a small sigh of contentment.

'Want to go for a walk?' he asked as they alighted from the train in Sorrento. He didn't want the night to end yet.

'Sure.' Her cheeks were flushed and she sent him a heated glance.

As soon as they were out of sight of the train station, he pulled her into a narrow alley and into his arms. He couldn't wait another second to kiss her again, and she didn't protest. Her petal-soft mouth welcomed his eagerly, and he simply couldn't get enough of the taste and feel of her. He tried not to get too carried away, but it was a long time before they stopped.

After that, they took a very long route back to the hotel, pausing to kiss some more in various nooks and crannies along the way. It wasn't until they came closer to their destination that Cat sighed and said, 'We'd better behave now. Someone might see us.'

It was late, so he doubted it, but he was willing to follow her lead. The most important thing was to earn her trust. For now, what they had shared this evening was enough.

Chapter Twenty-One

Pompeii, 14 October AD 79

Raedwald

Raedwald's leg took longer to heal than he would have liked, and it was almost a full week before he was able to resume his guard duties. He was still sore, and favoured his other leg, but tried not to show it. Aemilia hadn't risked another visit to his quarters, and he was grateful for that. Even if other Roman ladies came and went, he didn't want her to be seen there. He sensed that Lucius would be incandescent with rage if he ever found out. That was best avoided so that he didn't take it out on his wife. A plan was brewing in Raedwald's mind, and while he mulled it over, he wanted to be sure that she was safe.

That didn't mean he wasn't longing to see her. Those stolen kisses had stoked the fire burning in his veins, and his blood was near boiling point. He'd chafed against the enforced rest the wound had brought, and although he trusted Duro to look after her in the meantime, today he'd brooked no arguments. Healed or not, he was going.

'You know you might rip the stitches,' Duro grumbled, but his eyes danced with amusement. He hadn't stopped ribbing Raedwald since the 'respectable matron', as he called Aemilia, had come for a midnight visit. He found it hilarious that his friend's defences had crumbled for the sake of a pretty face.

Well, she was a lot more than that, but nothing Raedwald said made Duro shut up.

'Yes, yes,' he replied testily. 'I'm sure the lady will walk slowly if I ask her to, since she seems to care about my well-being.'

'She'd probably do more than that if you asked *really* nicely.' Duro chuckled and jumped out of the way of a punch.

'I hope you're not going to carry on like this once she's within hearing.'

'I'm not that stupid and you know it. I'll have your back.'

He would, and Raedwald would trust him with his life.

Aemilia was waiting for them, and they left the house in silence. She walked in front with the two of them a few steps behind. No slave women had been brought as an entourage today, and Raedwald wondered if that was on purpose. She ambled along as if she had all the time in the world, and he suspected that was for his benefit. He hadn't needed to tell her to take it slowly. Sure enough, a few blocks away from her home, she stopped and peered at him.

'Are you well, Raedwald?' Her gaze swept down his leg, as if she wanted to look through his barbarian trousers to check the wound for herself.

'Yes, thank you, *domina*. A few twinges now and then, but I'll survive.'

'I'm glad to hear it.' Her smile, and the soft look she sent him, warmed his insides. 'I am going to the Temple of Isis. Can you manage to walk that far?'

'Of course,' he answered automatically. Whichever temple she wanted to visit, he'd make it if it was the last thing he did.

She turned off the main street and headed south onto a narrower one. The Temple of Isis was actually not very far from the gladiator barracks, and the two men had passed it on their way to Aemilia's house earlier. It was hidden away behind a high wall and there was only one entrance. The area beyond wasn't visible from the street, but as far as Raedwald could make out, it was narrow and not overlarge. He had never been inside this or any other such precinct. As and when he felt the need, he honoured his own gods, but he'd been past this building many times. He'd been told it was the only temple in the town to have been completely rebuilt following the earthquake sixteen years before.

He knew Romans paid a lot of attention to their deities, and he'd heard that they even had special family ones for each home. There were gods and goddesses for everything here, controlling each aspect of life, though he'd only registered the names of the main ones, such as Mercury, Jupiter, Venus and Minerva. Foreign deities like Isis, who was apparently from a faraway country called Egypt, were also sometimes invoked. He found this confusing. Hundreds of statues and images of them were strewn around the city. There were even places set up at various crossroads where sacrifices could be made. All the gods had to be appeased with offerings and rituals, and he'd witnessed several of these where an animal was sacrificed outside a temple by special officials. There had been chanting and music involved, but he hadn't stayed to watch for long.

'I'll wait outside. Keep my eyes open,' Duro said when they arrived.

Raedwald nodded and followed Aemilia in through the gate. Wedged into the cramped area stood a small temple on a tall podium, with columns at the front topped by a triangular pediment. Steps of dark stone led up to the entrance, and inside, vivid frescoes could be glimpsed. The temple was surrounded by colonnaded walkways, and there was a second building behind it. The entire complex was painted in white and red, accentuated by the red-tiled roofs. In sunlight, the whiteness was almost blinding in its intensity.

Climbing the stairs hurt his leg, but he gritted his teeth and made it to the top, where the floor had a beautiful mosaic pattern. Tendrils of smoke from incense burners drifted around the inside of the temple, the spicy scents teasing his nostrils. The wall paintings of Egyptian scenes and various gods sprang to life in the light of oil lamps and any sunlight that reached in through the doorway. There were only a couple of people there: one male and clearly a slave, the other a female of higher status like Aemilia. The followers of Isis were apparently a mixed lot. The goddess was not just for the elite, but was especially beloved of women, freedmen and slaves. She was said to be compassionate, loving and merciful, and promised hope and rebirth after death to anyone who followed her. She had, after all, allegedly managed to bring back her husband, Osiris, from the dead, so why not everyone?

He stared at a statue of the goddess, whose diaphanous gown left nothing to the imagination. It must have been carved out of marble by a master craftsman, as it was very lifelike. The gilding in Isis's hair and other areas added to her ethereal appeal. In one hand she held a symbol that he'd been told was called an *ankh*, the key of life. She was supposed to be the epitome of feminine beauty, but in Raedwald's opinion she couldn't hold a candle to Aemilia. He wanted to tell her so, but there were people about who might hear.

Instead he asked quietly, 'Why this particular temple?'

Colour flooded Aemilia's face and neck, and she bit her lip. It made him want to pounce on her and kiss that luscious mouth, nibbling it himself.

'Oh, um . . . I'm making a vow to the goddess and asking for a favour.' She waved the lead tablet she'd been clutching. 'I've written it on here. If she helps me, I will give her my best gold bracelet.'

'Must be something important you're asking her to do,' he commented.

The goddess was by all accounts a wife and mother, but had also been a whore, and was therefore associated with eroticism and lovemaking. Raedwald couldn't help but wonder whether he was mentioned on this tablet of Aemilia's. They had only shared a few kisses, and he'd never believed in love before, but somehow he didn't feel quite so averse to the concept now.

She nodded. 'Yes, but I can't tell you about it. This is between me and the goddess.'

'Very well. Carry on.'

He followed her as she went to place her vow by the statue's feet, then bent her head as if in silent communication with the goddess. Other people were doing the same, and he leaned on a wall while he watched. When Aemilia was done, they descended the stairs. His breath hitched as one particularly uneven bit caught him out and pulled at the wound in his leg.

'Raedwald?' Instantly she was beside him, putting a hand on his arm, and looking at him with an expression of deep concern.

'I'm fine. It's nothing.'

'No, it isn't.' She held on to him until they reached the courtyard once more. 'Let's find somewhere to sit down for a while. You need to rest.'

He was about to protest, but she swept him along to the back of the central building, tutting in annoyance as she scanned the area, which was devoid of seating.

'I can just lean on this wall for a moment,' he told her, putting his back against the nearest one. The building felt warm on his skin, and he let the heat seep through him and into his aching leg.

'You shouldn't have come, you stubborn man,' Aemilia chided. 'You ought to be resting.'

She was standing so close, he could see gold flecks in her beautiful amber eyes. He allowed himself to drown in them for an instant before replying. 'Of course I had to come.'

There didn't seem to be anyone about back here; most of the temple visitors were on the other side. In fact, it would appear everyone else had gone home, as he couldn't hear any signs of life at all. After a quick glance, he put his arms around her waist and pulled her in. 'I couldn't stand another day without seeing you,' he whispered in her ear, smiling as he caught the shiver that went through her.

'Raedwald, this isn't—'

He cut her off with a kiss, fulfilling the wish he'd had earlier and sucking on her full bottom lip before delving inside to explore more thoroughly. It had only been a week, but by all the gods, he'd missed the taste and feel of her so much, he was like a starving man.

She made a noise, and he stopped to make sure she wasn't protesting. Her eyelids were lowered seductively and her gaze was unfocused. He could imagine exactly how she'd look after he made love to her. That thought went straight to his groin, which was already uncomfortable enough. They were still alone, and he dared to kiss her some more, losing himself completely in the moment. He forgot that she wasn't his woman, that he didn't have the right to do this, and that they might be discovered at any time.

Eventually, some semblance of rational thought reared its head and he drew back, breathing heavily. 'I don't know what you asked of the goddess, but I think she granted my wish at least,' he murmured, taking her face between his hands for one last kiss. Her *palla* had fallen down and he pulled it up to cover her head, pushing a few strands of hair into place. It wouldn't do for her to look tumbled. Not here, not now.

She blinked at him. 'That wasn't what I asked for, but it was part of it.' Grabbing the front of his tunic with both hands, she shook him slightly. 'Oh Raedwald, what are we going to do? This is madness. I can't eat, I can't sleep, I can't *think*! What are you doing to me?'

He gave her a lopsided grin. 'I haven't done anything to you yet.' She looked as though she was about to hit him out of sheer frustration, so he grew serious. 'But I would very much like to, even though I know it's wrong.' He sighed. 'I've not known you for long. Perhaps I'm moving too fast. Do you want me to leave you alone? Not escort you around town any more?'

'Yes. No. I don't know!' There was anguish in her voice, and he wanted to soothe away the crease of worry between her brows. She shook her head. 'No, I couldn't bear it if I never saw you again. I don't care if it's wrong. I just wish we could be alone. I feel as though everyone is watching us, and if Lucius found out . . .'

'Then we'll find a way.' He considered their options, which were limited at best. 'Do you ever wander your garden after dark?'

Her eyes lifted to his as understanding dawned. 'Sometimes, when I can't sleep. But how would you gain access? I can't take a chance on unbarring the back gate again.'

'I'll scale the wall. Isn't there a broken section? That'll make it easier.' He smiled and dropped one more swift kiss on her lips. 'Come to that hidden bench tonight after midnight and I will be there, then we can make plans.'

Seeing the way her eyes lit up made it worth the risk.

Aemilia

'Aemilia. A moment of your time, if you please.'

Lucius was waiting for her in the *atrium* when she returned from the temple, and turned to lead her into one of the side rooms without waiting for her reply. By the frown on his face, she gathered he'd been expecting her back earlier, and wasn't best pleased at the delay. Entering the room behind him, she stopped dead in the doorway. A crowd of people were sitting and standing around the walls. She counted eight men, all of them high-ranking by the looks of it. They were staring at her with varying expressions of impatience and disdain. Some she had met at supper parties, while others were strangers.

What on earth was going on?

Lucius did not introduce them. 'Sit,' he commanded, indicating one of two chairs that were not currently occupied. He took the other after he had dropped the thick curtain across the doorway. If he wanted privacy, that wouldn't do much good, as sound would still carry. Hopefully none of the slaves were around, though, and this would be over quickly.

'What is occurring?'

She held her hands still in her lap and her head high, not wanting to let on that she was supremely uncomfortable and quaking on the inside. Had someone seen her kissing Raedwald at the temple and she was about to be accused of adultery? Or noticed the heated glances she'd thrown him? She didn't care if Lucius was angry with her, but legally an adulterous wife had to be reported to the authorities and punished. There would be much more serious repercussions for the gladiator. As a slave, he could be put to death for daring to touch a free woman. It was her understanding that Lucius had the right to kill them both, if he wished, although that was a very old law and an uncommon occurrence these days.

Not that they'd gone that far yet, but she was honest enough to admit it was only a question of time.

Lucius interrupted her frantic thoughts. 'I think I've found an heiress who will suit me admirably,' he informed her without pre-amble. 'My patron has agreed to propose a marriage between me and Flavia Antonia, so you are to consider yourself divorced forthwith. These men are here to act as witnesses to this fact.' He held out a wax tablet encased in wood. 'Here, have your own property back.'

A quick glance at the tablet showed that it was the agreement made between her father and Lucius, recording the details of her dowry. It also served as proof that their marriage had existed and was legal. By returning it, he was effectively saying that the coun-try estate belonged to her henceforth, and the marriage was over.

'Wh-what?' Momentarily stunned, it took her a few moments to collect her thoughts, but when she did, anger surged through her. 'You've arranged a marriage while still wedded to me?'

'It's only been discussed privately so far. No need to kick up a fuss.' He gestured to the silent men surrounding them. 'I merely invited these witnesses to make sure everything is done properly. Now I can go ahead with my plans.'

'No need to . . .?' Words failed her momentarily.

It wasn't that she wished to stay married to him, but to discard her so callously, so easily, after five years of marriage, made her furious. And to humiliate her in front of strangers, on top of everything. It was as if they'd shared nothing, and she was worth-less. A mere nuisance to be cast aside at his whim. She clenched her hands and stood up, piercing him with a hard stare. 'And what about the fact that you have bled my estate dry? How am I to manage?'

Lucius shrugged. 'This year has been difficult for everyone, as you well know. The crops failed spectacularly, but I'm sure they will recover. You must speak to your overseer. It is your business now. I expect there's enough there for you to live on. The house is habitable, I understand.'

'I see.'

And she did. He thought she'd just go quietly and live in the countryside, where he wouldn't have to see her. On an estate that he had more or less bankrupted, to the point where there was no more profit to be had. The sad truth was that with no father or other male relatives to stand up for her, he was free to dispose of her as he wished. She could go to a magistrate, but that was unlikely to help. Divorce was a private matter.

And what of Caia? She considered mentioning their daughter, but decided against it. Since he didn't seem to have given the child any thought, she'd simply take her when she left. There was no way she'd leave her behind. She raised her chin, giving him her frostiest look. 'Very well, but I shall stay here until such time as I can arrange everything. Unless you object?'

He hesitated, then nodded. 'Fine, but don't take too long.'

And that was the end of their marriage, it seemed. Not that she minded. She felt only relief that it was over. There were hopefully better things in her future. Starting with a man with red hair . . .

But would he want her as anything other than a brief liaison? Given that he was a slave, was it even possible for them to have any other sort of relationship? She would have to wait and see what his reaction was to her news before discussing the future with him.

Chapter Twenty-Two

Naples, 9 October 2022

Cat

'Suzanne, how wonderful to see you! Are you well?'

Cat had dared to take a trip into Naples to have Sunday lunch at her uncle Pietro's apartment. Her mother hadn't mentioned anything more about any stalkers skulking round the place, and she was desperate to see Bella. Seeing Suzanne there too was a bonus. She'd come over for a short holiday and was staying at a small hotel nearby. They'd been in touch almost constantly by email since Cat had left the UK, but it was lovely to meet up in person again.

'Yes, very well, thank you.' Suzanne gave her a hug and held on to her hands in order to study her closely. 'And you look a hundred per cent better than last time I saw you. I'm so glad.'

Cat smiled. 'Being here has really helped. I can't thank you enough for your support. I might not have got this far without you.'

'Oh pish. I'm sure you would. But who's that?'

Connor had arrived separately, in case the house was being

watched. Perhaps that was taking paranoia a bit too far, but Cat felt it was better to be safe than sorry. She'd invited him because she knew he would be spending the day alone otherwise, and that seemed wrong. He was just coming through the door and being greeted by Giovanna. His mere presence made heat stir inside her, but she tamped it down. This was neither the time nor the place to think about all those wonderful kisses they'd shared.

Still, she knew her cheeks were tinged pink as she replied, 'Oh, that's a new friend of mine, Connor Drake.' She called to him. 'Hey, Connor, come and meet my saviour and former neighbour, Suzanne Trent.'

He made his way over to them. 'Pleased to meet you. I've heard a lot about you.' He shook hands politely, and Cat saw Suzanne's eyes open wide as she took him in.

'Well, I haven't heard anything about you,' she murmured, and threw Cat a smiling glance. 'Do you live here?'

He started telling her about his thesis, and how he'd met Cat at the hotel where she worked. Cat left them to it.

She spent the next half-hour with Bella and her second cousins, but she wasn't worried about Connor. He was clearly at ease in any social situation, and her relatives were all friendly and chatty. Most of them spoke good English too. He'd be fine.

Eventually he came and hunkered down next to her. 'There you are. Thank you for inviting me today. Definitely beats sitting alone in my room all day.' He nodded towards the dining room and kitchen with a grin. 'That's quite the clan you've got there.'

'You could say that. I hope they haven't teased you too much?'

'Teased me?'

'Mamma has been telling them that you're my boyfriend, and some of them have a tendency to joke around.'

'And am I?' He reached forward to push a strand of hair away from her face, looking into her eyes.

'Are you what?' She was finding it hard to concentrate on his words when he stared at her like that. A shiver of awareness sparkled through her, making her sway towards him.

'Your boyfriend.' His knuckles grazed her cheek in a languid caress.

'Oh, I . . . er, I don't know. I mean, we have only been on a few dates, right? You probably have other women friends back in the UK and—'

He cut her off by putting his fingers over her mouth. 'No other female friends. At least none that I want to kiss or do anything remotely romantic with.' He checked to see if anyone was watching them, but the others had all moved into the other room now, and the children were busy arguing over some toy or other. His mouth captured hers in a searing kiss, as if he was branding her right there. 'I'd like to be,' he whispered. 'Your boyfriend. Your man. Whatever. Yours.'

Cat was speechless. 'That's . . .' She couldn't find the words, and he smiled and stood up, taking her hands to pull her to her feet too.

'You don't have to decide right this minute,' he murmured. 'I can wait, and I'm aware things are complicated. Just know that I'm here if you want me.'

'OK.' It sounded inadequate, and didn't in any way express what she was feeling, but it was all she could manage before they were called to the table.

The lunch was as noisy and long as only a proper Italian family meal could be. *Antipasti*, pasta, main course, salad, cheese and a sweet, accompanied by wine and followed by coffee. Everything savoured to the full and debated loudly with wild gestures. Throughout, Cat was supremely aware of Connor sitting beside her, his well-muscled thigh rubbing against hers every time they moved. The scent of his shampoo and cologne nearly drove her to distraction. She tried to concentrate on her daughter and chatting to Suzanne, but all the time his nearness sent tingles through her.

He seemed to fit right in, laughing and chatting with everyone, and even trying out a few words of Italian that he'd picked up. Cat's uncles, Pietro and Luca, and their sons and sons-in-law included him in their talk of football and other such manly topics, and he held his own. He jokingly declared that British and Scottish beer and football clubs were far superior to Italian ones, and laughed when he was shouted down with a stream of denials.

'Never! Roma all the way!'

'No, Juventus!'

'AC Milan, you moron!'

It made Cat laugh too, especially as her relatives couldn't seem to agree between them which was the best of the Italian teams.

She was struck by how right this felt. The one and only time Derek had met some of her mother's relatives, at their wedding, he'd been stiff and formal with them. There hadn't been any of this male bonding stuff. Connor had known these people for less than a couple of hours, and already he was at home, welcomed as one of them. It drove home the point of how right she'd been to leave Derek, and how wrong he had been for her.

If only she could be free of him for ever, and not have to constantly watch her back.

Connor left soon after the meal, obviously trying to be tactful so that Cat would be able to spend precious time with Bella. He thanked his host and hostess, said goodbye to everyone, and drew Cat into the hallway, away from prying eyes. There, he pulled her into his arms and kissed her, long and slow, until she wanted to practically climb on top of him.

'I'd better go,' he whispered. 'You won't see me for a few days, as I'm heading back to London to meet with my supervisor.' At her sharp intake of breath, he caressed her cheek and smiled. 'But I'll be back, and I'll text you while I'm gone. Take care, yeah?'

She nodded. 'You too. I'll . . . miss you.' And that was definitely an understatement, but it earned her one last scorching kiss that would have to last until his return.

London, 11 October 2022

Connor

Connor exited Imperial College and turned right onto Exhibition Road, heading towards South Kensington. He passed the Science Museum, then the imposing Victoria and Albert Museum on the left. As always, he was tempted to pop in there for a quick look around – there was never a shortage of new things to discover among their eclectic collections – but he didn't have time today.

He took the number 14 bus to Green Park Tube station, and walked past the Ritz Hotel, then took a right down St James's Street and into Pall Mall. A short way along on the right-hand side lay the imposing Oxford and Cambridge Club. It was an establishment he could have been a member of if he'd wanted to, as he'd attended Cambridge University for three years. Because that was his father's wish, however, Connor had never applied to join. The old man was a snob, and there was no way Connor would play along with such outdated nonsense.

Sir John was waiting for him at a table in the so-called Coffee Room, a name that in no way did it justice. Featuring a soaring ceiling, ornate cornicing, full-length windows with swagged curtains, and oxblood-coloured walls hung with paintings of famous club members, it was as opulent as it could be. Connor had to admit he liked it, but he'd never tell his father that. The wall colour reminded him of the Roman restaurant he had taken Cat to. He'd only been gone two days, but he was missing her already.

He had it bad.

'I hope I'm not late?' he said by way of greeting, giving his father a perfunctory man hug that felt limp at best.

'Not at all. I just arrived myself. Have a seat and see what you'd like.'

They made stilted small talk while they ordered lunch, and Connor told his father a little of what he'd been doing in Naples.

'Vesuvius is monitored twenty-four/seven by sensors set up around the crater. There's a surveillance centre in Naples, and I'm working alongside members of the National Institute of Geophysics and Volcanology. They're very kindly allowing me access to their data for my thesis, and it's exciting stuff.'

'I'm glad. Sounds like you're making good progress.'

'Yes, I'm hoping to be done in a couple of months.' He had no idea what he was going to do once he'd finished, but he supposed a job teaching at some university or other was the expected way forward.

As their food arrived, he steeled himself to broach the subject he'd really wanted to discuss, and his father gave him the opening he needed.

'So what brought this on?' Sir John regarded him across the table. 'Asking to meet up, I mean. As I recall, that hasn't happened for a while.'

An understatement, or perhaps a dig at Connor, since every meeting between them in the last ten years or so had been at Sir John's instigation.

'Well, actually, I wanted to ask your advice on a legal matter. As a judge, I thought you might have some insight into a problem a friend of mine is having.'

'Oh? And what's that?' Sir John looked surprised and mildly

intrigued. Connor had never shown any interest in his father's work before, and they both knew it.

'My friend has just come out of an abusive relationship. Quite frankly, her husband beat her black and blue. And although she suffered this treatment for years, she decided she needed to get away when he started threatening their three-year-old daughter as well. She's applied for a divorce and sole custody of the child. I just wondered if you could tell me what her chances are of getting that. As I understand it, most spouses are awarded joint custody.'

He gripped his cutlery tightly, waiting for the reply. He badly wanted to be able to reassure Cat, and give her some good news. She was bound to be worried that her ex would mistreat Bella if he was awarded any sort of custody or access.

Sir John dug into his steak and kidney pie and chewed for a moment, a frown creasing his brow. 'That depends, I suppose. Can she prove that she and the child were mistreated? Did she lodge a complaint with the police?'

'Oh yes. She has evidence from a doctor at the Royal Free Hospital, and lots of photos of the bruising she sustained. Her neighbour also had the presence of mind to film part of her husband's last attack on her. It was vicious, and the police have been sent the clip. There's no proof that he ever hurt the child, though.' Connor took a mouthful of his own food, although he wasn't particularly hungry.

'It sounds to me as though your friend stands an excellent chance of being awarded sole custody, not to mention a restraining order against the husband. If there is a film of the attack, it's not just her word against his, as happens in a lot of cases.' Sir John took a sip of his wine. 'I take it she's in hiding until the case goes to court?'

'Yes, she's in Italy. That's where I met her.'

'What? With the child?' When Connor nodded, his father

shook his head. 'Oh no, no, no, that's not good. She shouldn't have taken her daughter out of the country. Her husband could use that against her. She's not allowed to do it without his consent.'

Connor swore under his breath. 'She is aware of that, but felt it was too great a risk to stay in the UK. The husband has been searching for her, and if he finds her . . . Anyway, she's ready to come back at a moment's notice as soon as she's needed here. As long as her ex isn't aware of her whereabouts—'

Sir John cut him off. 'Doesn't matter. Make her return immediately, or she risks losing the case. That is my advice.'

'OK, I'll see what I can do.' Connor closed his eyes for a moment, taking a large swig of the beer he'd ordered.

'She means a lot to you, this woman.' It was a statement, and he knew he couldn't fool his father.

'Yes,' he admitted. 'I mean to marry her if she'll have me.'

It sounded hasty and impetuous even to him, as they'd known each other for such a short time, but he'd never been more sure of anything in his life. A bone-deep certainty told him they were meant to be together, and he would be patient until she felt the same. He wasn't stupid enough to imagine she'd want to jump into marriage again any time soon, but he'd wait.

'I see. Well, I hope it all works out.' His father sounded like he actually meant it, which surprised Connor somewhat. He hadn't thought he cared much about his life. The older man added with a small smile, 'Good luck with being a stepfather. That's not an easy role, I can tell you.'

'You've had problems with Sophie?'

Sir John's smile grew into a genuine, warm and self-deprecating one. 'And how! As a teenager, she was a nightmare. Kept telling me I had no right to decide over her life as I wasn't her real father. Never mind that that wastrel didn't bother to so much as send her a birthday card, and weaselled out of paying any maintenance. I sent her to the most expensive schools, bought endless amounts of clothes, and tried to treat her as though she were my own, but it was never enough.' He sighed. 'As you've probably noticed, I'm not good at displays of affection. I hadn't had any dealings with little girls and had no idea how to handle that side of things. She probably needed more from me than I was able to give at the time. Thank goodness she's matured a bit now and realised I do care about her, very much. We rub along tolerably well these days.'

'Wow, I never realised.' Connor almost felt bad for not knowing, but then he'd avoided visiting his father's new family as much as he could. He hadn't even been interested in his stepsister and half-brothers until recently, when they had made the first move and contacted him.

'No, I don't suppose you did. I understand you and Sophie are in touch?'

'Yes. As a matter of fact, we're meeting for a drink this evening. James and Jolyon might tag along too, apparently.'

He watched Sir John's eyebrows rise. 'Never thought that day would come. Amanda was so pleased to hear about you and Sophie, but she'll be absolutely delighted that you're talking to the boys as well. It's what she's always wanted. Thank you.'

Guilt stabbed Connor. He probably hadn't given his father's second wife much of a chance, and never realised it would mean a lot to her that all the children got on. He shrugged, feeling his cheeks heat up a bit. 'We're adults now. It would be childish of me to blame them.'

'Yes, about that . . .' Sir John fixed him with an intense gaze. 'I know it's probably much too late, but I want to apologise to you for the way I handled things after your mother died. I wasn't thinking straight. I felt as if it was somehow my fault that she died; as though her illness was accelerated by the fact that we were heading for a divorce, you know? I never wished her ill, we just weren't suited to each other. When the funeral was over, my only thought was to escape the past. I met Amanda and fell head over heels in love, but that doesn't excuse the way I forgot about you. I should have been more supportive. You were grieving by lashing out, and instead of getting angry when yet another school expelled you, I should have sought help for you. I'm so sorry. It wasn't until your grandmother stepped in and told me off right royally that I understood, but by then it was too late.'

The apology was long overdue, but was it ever too late? His father looked and sounded sincere, and as he'd never spoken so openly about emotions before, Connor was sure it had cost him dear to utter this explanation. The least he could do in return was to meet him halfway.

'Thank you,' he said. 'And I'm sorry I caused you so much trouble. It was a difficult time for us both, but as a teenager, I only saw my own side of things.'

Sir John smiled. 'Perhaps we can put it in the past and try a bit harder going forward? I'm willing if you are.'

'I'd like that.' And Connor meant it. Somehow he felt lighter knowing things might be less strained between them in future.

They chatted for a while longer, and Sir John promised to look into Cat's case to see if he could find out more. When they parted outside the front door, he gave Connor a longer, more genuine hug and clapped him on the back.

'Good luck with Caterina. I hope to meet her soon. Just make sure she returns to the UK as soon as possible.'

Connor promised to do his best.

Chapter Twenty-Three

Pompeii, 15 October AD 79

Aemilia

The garden wall was high for a reason – to stop intruders from entering the house. If it had been easy, there wouldn't have been any point in all those bolts on the gate. But Lucius still hadn't engaged a builder to repair the broken section, and Aemilia was extremely grateful for that now. As she waited nervously in the shadows, she thanked the gods that there were no funds for such work at the moment.

She had no idea how the red-headed gladiator had become so important to her in such a short space of time. It was as though she'd been asleep, and suddenly she was wide awake, seeing how empty her life had been up till now. With Lucius, everything had been about duty and convenience. He was attractive enough, and to begin with they'd rubbed along tolerably well, but she'd never once felt even a tiny spark of desire for him. Whereas with Raedwald, there were so many sensations and emotions, they threatened to drown her. Just being near him made her tingle, as if there was some magic emanating from him that went straight through her skin and into her blood.

It was terrifying. And it was also incredible and addictive.

She peered out from behind the dense bushes now, and was pleased to see that no one stirred in the house. A short while ago, Lucius had come home in an inebriated state yet again, looking very much the worse for wear. She'd seen him slumped on his bed, snoring fit to wake the dead. As for the slaves, they took the chance to make themselves scarce and sleep as much as possible whenever they were not wanted for any tasks. They wouldn't stir unless she sounded a horn next to them.

Where was Raedwald? Would he come? She chewed on a fingernail, even though she hadn't done that since she was a child.

An arm snaked around her from behind, and a warm mouth placed a kiss in the hollow between her neck and her shoulder. A delicious shiver rippled all the way down her arm. She twisted on the bench and threw her arms around him, pulling him close. 'You came,' she breathed.

His white teeth glimmered in the faint light from the moon as he smiled at her. 'Of course. Did you doubt me?'

'No.' She really hadn't. He was a man whose word you could trust. An honourable man. She sensed it with every fibre of her being. Well, apart from coveting another man's wife, but she didn't care about that because she wanted him too. And she was no longer married, so it was a moot point.

He lowered his mouth to hers. The kiss was gentler than the ones they'd shared at the temple, almost as if he was asking permission this time. 'Are you sure this is what you wish? We really shouldn't . . .'

'Raedwald, I want you. Absolutely.'

'Good. Then will you come with me? I want to take you somewhere private, where we can talk without fear of discovery. Fetch your cloak, please, and your *palla*.'

She did as he'd asked, and he led her over to the broken section of the wall, which he helped her to scale. His strong hands gripped her waist and lifted her to the ground on the other side, then he took her hand and pulled her along the alley. 'Cover your head, my love,' he whispered. 'We don't want anyone to see you.'

She followed him along the dark streets, keeping her head down so that no one would catch a glimpse of her face if their torches should happen to shine on her. Raedwald held her hand, meshing his fingers with hers. After a while, she noticed that they were heading towards the sea. They crossed the Forum, and continued down a street that led to the gate that faced the harbour. The pavement here was a mosaic of small rounded stones, and she almost slipped at one point. He steadied her, putting an arm around her waist until she was upright again.

'Are you all right?' he whispered.

'Yes, thank you. Where are we going?'

'You'll see.' She heard amusement in his voice, and wondered where he was taking her, but she trusted him. It wouldn't be anywhere dangerous.

The gate itself was like a long, dark tunnel, sloping steeply downwards. It was paved with lava stone, just like the streets, worn smooth from centuries of use. As they passed through, their footsteps echoed on the vaulted roof. No one challenged their progress, as the gates weren't guarded. On the other side, the tang of the sea mixed with the scent of wild rosemary and pine hung in the air. Aemilia breathed deeply, trying to calm her racing heart. She wasn't afraid, but excited.

At the bottom of the hill, they turned sharp right and Raedwald led her to a sprawling building that was tucked into the cliffside. They entered a doorway on the right, and she found herself standing in some sort of entryway with beautiful mosaic flooring and a counter on one side. An older woman greeted them, but Aemilia kept her eyes lowered and her face hidden from view.

'I have an arrangement with Marcia. A room upstairs for a few hours?'

She heard the clink of coins, and gathered he must have slipped the woman a bribe.

'Ah yes, she told me. Turn left, then proceed up the stairs. Third room on your right.'

'Thank you.'

Without looking up, Aemilia followed as he tugged her along into another room, which appeared to be some sort of changing area. She came to an abrupt halt as she caught sight of the unusual frescoes that ran around the top of the walls. Her eyes widened and she drew in a sharp breath.

'What is this place?' she whispered.

Each fresco was numbered, as if to remind the user of the niche below where he or she had left their clothes, but that wasn't all. The paintings depicted people – mostly couples, but sometimes groups – in what appeared to be sexual positions. She felt her cheeks turn scorching hot, and blinked at the various images. She had never imagined the act could be performed in such ways, and had no idea why anyone would want to do that. Some of them looked even more uncomfortable than what she had done with Lucius.

Raedwald's arms came around her waist from behind, just like earlier. She felt a chuckle rumbling through him while he gave her a reassuring squeeze. 'This is a bath house,' he murmured. 'But they offer certain other activities too. Don't worry, we won't be joining them. I merely thought to speak with you privately, and we won't be disturbed here. Come, my love.'

Still glancing over one shoulder at the frescoes in horrified fas-cination, she went with him through a short corridor, then up a staircase and into the room the woman had directed them to. It was small and cramped, furnished only with a bed, a couple of chairs and a table. This held a tray with a flagon of wine and two cups, as well as an assortment of fruit. Raedwald closed and barred the door, then turned to her and smiled.

'Don't look so worried. I won't do anything you don't wish me to.'

'But this is a . . .'

'Brothel, yes. In a way. It is only for rich people who want their bathing to come with a little extra. Marcia is one of the girls who provides entertainment.' He held up a hand as if to forestall her next question. 'And no, I have not indulged, with her or anyone else here. She owed Duro a favour, as he once saved her from a beating. It's a long story, which I'll tell you later. Suffice it to say that she agreed to arrange for us to borrow her room for a few hours. Do you mind? It was the only way I could think of to spend time alone with you, away from prying eyes.'

A knot inside her loosened and she walked into his arms, burying her face in his chest. She inhaled his now familiar scent, and suddenly all was right with the world. 'No, of course I don't mind. Thank you.'

'Do you want to discuss—'

She cut him off by placing a finger on his mouth. 'No. Later. Please, kiss me first, Raedwald. I need you.'

He nodded, as if he heard the rest of what she was silently asking for. When he crushed his lips to hers, she forgot all about her surroundings. There was only him, nothing else existed.

He kissed her hungrily, and she gloried in the sensations running through her. She had never realised that just kissing a man could make you feel so much. At the beginning of their marriage, Lucius had made a few attempts to ready her for their coupling, but he'd never kissed her like this. He'd mostly run his hands over her body in ways she didn't like, and then taken what he wanted, as quickly and efficiently as possible.

Her gladiator didn't rush anything. His lips made their way along her chin, her collarbone, her shoulder, then lavished attention on other parts of her. First with his callused fingers, then his mouth, licking, sucking, stroking, until she writhed in pleasure. She trembled all over, and didn't protest when he divested her of most of her garments. He also shucked off his own tunic, and she was left breathless at seeing the glory of his naked torso up close once again. This time he wasn't wounded. There was nothing to stop her from running her hands all over his chest, shoulders, biceps and abdomen. She made the most of this opportunity, her fingers trailing the hard ridges of his muscles, exploring and caressing as she had longed to do. He closed his eyes and groaned.

'Aemilia . . .' He backed them up towards the bed, where he lay down and pulled her to sit across his legs.

'Straddle me, my love,' he breathed. 'There's very little room in here, so this will be easiest.'

She did as he asked, putting one knee either side of him, even though she didn't quite understand why he wanted her to. Her tunic was bunched around her waist by now, and her nakedness felt unbearably sensitive against the rough material of his trousers.

'Wait,' he murmured, undoing the drawstring at his waist and lifting his hips while he tugged at the garment. She sank down again, her exposed skin brushing against the hard muscles of his thighs. The hairs covering them tickled in a delicious way. A small shift higher up and his arousal pushed against her, just where she wanted him, making a thrill shoot through her.

'Are you sure you want this?' he asked one more time, his voice strained, as if he was barely holding himself in check. 'There's no going back after this.'

'Yes! Yes, Raedwald, please.'

'Thank the gods!'

He moved her with his big hands, showing her what to do until she took him inside her, slowly at first, then further and further until he filled her entirely. It felt insanely good, and at his urging, she experimented with sliding slowly up and down. He drew in a harsh breath, then surged up to cover her mouth with his in a fierce kiss. He helped her to find a rhythm that drove her towards something – she didn't quite know what. She was only aware of the fact that she didn't want to stop, had to go faster, harder, until she reached this unnamed goal. When she was almost sobbing with the intensity of it, he inserted his thumb between them to rub at her most sensitive spot. It sent her over the edge so hard she thought her entire body had exploded. He took over setting the pace then, and with a few hard thrusts found his own release with a barely stifled groan. She was still convulsing around him, and couldn't stop shaking. The wonder of it was blowing her mind.

'By all the gods,' she breathed. 'I had no idea.'

She felt rather than saw him smiling against her mouth, as his lips lingered on hers. 'You enjoyed that then, love?' There was a certain masculine smugness in his voice, but she'd allow him that.

Collapsing on top of his chest, she crushed him to her and nodded. 'You know I did.'

And 'enjoy' was an epic understatement. She'd revelled in it. Was ecstatic with the joy of proper lovemaking. At last she understood what all the fuss was about. And now that she realised what she'd been missing out on, she never wanted to go without again.

She slid off him to lie next to him on the narrow bed, encircled by his arms. It was a tight fit, but she didn't mind in the least. She stayed like that for a while, her cheek resting on his chest, the sound of his heartbeat steady and reassuring. Her body was relaxed, still humming with a residue of pleasure, and she didn't want to move. In fact, she'd love to remain right where she was until the end of time.

'Raedwald . . .' She whispered his name reverently, and allowed her fingers to trail across his taut abdomen. This was the first time in her life that she had truly desired a man, wanting all of him. She couldn't stop touching him. He was magnificent.

'Yes, my love?' He pulled her in tighter against him. She delighted in his nearness and those strong arms holding her close.

'What happens now?'

There was no doubt about it, she wanted this man in every way, but how would that work? He was a gladiator, a slave, and she'd been born into a high-ranking family. Although gladiators were allowed to have wives and families, everyone would consider that she'd married beneath her. She wouldn't care, but would he even want her? There would be talk, malicious gossip. Would that harm him?

His thoughts must have been going in a different direction. 'You mean, if there is a child? I'm sorry, I should have thought of that. Apparently there are ways of preventing it. Duro has told me what he asks his women to do. They use a sponge soaked in vinegar or lemon juice, shoved up into . . . er, inside you. He learned the trick from a tavern wench he befriended who swore it works every time.'

Aemilia was momentarily diverted from thinking about the future. 'A sponge? I had heard there were ways and means, but I didn't know how.'

A wife didn't deny her husband children – it was more or less her whole purpose in life – but quite a few families decided that one or two were enough, so she knew it was possible to prevent pregnancies. Her mother had taught her that swallowing silphium would get rid of unwanted ones, but she'd never contemplated that either. Thankfully she hadn't needed to because after Caia was born, she hadn't conceived again.

'No, listen, it doesn't matter.' She swallowed hard. It was time to tell him her news, but she was afraid to find out how he'd react. 'I . . . that is to say, Lucius has divorced me. He informed me last night, in front of witnesses, and said that he'll be marrying someone else soon. I'm to go and live on my estate, up on the slopes of Vesuvius. Or at least that is what he has planned.'

Would Raedwald want to join her there, in between his duties? It was a lot to ask, and she had no idea how it would fit in with his training regimen.

'You're divorced?' He sat up abruptly and blinked at her, then a huge grin stretched across his face. 'Excellent!'

'It is? I mean, yes, but . . .'

The grin faded, and his expression turned serious as he looked into her eyes. 'Is it not? You wished to stay married to him?' A frown marred his brow, and she could almost see him withdrawing from her in an instant.

She sat up too, and put her arm around him to tug him back against her, staring at him and imbuing her gaze with as much love as she could. 'No, absolutely not. I was merely surprised that you're so pleased.'

'Of course I'm pleased! I want you to be mine, Aemilia. In every way.' He lifted his hand and caressed her cheek. 'I wish for you to be my wife, if you'll have me.'

'Oh, thank the gods!' She threw herself at him, knocking him flat, and kissed him for all she was worth. In between kisses, she mumbled, 'I thought . . . maybe you didn't . . . want more than . . . a tumble. And I want . . . so much more.'

A chuckle shook him underneath her, and his well-muscled arms banded around her, holding her to him. 'Foolish woman. Of course that wasn't all I was after. Have you not heard? I've resisted every woman who's ever thrown herself at me since I arrived on these shores. There's only one I couldn't resist. You, my beautiful temptress.'

It was some time before they were able to speak coherently again, but when they were settled once more, Raedwald stroked her hair and whispered, 'My sweet, can you keep a secret? Swear an oath not to tell a soul?'

'Of course. I swear on my father's grave.' She looked up at him, hanging on his every word.

'Duro and I are planning to leave this place and escape to our homelands. We've bought a boat, and a fisherman is keeping it in readiness for us. We've been waiting for the right time to go, and it is fast approaching. Would you come with us? Please? As my wife. We can start a new life elsewhere. Perhaps in my homeland.'

Aemilia heard the sincerity of his words. He truly wanted to take her away from here for ever, to create a future together. Somewhere no one from Pompeii would find them, and where people wouldn't care what social strata they came from. There was only one problem.

'I can't leave Caia,' she whispered, her heart constricting at the thought. 'And what would your family think of me? I assume they believed you were captured by Romans, so they'll hate me on sight.'

'Caia is coming with us, of course,' Raedwald replied, kissing her softly. 'I would never take you away from her, and I doubt your former husband will care what becomes of her. And I give you my oath, I will treat her as my own child. She's delightful. As for my family, some of them were responsible for my capture, and they'll be paying for that. Trust me, they will have no choice but to accept you.' He sighed. 'But perhaps it is wrong of me to ask you to come and live in what will seem to you like a hovel. My home is a wooden building with dirt floors. No stone, marble or paint, no running water, no baths.' He pushed a hand through his hair. 'It was foolish of me to suggest it. Forgive me.'

'No! No, Raedwald. I'd go anywhere with you. I honestly don't care. As long as we're together. You are sure you don't mind about Caia?'

'She is a part of you. I love her already.'

'Then yes, please. I want to come. I'll just need to arrange for the sale of my estate, so that I have something to bring to our marriage. A plot of land here won't be much use where we're going, will it?'

He smiled. 'No, not really. That sounds like an excellent plan. We'll leave in a fortnight. How does that sound? Will it give you enough time?'

'Amazing! Now please, teach me some more about those frescoes downstairs.'

'With pleasure, my love.'

Chapter Twenty-Four

Naples, 15 October 2022

Cat

'This was a lovely idea, Connor. Much nicer than trying to swim in the sea this time of year. It's getting too cold now.'

Cat was floating in a large thermal pool at the Stufe di Nerone baths, situated just outside Naples, and the water was as warm as in a bathtub. Her limbs were pleasurably relaxed. She'd been told it was also cleansing, and her skin would feel like velvet after a lengthy immersion. Either way, it was as though her body was soaking up the restorative effects of the natural spring water, storing it up for future well-being. It was, quite simply, wonderful.

'You don't mind missing out on an afternoon with Bella?' He swam closer to her and gripped the edge of the pool, turning to lean his head against it.

When he'd first suggested the outing, she'd been poised to refuse, because she usually only got to see her little girl twice a week. But then her mother had rung to say that Bella was invited to a children's birthday party that day. That meant there wouldn't be any opportunity for Cat to spend time with just her. This news gave her mixed feelings. On the one hand, it was great that Bella didn't need her to the same extent as before, and was growing up into an independent little lady. On the other, she wanted to be with her baby every second she possibly could.

Then again, she felt that way about Connor too, and she wasn't sure she should.

'No,' she replied now, coming to rest next to him. 'With party games, cake and ice cream on offer, I doubt she would have even noticed I was there.'

He nudged her with his shoulder. 'That's a good thing, right? You said she's always been a bit clingy.'

'True. She hardly ever got to play with other kids. I was dreading having to send her to school in a year or so.' She smiled at him. 'Ignore me. I'm having a hard time letting go. I should be thrilled.'

He put an arm around her shoulders and steered her so that her back was against his broad chest. 'It's natural instinct. She'll be fine. And I for one am very grateful to have you to myself.' His mouth grazed her ear playfully and she leaned into him, a delightful shiver snaking through her.

'Oh yeah?' He was even warmer than the water, and she turned to put her arms around his neck. When she looked up, his eyes were intensely green in the late-afternoon sunlight, and they were searching hers as if he wanted to probe her very soul.

'Mm-hmm,' he murmured, pulling her close so that they were chest to chest. He glanced down and groaned. 'Do you have any idea what you're doing to me right now? That bikini is sheer torture. It should be illegal.'

She followed his gaze and saw her breasts squashed up against him, almost spilling out of her bikini top. It should have made her embarrassed, the way it would have done only recently, but instead she felt powerful, sensuous. 'Not really,' she whispered, checking to make sure none of the other bathers could hear. 'But maybe I'd like to find out.'

'Jesus, woman, you're killing me!' He closed his eyes and took a couple of deep breaths. 'I hope they have very cold showers in this place.'

Cat giggled, then on impulse she wrapped her legs around his middle and leaned forward to kiss him. It was meant to be a short, playful touching of mouths, but it soon turned into much more. She had no idea how long they were locked together for, but she eventually pulled away after she heard a muttered imprecation in Italian from somewhere behind her.

'Oops! We're causing a scene.' Her cheeks were turning hot, and she ducked under the water for a moment to try and cool them off. Not easy in a pool that was thirty-five degrees Celsius.

When she surfaced, Connor had his eyes closed again and had sunk low in the water. 'Minx,' he muttered. 'I won't be able to get out of here for hours now.'

'That bad?' she teased. She had no idea where this daring was coming from. Never in her life had she flirted so overtly with a man, especially one as clearly turned on as Connor was. She was playing with fire and she knew it, but she didn't want to stop.

He cracked open one eye and glared at her playfully. 'Just you wait till I get you on your own somewhere. Anywhere!'

Laughter spluttered out of her, and she felt ridiculously happy. So this was what wanting felt like. Desire. Lust. It was as though her entire body was fizzing with anticipation, and it could only have one ending. A few short months ago she would have dreaded that, but now she welcomed it. Wanted it. And it was a heady sensation to know how much Connor wanted it too. She had done that to him. She wasn't a doormat to be used, but a powerful, desirable woman.

It was amazing.

'I'm going to try the natural sauna, then go in the indoor pool for a bit,' she said. There were two so-called natural stoves, apparently heated by the thermal waters as well, and she was curious to see what they were like. The indoor pool was supposedly even hotter than the outdoor one, but she'd take a quick dip just to be able to say she'd experienced it. 'Then I'm having a massage.'

'Good. Get out of my sight, woman, so I can calm down.' His words sounded harsh but were accompanied by a mischievous grin. 'And if it's a massage you want, I'm sure I could oblige later . . .'

'I just might take you up on that,' was her parting shot. She thought she heard a string of swear words, but it only made her smile. She had a feeling this evening was going to be one she'd never forget.

Connor

By the time they headed back to the hotel, Connor was feeling languid and relaxed after a massage and a swim in the incredible indoor pool. He'd managed to avoid being in the water at the same time as Cat, which had helped preserve his sanity. He didn't think he could take another second of being near her when she wore that black bikini. She'd been threatening to burst out of it with every stroke she took. Perhaps he ought to buy her a new one, but images of her in even skimpier attire didn't help, so he pushed such thoughts out of his mind.

'Are you sure you're OK with coming to my room?' he asked, for at least the third time as they made their way along the winding lane towards the hotel.

Cat threw him an amused glance. 'Yes, Connor. I know by

now that you're not going to hurt me or do anything I don't want. I trust you.'

That trust was a precious thing, but it was also a burden. She'd been so badly mistreated, and although she didn't flinch away from him any longer, he wasn't sure how she'd feel if he tried anything other than kissing. Mind, she had wrapped her legs around him in the pool earlier, as if . . . He took a deep breath. No, she might just have been playful, nothing else. He shouldn't assume.

'Fine. I'll see you there in ten minutes, then. Bring a glass. I've only got the one.'

They'd bought bread, cheese, tomatoes, grapes and wine, and were planning a light supper. Neither of them was very hungry, and it seemed the ideal meal. It would save having to ring for room service for two, which could be embarrassing. Cat had to be careful not to be seen entering his room either, as it might cost her her job.

He allowed her a head start. They'd made it a habit never to leave or enter the hotel at the same time so as not to arouse suspicions. Although Cat often served his breakfast and dinner, if he took it in the dining room, they managed to keep those interactions professional. Hopefully none of the hotel staff suspected anything was going on between them.

Fifteen minutes later, they were seated next to his small Juliet balcony, overlooking the Bay of Naples. Lights glittered across the water like a sprinkling of stars fallen to earth, and they were reflected in the dark, restless sea. Cat sat hidden by a sheer curtain where she couldn't be seen from outside, while Connor had his feet up on the railing.

'It's so lovely here, isn't it?' Her gaze was on the view, but Connor couldn't take his eyes off her.

'Not as lovely as you,' he blurted out, then almost groaned as he heard the desire in his voice. She couldn't have missed that.

Smooth, Connor, real smooth. Way to spook her, now that he finally had her on her own. 'I'm sorry, I—'

'No, it's fine.' She smiled at him, and sipped her wine before taking a bite of bread. 'I like it when you say things like that. It's . . . a novelty.'

Taking his feet off the railing, he sat forward and took her hand, caressing her slim fingers. 'I don't want to make you feel uncomfortable in any way, Cat. You said earlier you had no idea what you're doing to me. I want to show you so badly, but it has to be on your terms. I'm not an animal, like your ex. I need you to want me too. I won't do anything unless you give me permission.'

She stared at him for a moment, then nodded. 'I know. I'm not afraid of you the way I was with . . .' Clearing her throat, she went on. 'Um, perhaps you could start by giving me that massage you promised? The one I had at the spa was great, but I kept trying to imagine how it would feel if it was your hands on me.'

Connor swallowed hard. 'Massage. Er, sure. I can do that.' Although it might definitely kill him. 'Let's finish eating first.' That would give him time to gather his strength.

Once he'd put the leftovers in the tiny hotel fridge, she walked over to his bed. Connor tried not to look, because Cat on any bed was something he'd fantasised about so often recently, it had become a recurring dream. He turned to say something joking, but the words died on his tongue and he swallowed a curse. She was lying face-down on top of the covers and her upper half was completely bare. Her silky skin glowed with a golden sheen in the light from the only lamp that was currently lit, and he could see the white tan line from her bikini top. All the blood in his body headed south, painfully fast.

She turned her head to look at him with a smile. 'I'm ready.'

'You're not the only one,' he muttered under his breath.

Although none of his neighbours could see into his room, he

pulled the long curtains across the windows. It made the space feel a lot more intimate, but he didn't want to share Cat with anyone.

Climbing onto the bed, he straddled her thighs, although he didn't actually sit on her. He was a big man and didn't want to crush her. Almost reverently, he began to trail his fingers over her back, starting at the neck and shoulders and proceeding down the bumps of her spine. She shivered, but didn't protest, and he used his fingernails to increase the sensation. When she squirmed a little, he started to massage her properly, shoulders first, then working his way down towards her slim waist. She was perfect, and he wanted to do so much more, but he had to take it slowly.

While rubbing his way back up, he leaned forward to kiss her neck and the sensitive spot underneath her right ear. 'The masseuse this afternoon didn't do that,' she murmured, a smile in her voice.

'Maybe she didn't fancy you,' he replied, doing it again on the other side. His fingers skimmed dangerously close to the sides of her breasts, which were spilling out beneath her, giving him a glimpse of ethereal white skin. It was his turn to shiver, and he gritted his teeth, forcing himself to sit back and return his hands to her shoulders.

'Connor?'

'Yes?' He stopped, waiting to see if she'd had enough. *He* hadn't. Not nearly enough, but he wouldn't carry on without her saying so.

To his astonishment, she turned over abruptly, scooting up to lean back on her elbows. Her breasts were displayed for him in all their glory, and his mouth went completely dry. 'How about this side?' she asked, looking at him from under her lashes.

He felt his eyebrows rise. 'You want me to massage those as well?' He couldn't take his eyes off her. She was so beautiful it hurt.

'Mm-hmm. But only if you take your shirt off too. I feel at a disadvantage.'

Connor had never ripped a T-shirt off so fast in his life. Then he leaned over her, scraping his knuckles along her body from her waist up to the underside of one breast. 'You, my love, are a dreadful tease. I hope you don't live to regret this.'

Just before his mouth closed on hers, she whispered confidently, 'I don't think I will.'

He wasn't as sanguine, but he'd do his best to make sure she enjoyed this evening to the point where she forgot that any other man existed in the entire universe.

Cat

Cat had no idea where this inner vixen was coming from, but the way Connor had stared at her as if she was a goddess gave her the confidence she'd so badly needed.

While he kissed her, deeply, languidly, his hands touched her breasts with a reverence she'd never experienced before. He palmed them, and rubbed her nipples with his thumbs, before bending down to replace his fingers with his mouth and tongue. She felt worshipped, adored and seen in a way she hadn't ever expected to experience. And when he moved further down, removing the rest of her clothing to do the same to other parts of her body, she closed her eyes and just delighted in the sensations he created.

'God, you're so gorgeous,' he murmured. 'I don't know what I've done to deserve you.'

'I should think it's the other way round.' She didn't feel as though she'd ever be worthy of this man.

'We were meant to be.' His lips moved lower, touching her in a way Derek never had. 'Is this OK?'

'Yes. Yes, please!' She was lost to the incredible sensations coursing through her, gripping first the sheets, then Connor's thick hair as he brought her to an explosive release.

He moved up her body, settling on top of her, although he was leaning most of his weight on his elbows so as not to crush her. 'Do you want me? All of me?' he whispered, looking into her eyes. His green gaze was hazy with desire, but she knew instinctively that he'd back off if she told him to.

'Yes. I want you. Now!'

She heard the crinkling of a condom wrapper, and soon afterwards, he surged inside her with a groan. 'Oh, you feel so good, baby. So good!'

'Mm, you too.' He'd started to move, and for the first time in her life, she welcomed the feeling. Little darts of pleasure shot through her, building towards another peak. 'Don't stop,' she breathed. 'Just . . . don't stop.'

'Never,' he vowed. 'Not until . . . Yes, that's it.'

Another explosion rocked her, and waves of ecstasy rolled through her body, one after another, until she couldn't think straight. She was vaguely aware of him following her over the cliff, groaning out his own release. Then he kissed her, gently, while they floated down from the peak.

Afterwards, he gathered her into his arms and held her tight. 'Sleep, sweetheart. I'll wake you before dawn, I promise, so you can go back to your room without anyone noticing. Trust me.'

She did.

Chapter Twenty-Five

Pompeii, 22 October AD 79

Aemilia

An ominous rumbling sound filled the air, and the ground began to shake without warning.

'What is that, Mater?' Caia threw her arms around Aemilia's legs and looked up at her, eyes huge with fear. 'Is Pater angry?'

They were in the back garden, and Aemilia had been playing with her daughter so that she'd have an excuse to be out here alone. She was expecting a notary with the payment for her estate. With the help of a middleman, she'd managed to sell it amazingly quickly, although that probably had more to do with the fact that she had agreed to a ridiculously low price. It was still a considerable sum, and she'd been promised it in gold and silver.

'No, he's not. I promise.' She grabbed Caia and hoisted her up onto her hip.

Another piece of the garden wall tumbled into the flower bed below. A jagged crack appeared in the back wall of the house too, and a couple of roof tiles crashed to the ground. Her heart began to beat faster. She scanned the area for danger. As they were in the middle of the garden, there was no risk from falling masonry, and no trees large enough to crush them. Their best option was to stay exactly where they were. It was terrifying, but she had to keep calm for her daughter's sake.

She kissed the top of Caia's soft curls, and stroked her back in a soothing rhythm. 'It's nothing, my sweet. The gods are a little angry with some people – not us – but they will soon get over it.'

But would they? These past few days, the town had been plagued by an increasing number of earthquakes, and there didn't seem to be any end in sight. What was happening? Surely the deities would not concern themselves with just one person? She refused to believe it. Even if they disapproved of her plans to run away with Raedwald and take her child from Lucius, this wasn't her fault. Why would they punish an entire town because of her? That made no sense. No, it had to be an accumulation of sins. Pompeii had been growing increasingly lawless, or so she'd heard. There was more crime, and gangs roaming the streets at night. It was one of the reasons Lucius had hired Raedwald and Duro. Had it become so bad that the gods were involving themselves?

She shuddered and ground her teeth together. It was as well she and Caia were leaving. Although she hadn't been living here when the huge earthquake had happened sixteen years ago, she'd heard enough about it to know that she didn't want to be around if it occurred again.

After yet another earth tremor, the ground stilled, and she breathed a sigh of relief. With a bit of luck, that would be it for now.

She put Caia down and took her hand. 'Come, my love. We are going to talk to a man by the back gate.'

When she opened it to peer out, the *scriba* was there, waiting for her. *Thank the gods!*

'Your payment, *domina*. As per your instructions, this transaction shall remain secret until the end of the month.' He made a face, as if he didn't hold with ladies making such demands, but it wasn't for him to comment. She could do as she pleased.

'Thank you. I appreciate your assistance.' She smiled graciously at the man, who bowed and left without returning her smile.

'What's that, Mater?' Caia tried to reach for the pouch of coins, but Aemilia held it out of her reach.

'This is a new flower that we're going to plant in the garden,' she lied. 'Do you want to help me dig?'

'Oh yes, please!' The little girl jumped up and down. She snatched the small trowel Aemilia retrieved from her pocket, where she had placed it earlier. 'Mine, mine. I want to do it!'

The two of them went to a far corner of the garden, out of sight of the house, and Aemilia let Caia dig several holes.

'Why don't you go over there and pull up one of those flowers, then we can plant it here instead. It will look better.' She pointed at some wilted blooms a few feet away. Caia skipped off eagerly, and while her back was turned, Aemilia placed the bag of coins in one of the holes and covered it swiftly. She placed a small whitish stone on top so that she would remember the exact location.

Together they replanted the flower Caia had dug up, and then repeated the exercise with a few more. She hoped her daughter would forget that there had been another hole nearby, and didn't notice that the pouch was gone.

That was yet another treasure she didn't want Lucius to get his hands on.

Pompeii, 23 October AD 79

Raedwald

'I don't like this. We need to put our plans into action sooner rather than later.'

Raedwald had earlier escorted Aemilia to the Temple of Isis, where she'd left a gold bracelet in the shape of three laurel leaves for the goddess. She had whispered that her wish had been granted when he'd asked her to marry him and leave this place with him. It was exactly what she'd hoped for, and now it was time to fulfil her obligation. He was pleased that she had wanted him so much she'd ask the gods to intercede, but he was too preoccupied with all the earth tremors and didn't allow her to linger. He'd ushered her out of the temple precinct as soon as she had paid her debt to the deity.

Now they were in the Forum, where she'd wanted to make some essential purchases for their journey. The place was unusually crowded, with people congregating in groups discussing the earthquakes. Hundreds of voices were raised in anger and fear, hands gesticulating wildly, and there were one or two tearful faces. As Raedwald listened, he heard all manner of suggestions as to why this was happening. Most had one common denominator – the gods.

'They are angry with us. Have we not made the necessary sacrifices?'

'Or perhaps the *aediles* didn't organise them for the right day?'

'I'm telling you, that bull they slaughtered last week was not willing to go to his death. I was there! I saw the beast resist with all his might.'

Raedwald knew the Romans were extremely superstitious. They believed that it was a bad omen if the animal chosen to be sacrificed appeared unwilling. It was supposed to be docile, as if it had the courage of a gladiator when confronted with imminent death. Utter rubbish. As if a bull understood what was happening. He shook his head at such nonsense. There was no doubt the gods were angered, though. The earthquakes hadn't let up since the previous day, and were coming thick and fast. It was worrying in the extreme, and there was much talk of leaving the town to find safety elsewhere. Some people were already heading for the two nearest gates, by the looks of it.

He bent to whisper in Aemilia's ear. 'Can you bring Caia to the Forum Gate after dark, my love? I think we should leave tonight. I'll have Duro and Marcellus ready the boat and load it with provisions, and I will escort you there.'

She sent him a wide-eyed glance, terror lurking in the depths of her amber gaze, but she nodded. 'Very well. I'll be there as soon as I can after dark.'

There was such a crush, he dared to grab her hand for a moment to give it a squeeze, and rub his thumb across the top of it. He wanted to pull her into his arms and press her to him, to reassure her everything was going to be fine, but he dared not risk it. There would be time enough to hold her once they were away from this place.

He saw her swallow hard. 'You . . . you don't think he'll follow us, do you?'

'Who, Lucius? No. He won't know where you've gone, for one thing. And for another, he'll probably assume you've left on foot or in a mule cart, heading for your estate.' Under cover of the folds of the cloak she wore, he took her hand one more time. 'I love you. I won't let any harm come to either you or Caia. We'll soon be safe in Frisia, where he'll never find us.'

'I love you too, and you're right. I'm worrying unnecessarily.' Aemilia squared her shoulders. 'Let me just find the rest of the things I need, then I'll go home and pack.'

Raedwald battled to lock down his emotions. He had no idea how he'd fallen so deeply in love with this woman in such a short space of time. But she was special, unique, and there was no going back. She meant more to him than life itself, and he would do anything to keep her and her daughter safe. If only they could escape this town without any trouble.

He glanced in the direction of the Capitolium, and then to the brooding mountain in the background. If he wasn't mistaken, there was smoke or steam coming out of the ground on its slopes in several places. He'd heard of that occurring, and had been told it was due to the hot springs that abounded in this area. Yet he had never noticed it before. At least not to this extent. There were also strange clouds hanging around the top of the mountain, like hot breath in winter. Something wasn't right, and he really didn't like it one bit.

'That's it. I have everything I need,' Aemilia announced. 'Please can you take me home now?'

They turned to make their way through the increasing number of worried citizens flooding into the Forum. It was a relief to reach the side streets, although even there a larger than usual number of people were milling around. When they reached her home, she entered through the front door, but asked him to meet her by the back wall straight away. He bowed and pretended to leave as usual, then doubled back into the alley behind the house. The broken wall was even lower than before, and he was able to peer inside without being seen.

Anxious moments went by, and he wondered what she was up to. At last, a low whisper floated over the wall. 'Raedwald?'

'Yes, here. Should I climb in? There's no one about.'

'No. I'm going to throw something over. Catch.'

A heavy pouch closed with a drawstring came sailing across, and he managed to grab it before it hit the ground. He swore under his breath, and quickly stowed it under his tunic and inside his trousers, where he had a hidden pocket. From the feel of it, there was quite a large collection of coins inside, and they weighed him down.

'Another,' came Aemilia's voice, and soon after, one more pouch came flying through the air. Again he caught it, and glanced around before putting it in the same place. At a guess, this one contained jewellery of some sort, as odd shapes stuck out in places.

'Is that it?' He raised himself on tiptoe and peeked over the wall.

She was standing next to it, scanning the garden, which was mercifully empty. 'Yes. Please can you keep those safe for me? I don't want to risk Lucius finding them. He has no idea they exist, and I'd like to keep it that way.'

'Very well. I'll see you outside the gate tonight.'

'Yes, tonight. I can't wait.'

'Me neither.'

He listened to her footsteps as she returned to the house, then strode off towards the gladiator barracks. Duro and Marcellus would need to pack, then slip out unobtrusively and go to the harbour to make the boat ready. In order to avoid suspicion, Raedwald decided to stay a bit longer and go through the motions of an ordinary day. They mustn't let on that anything was afoot. The ground shook yet again, and that sensation of unease slithered through him once more. Danger crackled in the air and caused his senses to be on high alert. The sooner they could leave, the better.

Aemilia

'What are you doing?'

Aemilia froze in the act of folding one of her tunics. There was an open sack by her feet, with most of her other possessions inside, so it must be perfectly clear what she was up to.

Lucius leaned on the door frame, swaying slightly, and she could smell the wine on his breath from several feet away. It would seem he'd started this evening's carousing early. She turned away to hide her disgust.

'Packing,' she replied, trying to keep her tone even.

'Why? You're not going anywhere. Not yet. My new marriage

contract isn't finalised, and you said you'd stay here and oversee the household until such time as you were no longer needed.'

She'd never said that. Would not have agreed to it, even if he'd asked. That wasn't why he was saying it, though. Judging by the sulky expression, he was miffed that she wasn't more upset about going. That she was, in fact, happy to be packing and leaving. Knowing him, it hurt his pride. He always wanted to be the centre of attention, adored and respected, but she no longer had to pander to him. He had ended their marriage. Now he could face the consequences.

Besides, that was not the main issue right now. '*Everyone* is leaving,' she told him. 'Have you not looked outside? They're saying another massive earthquake is on its way. It's only a matter of time. Hours, perhaps. We're not safe here.'

It was true. She'd peeked out the front door earlier. Hordes of Pompeiians were heading for the gates, carrying what possessions they could. Some people had huge sacks on their backs; others had loaded carts with their worldly goods. There was noise and bustle, frantic activity and confusion, and the fear was almost tangible in the early-evening air. It was contagious, terror crawling across her skin like ants and making her restless.

'Rubbish.' Lucius smacked the door with his palm for emphasis, and she flinched.

'It's not! The tremors haven't ceased all day, and the water supply is already broken. Look at the fountain – it's stopped. The aqueduct must have been damaged. How are we to survive without water?'

'Don't be so dramatic. Someone will soon mend it. Now put those items back in your clothes chest. You're staying put, not running away like a coward. No Merula has ever lacked for courage, and we're not starting now. It's merely a question of waiting it out.'

'But . . .'

She wanted to shout that she was no longer a Merula. Had never really been one. Before she had a chance, however, he walked over and punched her, pushing her to the floor. 'Stay, I said!' Then he flung out of the room and shut the door, barring it from the outside.

Blinding pain shot through her cheek, and for a moment she was so dazed she couldn't stand. Eventually she lurched to her feet and ran to hammer on the door with her fists. '*Lucius!* Don't be absurd. *Let me out!* It is madness to stay. We'll be in danger, all of us!'

He didn't reply, and no one else answered her pleas for help either.

She sank to the floor with her back against the wall, cupping her bruised cheek with one hand. 'Swine!' she hissed, but calling him names was futile.

What was she to do now? Raedwald would be waiting. How long would he remain by the Forum Gate if she didn't show up? Would he guess that something was wrong, or would he assume she'd changed her mind and leave without her?

'Noooo!' A keening wail erupted from her throat, and she couldn't stop it, nor the tears that came after.

She'd been so close to freedom. So very close to happiness at last. To true love. And now Lucius had taken that from her as well.

The sound of the bar lifting gave her momentary hope that he'd changed his mind, but before she could even stand up, Caia was shoved into the room and the door closed again.

'Mater!' The little girl ran sobbing to her mother and threw her arms around her neck. 'Pater isn't being nice. He hurt me. Look.' She pointed at a bruise that was blooming on her skinny little arm.

Aemilia hissed out a furious breath. 'The gods help me, but he'll pay for that. I won't let him do that to you ever again.'

But how was she supposed to stop him?

Chapter Twenty-Six

Naples, 23 October 2022

Cat

For the next week, Cat walked around in a haze of happiness. Whether waitressing or cleaning hotel rooms, nothing could dim the glow inside her. It was as if she'd woken up from a long slumber, and suddenly she felt alive in a way she never had before. Connor had shown her that there were good men in the world. Men she could trust, and who put her needs before their own. She spent every spare moment with him, feeling like a naughty teenager sneaking around the hotel at night. It was sheer bliss, and even though they stayed awake much longer than they should have each night, she was never tired.

The following Sunday, she finally had a day off, and went to visit her mother and Bella. They had arranged to meet up outside the station in Piazza Garibaldi, in the centre of Naples. To save money, she had left plenty of time for the journey and took the slow commuter train. It was packed, and she had to squeeze into a corner to make way for a busker. The man seemed to be playing his way through every carriage, although not many of the passengers paid him any attention. Cat gave him some coins, feeling bad for him, and received a beaming smile in return.

Napoli Garibaldi station was a sleek modern building, always busy. She took the stairs up from the platform, two at a time, and pushed her way through the crowds. She emerged into the madness of Italian traffic, with honking and shouting drivers, and the hustle and bustle of the city. It was complete chaos. People darted between the cars as if they expected them to stop even when the lights weren't green. Cat hadn't quite become used to this yet, and was more cautious.

She looked for her mother outside the Starhotels Terminus, on the opposite side of the street from the station, where they'd arranged to meet. When there was no sign of her, she took out her phone to check for messages. Nothing. Just as she was about to type out a text, it rang.

'Hello? Mamma, where are you? Are you running late?'

The only reply was a wail and a huge sob, followed by an incoherent string of words half in Italian, half in English. She heard the name Bella in there somewhere, and her throat constricted.

'Calm down! I can't understand you. What's the matter? What has happened?'

Giovanna took an audible breath, then started again more slowly. 'Bella is gone. He took her. That . . . that hateful man! We had just come out of the front door. He appeared out of nowhere, pushed me to the ground. Then he grabbed her and shoved her into the back of a car that must have been waiting. They took off before I could even blink. Oh *cara*, I'm so sorry! This is all my fault.'

'No, no, it's not. It's mine. I should have known.' Cat could barely get the words out. A vice was gripping her lungs and she couldn't breathe.

Derek must have figured out where she'd gone. He was

cunning and methodical, and he'd finally guessed why there was no sign of her and Bella in the UK. *Damn it all!* She should have been more vigilant. Made sure her mother only stayed with obscure relatives he knew nothing about. Of course he'd be able to find Pietro and Luca. She'd sent Christmas cards every year and their addresses were on the home computer.

'Caterina, are you still there?' Her mother's voice sounded small and scared, exactly the way Cat herself felt right now.

'Yes, but I'm coming over. Stay there and we'll try to think of something.'

She strode off in the direction of her uncle's apartment building. She had to think, even though her brain was paralysed with fear. What could they do? Derek would want to take Bella to the UK, but did he have a passport for her? With a bit of luck, he wouldn't have thought of that, and he'd need Cat to hand over the one in her possession. That might give her some leeway to negotiate. But how?

Without thinking, she dialled Connor's number and blurted out what had occurred.

'Oh sweetheart, I'm so sorry. What can I do to help? Have you called the police?' Just hearing his voice calmed her down a little, and her frantic thoughts began to order themselves.

'No, I can't. I'm not supposed to be here, remember? You told me that's what your father said, and he was right. I should have made plans to leave already. I guess I thought I had a little more time, but now I've made everything worse. Derek has the upper hand here, and I can guess what he'll demand.'

'And what's that?' Connor sounded as though he was grinding his teeth together.

Cat sighed. 'For me to return and be his dutiful wife again. His . . . his punching bag. And to . . . to give him a son.' She couldn't stop a sob from erupting, and her vision blurred as tears filled her eyes.

'No! You can't. You're not going back to that scumbag. You have me now, remember? And Suzanne, and your mother and her relatives. You're not alone. We'll make him realise that.'

'But—'

'No buts, my love. Stay with your mother. I'm coming as fast as I can. If Derek contacts you, stall him until I'm there. We'll face him together, OK? I love you! I'm not letting anything happen to either you or Bella, do you hear me?'

'Yes. Thank you. I love you too,' she whispered, swallowing past the obstruction in her throat. She did. She loved this man so much, and she couldn't let Derek ruin everything.

She took a deep breath and reminded herself that she wasn't a mouse any longer. There was no way she could go back to being the meek little wife. She had escaped once, and she was determined to do it again. One way or another, she'd break free.

Connor

By the time Connor arrived at Pietro's apartment, he had managed to calm down. He still wanted to tear Derek limb from limb for what he was doing to Cat – and the Lord only knew what damage it would do to Bella, too – but he knew that wasn't the answer. They had to be cunning and beat the man at his own game.

If only Cat hadn't taken Bella out of the UK without permission. It meant she didn't have a leg to stand on legally, and the bastard probably knew that. *Damn it!* Although in that scenario, Connor would likely never have met them, and selfishly that wasn't something he wanted to contemplate.

As soon as the door opened, Cat threw herself into his arms and he hugged her close. 'Thank you for coming. I'm so scared.

I'm going out of my mind!' That was very apparent from the way she was trembling, and there were tears running down her cheeks.

'I know, I know. Shh, it's going to be OK.' He kissed her, not like a lover, but to soothe her and reassure her that he was there. 'We'll figure it out. Has he been in touch?'

'No, not yet. I—'

She was interrupted by the sound of the doorbell ringing, but when they opened the door, there was no one there. On the mat outside was an envelope, though, and Connor picked it up and handed it to Cat. With shaking hands, she tore it open and pulled out a single sheet of paper. It read:

> Meet me at the Marina Grande pier in Sorrento harbour
>   tomorrow at 5 p.m. sharp.
> Come alone, or you know what will happen.
> Bring your suitcase. You're coming home with us.

The note wasn't signed, but it wasn't hard to guess who it was from.

Cat burst into tears again, sobbing harder. He gathered her into his arms, stroking her back and murmuring endearments. Eventually they ended up in the sitting room, where it seemed the entire Rossi clan had assembled. If nothing else, it was definite proof that Cat was no longer alone with her problems.

'What are you going to do, *cara*?' Pietro's dark brows were lowered in a formidable scowl, and he looked as though he too would like to wring Derek's neck. His brother, Luca, who was sitting next to him, wore an equally fierce expression. 'You want us to call in our friends?'

Connor had a vague idea that the men had connections with the local Mafia, but the less he knew about that, the better. He wasn't sure violence was the answer – if that was what Pietro was offering – but it was tempting. So very tempting.

'No, he'll hurt Bella. We have to try and persuade him some other way,' Cat replied, wiping her cheeks with a tissue Pietro's wife handed her.

Connor had been thinking. 'He's asked you to meet in a public place, right? So if there should happen to be a few other people around – like tourists, I mean – he can't object to that. How about if I pretend to stroll out onto the pier while you're there, and try to grab Bella? I don't think he knows I exist, so hopefully he won't be on his guard against me. He's clearly figured out you came here, but he probably doesn't realise you live and work elsewhere. That means he won't have seen us together.'

'That's true. He's insanely jealous, and he would have made some comment about me being a whore if he had.' Cat's cheeks turned pink, and Connor gathered this had happened in the past.

'Pietro, Luca and their sons can be waiting somewhere out of sight, and as soon as Bella is safe, they can come running,' he continued. 'Together we'll threaten Derek and force him to back off.'

'*Si*, *si*, that sounds like a good idea.' Luca nodded. 'He will be outnumbered, and no matter how *stupido* he is, he will realise he has lost.'

'Yes, and as soon as we're out of there, you and I will take Bella to the UK,' Connor added.

'It might work.' Cat's tears had dried up, and she was only trembling intermittently now. 'Although if Derek gets his hands on our Italian passports, he'll be able to prove we were here. I'll have to destroy them. But I can't think of anything better, so let's try that. If the worst comes to the worst, you'll know where I am. Perhaps you can rescue me in the UK.'

'Oh, you better believe I'll come for you wherever you are,' he vowed. 'Hopefully that won't be necessary, though. Now, how about we buy you a cheap mobile that you can hide in your bra or something. Then if he takes yours away, you'll still be able to communicate with us.'

'*Eccellente!* I will go and buy now.' One of Pietro's sons jumped to his feet. 'I'll be back in *un momento.*'

They sat around discussing the plan for a while longer, but couldn't think of anything to add. In the end, Cat and Connor left separately and returned to the hotel, where they met up after dark. He held her almost until dawn, and prayed to whatever gods there were that everything would work out.

Sorrento, 24 October 2022

Cat

The sound of the suitcase wheels on the uneven paving stones grated on Cat's ears as she dragged it behind her. The Marina Grande area of Sorrento was reached via a very steep alleyway that led downwards in a series of wide steps and sharp bends. There were houses and high walls either side, making the noise echo around her ominously, but once she passed through an archway, the sea spread out before her and the walkway opened up. As usual, Mount Vesuvius brooded in the distance, but for once it didn't scare her. She was too focused on what was about to happen here.

Towards the bottom of the hill, the route doubled back on itself and ended up on a wide paved area that ran along the seafront like a promenade. A former fishing village, the Marina Grande was a jumble of tightly packed houses facing the water. They were painted in the usual local colours of bright yellow, ochre, white and terracotta. Cars were parked haphazardly in front of them. On one side, a precipitous cliff face towered over everything, with more buildings clinging precariously to its side.

There was a beach with boats of various kinds pulled up onto the sand, and two piers jutting out. The largest was T-shaped, and had tables and chairs set out on it like at a restaurant. The whole structure rested on enormous boulders that stuck out underneath on either side.

As Cat descended the final part of the hill, she scanned the pier and saw Derek seated over to one side. Her stomach muscles clenched at the sight of him, the familiar fear pooling in her gut and making her limbs shake. She forced herself to take some calming breaths, pushing the terror away. This was not the time to freak out; she had to stay alert. The tiny figure of Bella could be glimpsed in a chair next to him, her bright pink hoodie unmistakable. Cat's insides turned to ice. Had he hurt her? Was she scared? She really hoped he'd kept his temper in check. The little girl had been forced to spend a whole night with him, wherever he was staying, and that could have been fraught.

'Please let her be OK,' she prayed, looking to the heavens for help from anyone who might be listening.

Connor was here somewhere already, although she couldn't see him yet, and that thought calmed her. Her uncles and cousins were also in the vicinity. They'd mentioned something about hanging out in one of the restaurants, which was owned by a friend of theirs. Fingers crossed they could come to the rescue if necessary.

Her arm was getting tired from dragging the heavy suitcase behind her. She hadn't dared to fake it and bring it empty, so she'd packed everything she owned. Now she regretted it. She should have just brought half her things for now. It wasn't as though Derek knew how much she'd taken with her in the first place.

She made her way along the seafront, and stopped to catch her breath before stepping onto the pier. As she began to walk across the planks, she caught sight of Connor sitting at another table with an Italian newspaper held up in front of him. That almost made her laugh, as she knew he couldn't read a single thing in it. It also had her swallowing down a sob of gratitude because he was there for her. She trusted him to have her back, even if she was forced to return to the UK with Derek temporarily.

Drawing in a deep breath, she strode more confidently towards Derek.

'Mummy! You ca—' Bella's joyful cry was cut short as Derek grabbed her upper arm and prevented her from running to her mother.

Crossing the final few yards in a hurry, Cat crouched down to hug her daughter and kiss the top of her head. 'I'm here, sweetheart. I'm here. Are you OK?'

'Of course she's OK.' Derek's voice cut in, and she rose to face him.

'There's no "of course" about it. In your note, you threatened to harm her,' Cat said, glaring daggers at him. 'Well, indirectly.'

He narrowed his eyes at her. 'Oh, so you've suddenly grown a backbone, have you? Well, we'll soon sort that out. Let's go. And don't try anything stupid, or I really will hurt her.'

He still had Bella's arm in a vice-like grip and tugged her to his side.

'But I haven't finished my *gelato*!' Bella whined.

'Yes, you have. You shouldn't be eating rubbish like that anyway.' He turned accusing eyes on Cat. 'And I see you've been teaching her Italian. That will have to stop. I told you, my daughter is not to be tainted with your foreign ways. She's English.'

'It's part of her heritage,' Cat said. 'Learning a second language can be useful.'

He took a step towards her and raised his hand. She automatically flinched, and stumbled back. That made him smile.

'I see you haven't forgotten what happens when you disobey

me or talk back. Believe me, you're going to learn that lesson again as soon as we're back home. Properly this time.'

Cat clenched her teeth together and refrained from replying, but she couldn't stop a shudder from coursing through her. She had to hope that the plan would work so that she didn't have to go with him. She had a feeling she wouldn't survive his next attack. He'd had weeks to feed his fury and would be vicious in the extreme.

Bella started to cry, but Cat didn't dare console her. Instead she turned to walk next to her husband as he strode off along the pier. When they passed Connor, she pretended to stumble, and knocked into Derek.

'Watch what you're doing, you clumsy bitch!' he snarled, and she almost smiled, because surely this was the opportunity Connor had been waiting for.

But in the next moment, it all went wrong. Bella must have caught sight of him too, and cried out, 'Connor!', sounding very happy to see him.

Never slow to catch on, Derek yanked his daughter towards him at the last minute, just as Connor made a grab for her. To Cat's horror, he lifted the little girl up high and held her out over the nearby railing, as if he was going to toss her onto the boulders below. Bella screamed, then grew still. Her small figure was like a frozen rag doll, eyes huge with fright.

'Derek, no! Please, no! Don't hurt her! Take me instead,' whispered Cat, but he sent her such a filthy look, she closed her mouth and didn't say anything else.

'I'm having you both, you stupid woman. Make no mistake. Now call off your friend, unless you want Bella to die,' he ordered.

Cat stared at Connor, her eyes stinging with unshed tears. A look of devastation passed between them, but they both knew there was no choice. 'Go,' she said quietly.

He nodded, and backed away, keeping his eyes on Derek. When

he'd retreated a few yards, he sprinted off towards the shore, and Cat swallowed past the huge lump that had risen in her throat.

Derek waited until Connor had ascended the first part of the walkway before he put Bella down. Cat breathed a huge sigh of relief that the danger was over for the moment, but she was aware that this was only the beginning. Her husband had the upper hand, and he knew it. It was clear he was prepared to do whatever it took to get his way.

'Come on, we're getting out of here. I really hope you weren't stupid enough to bring anyone else. Didn't I tell you to come alone?'

He ended up carrying Bella, as she was still traumatised and seemingly unable to walk. That put him in an even worse mood, and he muttered to himself as Cat trailed after him pulling the suitcase.

When they reached a little Fiat, he stopped and unlocked the doors. 'You'll have to put your case in the back seat. It won't fit in the boot. Trust a woman to bring way too much unnecessary stuff.'

Somehow Cat managed to haul the bag into the car. When she started to climb in after it, Derek tugged her out of the way and shoved Bella in instead. 'She's smaller. She can go in the back. You get in the front where I can see you,' he snarled.

She helped Bella buckle her seat belt, then did as she'd been told. While she was doing up her own, he held out his hand. 'Give me your phone,' he demanded.

'What?'

'Your mobile, idiot! Give it here.'

She fished it out of her handbag, and he threw it straight out the window. 'There, now your relatives can't follow you, even if they were smart enough to put a tracking device on it, which I doubt,' he muttered.

Cat remained silent, but made sure to put on her most

aggrieved and devastated expression. She had to make him believe he'd won that round. The extra mobile was securely nestled between her breasts, and hopefully he wouldn't be asking her to strip any time soon. She shuddered at the mere thought.

He manoeuvred the car out of the tight parking spot and took off up a hill. Bella was crying softly in the back, but Cat didn't dare to so much as look at her. After a while, the sobs turned into sniffles, then stopped altogether.

Derek seemed to be heading past Sorrento and back around the Bay of Naples. Soon he took a turning towards Sant'Agnello, the next village along the coast. Weaving his way past apartment blocks and hotels, he pulled into the car park of a dilapidated four-storey building. It was painted ochre, with green shutters and balcony railings that had seen better days. She guessed he'd rented an Airbnb property, as that would be the most sensible option when on a mission such as his. At a hotel, people would ask questions if he came in dragging a woman and child, but in an apartment block, who would care?

'Get inside,' he ordered. 'You can leave the suitcase, as we'll be heading to the airport as soon as I've bought us plane tickets.'

In silence, she extracted a subdued Bella and carried her into the building. On the second floor, Derek unlocked a door and gave her a push towards a brown corduroy-covered sofa. 'Sit over there where I can see you, and don't try anything.'

She did as she was told, and waited to see what would happen next.

Chapter Twenty-Seven

Pompeii, 24 October AD 79

Raedwald

'Still no sign of her?' Marcellus's worried gaze lifted to Raedwald's, and the youth shifted from foot to foot, anxious to be gone.

'No. Perhaps she got lost or went to the wrong gate?'

'I already checked the others. You sent me ages ago.'

'I know, but . . .' But nothing.

They stood to one side of the Forum Gate, trying to stay out of the way of the flood of humanity rushing past on their way to the harbour. All through the night they'd kept coming. It was a miracle they all remained on their feet and no one was trampled to death. Raedwald had had to steady more than one person when they almost fell in their haste to escape the wrath of the gods. Yet no matter how many times he scanned the crowd, he couldn't see Aemilia. Where was she? The night was almost over. Dawn was creeping over the horizon, but she hadn't come.

He swore softly under his breath and fought the icy sensation in his gut.

Duro and Marcellus had been waiting in the boat, ready to

leave at a moment's notice. They'd had to stay vigilant all night. People who were hoping to escape by sea would have stolen it otherwise, as there weren't enough ships to go round. He should have been there to help them, but he refused to go without Aemilia. He didn't want to believe that she'd changed her mind. She loved him as deeply as he did her. He'd seen it in her eyes, felt it in every touch when she caressed him. But would that love fade once she realised the poor bargain she'd made in swapping this amazing town for a cold *terp* in Frisia? Had rational thinking already made her decide it was madness?

Closing his eyes momentarily, he paced away from the gate, then back again. No, he wouldn't believe it until he heard it from her own lips. If she was too much of a coward to come and tell him, he would seek her out. Only then would he be able to leave.

'I'm going to find her. Go back and wait with Duro. I'll return as soon as I can, I swear.'

'Very well, but hurry.'

Marcellus took off at a sprint, weaving his way through the crowd, while Raedwald set off into the town with determined strides. He had to battle his way through, as he was heading in the opposite direction to everyone else. Some even told him he was mad to do so, and tried to make him turn around, but he resisted.

'Let go of me!' he snarled at one particularly persistent man. 'I'm not your concern.'

The main street had a steady stream of refugees moving along it, but at the same time there were people carrying on with their lives as if nothing was amiss. The *cauponae* and *thermopolia* were still busy, even though it was long past the hour they normally closed. It was as if people were taking the chance of one final night of carousing, clutching at normality with desperation. Customers spilled out into the street. The ruckus from inside could be heard above the noise of those fleeing towards the town gates.

Raedwald couldn't believe anyone would be that sanguine about a possible major earthquake. Could they not see what was happening? The danger they were in?

'To each their own,' he muttered, shaking his head at a group of inebriated men who started up a chorus of a bawdy song. They were joined by prostitutes from a nearby brothel. Clearly the women weren't going anywhere either, but perhaps their owners were forcing them to stay. They were chattels, the way he himself had been. Well, no more. So far no one had come looking for him or Duro, and in the current chaos he doubted they would. By the time Antonius Varro realised they weren't coming back, they'd hopefully be far away.

Yet another earth tremor shook the pavement underneath him as he ducked into a side street. Here, it was more peaceful. Everyone who wanted to run must have done so already. When he reached Aemilia's house, the front door was closed. He wasn't sure if that meant the occupants had left, or were barricaded inside. Only one way to find out. If a servant opened up, he'd claim to be concerned about them in his capacity as bodyguard. That way, he should at least find out if she was still here.

'Hello? Anyone there?' He banged on the door as loudly as he could. No answer, apart from the barking of a dog. Surely they wouldn't leave their guard animal behind? But somehow he could believe it of Lucius.

He tried knocking for a while longer, but when there was still no response, he made his way to the back alley instead. The crumbled wall was even easier to scale now, and he had no trouble gaining access to the garden. Inside, all was quiet, and he frowned. Where was everyone? He walked along the paths to the back of the building, and noticed that the doors to the storerooms and kitchen were closed and barred from the outside. Opening one of them, he peered inside, and was met by the blinking eyes of half a dozen slaves.

'What are you doing here?' he barked, shocked to find them locked in.

'The . . . the master said to stay here until the earthquakes finished,' one of the older men said. Raedwald recognised him as the one who usually guarded the front door. 'He said he'd be back, but it's been ages . . .'

'And he locked you in? Unbelievable!'

It made his blood boil. The storeroom was small and cramped, with shelves and amphorae stacked around the edges, and only a tiny window high up. If a really big quake hit, this was nothing but a death trap. In fact, most of the slaves were already covered in plaster dust from cracks in the ceiling.

'Get out!' He motioned them all to stand up and head outside. 'Take your belongings and leave this town. Now! It's too dangerous to remain.' When someone opened their mouth to protest, he added, 'I don't care what Lucius says. If you stay here, you'll all die, I'm sure of it.'

No one argued further, and the slaves scurried off to find what little they owned. If they could get away with it, they'd probably steal a few items as well, but Raedwald couldn't care less. Any man who treated his slaves this way deserved it, in his opinion.

Leaving them to sort themselves out, he carried on towards the peristyle garden. Some of the rooms leading off this area had their doors shut as well, although most weren't barred. He opened and closed a few of them, and checked others, but they were all empty.

'Aemilia? *Domina?*' he called out, hoping against hope that she was somewhere nearby. He thought he heard someone reply, and the sound of muffled banging reached him. 'Where are you?'

Circling the courtyard, he came across one door that was barred, and made quick work of opening it. It was pitch black inside, without so much as a tiny slit of a window, but before his eyes could adjust, a shape detached itself from the shadows and threw itself at him.

'Raedwald! You came! Oh, thank the gods.'

'Aemilia!' Her arms twined around his neck and he crushed her to his chest. 'What happened, my love? Why are you in here? And where's . . . Oh Caia, come here, sweetness.'

He'd caught sight of the little girl lurking behind her mother, hanging on to her skirts. Bending down, he lifted her up with one arm, then encircled Aemilia's waist with the other. They huddled together for a moment, before she pushed at his shoulder.

'We need to leave. Now. Before Lucius—'

'Before Lucius what? Didn't I tell you, you're not going any-where?' The voice of the man in question rang out behind them. 'And what exactly is going on here? You're consorting with a slave? How dare you!'

She gasped and whirled around, still with Raedwald's arm around her torso. He looked over her head at the man standing before them, brandishing a *gladius*. The short blade glinted in the pale light, vicious and deadly.

'It's not safe here,' Raedwald said, imbuing his voice with a calm he didn't feel. The man had caught him hugging his wife and child, but he refused to feel embarrassed. *Former wife*, he reminded himself. Lucius had divorced her. It was none of his business what she chose to do now.

'Never took you for a coward, barbarian,' Lucius sneered. 'There's no need to flee like cockroaches in a beam of light. I sur-vived the last earthquake just fine. This one will be no different.'

'You can do as you please, of course, but Aemilia and Caia are leaving now.' Raedwald slowly let go of them both, and shunted them behind him. 'Let us be on our way, and no harm will come to you.'

Lucius laughed and waved the *gladius* around. 'To me? I'm the one holding a sword, while you're unarmed. And you're not taking my possessions anywhere, slave. Caia is mine and she stays. As does Aemilia, for the time being. In fact, I'll have you put to death for this. Touching a free-born woman! Outrageous. My patron is very influential. He'll have you—'

Raedwald didn't wait to hear what the man had in store for him, because it wasn't happening. He pulled a knife out of his boot and lunged at him. The Roman had been drinking, judging by his slightly slurred speech, and wasn't trained in combat the way Raedwald was. Plus, he was puny in comparison. Still, he managed a creditable jab, which Raedwald had to fend off with his much smaller knife. The clash of the blades reverberated up his arm, but he took no notice. While Lucius gathered himself for another attack, he punched him on the side of the head, making him stumble.

'No! I won't let you take them. Foreign scum!' Lucius shouted a string of insults, but Raedwald ignored him and landed a couple more punches.

The *gladius* nicked his arm, but he barely felt it. He was filled with rage that this pompous little fool had tried to force Aemilia and Caia – not to mention his slaves – to remain here against their will. Had deliberately put them in danger and locked them in a room as dark as the god Hades' domains. It wasn't to be borne. Again and again he hit the Roman, until he slumped on the ground, the *gladius* lost in the nearby bushes.

'You stay, if you're so sure it's not dangerous. We're leaving now,' he snarled. Turning to Aemilia, he put his hands on her shoulders and turned her towards her room. 'Please, my love, grab your possessions and let's go. There is no time to lose.'

The urgency in his voice must have worked, because she scurried inside and came back with two sacks. He took one of them from her, then picked up Caia. The little girl had remained silent throughout the fight. She was no doubt in shock. Soothing her would have to wait, though. First they needed to reach the harbour, before it was too late.

With a final glance at Lucius, who was beginning to stagger to his feet, he hustled his beloved towards the back gate.

'You'll regret this!' Lucius shouted, his words even more slurred. Whether that was from the wine, or the fact that he had a split lip and a few broken teeth, wasn't clear. 'My patron will see to it that you're crucified. Soon as this is over. Just you wait . . .'

Raedwald could see the fear in Aemilia's eyes, but he bent to give her a swift kiss. 'Ignore him. He will never find us, I swear it.'

She nodded, then, like the courageous woman he knew her to be, followed him into the street.

Chapter Twenty-Eight

❦

Sant'Agnello, 24 October 2022

Cat

Derek shrugged out of his jacket, and threw it over the back of a chair, then sat down at the dining table. His laptop was already on it, the lid open. Cat guessed he had been searching the airline sites earlier and had bookmarked the various possibilities. Knowing him, he'd go for whatever was the cheapest. Especially now he no longer had a job.

The apartment was small, with an open-plan kitchen and living room. There was one bedroom at the back, which could be glimpsed through an open doorway, and a bathroom next to it. The floors were polished marble, but dull, as if they'd been around for decades. The furniture and decor were outdated and tired, but reasonably clean.

He glanced at her. 'So who was that man? How does my daughter know him? Have you been screwing the locals while you were here? Or is he another one of your infernal cousins? Jeez, they breed like rabbits, these spics.'

She could have told him the racial slur was outdated and

inaccurate, as well as offensive, but it didn't matter now. 'Connor is a family friend,' was all she said.

'Connor? That doesn't sound Italian. Friend, my arse,' he muttered. 'I saw the way you looked at him, slut. But we can discuss that later. Give me your passport. I assume you must have obtained a new one somehow, or you wouldn't have got out of the country.'

Cat rooted around in her handbag until she found it, then walked over to place it on the table next to him. He scowled at the burgundy-coloured Italian document. 'I should have known. Gone back to your roots, have you? Huh.' He focused on the screen for a moment, tapping something on the keyboard, then picked up the passport. Flipping through the pages, his scowl grew more pronounced. 'Where's the bit where Bella is added? I can't read this infernal language.'

'She's not in there. She has her own,' Cat informed him.

'Well, where is it? Give it to me!' He held out his hand, waving at her impatiently.

She shook her head. 'I can't. My mother has it. I left it with her for safekeeping when we arrived here and I forgot to get it back from her. I assumed you'd obtained a British one for her, or added her to yours.'

That was the truth, but she had no doubt she would be punished for it. She really had forgotten, as she'd been too busy panicking about her daughter's whereabouts.

'For fuck's sake! Unbelievable!' He surged out of his chair and punched her in the face.

'Ow! Don't!' She tried to duck out of the way, but several more blows followed, and she put up her arms like a shield. Bella started to cry again, shrinking against the sofa cushions and staring at Derek with wide, terrified eyes. 'Stop, or they won't let me on the plane!'

That got through at least, and he ceased hitting her. 'You do realise you're delaying our plans? Wouldn't surprise me if you did it on purpose. Well, you'll have to get her to bring it.'

'What, here?' If Giovanna was given this address, the rest of her clan would come with her and make a rescue attempt. Cat wasn't sure if that was a good idea right now, with Derek on high alert. Someone would get hurt.

'No, I'm not that stupid. If that was your plan, you've failed. We'll have to meet her in Sorrento again, just before we leave for the airport.' He held out his mobile. 'Call her and tell her to be at that pier at eight p.m. Alone! There's a plane that leaves at eleven thirty. We'll have time to catch that.'

Cat took his phone with shaking fingers and managed to dial. Giovanna picked up almost immediately. '*Cara*! Where are you? Are you OK? I—'

'Mamma, listen. I don't have time to talk. Please can you bring Bella's passport to the pier tonight at eight? Our lives depend on it. And come alone.'

'Fine, I will, but—'

Derek snatched the phone away and hissed, 'Just do as she said, bitch, or your granddaughter dies.' Then he hung up.

He paced back and forth for a moment, then went back to his laptop. Cat returned to the sofa and pulled Bella close. She rocked her gently, hugging her and stroking her back. 'Shh, baby, shh. We'll be leaving soon. It will be OK, you'll see,' she murmured, even though she didn't believe it herself.

After what seemed like ages, Bella said she needed the bathroom. 'Can I take her?' Cat asked Derek.

'Yes, yes, but hurry up!' He barely looked up from whatever he was doing, and she and Bella scurried off before he could change his mind.

While Bella was washing her hands, Cat retrieved the phone from her bra and typed a short message to Connor.

We're OK. In apartment in Sant'Agnello. House ochre colour with green shutters. Near seafront and a hotel called Mediterraneo. We came in a white Fiat 500. Taking a flight at 11.30 p.m. Don't do anything rash this evening on the pier. C x

She hadn't been able to see any street names, but she'd noticed the hotel as they passed it and hoped that was enough for her relatives to find her. What, if anything, they could do even if they did, she had no idea. Derek still had the upper hand, and she couldn't risk Bella's life. If nothing else, perhaps they could intercept them at the airport. The mobile vibrated in her hand and she checked the screen while her daughter dried her hands on a worn towel.

We'll be careful. Be ready to pull Bella out of the way. Remember the moves I taught you. We won't let you get on that plane. C xx

She quickly deleted both messages. As she hid the phone once more, a memory surfaced. One night, after they'd finished making love, she had admitted to Connor how helpless she'd always felt when her husband attacked her.

'But you don't have to be,' he'd told her gently. 'You can fight back, you know. Women may be the weaker sex, but they can learn to defend themselves. Here, let me show you some easy moves.'

He'd started with a backwards headbutt, to be used if she was being held from behind. 'With any luck, that would break the bastard's nose and you could run,' he had said.

He had moved on to how to disentangle yourself from a front hold, how to grab and twist a man's balls to best effect, and how to stick your fingers into someone's eyes. Finally, there was the throat punch.

'You just jab your elbow back into his Adam's apple, and that should make him choke.'

Gritting her teeth, she vowed to do whatever she could to keep her daughter – and herself – safe from the monster that was her husband.

Sorrento, 24 October 2022

Connor

Connor paced inside the restaurant, unable to keep still. He couldn't believe they'd failed so spectacularly earlier that afternoon. They should have realised that Bella would react to the sight of him, or any of the others. They'd all treated her well during the past few weeks, played and laughed with her. As it was so very different from the way her father behaved, the little girl had started to trust them and become attached.

'Sit down, man. You're going to make a hole in my friend's floor, you know.' Pietro put a hand on Connor's shoulder and guided him to a chair. 'We will manage it this time.' He glanced at his watch, an expensive Rolex. It was probably best not to ask where it had come from or what he had done to earn it. Connor was glad Pietro was on their side. He wouldn't want to be up against him. 'Only a few more minutes, then we will go and get into position.'

It had been decided that the two uncles would sit at a table outside and have a drink. They were dressed like American tourists in baseball caps, bomber jackets and brightly coloured sneakers, and both sported fake glasses. Their sons and daughters, Cat's cousins, were out on the pier with a group of friends, having an impromptu party. They'd brought music and wine, and were pretending to be carefree teenagers, messing around. With any luck, Derek had no idea what they looked like. Giovanna had told Connor that her son-in-law had only met them once, at Cat's wedding five years earlier, when the cousins were much younger.

Luca came over and grinned at Connor. 'You look . . . er, inter-esting.'

'You mean I look like a prat.'

It was true. He too was dressed like a teenager, in big baggy trousers and an even baggier hoodie, but since Derek had already seen him earlier, they'd added more of a disguise: a long blond wig and a slouchy hat, as well as a dangly silver earring in the shape of an ankh symbol. He'd had to have his ear pierced for this purpose, but it was a minor inconvenience in the circumstances.

'I hope it's enough,' he said.

'It is. Don't worry. Your own *mamma* wouldn't recognise you.' Pietro laughed.

Luca's mobile rang and he listened before answering with a quick burst of Italian. He turned to Connor. 'They're on the move. Let's go. You know what to do.'

They'd found the house Cat had described, and someone had been keeping an eye on it to make sure Derek didn't do something unexpected. It had been decided that it was too risky to rush in and try to free Cat and Bella. Better to do it in the open, among people, where there were witnesses.

Luca and Pietro exited the restaurant, each carrying a bottle of beer and some snacks. Connor followed them and walked over to where the party was in full swing. The cousins were dancing and chatting with their friends, and a group of three girls were twirl-ing sinuously to the thumping bass beat blaring out of the speakers. One of them tried to grab Connor's hand and drag him into their circle, but he shrugged her off. He had to keep his wits about him, and in any case, he was way too old for them.

There was only one woman he wanted, and she was on her way.

He sank down to sit on the planks of the pier with his back against the railing, facing the shore. With his hood up, he could look under the rim of the hat and see them coming. Pietro and

Luca were also in position now, at a table a little further along. And Giovanna was standing in her place at one end of the T-shaped pier. Somehow an opportunity would present itself to mess up Derek's plans.

One of the cousins, Flavio, bent down to hand Connor a bottle of beer and whispered, 'Here they come.'

'Thanks.'

A frisson of adrenaline ran through him, and he gripped the bottle tightly. This had to work. He couldn't let Cat go back to that bastard. It simply wasn't an option.

Chapter Twenty-Nine

Pompeii, 24 October AD *79*

Aemilia

'I thought you would have left without us.'

Aemilia was hurrying along next to Raedwald, clutching one of the sacks containing her and Caia's belongings. With her other hand she held on to his belt to prevent them from becoming separated. As soon as they'd reached the main thoroughfares, they'd been engulfed in a tide of other refugees. They were having to battle their way forward, and were constantly being pushed and shoved in various directions.

'Never!' He shook his head and sent her a look so intense her legs almost buckled. 'I would never leave you, unless you wanted me to. But I thought perhaps you had changed your mind. I was coming to check, because if so, I needed to hear it from you.'

'No, no! I was so scared when Lucius shut us in, but I was hoping one of the earthquakes would make the walls crumble so we could escape. Thank the gods you came looking for us.'

They had finally reached the Forum, and he was about to answer her when a loud noise was heard, followed by gasps and screams of pure terror. Turning to see what everyone was looking at, Aemilia could only stare with dawning horror at the previously scenic Mount Vesuvius. An enormous column of something like steam or cloud matter was rising from its depths, shooting so far into the sky it was impossible to see the top. She finally understood that all the earth tremors had merely been a precursor to something far worse. The very ground they stood on was exploding, boiling out of the top of the mountain. They were all doomed.

'Oh, dear gods – we're going to die!' she cried. A vice was closing around her chest and she felt as though she couldn't breathe. They'd been too late. If Lucius hadn't locked them in, she and Caia would be far away by now with Raedwald and the others. But now . . .

'Aemilia, *move*!' Raedwald's voice pulled her out of her trance. 'We have to get to the boat *now*!' As if he'd read her mind, he added, 'It's not too late. Hurry and stay close to me!'

She forced her legs to move, and followed right behind him as he forged a way through the chaos. In the midst of people panicking and running blindly in every direction, he was a rock to cling to. Taller than most, his large frame created a path. He stood firm against those who bumped into them, or tried to shove them out of the way. Her fingers were numb from gripping his belt so hard, but she dared not let go. Keeping her gaze on him, she trusted him to get them where they needed to go.

'Have a care here. The hill is steep,' he warned, as they surged through the Forum Gate among a sea of others.

The paving stones beneath their feet were worn and slippery, but she steadied herself against his broad back. Caia was clinging to him like a frightened monkey, her face buried in his shoulder, but she wasn't crying. Aemilia gathered that her little girl felt safe in his arms, the way she always did herself.

After what seemed like hours, they finally reached one of the jetties, where a crowd had gathered. There were scuffles and heated exchanges, pleading and wailing. Curses streaked through the air as the refugees fought to get on board the few vessels that were left. One of them was Raedwald's. Aemilia spotted Duro and a lanky youth fighting off a swarm of people, using oars like weapons to push them away.

'You have to take us!'

'We'll pay you!'

'You can have all my gold and silver – anything! *Please!*'

'By Baduhenna, this is madness!' Raedwald hissed.

He shoved his way through the crowd and lifted Caia into the boat, before helping Aemilia on board.

'What took you so long?' Duro was panting and red-faced, but at the same time there was the light of battle in his eyes, as if he relished this fight. 'We're about to be overrun.'

'I can see that. I'll explain later, and I'm sorry. Let's just get out of here.'

The boat was big enough to take at least ten people, even though it had been loaded with provisions for their journey, and there were only five of them. Aemilia caught sight of a couple with a baby and four children, ranging from a toddler to about eight or nine years of age. The mother was crying and clutching her baby as someone bumped into her from behind and bashed her shoulder with a travelling chest. Her husband was desperately trying to protect the three older children, while carrying the toddler. Short of jumping into the sea, they were trapped, unable to get off the jetty any other way. It was a disaster in the making.

She tugged on Raedwald's sleeve. 'Can't we take a few more with us? Look at that family. Those little ones are about to be trampled and killed, or maybe drowned.'

He nodded, and headed towards the back of the boat as Duro

284

and the youth, whose name she gathered was Marcellus, continued to fight off the angry crowd. She watched as he silently caught the father's eye and beckoned him forward. He lifted the mother and baby bodily into the boat, then swung the three older children in after her and held out his hand to the man. As soon as they were all seated, he sat down on a bench, gripping the second set of oars.

'Now, Duro!' he shouted.

The man and youth swiped the crowd one last time with their makeshift weapons, then placed them against the side of the jetty and shoved hard. One man made a final frantic attempt to join them, jumping towards the boat but missing and ending up in the sea, shouting imprecations as he sputtered to the surface. Raedwald started to row, and Duro and Marcellus scrambled to fit their oars into position. Then Duro joined him, and they were off.

Raedwald

'I can't thank you enough for saving us. Please, let me take a turn at rowing.'

'You can thank Aemilia,' Raedwald replied gruffly.

She was the one who'd noticed the family and their plight. While he had considered offering passage to some of the people on the jetty, most of them had been so angry and self-obsessed, he'd been disgusted. This man and his wife were clearly different; their only concern had been for their children.

'Oh, I have, and I'm sure Julia, my wife, is doing the same at this very moment.' The man nodded to where Aemilia sat chatting with the other woman. 'I'm Gaius, by the way. You are Rufus, are you not?'

'Raedwald,' he said. He was done being a slave and answering to a name that didn't belong to him. It was time he reclaimed his own. 'Rufus is dead. So is Drusus – he's Duro now, and that's Marcellus. My . . . wife is Aemilia.' He'd hesitated to call her his spouse, but they were married in their hearts. A ceremony of any kind wasn't really necessary.

'Well, we owe you our lives. For that, we will be forever grateful. Now, may I?' Gaius indicated the oars, but Raedwald shook his head.

'It will be faster if we pair up. Duro, come and join me here, and let Gaius row with Marcellus. We will be more evenly matched. I want to get round the headland as soon as possible.'

He was worried they weren't making fast enough progress. It was as if the tide was against them, even though this sea, the Mare Nostrum, was barely tidal at all under normal circumstances. At the same time a strong current tried to push them back towards the shore. They'd been rowing for hours, and still they were only halfway along the bay. His muscles ached, but that was nothing new. He'd pushed himself through gruelling training sessions for years; he could do this.

Having four people at the oars quickly made a difference to their speed. Raedwald was just breathing a sigh of relief that they were finally getting somewhere when there was an almighty booming noise. It was as if a multitude of thunderclaps sounded all at once, followed by a loud roar. They turned as one towards the mainland, where Vesuvius was erupting with the force of a thousand Greek fires. A large dark column of what looked like dust spewed into the air, rising to the heavens. Soon after, a shock wave of hot air hit them, although it could have been with only a fraction of the force they'd have felt if they were still on land. Even this far out, they heard screams echoing across the water, as more panic ensued in the towns and houses along the coast.

'By Teutates, that is . . . magnificent,' Duro breathed, gaping at the sight.

'And deadly,' Raedwald added. '*Row!* For the love of the gods, put your backs into it.'

They increased their efforts, their eyes fixed on the lethal column, which kept on rising as if it was headed for the gods themselves. Eventually, however, it must have reached a limit of some sort, and appeared to collapse on itself, forming the shape of an umbrella pine. It was a mesmerising sight, but it wasn't wise to hang around staring at it. Raedwald was sure they were still in danger.

'Keep rowing,' he urged, wiping the sweat off his brow with his sleeve.

The sky was turning black, as if night had descended on the area without warning, even though it couldn't be later than midday. Lightning bolts criss-crossed the heavens, and a thunderstorm started up. It was as though the gods were having a vicious battle with each other. Through the gloom, grey flakes and something that might have been hail began to rain down on the boat. He shook them off when they landed on him.

'What is that?' one of the children asked, a mixture of fear and wonder in his voice.

'It looks like ash and . . . some sort of soft stone,' Aemilia replied. 'Pumice?' Raedwald saw her smudge the flakes between her fingers, where they left a sooty residue. 'It's hot to the touch.'

'The inside of that mountain must be like a cauldron,' he guessed. 'It's spewing it out faster than we can blink.' A terrifying thought, and not one he wanted to dwell on.

'Where do they think *they* are going? Are they mad?' Duro was staring at something behind them, and Raedwald turned to see a group of Roman galleys sailing towards land, rather than away from the danger.

'That's the fleet from Misenum,' Gaius commented. 'Perhaps they are hoping to save people along the coast.'

'They must have lost their wits,' Raedwald muttered. 'No one in their right mind would head in that direction. But it's not our problem.'

They could see fires in the towns on shore now, and refugees milling around like ants without a purpose. He was incredibly grateful that they had managed to get this far, and hoped they would be out of range of whatever the mountain decided to throw at them next. It was clearly a curse from the gods, but he trusted his own deities, who had kept him safe so far. He wasn't a Roman, and ought not to be punished for their misdeeds.

But then again, did anyone deserve to live through something this terrifying? The people of Pompeii were no worse than anyone else.

He wondered if Lucius was looking at that deadly column and regretting his decision to stay in Pompeii. The mountain was unleashing its fury on everyone around, and there could be no escape now. It was too late for those remaining.

The ash and stones were falling faster now, joined by larger bits of rock that were black, as if charred by flames. No one in the boat could escape the deluge.

'Splash yourselves with seawater,' Raedwald ordered. 'And cover the children and yourselves with wet blankets.'

The women obeyed without question, and huddled together in the stern with the six little ones. The children were all unnaturally quiet, and obviously scared out of their minds. Hopefully once they rounded the headland they would begin to recover from the shock.

'Aemilia, if you can, please shovel some of those stones into the sea. We don't want to be weighted down too much.' They were piling up in the bottom of the boat, and he couldn't have that. Plus he didn't want to risk them burning a hole in the planks.

'I'll do my best.' She grabbed the scoop he indicated for her to use. It was really for bailing water, but it would have to do.

Many hours later, possibly towards evening, although it was hard to tell with the sky so black, they finally passed the port of Misenum. Continuing on round the headland, they entered the next stretch of coastline, where thankfully Vesuvius could no longer be seen.

'I think we can take turns now, and row one pair at a time,' Raedwald said. 'Gaius and Marcellus, you can rest for a while.'

They were too tired to do anything other than nod, and collapsed onto the planks at the bottom of the boat. Raedwald was just as tired, but knew he had to stay strong for now and carry on. He exchanged a glance with Duro, who nodded as if he understood. They moved the oars as one, their rhythm steady.

'Aemilia, you'll find some bread and cheese in one of those chests over there,' he continued. 'I'm sure we could all do with some sustenance. And I for one would kill for a drink. There is a barrel of watered-down wine too.'

'Of course. I'll bring you some in a moment, my love.'

He smiled at her, relishing the endearment. She smiled back. There was still fear lurking in the depths of her eyes, but she was staying calm. He was so proud of her, his fierce and wonderful woman. If possible, he loved her even more now than he'd done before. If they reached safety, he vowed never to let her go.

Another loud boom echoed across the sky, and they guessed the mountain had exploded once more. The gods help anyone who was still in the area. They didn't stand a chance. Thankfully, the wind had turned, and here on board the boat they were no longer being pelted with stones and ash. As long as they kept going, they should be safe.

Lucius

In the *atrium* of his once magnificent home, Lucius lay on a bench watching ash and tiny pellets of something else falling through the opening in the roof. The *impluvium*, the little pool beneath it, was filled with the stuff already, and there were drifts of it all around him too. Shaking some off his shoulders, he took a swig of wine directly from the flagon he was holding, and winced as the sharpness of it stung his split lip.

'Curse that barbarian!' he muttered.

But he knew he had no one to blame but himself. He should have fled with everyone else. Should have taken his former wife and their daughter to safety. But last time there was a huge earthquake, his mother had made him leave, and when they came back, they'd lost almost everything. He hadn't wanted to risk it happening again. Wanted to stay and protect what was his against looters and thieves.

And yet . . . here he was. Alone, in a house that was slowly collapsing around him.

He'd been outside once, and had seen the terrifying column rising from the mountain. Since then, he'd taken refuge in wine and morose thoughts. It should be safe here in the *atrium*. If the roof fell down, he'd stand in the pool. Provided he could stand at all by then.

He heard roof beams cracking, and walls crashing down.

His beautiful home! It was all being destroyed. *Curse it all!*

Everyone had left him, even the guard dog. He'd searched the house, but the slaves he had locked in had escaped, among them his new pets – the two beautiful girls he'd bought only weeks ago – despite the fact that he had promised them riches and jewels if they stayed. He had a suspicion they knew he couldn't deliver on that. Slaves saw and heard too much. They would have been aware of his precarious financial situation.

'Well, who needs you?' he shouted, the question echoing back at him round the *atrium*.

They were the last words he ever uttered, as the mountain chose that moment to unleash a far more deadly attack on the town – a wave of heat so fierce, no living creature could have withstood it.

Lucius, and his hatred, was gone.

Chapter Thirty

Sorrento, 24 October 2022

Cat

'Walk in front of me and grab the passport from your mother. One wrong move from you and I will throw Bella over the side, got it?'

Cat nodded and moved to walk ahead of Derek onto the pier. He had their daughter perched on his hip, one arm around her waist, ready to lift her. His other hand held her upper arm in a tight grip, a clear warning to stay still, and the little girl was sobbing again.

'Ow, Daddy, ow! You're hurting my arm!'

'Be quiet or I'll really give you something to whine about,' he hissed, giving her a rough shake.

Cat had to grit her teeth together hard to stop herself from hitting him. It was too risky, though, as he had lightning-fast reflexes and would no doubt hurt Bella in seconds.

'What the hell are all these people doing here?' he muttered, glaring at a crowd of young people who were partying up a storm.

Cat recognised her cousins, and gratitude welled up inside her.

They were all here for her, a safety net she should have remembered she had. If only she'd reached out sooner, they would probably have helped her years ago, but she had been ashamed. Embarrassed that she had let those things happen to her and been too weak to resist. Too cowed to stand up to Derek. Now she knew they wouldn't have blamed her. They'd have had her back.

Nearby she saw two tourists sitting at a table, and realised they were her uncles. And she almost did a double-take when she noticed a guy sitting on the ground sending her a quick glance. Was that Connor? What on earth was he wearing? And that hair . . . Hysterical laughter bubbled up inside her, but she swallowed it down. It wouldn't do to alert Derek to the fact that he was surrounded by Connor and the Rossi clan.

They carried on walking until they reached Giovanna. She sent Cat a look of intense concern, but handed over Bella's passport in silence.

'Glad to see that someone in your family is capable of doing as she's told,' Derek snarled. 'Now leave, woman. I don't want to ever see you again.'

Drawing herself up to her full height, which was a mere five foot nothing, Giovanna shot him a look of loathing. 'The feeling is entirely mutual.' She marched past him with her chin tilted up, and continued towards the shore.

'Heinous witch,' Derek muttered, then shoved Cat between the shoulder blades. 'Move!'

She took a few steps, pretending to be cowed, but made sure she walked close by Connor, whose legs were stretched out in front of him. As they passed, his foot shot up and kicked Derek on the side of one knee. Derek hissed out a curse and stumbled, but managed to hold on to Bella. Cat had swivelled round and knew that any second now he was going to throw their daughter over the side. Without hesitation, she lifted her arm and rammed her elbow into his Adam's apple with all her might. A strangled gurgle came out of his mouth, his eyes bulged and he fought for breath. One hand came up to clasp his throat, and while he was distracted, Cat tugged Bella out of his grip, just as Connor surged up and tackled him from the side. The two men stumbled and began to fight, snarling, fists flying.

'Run!' shouted Luca, while he, Pietro and four of her cousins converged on Derek and Connor.

She fled, but stopped a short distance away, peering past the group of youngsters, whose party had stopped abruptly. She had to see what was happening. There was no way she could leave yet. Her heart was beating madly, and her hands shook, but she couldn't look away from the scene playing out in front of her. A part of her wanted to haul Bella out of harm's way, but her legs refused to move. Her insides were frozen with fear for Connor. What if Derek somehow got the upper hand and killed him? She couldn't bear the thought of it.

'No, no, *no*!' she murmured. 'I can't lose him now!'

The two men grappled for a moment, then one of the cousins leaped forward and smashed a beer bottle over Derek's head. That ruined his concentration, but he hadn't given up. He was fighting like a madman, but with at least seven men against him, he didn't stand a chance. Connor soon had hold of his arms and twisted them up behind his back, forcing him to stand still and face Cat's uncles.

'You will leave my niece and great-niece alone from now on, understand?' snarled Pietro. 'We know some very important people, not just here, but in the UK too, and you won't stay alive for long if anything happens to Cat or Bella. Sign the divorce papers and move on.'

'What are you, the Mafia or something? Bloody typical!' Derek tried to act defiant, but Cat could see even from where she stood that it was all bluster. For the first time in years, he was on the receiving end of the violence, and he was scared witless.

'Do you really want to risk finding out?' Luca this time, trying to sound reasonable and calm. Cat could have told him there was no use. Once Derek got worked up, rational thought didn't enter into the equation.

'Hah! You think I care? I'm going to hurt Catherine because she's ruined my life. And I will, no matter what. She took everything from me! *Everything!*'

I took everything from him? *Hah!* What a hypocrite. Cat stared at him and loathing surged through her. She hated him with every fibre of her being. Tears spilled over onto her cheeks as she contemplated the fact that she would never be free of him. Even if he walked away and agreed to the divorce, she'd always be looking over her shoulder, expecting him to come for her and Bella. And he would. He was that deranged.

He started shouting obscenities, most of them about her, but she tuned him out. The man had gone insane. Stark raving mad. She was lucky he hadn't killed her or their child already.

Thumping footsteps were heard approaching along the pier, and Cat turned to see a group of policemen running towards them. When they reached Derek and her relatives, her uncles explained the situation in a rapid torrent of Italian.

'The police are going to take you away for questioning,' Pietro informed Derek. 'They will probably put you on the next plane to the UK. Don't even *think* about coming back. And remember what I said. We *will* find you if you try anything.'

Derek hung his head, as if he had finally accepted his fate, but in the next moment he suddenly managed to free himself by head-butting Connor and climbing up onto the railings. He was obviously intent on getting away, although where he thought he was going was anyone's guess, with the policemen cutting off any escape routes. He raised his arms for balance and tried to jump onto the boulders the structure was resting on. At the last moment, his foot got caught in the upper part of the railing, and he tumbled head-first onto the stones. Cat gasped as his body landed with a dull thud and went still. The others stopped and stood like statues for a moment, then surged forward. Luca's oldest son, Flavio, climbed across and bent down to check for a pulse. He shook his head.

'Oh my God.' Cat swallowed hard, but couldn't stop staring at the lifeless body. She was holding tightly to Bella, and was thankful the little girl had had her face buried in her stomach so she hadn't witnessed her father's fall. She blinked to try and take it in. He was dead. Derek was gone. For good. She hadn't wished that on him, but she couldn't help but feel relieved, as she knew he would never have stopped his vendetta as long as he'd lived.

In the next instant, Connor was by her side, swinging Bella off her feet and pulling both of them into his arms.

'I've got you, baby girl. You're OK,' he murmured to Bella, but Cat knew he was talking to her as well.

The little girl clung to him for dear life with her face now buried in his neck, but he still managed to give Cat a kiss. 'Come. Best if we're not involved further. Your relatives know what they're doing and the police have everything under control.'

She lifted a hand to his face. Blood was flowing freely from his nose, but he seemed otherwise unharmed. 'Is it broken?'

'No, I don't think so. I managed to turn my head slightly at the last moment.' He kissed her again, and she didn't care that it tasted like blood. 'You did well, my love. I'm proud of you,' he whispered. 'I'm so sorry I failed you the first time. I should have been quicker.'

Cat wrapped both arms around him and squeezed hard. 'Not your fault. We should have realised Bella would say something when she saw you. I didn't think about that.' She glanced at her daughter, so comfortable in this wonderful man's arms. 'She clearly likes you. A lot.'

That made him smile. 'The feeling is mutual. Not to mention that I adore her mother.'

Pietro and Luca came over. Pietro put his hand on Cat's shoulder. 'I'm sorry, *cara*. It was an accident. Don't worry, we will take care of this now. I'll talk to the police.' He nodded at Connor. 'Take them away from here, please.' He held out a set of keys. 'These were in his pocket. You can take the rental car. Go to my place and just leave it on the street. I'll make sure there's no fine.'

'Thank you, I will.'

Cat disentangled herself from Connor for a second and hugged both her uncles. 'Thank you. I'm so sorry to bring all this trouble.'

'Hey, hey, we are family. Is not a problem, OK? Everything will be fine, I promise. We have witnesses and friends. You go home and rest now. We'll talk more tomorrow.'

She nodded, and took Connor's hand. It hadn't sunk in yet that she was free, and she never had to worry again. But the warmth of his fingers as they tangled with hers brought it home to her.

They were safe.

Naples, 25 October 2022

Connor

'How are you feeling this morning?'

Connor was lying on his side, his head resting on the pillow as he watched the beautiful woman next to him. She had only just opened her eyes, and blinked at him sleepily. When her gaze focused on him, a smile spread across her face.

'Fine. I'm . . . fine. I think.' A little shiver ran through her, as if she'd remembered what had happened the previous day, but she shook it off. Her smile grew wider. 'As long as you're here. And Bella.'

'I am. We are.'

The little girl was lying in between them in the queen-size bed in Pietro's guest room. It was a tight squeeze, but Connor hadn't wanted to take them back to his hotel room last night. He wasn't sure what the future held, but if Cat was still planning to work there, it was best if the rest of the staff didn't gossip about her.

As Bella was still asleep, they were talking in hushed whispers. The need to touch Cat became overwhelming, and he reached across the child to caress her mother's cheek.

She leaned into his touch, rubbing herself against the palm of his hand as if she were indeed a feline. 'I can't believe it's over. That . . . he's gone.' Her eyes filled with sudden tears. 'I'm free!'

'You are indeed.' He hesitated, not wanting to push her too soon. 'So what are your plans now? Will you stay here for a while or go back to the UK? I'm assuming you can safely return to your house now.'

A frown appeared on her perfect brow, and she shuddered. 'No, thanks. I'm never setting foot in that place again. Knowing Derek, he's probably made a will in favour of his sainted mother, so it won't be mine anyway. Although as I was divorcing him, hopefully I'll be entitled to half of it.'

'I'm sure you are. I'll ask my father.'

'Thank you.' She was quiet for a moment, then looked up at him. 'How long are you staying here? You said you were almost finished with your work, right?'

He nodded. 'Yes. Technically I should have left last week, but I decided to have a little holiday. I didn't want to leave you. But I have to go back soon.'

'Oh. Of course.' She gave him a smile that didn't reach her eyes. 'I can't expect you to put your whole life on hold for me.

Maybe we can meet up when I've figured out where to live. Back in the UK, I mean.'

'So you're definitely going back? I thought you'd want to stay here, with all your relatives. Didn't your mother say she was buying a flat in Naples?' He'd heard Giovanna and Cat discussing it, excited about the possibilities.

'Yes, but my life is in England. My translation business, I mean. I grew up there. It's my home, no matter how welcoming everyone is here. And now that my mother will be based in Naples, we can visit her often.'

Relief coursed through him. This was excellent news. 'That sounds like a great plan. Then how about you come and live with me? I don't know how you feel about Norfolk. It might be too rural and out of the way, but I'd be happy to move elsewhere if you prefer.'

'M-move in with you?' Cat looked stunned, and half sat up to stare at him.

He followed suit, moving slowly so as not to wake Bella, and took Cat's hand. 'Sorry, sweetheart, I realise this might be going a bit too fast for you. You've just come out of a horrible relationship, and I'll give you all the time you need to recover. But you have to know, I want to spend the rest of my life with you and Bella. You're my world. My everything. I love you, and I want to marry you, if you'll have me.'

'Oh Connor! That sounds wonderful, but . . . maybe not right away? I really do need some time to sort myself out. It's sweet of you to want us to move in, but would you mind if we waited a while? I'd like to have my own place first. Stand on my own two feet, just to prove to myself that I can.' Cat's cheeks turned pink. 'Everything has happened so fast, but . . . I would be honoured to be your wife eventually. Could we perhaps just get engaged for now? I love you too, so much!'

He pulled her into his arms, awkwardly over the top of the sleeping child, but he couldn't wait another second to hold her. 'That sounds perfect. And of course I understand. I can't wait to have you both with me for ever, but only when you're ready. I would never push you into anything. I want you to be happy, so take your time. I'm not going anywhere.'

'Thank you.' The smile she gave him, and the kiss that followed, told him all he needed to know. He would be patient for as long as it took. Cat was worth waiting for.

Later that day, they discussed their future in more detail, and told Giovanna about their plans.

'I hope you won't be sad, Mamma,' Cat said, sending her mother a glance of uncertainty.

Giovanna merely smiled and patted her hand. 'Of course not, *cara*. I want you to be happy, and I can see that you really are this time. You are safe with Connor around, and it will be lovely for you to have a place of your own. We can visit each other as often as possible. There will always be room for you in my flat, even if it's a squeeze.'

'Or we can buy our own apartment close to yours,' Connor suggested. When Cat blinked at him, he explained, 'My grandmother left me a huge sum of money, which I have invested wisely. We can afford to buy an entire building here if we want. Just say the word.'

'Wow! I had no idea.'

'Well, it's good to know you won't be marrying me for my money, as and when we get around to it,' he joked.

Cat and Giovanna laughed and shook their heads. 'I think a small apartment will do fine. Thank you. You're full of surprises.'

He was rewarded with a lingering kiss, and decided that spoiling Cat and Bella would be his new mission in life. To that end . . .

'How about we go shopping for an engagement ring? You like

those antique ones, don't you? Much better if you choose one for yourself, rather than have me guess what you'd like. Oh, and we can buy a gold bracelet or something for Bella while we're at it.'

'One like this?' Cat held up her wrist with the Roman arm ring. But her glance was teasing, and he knew she wasn't serious.

'I think if we bought one of those, we'd be in big trouble. Let's choose something that's not a couple of thousand years old.' He added under his breath, 'And haunted.'

'Very well. Lead the way! Mamma, we'll see you later.'

Chapter Thirty-One

Frisia, 24 December AD *79*

Raedwald

After leaving Gaius and his family near Rome, where they had relatives who would take them in, the boat had continued north and west along the coastline. Raedwald knew that if they simply kept the coast in sight on their right-hand side, they would eventually reach his homeland. It was a long, long way, but that didn't matter. They had all the time in the world now.

Marcellus left them halfway up the coast of a land he called Gaul.

'I know where I am now. I recognise this place,' he'd said, a huge grin on his face. 'Thank you for taking me with you. Would you like to come and meet my family? I'm sure they'll want to express their gratitude too.'

'If you insist, but no thanks are necessary. You earned our trust with your hard work,' Raedwald said gruffly. He was going to miss the youth, but this was where he belonged, and he had no right to ask him to stay with them.

He was proved right when they had rowed a short way up a

river and arrived at a small settlement. People came running out of their dwellings, and as soon as they caught sight of Marcellus, there were cries of joy and a lot of hugging. His parents both had tears running down their cheeks.

'We never thought we'd see you again,' his mother sobbed, then threw her arms around both Raedwald and Duro as Marcellus explained how he came to be back. 'Thank you so much for looking out for my boy. You have no idea what this means to us.'

They were even more pleased when the youngster showed them his share of the gold and silver they'd brought. The two gladiators had always given him a cut of their earnings, and it was a considerable sum by now. After a feast to rival all feasts, they left Marcellus with his family, who vowed never to let him out of their sight again.

Weeks later, it was Raedwald's turn to recognise the coastline.

'We are getting close to my home now,' he informed the others. 'Duro, I trust you to have my back. This will not be anything like the welcome Marcellus received, I can guarantee you.'

The man-made island hove into view, and they tied the boat to a rickety jetty. Raedwald helped Aemilia and Caia onto dry land, but asked her to stay behind him and Duro. Walking up the slight incline, he couldn't see anyone out and about. As it was midwinter, and nearly dusk, he guessed everyone was huddled inside the main building for warmth. He couldn't blame them. The ground was covered with snow, and ice hugged the coastline. They'd been lucky to get this far before everything froze completely.

Without preamble, he threw open the door to the largest building. He'd made sure he had a *gladius* strapped to his belt and a long knife in his boot. Duro was similarly equipped. The chatter inside stopped dead as he entered and halted just inside, surveying the gathering. At one end, his father sat behind a table in the hall's only chair, while his wife and children were seated on benches either side of him. Others sat on benches along the long walls. Everyone gaped, their eyes widening.

'Good evening, Father.' Raedwald strode along the centre of the room until he stood in front of the table. 'I trust you remember me?'

'R-Raedwald? By all the gods . . .'

The man lost all the colour in his face and simply stared for a moment. He looked much older than last time they'd seen each other, and somewhat frail. Raedwald saw his hand shake as he put down the mug of ale he'd been holding. He was gawping at his oldest son as if he was seeing a ghost. Ignoring him, Raedwald swept his gaze over the two people on his father's right.

'Osbehrt and Hild. I wish I could say it's a pleasure to see you again, but it's not.' He sent them his most deadly glare and watched them both turn ashen.

'How is this possible?' his stepmother whispered hoarsely, one hand rising to cover her mouth. She blinked, as if by doing so she could make him disappear.

'You mean, why am I not lying dead in a Roman arena somewhere? Well, Hild, that would be because I fought to stay alive so that I could come back and kill you and your son, you lying bitch.'

'I . . . I don't . . .'

Osbehrt had apparently grown up somewhat since last time they met. He was taller and more muscular, although nowhere near as big as Raedwald or Duro. His face now went from pale to bright red, and he banged a fist on the table. 'How dare you show up here after all these years? You ran off without so much as a word, and Father thought you dead.'

Raedwald raised his eyebrows at him. 'Oh, is that the tale you spun? Interesting.' He turned towards his father, who was still clearly in shock. 'I trust you will allow me to challenge Osbehrt to a fair fight to prove that what he told you was a vicious lie. He and his conniving mother had me captured and sold to the Romans as a slave. I've spent the last six years trying to find a way to return and kill the little serpent.'

Some of the colour returned to his father's cheeks as well. 'That is not what he said, no.' He frowned and regarded his second son and his wife. 'You sold him? My heir?'

'Don't be ridiculous,' Hild sneered. 'Why on earth would we do such a thing?' She attempted a mocking laugh, but it came out sounding false.

'Hmm, yes, I wonder,' Raedwald mused. 'Could it possibly have been so that *your* precious son would be next in line to take over leadership of our tribe? No, I must have imagined that.' The sarcasm in his voice was obvious, and her eyes spat fire at him. He glared right back, his own gaze promising retribution. Whether his father believed him or not, he'd get his revenge. That was all he had come for.

'He was never trustworthy, Father,' Osbehrt interjected. 'Allow me and my brothers to eject him from the hall. We don't need him here. He has proved that his loyalties lie elsewhere. He's probably a Roman spy.'

The older man, Raedwulf, sat up straighter in his chair, scowling even more fiercely. 'If you're so sure he is lying, you won't be afraid to show us by fighting him fairly.'

'Wh-what? You cannot be serious,' Osbehrt spluttered, his face turning an even darker shade of puce. 'He doesn't deserve to—'

Raedwulf cut him off. 'He deserves a chance to prove his claim. If you wish to be my heir, you'll need to be strong enough to withstand any counter-claim. Now get up and show us all that you're a man to be reckoned with.' Something glinted in the older man's eyes. Raedwald could have sworn it was satisfaction, but why, he had no idea. Was it possible he'd seen through his second son?

That was probably too much to hope for.

'Move all the tables out of the way,' Raedwulf ordered, and a mad scramble ensued to make space for a fight.

Raedwald returned briefly to his travel companions. 'If things go badly wrong, please leave immediately. Duro, I trust you to keep Aemilia and Caia safe.'

'Of course. You have my oath.' Duro clapped him on the back and smiled. 'But you'll defeat that weasel in no time, unless he fights dirty. That wouldn't surprise me.'

'I'm on my guard. Aemilia – I love you. Please, stay with Duro and do as he says.' He kissed her hard on the mouth, clinging for a moment longer than he should have.

'I love you too,' she whispered. 'And I will, I promise.'

'Thank you.' He turned to face his half-brother, whose lip curled at the sight of him. It was going to be a huge pleasure to teach the pup a lesson. One long overdue. He couldn't wait.

Aemilia

Aemilia tried to breathe normally as she watched Raedwald stalk towards his half-brother, but it wasn't easy. There was something constricting her throat, and she swallowed convulsively. *Please let him be unhurt. Please let him win.* She chanted the prayers in her mind, hoping the goddesses of war and love were listening. She couldn't lose him now. Not when they'd come this far and had so much to live for.

Raedwald's sword was shorter than that of his brother, since he was wielding a Roman *gladius*. She was afraid he was at a huge disadvantage, but that soon proved to be untrue. He was so much more skilled with his blade than Osbehrt, and had the younger man jumping out of the way several times. If anything, it looked as though he was toying with him, the way he would an opponent at the gladiatorial games.

'Is that the best you can do?' he taunted. 'I would have thought you'd learned a lot more while I was gone. After all, you'll have had Father's undivided attention, just as you wished.'

'Shut up!' Osbehrt hissed. 'I've trained plenty. You're fighting dirty with that puny blade of yours.'

'Oh really? Like this?' Raedwald swiped his weapon across his half-brother's arm, drawing blood.

A gasp was heard from Hild, and Aemilia saw her move forward as though to help her son. Raedwulf's arm shot out and gripped hers, pulling her back. 'No you don't,' he hissed, and held on tight to her.

'Let me go! Are you going to stand there and do nothing while your heir is harmed?'

'Looks to me as though my true heir is doing very well on his own,' Raedwulf said, loud enough for everyone to hear. His gaze wasn't on Osbehrt.

'Why, you . . . you . . .' Hild struggled in his hold, but he must have been less frail than he looked, because she couldn't break free. Stamping one foot, she called out to her three other sons, 'Do something! Attack that woman over by the door. She and the child obviously mean something to Raedwald. Go on, get them!'

Aemilia's stomach clenched, and she pushed Caia behind her as the three young men glanced at each other before moving forward. One of them, the youngest, hesitated, and stopped to watch the ongoing fight for a moment, but the others continued. Duro moved to stand in front of her, pulling out his own sword. 'Don't worry, they can't best me,' he whispered.

'If any one of you takes so much as one step further, you are banned from these lands for ever and are no son of mine!' Raed-wulf's voice rang out loud and clear.

The oldest of the three sneered at him. 'Oh yes? And are you going to enforce that, old man? You can barely hold your ale mug these days.'

Raedwald must have been aware of what was going on, because he suddenly charged towards Osbehrt and sank his *gladius* into his brother's sword arm. In the next instant, he smashed his fist into Osbehrt's jaw, following that with an even harder blow to the head with the hilt of his sword. The man sank to the floor in a heap, bleeding profusely from the cut on his arm.

Duro charged towards the two brothers, who had by now almost reached the door. He wasn't alone for long, however, as Raedwald caught up with them from behind. The youngest brother nodded to himself, as if he'd made up his mind about something, then came to stand next to Raedwald and joined the fray fighting on his half-brother's side.

'You traitorous runt, Osric!' Hild shrieked. 'What are you doing?'

'I'm doing what is right,' Osric replied through clenched teeth. 'I heard you and Osbehrt whispering about Raedwald after he'd gone. You lied to Father, and what you did was plain wrong.'

With three against two, and two of them well-trained gladiators, it wasn't long before Raedwulf's middle sons lay dead on the floor. Hild was screaming like someone demented, until her husband backhanded her.

'Stop that infernal noise, woman. They got what they deserved.' He nodded at Osric. 'I'm glad I have at least one more honourable son. And where do you think you're going?' This last question was directed at Osbehrt, who'd stumbled to his feet and sprinted for the door. 'Raedwald, grab the coward!'

His oldest son obliged, catching his half-brother before he could reach Aemilia. He dragged his unwilling victim back to their father, who sent him a look of pure venom. 'I think you have proved Raedwald's point, you and your mother, whether you lost the fight or not. You will be the next sacrifice to the gods.'

That provoked another earth-shattering scream from Hild, but Raedwulf told someone to tie her up and put a gag on her. 'Confine her to our chamber for now,' he added.

Osbehrt himself was hauled outside by some of the other men of the clan, and locked into an outhouse until he could be dealt with.

'What will happen to him?' Aemilia asked, when Raedwald came over to check that she and Caia were unhurt.

'He'll be tied to a pole in the sea at low tide and left to drown. If Father is feeling extra vengeful, he will be castrated first. A fitting sacrifice to the gods.'

It sounded harsh, but everything Osbehrt and his mother had put Raedwald through meant he deserved it. 'And your stepmother?'

Raedwald shrugged. 'She has to live with the fact that three of her sons are dead. With any luck, my father won't let her have a say in the running of this household henceforth. Come, let me introduce you.'

He led her over to the chair where Raedwulf was now sitting with Osric next to him. The recent events had clearly been too much for him, and he was grey with fatigue. 'Who do you have there?' he asked, trying to summon up a smile for his guests.

'This is my wife, Aemilia, and our daughter, Caia.' Raedwald stood behind her and placed a hand on her stomach. 'And the gods willing, another little one will be joining us in the summer.' He indicated his gladiator friend. 'This is Duro of the Icenii tribe in Britannia. Loyal friend and travel companion.'

'I am pleased to meet you all. Please, sit down. I will call for ale and food.'

When some order had been restored, they shared a meal.

Things were awkward at first, and the conversation didn't exactly flow. Aemilia knew that Raedwald considered his father partly to blame for what had happened. The older man had apparently never put his foot down with his second wife and son, thereby leading them to believe they could get away with their plot. And they almost had. That thought made her shiver.

Osric came to the rescue, keeping up a steady stream of comments. He seemed pleased to have his oldest brother back. Aemilia remembered Raedwald telling her he'd liked this particular sibling. Osric had been a mere child at the time of the abduction, but it looked as though he'd idolised Raedwald. And having seen her husband with Caia, she knew he was good with children.

Eventually Raedwulf cleared his throat and looked his oldest son in the eye. 'I believe I owe you an apology. I should have seen what was happening and been sterner. There is no excuse, but I cannot tell you how sorry I am. And how good it is to have you back where you belong.'

'Thank you, but I'm afraid I'm not staying.'

That was news to Aemilia, who turned to stare at him. He gripped her hand under the table and squeezed it, as if to say he'd explain later. She gave an almost imperceptible nod. Whatever he decided was fine with her. She trusted him.

'What do you mean?' Raedwulf frowned. 'I thought—'

'That I'd come back to take up my place as your heir? I admit that was what I intended at first, but finding Aemilia has changed that. I want her to live the kind of life she would have had if we'd stayed in Pompeii. From what Duro tells me, the Romans have occupied his clan's territories and are busy foisting their society and way of life on the locals. We are both going to purchase land there and live more or less in the Roman style.' He shrugged and sent his wife a teasing smile. 'It's not so bad after all. I think I can put up with it for her sake.'

She smiled back at him, warmth filling her chest. He'd hated her people, but he was willing to live the Roman way for her. If that wasn't true love, she didn't know what was.

'I see. And what about us? You'll be leaving your clan without a future leader.' Raedwulf sounded confused and a little sad.

Raedwald's smile widened and he glanced at Osric. 'Not so. You have the perfect candidate here. He's always had more brains than the rest of your offspring with Hild put together. When it came time to take a stance, he weighed his options carefully before rushing into the fray. Ultimately he stood on the side of what was right. He is a worthy heir, and I am happy to call him brother. And I will only be a short boat ride away, should you, or he, need my assistance.'

Osric's cheeks turned rosy, but his eyes glowed. 'I would do my utmost to be a good leader, but it is up to Father,' he said.

Raedwulf regarded him with pursed lips for a moment, then smiled broadly. 'I do believe your brother is right.' He stood up and banged his mug on the table until everyone was silent. 'Listen and hear me! I hereby name Osric my heir and ask that you treat him with due respect. I shall begin his training on the morrow.'

He sat down again and held up his mug towards Raedwald. 'Let us drink to that.'

Chapter Thirty-Two

Norfolk, December 2023

Cat

'Are you ready? Everyone is waiting for us. And oh, don't you look gorgeous, *cara!*'

Cat stood in the porch of a tiny Norfolk church, listening to the organ music that was spilling out from inside. She handed her white fake fur coat to a church warden, who had promised to hold on to it until it was needed again after the ceremony. Drawing in a calming breath, she smoothed a hand down her exquisite lace dress. She'd chosen it on a shopping trip in the company of her mother, Bella, Suzanne, and Connor's stepmother Amanda and stepsister Sophie. They'd had a wonderful day together, and she had ended up with her dream dress. Nothing like the frumpy cream-coloured skirt suit Derek's mother had insisted she wear for her first wedding.

That had been at a registry office, as Derek didn't believe in religion and thought the expense of a big white wedding was a complete waste of money. At the time, no one had asked Cat's opinion, and she'd been too overawed to protest. This time Connor had insisted on her deciding everything.

'I'll just turn up wherever you tell me to, dressed however you want, my love,' he'd told her. 'And don't worry about the cost – I'll pay for everything.'

She'd taken him at his word, and she appreciated his generosity more than she could say, as it was in stark contrast to her experiences with Derek. Her days of enforced penny-pinching were over. Still, she hadn't gone completely mad with his credit card. It wasn't necessary, and it would be a day to remember no matter what.

'I'm ready.'

She took her mother's arm and started to walk up the aisle. Bella trailed behind them, looking solemn in her sky-blue satin princess dress, as she'd called it. She was taking her bridesmaid's duties very seriously indeed, and held on to one corner of Cat's long veil. The other corner was lifted by Sophie, who was the maid of honour.

Giovanna had agreed to walk her down the aisle. She knew that Connor's father would have performed that duty if she'd asked, since they got on very well, or one of her Italian uncles, but it felt right to have her mother by her side.

Waiting at the front of the church, Connor looked incredibly handsome in a morning suit and a primrose-yellow tie that matched Cat's bouquet. The pale rays of the winter sun slanting through a nearby stained-glass window lit up his hair, turning it to burnished copper. But it was the expression on his face and the love shining in his eyes that drew her gaze. As he held out his hand to her, she couldn't believe how lucky she was to have found this amazing man. He was her true love, her soulmate, and she never wanted to leave his side.

'You are stunning, and I am the luckiest man in the world,' he whispered, his fingers closing around hers, and then they turned to face the vicar.

One year later

Cat

'I've never celebrated Christmas in Italy before. This should be interesting!'

Connor led the way to the taxi rank outside Naples' small airport, carrying a car seat containing their two-month-old son Callum in one hand, and dragging a suitcase behind him with the other. Cat followed with another suitcase, some carry-on luggage, and Bella, who had a bright pink backpack.

'Well, at the very least we might get some sleep,' Cat commented with a smile. 'There will be plenty of people to help soothe his little majesty when he decides he wants to exercise his lungs.'

'Sleep? Oh yes, please! What utter bliss that would be.'

Connor sounded as if he'd give a kingdom for just a few hours of that precious commodity, but Cat knew he didn't really mind. He'd been a rock ever since Callum was born, and had done his fair share of baby duties. He was a wonderful father, and not just to their son, but to Bella as well. No one could have asked for a better one. Bella called him Dad and, with the resilience of the very young, seemed to have forgotten that Derek had ever existed. Both she and Cat had had some counselling to help them process everything, but they hadn't needed it for long. Cat would eventually talk to her daughter about her real father, but it could wait. And Connor had adopted Bella, so she was legally his now.

As she sank into her seat in the taxi, she adjusted her Roman bracelet, which felt too tight. She smiled and glanced down at it. Most of the time she forgot she was wearing it, but occasionally it was as if the previous owner sensed a link between them and wanted to remind her. Sometimes she had dreams, other times simply a feeling of déjà vu. She guessed it meant that there were things they had in common. Had the Roman woman felt the same? Was her man a fantastic father too? Cat hoped so.

Connor's phone beeped with an incoming mail. 'What now?' he muttered. 'Please don't tell me the pipes have burst or something.'

They'd left Sophie house-sitting for them. She was studying for her university finals and needed peace and quiet. She would go over to John and Amanda's place on Christmas Day for the traditional lunch, but the rest of the time she'd be sequestered away, working hard. It meant they didn't need to worry about their large Victorian rectory, which was undergoing renovations at the moment.

'Oh wow!' Connor stared at a photo that was appearing on his mobile screen.

'What is it?' Cat leaned over Bella, who was sitting in between them, to have a look. 'Is that . . . mosaic?'

'Yes! Sophie says the guy who is putting in the underfloor heating in the conservatory found this beneath the original tiles. It looks Roman!'

'Goodness! That's beautiful! And you had no idea it was there?'

Cat's bracelet tightened on her arm yet again, and she moved it automatically. The mosaic looked familiar. *As if I've seen it before.* Maybe she had, in another life. The thought no longer scared her, but made her smile.

'Well, we had been told that some Roman stuff had been found in the garden back in the eighteen hundreds, but no one has ever done a dig. I think they'll have to now, though. The underfloor heating will have to wait. This is a job for the local archaeologists.'

'Absolutely. Tell Sophie to call them immediately.'

Connor smiled, his eyes twinkling. 'I don't think they will come out at Christmas, but hopefully soon. Isn't this amazing? Such a coincidence, with you being sort of Roman by descent.'

'Indeed.'

But Cat didn't believe in coincidences any longer, and when her bracelet gave her another squeeze, she knew that the mosaic floor hadn't ended up at their house by accident.

She closed her eyes, and an image of two people popped into her mind. They were dressed in Roman outfits – the woman in a flowing dress and head covering, the man in a tunic with what looked like trousers underneath – and were standing at the top of a hill overlooking the sea. Cat knew that hill. Had stood on it herself and enjoyed the very same view. It was behind their home in Norfolk.

Whoever you were, I hope you were as happy as Connor and me, she thought.

From the way they turned to gaze at each other, she was sure they had been.

Epilogue

Britannia, August AD 80

Raedwald

'Are you happy, my love?'

Raedwald was standing behind his wife, with his arms around her waist. It was almost back to its former circumference since the birth of their son a couple of months earlier. He had loved watching their child grow inside her, though, and hoped that she would soon be expecting again. She was beautiful in any shape or form, and he adored her.

'Yes. It's so lovely here. Thank you for putting my wishes first and settling in Britannia, instead of where you rightfully belong.'

She rested her arms over his and wrapped her hands around his forearms, which made her favourite gold bracelet glint in the sunlight. It was the remaining one of an identical pair, in the shape of three laurel leaves. She had told him that the other was the one she'd given to the goddess Isis as a thank you for granting her wish and helping them to be together. It was a sacrifice that had been well worth it. He would have given a hundred such armbands for the privilege of having Aemilia as his wife.

They were on the top of a hill overlooking their new domains. As luck would have it, a rich Roman had been recalled to his country to serve in the Senate, and had been willing to sell them his entire estate, including a substantial villa, close to the east coast. As Raedwald had said, he was only a short boat ride away from his clan in Frisia, yet here they lived as Romans. And they still had enough riches left over for whatever luxuries they might wish.

The land around the villa was fruitful, and they had fields full of wheat, and herds of cattle and sheep. They lacked for nothing. His days were filled with tasks around the farm, which he enjoyed greatly. And his evenings and nights were spent with those he loved.

'I belong wherever you are,' he told her, and turned her in his arms to give her a lingering kiss. 'If you're content, so am I. And you are everything I could ever want.'

'I feel the same. You know I would have happily lived in that draughty hall as long as you were by my side.'

'Yes, but I wanted better for you and our children. You deserve only the best.'

'Thank you – for this, for protecting me and loving me.'

'Always, my love, always. We will be together for eternity, you have my oath.'

Author's Note

I have tried to stay as true as possible to the real events of those fateful days back in AD 79, and to stick to the order in which they happened. Walking along the peaceful streets in the ruins of Pompeii, I could only imagine the sheer terror of the poor people who lived through that time, and those who perished. I hope my story does them justice and conveys the scale of the tragedy they experienced.

There is some debate about the exact date of the eruption, however. For the longest time, everyone took it for granted that Pliny the Younger's account of events was correct, including the date in late August that he mentioned. This is now in doubt for various reasons:

- Large amounts of autumnal fruits have been found around the area, such as pomegranates, which are usually only ripe in late autumn.
- Many of the victims were wearing woollen clothes not suitable in August, as it would have been very warm then.
- More than a dozen versions of Pliny's text exist and some may have been changed or misinterpreted by medieval scribes, including the dates.

- A hoard of silver denarii was found with the Emperor Titus's titles on the reverse, including one it is possible he could not have claimed before September of AD 79, which would mean the eruption had to have happened later than that.

On the other hand, there were leaves on some of the trees at Herculaneum that should have been bare if the eruption happened in October, herbs that should have finished flowering by then, and fresh broad beans found. Those would have been ripe in late summer, and once you have picked them, they don't stay fresh for long. Some scholars also say that the aforementioned pomegranates could have been picked before they were ripe and then preserved somehow, and that people might have put on their woollen clothing to protect them against the pumice stones falling on them as they fled.

For the purposes of this novel, I chose the later date of October, as it fitted my story better. The excavations at Pompeii and Herculaneum will no doubt go on for many years to come, and hopefully the archaeologists will eventually find the definitive answer. Until then, we can only guess.

Acknowledgements

After five books set during Viking times, this novel is a slight departure from my previous Headline stories, and I want to thank the team for letting me branch out and turn to the Roman era for a change. It's been very exciting, and I'd like to say a huge thank you to my new editor, Nicola Caws, who has been wonderful to work with! Thank you also to the rest of the Headline team, including the talented cover designer, Caroline Young, and as always, the brilliant audio book narrator, Eilidh Beaton. And heartfelt thanks to Lina Langlee, my lovely agent, who always has my back. It is a great pleasure to work with you all!

I first heard about Pompeii and the fateful eruption of Mount Vesuvius when I was a child, and the event caught my imagination. Seeing photos of the bodies frozen in time inside the layers of ash was poignant and very moving, and I dreamed of going to see the place for myself. Last year, that dream finally came true when my husband, Richard, and I travelled to the Naples area. I got to visit Pompeii, Herculaneum and the mountaintop itself, as well as other areas around the Bay of Naples. It was definitely one of the most memorable holidays/research trips I have ever been on. I'd like to thank Richard very much for coming with me and putting up with following my schedule to fit in with the research, including trying an authentic Roman meal. Such fun!

A special thank you to my wonderful friend Alison Morton for beta reading the manuscript to check for mistakes – her knowledge of Roman times is second to none and I appreciate it very much!

As ever, thank you to my lovely friends – Gill Stewart, Henriette Gyland, Sue Moorcroft, Myra Kersner, Tina Brown, Carol Dahlén, Nicola Cornick, and the other Word Wenches: Anne Gracie, Andrea Penrose, Patricia Rice, Mary Jo Putney and Susan Fraser King. Having you all to talk to is invaluable!

To my amazing girls, Josceline and Jessamy – loads of love!

And finally, a massive thank you to all the readers, reviewers and bloggers who help to spread the word about my books – you have no idea how much I appreciate your support, and I hope you won't mind reading about Romans for a change!

Christina x

PS If you want to keep up with news, behind-the-scenes information and special deals, please sign up for my newsletter – you'll find the details here: https://tinyurl.com/mr3fu9ch

Bonus Material

Alaric's Dilemma

⚜

Frisia, AD 94

Alaric had forgotten how to breathe and he was sure he was dreaming. He had never seen such a beautiful girl in all his life, and she was so far out of his reach, she may as well be a goddess. He swore softly to himself and tried to stop staring, but his eyes refused to obey. He simply couldn't look away. The dark-haired vision was being helped onto the jetty by his stepfather Osric, and greeted warmly, as was the rest of her family. She was the daughter of Osric's older half-brother Raedwald, who lived in Britannia, and they'd all come for a visit from across the sea. Alaric had never met them before as last time they came, he'd been away.

He wished he hadn't been here this time either, because this was going to be torture.

Standing next to his mother, who had been a widow with a five-year-old son – him – when she married Osric, he watched the group approach. His younger half-brothers snickered as they were at that awkward stage where girls were still an exciting mystery. And there were three of them – not just the dark-haired beauty, but two younger ones with different shades of auburn hair. They were pretty too, but of no interest to him whatsoever.

'Alaric is smitten,' his older half-brother whispered in a teasing, sing-song voice, while elbowing him none too gently.

'Shut up,' he hissed back.

'Behave, Oswald!' their mother muttered. 'You're too old for such childishness.'

At fifteen, the boy really was, but Alaric refrained from agreeing out loud. He knew better, and having seen twenty winters now, he was above pettiness.

Osric and the others had reached them. 'Raedwald and Aemilia, you remember my wife Ada, and my children. But I don't think you met Alaric, Ada's son from her previous marriage, last time you were here?' He made the introductions, and Alaric tore his gaze away from the goddess long enough to bow to his step-uncle.

'I'm pleased to meet you,' he murmured. The man was big and scary, and still powerful despite having seen at least forty winters. Alaric had heard many a tale about Raedwald's days as a fearsome gladiator, fighting in Roman arenas. He was a legend and it was easy to see why. When Alaric dared look him in the eye, though, there was a distinct twinkle of good humour.

'Very happy to meet you at last as well.' He indicated a woman by his side, who was still lovely and with a striking resemblance to the girl who had struck him dumb. 'This is your aunt Aemilia, and these are our children Caia, Maximus, Marcellus, Carina and Cassia. We have three more, younger ones, but left them at home this time.'

Alaric bowed again, while his stepfather waved them all up the slight incline towards the main building. To his surprise, Caia – the goddess – fell into step beside him as they began to walk.

'I'm glad to see there is someone in the family my age to speak to this time. When we were here last, your younger brothers turned bright red every time I tried. I ended up sitting with the older women the whole time.' She made a slight face and leaned closer to whisper, 'Not my idea of fun. All they chat about is childbirth.'

He spluttered a surprised laugh at that comment and found his voice, although he had to clear his throat before his vocal cords would work properly. 'That does sound tedious, cousin,' he agreed. 'Not that I would know as I spend most of my time outdoors.'

They had reached the doors, and he waited politely for her to step through first. 'Oh, we're not cousins, Alaric,' she told him with a smile that nearly slayed him on the spot. 'As I understand it, Osric isn't your father, and Raedwald isn't mine. Not by blood anyway, although I call him Pater.' She took a seat on a bench and he sat down beside her. 'So what do you do outdoors then?'

For an instant, he forgot the question. Being so close to her, he was able to study her features properly. Huge amber eyes under delicately curved eyebrows regarded him with the same twinkle he'd seen in her stepfather's gaze earlier. Her nose was patrician and proud, but suited her face to perfection. High cheekbones, porcelain skin and a lush mouth that was fairly begging for attention, red and ripe as the finest berry. An incredible figure he dared not let his eyes linger on, and hair that was a gleaming black mass trying to escape from the strange bands woven into it to hold the tresses in place. He longed to thread his fingers through it to see how soft it was and . . .

'Alaric?'

'Huh? Oh, I'm sorry. Outdoors? I help to oversee the cattle and field work, and of course I do my fair share of anything that needs doing. I also hunt further inland, and I love fishing and swimming.'

He could feel his cheeks heating up. What must she think of him? An unpolished country boy who couldn't string a coherent sentence together in her presence.

She merely smiled. 'I love being outside too, and farming is a passion of mine.'

'It-it is?' He'd never heard of a female being enamoured of farming. It was simply something you did to subsist.

'Yes. Pater has large flocks of sheep and cattle, and I always help with lambing and calving. He has taught me about crops and all manner of things, and he has bought me my own property as a dowry for when I marry.' Her eyes dimmed momentarily. 'Although I suppose my future husband will want to run things his way and might not let me have a say.'

Alaric frowned. 'Marriage is a partnership. A husband and wife run things together. Here, if the menfolk have to go away, the women are perfectly capable of overseeing everything.'

'Really? Hmm, I like the sound of that.'

They were interrupted by a thrall bringing them mugs of ale, and Caia's attention was claimed by her mother for a while. Alaric sat and sipped his drink, trying his best not to cast surreptitious glances at the young woman by his side. He caught his step-uncle's gaze on him once or twice, and wondered if he ought to leave. The man probably didn't think him good enough to speak to his adopted daughter. At least, not for any length of time. When Alaric's mother had married Osric, it was on the understanding that her son would not inherit the title of chieftain here when he grew up. That honour would fall to Ada and Osric's oldest son, as was right and proper.

He had never resented it as such, but it did put him in an awkward position. As stepson to the chieftain, he had a certain status, but he had nothing much to offer a prospective wife. Certainly not a girl like Caia, whose family was clearly wealthy. He sighed and stared into his ale mug. It would be better for his peace of mind if he stayed out of her way. Then perhaps he wouldn't yearn for what he couldn't have.

And yet, how could he possibly keep away from her?

'Seen something you like, daughter?'

Caia felt her cheeks turning pink, but she refused to rise to her stepfather's bait. 'I don't know what you are talking about.'

She fixed her gaze on her little brothers, who were doing their best to beat Alaric and their other cousins at spear throwing. He towered over them, his white-blond hair bright in the sunlight, His shoulders and arms were much more powerful than the young boys', and he could probably have bested them blindfolded, but he was holding back. So not only was he handsome, but kind and good-natured as well. A powerful combination. She'd been leaning on a fence, watching them – well, watching Alaric really – when Raedwald had wandered over to stand next to her.

He chuckled now. 'You seem to have got on well with Alaric these last few days.'

They'd been here for a week now, and she had made it a point to sit next to him each evening. She'd had to be the one to take the initiative, because he had appeared reluctant to approach her. Why, she wasn't sure, but she was too fascinated with him to allow such reticence. And once they started talking, they lost themselves in conversation and time flew by. Everyone else faded into the background and there were only the two of them in perfect harmony, and with a shared sense of humour.

She shrugged, pretending nonchalance. 'He is tolerable. At least he doesn't snicker the whole time like the others. He is a man, after all, not a silly youth.'

'Oh, so you noticed that, did you?'

Caia's reply was to punch him on the arm. They had a warm

relationship and frequently ribbed each other, so she knew he would not take offence. As she could have predicted, he only laughed.

'And is not snickering the only good trait he has?'

She frowned at him. 'Why are you asking me?'

'My brother was telling me Alaric is great at helping to run things here. Always willing to work hard, even though the land will never be his. A shame. A man such as that should have his own domains. Osric wishes there was something he could do for him.'

Caia only raised her eyebrows and waited.

Raedwald cleared his throat. 'I, um . . . that is to say, we wondered if perhaps a match between you would suit. You'll bring the property and he the skills to manage it. Osric assures me he's a good man, but you know I would never force you into any marriage that is repugnant to you. That's why you're still unwed, even though you've seen eighteen winters already.'

She nodded and took his arm, leaning against him. 'I know, and I appreciate your kindness in allowing me a choice, Pater. You've always been a wonderful father to me.'

He patted her hand and dropped a kiss on the top of her head. 'You know I love you and I've always regarded you as my daughter. I want you to be happy and settled, but you've shown no interest in any of the men we regularly meet back home. What do you think? Would Alaric be to your liking?'

She took a deep breath. 'I suppose that depends. I'm not sure I'd want him if he's only marrying me to gain property.'

'I understand. How about if we test him a little?' Raedwald's eyes held a glint of mischief. 'Then you can make your decision based upon that?'

'That sounds fair. What do you have in mind?'

'Come for a walk down to the shore and I'll tell you . . .'

* * *

Alaric could have easily won the spear throwing competition, but he allowed Oswald that honour, while Raedwald's oldest son Maximus came second. He had a feeling Oswald knew very well that he'd held back, as he threw Alaric a grateful glance when they walked towards the hall. Alaric smiled back and ruffled the youth's hair affectionately. The young one would make a good chieftain one day and he didn't begrudge him the status of heir one bit.

Well, only insomuch as it could have made a difference to his chances of marrying Caia, which at the moment were entirely non-existent. Still, he couldn't imagine her living here on the little man-made island by the sea in a draughty wooden hall. He'd heard a lot about the fabulous buildings Raedwald and his family inhabited, all built in the Roman style. Apparently, they even had a heated bath house that could be used all winter. Unbelievable luxury.

This evening he took a seat as far from Caia as possible, since he didn't want to torture himself by being close to her. He'd spent far too much time with her already, talking about all manner of things, most of which he couldn't even remember now. Hearing her husky voice and being enveloped in her flowery scent was both bliss and exquisite pain, and more than he could bear. Much better to stay away altogether. That way he'd be used to it by the time she went home again, which was soon, unfortunately.

That plan went out the window when she sank down next to him yet again, shooing one of his younger half-siblings out of the way. She leaned close and whispered, 'Are you by any chance avoiding me, Alaric?'

'I . . . no. No, why would I?'

'Hmm, yes, that's what I was wondering.'

He scowled at her, hoping to scare her away. Her arm was brushing his, sending little darts of lust through him whenever they came into contact. That enticing scent of hers teased his nostrils, and tendrils of her hair tickled his cheek whenever she moved, as they were escaping those bands yet again.

'I thought we'd been getting on well,' she commented, taking a dainty sip of her ale. 'But perhaps I was mistaken.'

'We did. I mean, we do,' he bit out, clenching his teeth so as not to spill the secret of how very much he enjoyed talking to her.

'Then it must be something else.'

She put a finger on her lower lip, pushing at it in a way that made him squirm. He wanted to kiss that mouth so badly and . . .

'Are you courting someone?'

'What?' The abrupt question threw him and he blinked.

She gave him a small smile. 'Well, since you don't seem interested in talking to me this evening, I can only assume you are done being polite and your interest is engaged elsewhere.' Glancing around the room, she nodded surreptitiously towards a couple of young women who were giggling together in a corner. 'One of them, perhaps? That red-headed one is quite pretty.'

'I'm not interested in them,' Alaric stated firmly, scowling even harder. 'And I'm happy to talk to you, but we both know that's all it can be.'

'Oh? And why is that?'

'Don't be obtuse.' He stared at the floor, refusing to look into those amazing amber eyes. 'Your father is wealthy. I have nothing.'

'What if the opposite was true – would you be interested then?'

He forced himself to turn to her. 'I'm fairly sure you know the answer to that. Now would you please stop tormenting me and go and eat your supper? I'm going outside for a while.'

He downed the rest of his ale and stood up abruptly, making his way out the double doors. Once outside, he gulped down huge lungfuls of cool evening air, while clenching his fists. There was only so much a man could take.

* * *

The following morning, Osric called out to Alaric, just as he was about to head outside after the morning meal. 'Hold on. Can I have a quick word, please? In private. Let's go down to the jetty.'

'Of course.' Alaric followed his stepfather, but frowned when he saw Raedwald waiting for them down by the sea. Uneasiness stirred inside him. Was the man angry because Alaric had spent too much time with his stepdaughter? Perhaps he'd inadvertently flirted too much with her? He'd been so mesmerised he couldn't remember half of what he had said and done.

'Raedwald has a proposition for you, son,' Osric said, clapping Alaric on the shoulder. 'Hear him out, won't you?'

Alaric only nodded, while the big former gladiator seemed to be measuring him with his gaze.

'As I'm sure you have noticed, my stepdaughter Caia is of marriageable age. Has been for some time now, but I've been lenient and not forced her into any unwanted alliances. There is only so long I can be patient, however, and now I must put my foot down. Osric tells me that you are in need of a wealthy wife and we feel that a union between you and Caia would benefit you both. Her dowry consists of a large property that borders mine, and Osric also informs me your management skills are second to none. What do you say? Would you be willing to marry Caia in order to gain your own domains?'

Alaric swallowed hard. The man was offering him everything he'd ever wanted and then some. A veritable dream come true. His own property, where he'd be beholden to no one, and a goddess for a wife. But the price was too high. He would have to sacrifice his pride, which he could perhaps have managed, but he would also be robbing Caia of a future with a husband who was her equal. And by the sound of it, she wasn't to be given a choice in the matter any longer.

He shook his head. 'It is most generous of you to consider me, but I am not worthy. I can bring nothing to such a union other than myself. Caia deserves better. Thank you for the offer, but my answer must be no.'

Unable to bear looking at the two men an instant longer, he turned on his heel and walked swiftly away from them. He was breathing heavily, wanting to punch something hard until his knuckles became bloody. The pain inside him was eviscerating him, and he didn't know how to stop it. There was nowhere to hide either. In the end, he went to the only place where he was out of sight – the hayloft – and sank down with his back against the wall. Knees bent, he put his arms around them and leaned his head down, trying to stop himself from uttering a sound.

It would pass. All bad things always did. It was only a matter of surviving.

Caia climbed the ladder to the hayloft as quietly as she could. She didn't want to spook Alaric into fleeing before she'd had a chance to talk to him. As she crested the upper floor, she saw him sitting motionless over by the wall. He was bent over and utterly still, as if frozen in time, his face hidden. She pulled herself up the rest of the way and padded over to him, sinking down beside him. To make sure he didn't bolt, she threaded her arm through his and held on. He flinched, but stayed put.

'Alaric,' she whispered. 'Everything is going to be fine.'

He turned his head slowly to look at her, his sky-blue eyes bleak. 'What do you mean? You shouldn't be here,' he said, his voice hoarse as if he was forcing the words out.

'Yes, I should. Pater told me about your meeting earlier. I knew what he was going to say to you as he'd asked me about it first. He wanted my approval to make you that offer.'

Alaric frowned. 'That's not what he said. He . . . he was going to force you to marry me because he's tired of waiting for you to make up your mind.'

Caia smiled. 'He lied. He would never force me to do anything I didn't want. It was a test to see whether you were greedy enough to accept such a proposal without taking my feelings into account. If you had said yes, he would have changed his mind.' She shook his arm a little. 'But you didn't. You put me first and refused, even though you must want nothing more than a property of your own.'

'I . . . what?' He looked adorably confused, but he was sitting up straight and listening to her properly now. 'A test?'

'Yes. You apparently said you're not worthy because you can bring nothing but yourself to a marriage.' She moved closer and looked him in the eyes. 'But what if that is enough? What if it is all I want? You have proved that you're not selfish but an honourable man, but would you want *me* if I had nothing? You didn't reply to that the other night. Not properly.'

'Caia, I would *prefer* it if you didn't own a thing. I want you more than I've ever wanted anything. Just you.' He was staring at her intently, and she was drowning in his gaze.

'Then all is well. We both get what we want.' She looked away and added, 'Could you . . . learn to love me, do you think? I've always dreamed of the sort of marriage my parents have.'

He pulled his arm out of her hold and turned her face towards him with gentle fingers. 'I already do, Caia. But do you truly want to marry a man who has nothing?'

'If that man is you, then yes. It's not as if I have earned my dowry in any way – I am just as unworthy of owning anything and I've merely been lucky enough to have wealthy parents. I'd be very happy to share.'

He shook his head as if he couldn't believe what he was

hearing. 'I want that, so much, and I will love you – no, worship you – for the rest of your life, you have my oath. Are you sure?'

'I have never been more sure of anything, ever.' She put her arms around his neck and threaded her fingers into his hair, pulling him closer.

He studied her expression for a moment longer, as if making certain that she wasn't joking. 'Very well then. Caia, please will you do me the enormous honour of becoming my wife?'

'Yes! Yes, I will. And from now on we share everything equally, agreed?'

He nodded. 'Agreed. We will run things together and I promise to consult you at all times. How does that sound?'

'Absolutely perfect.'

His arms came around her waist and his mouth found hers in a kiss that sent shockwaves all the way down to her toes. She wanted this man so much and couldn't wait to marry him. Together, they would make a wonderful partnership, and he was the man she had been holding out for all this time. At last, she had found him.

Don't miss the sweepingly romantic, epic dual-time standalone novel from Christina Courtenay!

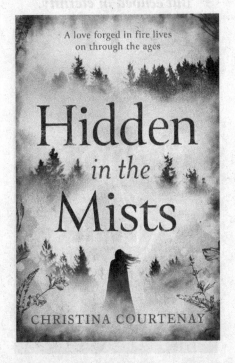

A love forged in fire lives on through the ages . . .

Available now from

Discover Christina Courtenay's Runes novels!

Their love was forbidden.
But echoed in eternity.

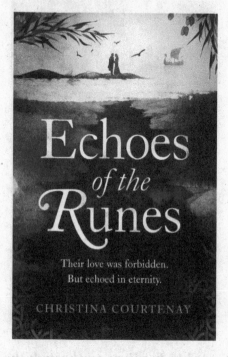

Don't miss Christina's classic sweeping,
epic tale of forbidden love . . .

Available now from

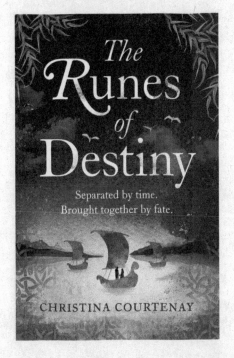

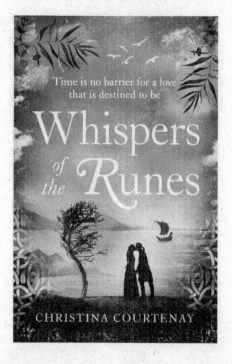

Born centuries apart.
Bound by a love that defied time.

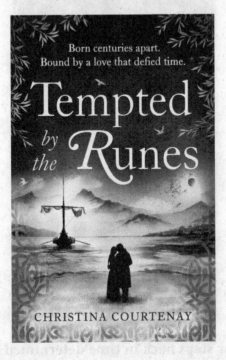

Amidst the perils that await on their journey to a
new land, the truest battle will be to win Maddie's
heart and convince her that the runes never lie . . .

Available now from

REVIEW

He travelled through time to capture her heart.

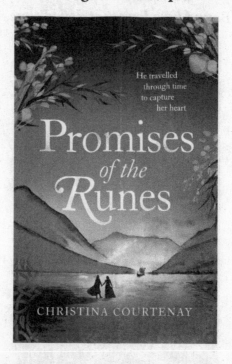

Ivar steps back in time determined to follow his destiny, and find the woman who has called to his heart . . .

Available now from